# *Broken*

C.H. Garrison

Robert Allen

Cover art by Mule Kimber
Editing contributions: Harry Althoff

For my sister Eva, who showed me how to be a parent,
my daughter Teresa, who helped me practice,
and my nephew Andy (the real Tahvi), whose spirit is unbreakable.

*C.H. Garrison*

# CONTENTS

*This story occurs in another time, another place.*

# FIRE IN THE SKY

The cold night brightened as the sky exploded with fire. A bright sphere of yellow, surrounded by a green glow, raced toward the planet. It shot sparks and flames seemingly at random while it descended, determined and eager to reach its destination. About 100 kilometers before impact the sphere suddenly changed its course. It shattered, sending pieces of itself into the lonely sky. They brightened the night briefly and then, just as quickly, they vanished.

The largest piece of the object flew through the night, headed towards a long stretch of flatland surrounded by immense rock formations. Animals within and around the canyon felt vibrations in the ground and a thickening in the air. They fled the area as the object approached. The force of the wind wrenched leaves from the branches of the few trees in the canyon. The ground shook as the object skidded along the planet's surface for several hundred meters before it crashed into a thick layer of red rock embedded in the ground. The red rock did not stop the object immediately: it tore through the rock and obliterated the top layer. The sky filled with a dust that coupled with the fire, burned a bright reddish-gold color. Once the smoke and fire diminished, the canyon was nearly silent except for the crackling of the charred pieces of material that protected the outside of the object.

After the crackling stopped the night was awakened again by a loud CRUNCH!

The large mass shed the charred formations on its outside, revealing a broken, metallic-black egg-shaped case on the inside.

Suddenly, beams of light shot through the small crevices that covered the surface. One of the cracks grew larger until it formed a kind of semi-circular shape, and then the broken piece split off completely, falling to the side. As soon as it did, the beams of light merged into a singular stream of light that brightened the darkness.

The animals, still running from the object, stopped abruptly and turned to sniff the air around them. All living things in the area, no matter how small, now were drawn to it.

A young ring-tailed cat searching for food in the canyon was not far from where the object landed. After sniffing the air, the ringtail cautiously began moving toward the object. As it got closer, it picked up its pace until it was running as fast as its little legs would allow. It stopped about a meter from where the object had burrowed into the ground. The light radiating from the object looked warm and inviting, but still the ringtail hesitated. It twitched its nose, rubbed its front paws together and then scratched its left ear.

As the ringtail looked at the object it bent its head to one side, then the opposite side, then it sniffed the air again. The light from the object was different from anything the ringtail had seen before. The light undulated, pulsing with a consistent rhythm.

The ringtail peered into the egg-shaped case and saw something its mind could not grasp. The sight didn't register in any memory it had collected thus far, but the animal did not sense danger. Instead, it felt very safe. It reached into the case, and when its paw touched the beam of light, the light changed to a brilliant, blinding green. The ringtail made a sound like a hiccup and its body melted into a relaxed position, as if all the energy in it had been depleted.

Within seconds, the light disappeared.

The ringtail was sluggish for a bit and then regained its composure. When it realized the light was gone the ringtail whimpered and then began to sniff the air excitedly. Its nose twitched as it caught the scent it was looking for, and then ran off into the night to follow it.

Long after the ringtail was gone—so long that the ground around the object was now cold and damp—a faint green light appeared in the case. The light was just as beautiful, but this time not nearly as intense, and could not be seen by anyone or anything more than a few centimeters away.

The light remained for several seconds and then disappeared. Like before, it pulsed as if it was breathing, as if it was … alive.

# TAHVI OF STEFAN AND EVANGELINA

Tahvi squints and lazily tosses his arm over his eyes in an attempt to keep the light out. He hears his mother calling to him, so he knows it is time for him to wake, but the bed feels so comfortable that he merely stirs.

Then he remembers what today is. He rubs his eyes and blinks several times to help them adjust to the brightness. A wide smile appears on his face.

"Mother!" he yells.

"Tahvi, are you not well?" she yells from another part of the house.

"Do you know what today is?"

"Tahvi!" she shouts, relieved, "Of course I know what today is. We've been preparing all week."

"I have eight years. I am nearly a man!"

Evangelina pokes her head into his room and sees him trying to sit up on the bed.

"Hmm … not a man yet, but you are growing. Happy day of birth, my little joy."

She enters the room, helps him sit up and gives him a lengthy hug. Still loosely wrapped in his sheet and blanket, she can feel him trying to hug her back with one arm.

"I can hardly wait for you to open your gifts and see what we've planned."

"I should open one now."

"Oh no, we'll have none of that. No gifts until after the

4

celebration. We'll have an early supper, then a surprise, then gifts."

"Just one? Please?"

"Do I seem like the kind of mother who surrenders because a child pleads—even one as handsome as you?"

He gives her a look that shows he's seriously considering the question.

"If I say no may I open a gift?"

They both laugh at this and Evangelina hugs him again.

"My dear boy, my answer is still no. Would you like me to help you dress?"

"Yes. I'm eager to see Sheree and Humbul—and Kaco. They still have Kaco. May I visit with them?"

"Yes. After you break fast."

Evangelina removes his sheet and blanket. The boy is wearing his sleeping clothes. The left sleeve is of regular length and his little hand and fingers poke out of the bottom. The right sleeve ends where the elbow would be if he had one.

His mother helps him remove his sleeping clothes but leaves his loin garment. She opens the trunk next to his bed and pulls out a lightweight wooden arm with a bendable elbow, a forearm and a carved wooden hand. The hand is covered with a glove that spans the length of the wooden forearm, which is fastened tightly just below the elbow. She attaches the forged arm by fitting it around his right stub and then fastening the buckles to his shoulder and neck. Then she puts his tunic on. As he shuffles and adjusts the sleeve on his left arm, the gloved wooden arm on his right sits limp next to his body.

"You forgot to check," Tahvi says.

"Oh." She tugs on his forged arm firmly enough to make sure it's connected well, but not so hard that it will hurt him.

"Is that comfortable?"

Tahvi nods emphatically.

"Ready for the leg?"

He nods emphatically again.

"Tahvi, if you keep nodding like that we'll have to make something to hold your head on, too."

The boy giggles, rolls his head then lets it drop to the side as if it's about to fall off his neck.

Evangelina laughs and reaches for her son's forged leg from the trunk. Tahvi's left leg is missing just above the knee. He sits on the bed anxious for his mother to attach the partial leg, moving it in a circling motion so she can see the muscles in his thigh flexing.

She imagines what it would be like if he had the rest of his leg. She frequently does this before she touches the stump.

Now she's thinking about how smooth and flat the stump is, as though someone has purposefully sculpted it that way. She can't help but think, *What does it mean? Does it have anything to do with*—but she pushes that thought away instantly. She's still distracted when she realizes Tahvi is speaking.

"Mother?"

"Oh, forgive me," she says with a smile.

She repeats a practice similar to what she did with his forged arm, only this time she fastens buckles around his upper-left thigh and then more buckles around his waist. She had previously tried buckles around only the thigh, but unless they were fastened tightly, the leg would sometimes fall off. Putting fasteners on both was the best way to make sure Tahvi didn't get injured. He wouldn't need the buckles on the waist if the forged leg could provide suction where the stump meets the artificial limb, but the stump is too flat to try. Evangelina often feels frustrated that she can't think of ways to make the limbs fit better, but she reminds herself that being able to find a toymaker who could make *these* limbs for Tahvi is nothing short of a miracle. Evangelina is grateful, but she can't help wishing that Tahvi had been born with the limbs of an ordinary child.

When she finishes tightening the buckles around his waist, she has him stand and test the leg to see if it fits comfortably. He takes a few steps and is satisfied.

"Ready!" he yells.

"What about your pants, Tahvi?"

"Oh!" Tahvi giggles.

His mother helps him put his pants and slip-shoes on. "*Now* I believe you're ready."

"Thank you." He kisses his mother on the cheek and leaves the room.

Tahvi quickly breaks his fast and then puts his bowl and spoon in the wash bucket.

"May I leave now?"

"Yes, but you should return soon. You have chores before the celebration. Remember to stay where I can see you."

Tahvi nods. As he's about to leave he looks back at the bucket. He notices the only dishes in it are his. He looks at his mother, already working on the day's chores. She owns a tailoring shop, where she also sells and barters clothes, fabric and jewelry. His father used to help her manage it. He furrows his brow at that thought. People still talk about his father, who died before Tahvi was born. Every so often, he sees people holding his mother's hand in a comforting way when they mention him. Or they hug her and say things like, *I hope someday you find another who loves you as he did.*

On numerous occasions he'd seen a look in his mother's eyes that showed a longing he believes even she is not aware of. In those moments if he were near her he would hold her hand and her eyes would light up once she felt his tiny fingers.

Tahvi knows she purposely doesn't talk about how much she misses his father, not when she thinks he can hear her. Tahvi also knows she tries to keep him sheltered from her grief, thinking it might hurt him if he sees her that way. But he understands much more than she realizes. He knows how much pain his father's death has caused her. He also feels the pain of his own loss, which he can't explain to his mother. Though he is capable of communicating this to her, his instincts tell him not to.

Tahvi's eyes return to the mostly-empty wash bucket. He limps back to the table and cuts a piece of fresh bread for his mother. He sprinkles it with cinnamon powder and puts it on a plate. Then he goes to her and takes her hand as she is folding clothes in his room. She smiles at him and allows him to lead her into the cooking room.

"What is it, Tahvi?"

"Here." He hands her the bread. "You must break fast."

"I will, as soon as—"

"Mother, you have to eat. I know you don't want to, but if you don't eat now, you will be tired. You have so much to do, and I know you'll forget. I love you, so please eat."

She looks into her son's eyes and finds it hard to believe that this is the little boy she helped dress just a short while ago. Sometimes the way Tahvi speaks to her makes him seem much older. As she eats the bread she wonders about the things she doesn't know about her son, and if those answers will ever reveal themselves. She eats the bread quickly, surprised by how hungry she is. Once she's finished, Tahvi kisses her on the cheek again and starts to walk out of the house.

"Tahvi?" She stares at him a moment, not sure what she wants to say. As he turns to her she says, "Be safe."

"I will. My heart is with you."

"And mine is with you."

## SHEREE, HUMBUL AND KACO

Sheree, Humbul and Kaco are waiting for Tahvi outside his home. They welcome him with a group hug and exchange the common greeting for all those who live in the village of Padhraig.

"Good day and good health to you," Tahvi greets Sheree first.

The fraternal twins return the greeting.

Tahvi feels something tapping his foot. He looks down and sees Kaco, his ring-tailed cat. With his body measuring only 25 centimeters in length and his tail measuring 10, Kaco is smaller than the average ring-tailed cat. Light-brown fur covers most of his body except for his tail and large ears. His tail has thick black and white stripes and his ears are a deep black color as well, matching his eyes. The white of his tail is sprinkled with gray hairs that can't be distinguished unless one is very close to him. The animal reaches for Tahvi, wanting to be held.

"Kaco!" Tahvi scoops him up and pets him. "I missed you so much. Did you enjoy your night with Sheree and Humbul?"

"He enjoyed running back and forth from our home to yours. I woke three times during the night and he was with me only once," Sheree says.

"Maybe he was in Humbul's room," Tahvi guesses.

"I don't think so," she says. "The little elfkin must have jumped into that blue powder you made. I saw his tiny footprints on my bed, the floor and my window this morning. So I know he didn't spend the full night with me or Humbul."

Humbul nods.

"I think Kaco finds it difficult to be away from you, Tahvi," Sheree says.

"I do miss him very much when he's away." He rubs the ringtail behind the ears and Kaco brings his face closer to Tahvi's. Kaco can smell the scent of Tahvi's meal and gives his nose several quick licks.

"You must be hungry, little one?"

Tahvi puts Kaco on the ground, and when Kaco walks all three follow him. As Kaco starts running they can no longer see his body, but they see the grass part and the tip of his tail as he approaches the spring nut bushes behind Tahvi's home.

"Time to break fast, Kaco?" Sheree asks sweetly.

"Since Kaco is a night walker, wouldn't this be his supper?" Humbul asks, pronouncing the creature's name *Kah-coh*.

"It's *Kay-co*, Humbul. *Kayyyyy-co*. You know he doesn't like when you don't pronounce his name well," Tahvi says.

"I'm only teasing. I don't see why he cares."

"Would you like it if someone called you *hume-bool* instead of *hum-bul*?" Sheree asks.

Humbul wrinkles his nose and lifts his upper lip. It makes him look very unpleasant, and Sheree and Tahvi can't help but laugh.

"Kaco's name is important to him," Tahvi says, still giggling a little. "It says a lot about him."

"To who? Aren't we the only people who play with him?"

Tahvi and Sheree both shake their heads.

"This is beyond you, Humbul. It's fitting that you don't understand," Sheree says playfully.

Humbul pushes her gently and she smiles at him.

When they arrive at the spring nut bushes, they watch Kaco pick some nuts and open the shells with his little claws. They're awed by how much his claws look like little fingers and how well he uses them.

"We don't have long. Evangelina will be calling me soon. What would you like to do?"

"Why do you sometimes call your mother by her proper name?" Sheree asks.

"Because it's such a beautiful name. Don't you think so? I would call her by her name every day if she would allow it."

"It's a sign of respect to address our parents with traditional titles," Sheree says.

"I don't see why it matters," Humbul says. He is using the end of a stick to draw circles in the dirt.

"Do names not matter to you at all?" Sheree asks.

Humbul smiles but doesn't respond.

"I'd like to make more powders," Sheree says. "I would enjoy making a red and maybe a yellow."

"I'd like to see Kaco do some tricks," Humbul says, pronouncing his name correctly.

Kaco turns toward Humbul when he hears his name. He brings Humbul a nut and places it by his shoe, then makes a clicking noise before heading back to the bushes.

"Thank you," Humbul says.

"I told you he likes it when his name is pronounced rightly," Tahvi smiles. "What about something … new?"

Humbul and Sheree nod with enthusiasm. Of all the people in the village, Humbul and Sheree have known Tahvi the longest. They know that Tahvi is unusually kind-hearted and his cleverness far surpasses those of the twins despite the fact that they have four more years than he.

But more than that, they're the only children who have seen proof that Tahvi is *special*. They'd learned at a very young age that he could do things that others in the village can't. They'd also learned his mother had no knowledge of his abilities—the day they'd learned that was a day they would never forget.

*  *  *

Sheree and Humbul were born to Josephine and Gaelan. Josephine, known to most everyone as Sephine, was a long-time friend of Evangelina's and one of the few village birth wives, so the twins began visiting Tahvi even before he was born. The first time they saw him move while he was still growing in Evangelina's belly, they gasped in unison. After that day, time and again they would ask to feel her belly and would sit next to her with their ears pressed against her stomach. Humbul would ask her to make the baby move and Evangelina would explain that little Tahvi or Isabella already had a strong will. She told them that the baby made his or her own choices and would only move when it was ready. Evangelina often called it "he," even though she didn't know for sure that it would be a boy. But the name of the child, be it boy or girl, had been decided long ago when she and Stefan decided to have children. Sheree often hoped it would be a girl, but when the baby was born it no longer mattered to her.

Because of Tahvi's limitations, Josephine eventually spent most of her time working for Evangelina, so Josephine and her children visited Evangelina's home daily. By the time the twins had eight years, they were often told to look after Tahvi for short periods of time while their parents brought water from the well, tended to the horses or finished other errands that consumed lots of their time. Being the twins of a mother who was both a midwife and herbalist, they were already used to being around and assisting with children, but of all the toddlers they helped with, Tahvi was absolutely their favorite.

Tahvi was extraordinarily happy and agile for a child with his challenges. It didn't seem to matter that he was missing almost an entire leg and arm, and it didn't slow him down: by the time he had one year Tahvi could move by scooting his backside along the ground or by crawling with his alternate limbs. With the latter, he could use his hand and knee or his hand and foot, but when he did this he often looked like a little spider. It sometimes made Sheree feel uncomfortable to see him that way, but it didn't bother Tahvi.

When Tahvi had two years he was able to hop quickly using his right leg while using his left arm for balance or by grabbing whatever he could get hold of. His energy and spirit made him fun to be around. The twins felt comforted in his presence and always looked forward to spending time with him.

When Tahvi had four years, Sephine asked the twins to watch Tahvi for a period of time that was longer than usual. It was during this visit that the twins discovered how special Tahvi was. He was seated on the floor atop a large bright blue quilt. It was early in the morning. Evangelina was working within her home more often and was beginning to receive unexpected visits from patrons, so though Tahvi was still in his nightclothes his false limbs were attached. She had left him a few toys. Her instructions to the twins were to ensure he didn't play any further than the boundaries of the quilt and to practice his letters and numbers. Tahvi cooperated, counting as high as Sheree wanted him to count or saying the letters in the alphabet with Humbul until he noticed his mother and Sephine walk out the front door. As soon as they did, Tahvi stopped abruptly.

"I have a secret," he said softly to the twins, "Do you want to know what it is?"

Sheree and Humbul exchanged a quick glance, startled by the way Tahvi had asked the question. Something about his tone made him seem as though he was someone else, someone older. Then they nodded at the same time. They often did this and Tahvi smiled as they did. It was one of his favorite characteristics about them.

"You must promise not to tell."

"I promise," Sheree replied.

"I promise too," Humbul agreed.

Tahvi looked toward the open window and said, "Come in. Meet my friends."

The twins stared at the window. Within seconds, two small paws appeared over the edge and a small head followed. It had big black eyes and ears that were twice the size of its face. It hesitated, looking uncertain. It sniffed the air and held its position. The twins had seen this kind of animal before, but never so close.

"It is all well," Tahvi said. "They won't hurt you."

The animal crawled onto the window ledge, jumped to the floor and ran towards Tahvi. The animal sat next to Tahvi, looked him in the eyes and then looked at Humbul and Sheree. His nose twitched and he put his paws together as if he were praying.

"This is Kaco," Tahvi said. "He is glad to meet you."

The twins looked at Kaco and smiled.

"It is good to meet you, Kaco. Good day and good health to you," Sheree said.

"Kaco visits me every day. Mother doesn't know yet. I will tell her when I have seven years, maybe six. It would worry her if I told her now. But he is my friend. He would never hurt me. He told me so."

"He speaks to you, does he?" Humbul asked.

"Yes, often."

Humbul smiled. He believed the animal must be familiar with Tahvi's voice to come when summoned, but it was clear that Tahvi was simply imagining he could talk to it. Still, Kaco was an interesting-looking creature, and Humbul was curious to learn more about him, so he played along. "What does he say?"

"He doesn't speak in the way that you and I do. But his body speaks. It tells me about what he does when he's not here. What he likes to eat and see. He used to live in a canyon. Now he lives in the barn. He has not seen his family since he was a baby. My uncle says he is a ring-tailed cat, named this because of the stripes that look like rings." Tahvi patted the animal's tail.

The twins sat in silence. They had never heard him speak this way. They were surprised by how articulate he was. The language flowed from his lips comfortably, as if he had been speaking this way for years. Although they thought it odd, they were eight-year-old children with imaginations more flexible and tolerant than those of adults, so they continued to indulge him.

"Why did you name him Kaco?" Sheree asked.

"I didn't name him, not really. He already had a name. He tried to tell me what it was, but I couldn't see how to make what he told me into a word, so I gave him my closest understanding of it, which is Kaco."

"That is very sweet," Sheree said sincerely.

Tahvi smiled—the smile made both Sheree and Humbul uneasy. It reminded Sheree of the way her mother would smile at her when Sheree was trying to fool her about something.

"You don't believe me," Tahvi said candidly. "What will help you believe me?"

Sheree began to speak but Humbul interrupted her. "Make him do a trick!" he said excitedly.

"Humbul!" Sheree exclaimed, shocked at his response. Sheree was kindhearted and she loved Tahvi very much. She didn't want him to be embarrassed. She found it endearing that Tahvi had such an imaginative relationship with Kaco.

"What kind of trick?" Tahvi asked.

"Can he fetch things?"

"Yes. What would you like him to fetch?"

"Tahvi, he doesn't have to fetch anything. Humbul, that was rude of you to ask." Sheree glared at Humbul, wrinkled her brow, and nudged him, urging him to take back his request.

"No," Humbul said to Sheree. He was kindhearted as well, but he also had a playful nature, and it didn't occur to him that Tahvi might be embarrassed when Kaco was unable to fulfill Tahvi's expectations. Mostly, he just wanted to see what the ringtail would do.

"Tell him what you would like," Tahvi said.

"I would like some bread," Humbul said. When he said it, he rubbed his stomach, acting like he was famished.

When Humbul finished speaking, Kaco looked at Tahvi and rubbed his ear with one of his paws.

Tahvi petted Kaco on the head. As he did, he said, "Kaco, bread please?"

Kaco skipped off the quilt and looked toward the cooking room. He sniffed the air for the smell of bread and to check for other person-scents. Sensing it was safe he ran toward the cooking room, his tail moving in a wave-like pattern.

Sheree and Humbul were sitting cross-legged, and when Kaco scampered off they simultaneously tilted their torsos backwards to follow him with their eyes. He disappeared into the cooking room. Shortly after, there was a scratching sound and then a noise that sounded like a plate or bowl had been knocked off balance. Kaco reappeared, walking back toward the children. This time he was standing on his hind legs and holding a large piece of bread with his front paws. His gait was not nearly as graceful as before. Using only his hind legs, he wobbled toward them while maintaining a very inelegant rhythm. Kaco dropped the bread in Humbul's lap and sat next to Tahvi.

Sheree and Humbul sat with their mouths hanging open and their eyes wide. At that moment, Tahvi thought they looked like *identical* twins. He let out a short giggle.

"You were … speaking the truth," Sheree said, astonished.

"Yes. This is my secret. Will you still keep your promise?"

Sheree and Humbul nodded in unison.

"Let's see what else he'll do!" Humbul nearly screamed.

Tahvi and Sheree laughed.

The longer they spent with Tahvi the happier they felt, and when they were all together, it felt right and safe.

Kaco was the first of many secrets they would share. Over the years the twins came to regard Tahvi as family and they treated him as such. They learned that though he was younger than they were, his mind still childlike in many ways, he was also like an adult. He knew and spoke of things other children his age and their age did not know. They learned to trust each other and keep secrets from their parents that Tahvi said were best to keep, at least for now. He promised that someday they would be able to share those secrets with their parents. They trusted and believed everything Tahvi told them and he trusted them completely. As meaningful as their friendship was it was also fun and exciting. Tahvi helped them by entertaining their minds and they helped him a great deal through physical and emotional kindnesses.

After Tahvi had five years, it was rare to see him without Sheree or Humbul or both. It became routine for them to see each other nearly every morning, and every so often Tahvi would have something new to tell or show them. So, on the morning that he had eight years, when he asked if they wanted to see a new trick, as usual he was pleased when their answer was yes.

* * *

"First we must gather some rocks and place them in a circle," Tahvi says.

The twins begin to help him arrange the rocks. They also collect some leaves and sticks to put in the center at his request.

"Who will be the watchperson?" Tahvi asks.

"It is Humbul's turn." Sheree looks at Humbul and he nods in agreement. Each time they experiment with Tahvi's abilities someone is always assigned to be a lookout. Though Tahvi's home is near the outskirts of the village, they know it's important that they do their best to be careful. They agreed that no one in the village must learn about what he can do, not even his mother.

Tahvi and Sheree sit near the rocks but Humbul stays standing. He tries to appear indifferent, as if they're doing nothing of interest. He begins swinging the thin stick he'd been drawing in the dirt with earlier. Kaco has finished eating but he still holds two spring nuts, one in each paw, and he hobbles toward the circle of rocks to sit next to Tahvi. He places the nuts between himself and Tahvi, so he can guard them. He then lies in the dirt, folds his front paws in front of him and rests his chin on them.

"What's the trick?" Humbul asks. He keeps alternating between looking at the circle of stones and looking at the surrounding area. Tahvi's parents' land is slightly larger than 8,000 square meters and they are in the yard facing the back of the house, about 20 meters away. They will have plenty of warning time if they need to stop.

"We're going to make a fire."

"Awwww, Tahvi, you've already shown us how to make a fire. I thought this was a new trick."

"We've never made a fire like this."

Tahvi closes his eyes and takes deep breaths. He breathes in slowly for eight seconds and then breathes out for the same amount of time. He does this for only a minute or so, and then he opens his eyes and stares at the small pile of kindling. As he continues breathing deeply, various parts of his body start to twitch at random. Then he experiences a light shudder. The twins are used to seeing this process when Tahvi uses his abilities and they are not afraid—it doesn't seem to hurt Tahvi, and he will do this again after a few minutes if the trick lasts longer than that.

The twins watch the kindling with anticipation, not sure exactly what Tahvi is going to use to start the fire. Then they notice the kindling looks different. It's moving in waves, like they're looking at it under water. They realize what they're seeing is the manifestation of heat. The wood starts to smoke but there is no flame or spark. Small puffs of smoke shoot out of the center like smoke from a pipe. Then they hear a crackling noise as sticks begin to burn. The sticks take on a reddish color as the temperature within them increases but a flame has yet to appear. Kaco smells the smoke and sits upright.

"The fire won't hurt you if you don't go near it," Tahvi says to Kaco as he pets him.

Kaco looks at Tahvi and makes a clicking noise. Then Kaco picks up one of his spring nuts and throws it into the circle. He presses his paws together and hops twice on his hind legs.

Tahvi increases his focus. Suddenly all of them feel the heat increase dramatically. They hear a quick buzzing sound and then see sparks, reddish-yellow flickers of light, appearing over the kindling but not in it. It's simply in the air. A fireball about the size of Tahvi's fingernail appears over the kindling and shoots straight out toward the spring bushes. Tahvi gasps and reaches for it instinctively. It burns a small section off one of the bushes before it extinguishes.

Kaco jumps into Sheree's arms, looking back and forth at her, Tahvi and the kindling. He grabs so tightly to her garment that he accidentally scratches her with his nails. Sheree pets him gently on the head and grabs his paws to loosen his grip.

The twins are speechless. They look at the spring bush, unable to believe what they have just seen. Sheree looks back at the kindling and it's no longer sticks and leaves—all that is left is a pile of ashes.

"I am sorry," Tahvi says solemnly. "I didn't mean for that to escape the rocks."

"We are all well," Sheree says as she pets Kaco's fur. "Tahvi, when did you learn you could do this?"

"Yesterday. I was excited about it … but it did not escape like it did today."

"That was fantastic!" Humbul says.

"I should be more careful," Tahvi says, sounding disappointed.

"Again!" Humbul nearly yells.

"Maybe we should—" Tahvi begins, but he is interrupted when he hears his mother calling to him. Sheree puts Kaco on the ground and helps Tahvi stand. She wipes the dust off his clothes and notices that Tahvi is warm to the touch.

"Are you feeling ill?" she asks.

"No."

Kaco's spring nut had landed between two of the rocks and Sheree asks Humbul if he will use the stick to get it out. He does so and afterwards tries to touch it with his fingers.

"Ow!" Humbul drops it and looks at Sheree. "It's hot."

"Didn't you know it would be?" Sheree shakes her head. She checks his hand for a burn mark and is happy not to find one.

"I will be more careful when we do this again," Tahvi says to them, eyes watery and solemn.

"Tahvi, no one was hurt. We know you are *always* careful. All is well. Truly it is." She smiles at him.

"Did you make it stop when it hit the spring bushes? Is that why it did not grow larger or burn anything else?" Humbul asks.

Tahvi nods. "As soon as I felt I couldn't control it I asked it to dissolve and I believe that's when it did." He inhales sharply. "I nearly forgot!"

Tahvi picks up the spring nut, which is still very hot.

"Tahvi, no!" Sheree cries.

The spring nut makes a sizzling sound while steam rises from it. At first the twins think it's smoke and that he's starting another fire. Instead, it now appears to be cooler than before. He hands the nut to

Kaco, who accepts it without hesitation.

Sheree grabs Tahvi's hand and looks at his palm. With her index finger she rubs his palm in a circular motion. The temperature of his hand is normal. She also notices he is no longer warm.

"You are not burned?" she asks, surprised.

"No." He smiles at her. "It is the same trick, really. We'd better start back."

They hear a crunching sound and see it's coming from Kaco. He's opened the roasted spring nut and is trying to eat it. Then, as quickly as he'd begun eating it, he spits it out. He shakes his head and wipes his nose several times with his paws. He pushes the rest of the spring nut away from him.

"Not good, my furry friend?" Tahvi asks.

Kaco responds by wiping his nose with both claws again, then running back toward the house. Tahvi and Humbul follow him but Sheree stays behind to dishevel the circle of rocks. As the boys continue toward the house Sheree uses her feet to move the rocks out of place. Then she walks over to the spring bush. The edges of the leaves are singed where the fireball had touched them. The burned ones look like a tiny person has taken bites out of them. She puts her hands near the leaves, testing them for heat. When she feels none, she touches one of the leaves and finds it cool. On her way back she stops to inspect the ashes. She picks some of them up, finding them cool to the touch. Surprised by how soft they feel in her hands, she lets them fall through her fingers, rubs her hands together and looks at her palms. She thinks about Tahvi's palm and how it didn't burn.

As she walks toward the house she watches the two boys ahead of her. She notices Tahvi limping on his wooden leg and sees how his forged arm moves differently than his real one. She tries to think of a time when he was injured and nothing comes to mind. She searches her memory but can't recall helping her mother mend any broken bones or wounds for him—not even after he's had one of his spells. The longer she thinks about it, the more she believes she's never seen him hurt. She can't remember ever seeing anything as minor as a bruise.

# SEPHINE

Josephine fills goblets with water and places them atop a wooden tray on the cooking room table. She and Evangelina had anticipated most guests would trickle in throughout the afternoon, but almost all the guests have already arrived, which is keeping them busy with arrangements.

Sephine carries the tray to the courtyard in front of the house, where a number of tables are set up for the guests. Music, chatter, laughter and playful screams fill the air. She invited half the village, nearly fifty people. Evangelina also invited a few from nearby villages, customers who have become close acquaintances over the years. There are at least forty people present, a third of those being children.

The young ones play games. The adults enjoy pleasant conversation, while also taking turns cooking the meat that Evangelina had spiced for them, each of them excited to cook on her huge iron plate. Nearly a square meter in size, it was a special gift from her husband's brother and the only one of its kind in the village. The band of wayfarers Evangelina hired as their entertainment makes their way around the guests. Three of them are playing instruments, one is juggling and another is performing a puppet show for the children. There is a fortuneteller there as well, for the adults, and another pretending to make magic.

Sephine keeps a wary eye on the magician, skeptical about things unknown to her. She, like many, has heard rumors that magic exists and knows of the widespread stories of its use. She's never met a *real* magician and has never actually seen magic that she was aware of, but she knows that does not mean it doesn't exist.

What Sephine does reluctantly concede, each time she hears the subject discussed, is that the cosmos holds many mysteries that people have yet to understand. It's more than possible that magic might be one of them.

She is watching the magician pretend to pull small trinkets and toys from the ears of little children when she suddenly hears a child crying. The child sounds very young, much too young to be one of her children. She looks for the source of the crying and finds it.

A tot of about five years, Eldgeon of Maryth and Stephen, is holding his head and pointing to a table with an accusing finger. Sephine watches as his father scoops Eldgeon into his arms and tries to comfort him. She scans the courtyard for the twins. She notices them out of harm's way in the far south corner of the lot with Tahvi. She puts her hand over her eyes to block the sun star from her face. Tahvi and the twins are surrounded by several other children. They are playing one of the games Evangelina set up. Sephine takes a deep breath and exhales.

Sephine is pleased that the twins and Tahvi are so fond of each other. With her husband travelling so often he is practically a nomad, Sephine had worried the twins might feel abandoned. Instead they spend so much time with Tahvi they hardly seem to notice that their father is away. When their father is home the twins always ask to include Tahvi in any plans they have together. As Sephine is thinking about how inseparable they've been she notices Evangelina standing beside her.

"What happened with little Eldgeon?" Evangelina asks.

"He hit his head on the table."

"Poor dear. Was he injured?"

"I don't believe so. His father is with him near the puppet stage now." She points to where they're standing. The boy has stopped crying, showing more interest in the puppets than his pain.

"And Tahvi—with Sheree and Humbul, of course?" Evangelina asks.

"Of course. Shall we frost the sweetened breads?"

Evangelina nods and they walk back to the house together, confident the guests have all they need outside. In truth, they're busy appreciating the food and entertainment. Many people have brought gifts, which Evangelina will let Tahvi open in the evening. The sweetened breads are all that is left to finish. Evangelina made many and she looks forward to having a moment to sit down and relax, especially since Sephine will be helping her.

"Eva, I can't believe how fast Tahvi is growing. It seems that just yesterday he was a baby."

"I was just thinking about that the other day. Tahvi was fastening his leg and I remembered there was a time he couldn't do that without me. Not only is he growing quickly, but also his dexterity and physical strength are impressive for a child born with his limits. And his learning, Sephine—he no longer needs a review of lessons learned the day before. I can't understand how he can be so gifted in these areas and still have ... "

"The spells?"

"Well, yes. But what I thought to say is that he's having so many. They've increased so much over the past year. I thought maybe my fear was impacting my memory, but I checked the log and I was right. I still don't understand why he has them, or what it means that he is having more. He seems so healthy otherwise."

"I don't know that they mean anything, Eva. They don't seem to hurt him. Did Ocran have any new thoughts on the matter?"

Evangelina sighs in frustration.

"None. I'm convinced he has almost no thoughts at all."

Sephine chuckles. Her chuckle is contagious and Evangelina laughs with her.

"You know I believe he's never been much help with Tahvi. With few exceptions, most of what I learned about how to care for Tahvi's condition I've learned from you."

"I hoped maybe as Tahvi grew older, that Ocran might learn more. But in truth, I sometimes wonder if being an herbalist is a true calling for him."

Evangelina shakes her head.

As they're frosting the sweetened breads one of the villagers asks if they have more spices for the next round of meat. Sephine gives them to him and returns to the table.

"I've been meaning to tell you something," Sephine says solemnly.

"I'm listening," Eva says, slightly concerned.

"I miss Gaelan very much. I'm sad, sometimes even bitter, that his work keeps him away from us for long periods of time. I find myself feeling very lonely when he's gone. It is easier to keep busy. That's what I tell myself, anyway."

"I understand." Evangelina smiles.

"Thinking of you, Stefan, Tahvi and what you have been through … I am sometimes filled with so much grief I can't explain it, and yet … I believe it makes me appreciate that my husband is still with me. That he's able to see and know his children. When Stefan died, I wasn't sure you would survive it. I was very afraid for you."

"I remember." Evangelina is about to say more, but instead she waits.

"And when Tahvi was born as he was, I wasn't sure if you would lose him as well. I felt overwhelmed with relief when you didn't lose him and grateful that aside from the spells, his condition did not seem to impede him much." She pauses, her eyes watering. "I'm not sure I'm saying what I want to say."

Evangelina smiles but says nothing.

"I believe what I'm trying to say is that I am grateful to have you as my friend, and I pray to the stars that you and Tahvi will continue to be blessed throughout your life. I know I've said this before, but sometimes I feel that I don't say it enough."

Evangelina puts the sweetened bread she is holding on the table and offers her hand to Sephine, who accepts it. As Sephine cries, Evangelina caresses the top of Sephine's hand with her thumb.

"Thank you for sharing how you feel," Evangelina says. "But I know that you know our friendship has always been important to me, even more so after Stefan died. And you're more than a friend, you're family."

"Yes, we're family."

"My heart is with you."

"And mine is with you."

They continue working in silence for a few minutes, when Sephine breaks it by asking,

"Do you ever feel life has cheated you, because of Stefan's death and Tahvi's limitations?"

Evangelina considers this question for some time before answering.

"Do you remember what I shared with you about when I was pregnant and it was nearly time for Tahvi to be born?" Evangelina asked

"Do you mean how often he would wake you in the night?" Sephine asked.

"Yes. I would feel the movement in my belly and would cup my hands over it. Tahvi would kick me and I'd feel joy just knowing he was alive and part of me. I would rub my hands on my stomach, anxious to hold the baby that Stefan and I had waited so long for. I'd see the moonlight shining on my nightgown and covering my belly, and I'd imagine that my baby was glowing. I would look up at the moon and how it brightened the night sky, and I remember feeling very small. I couldn't help but think of Stefan and couldn't help but to be scared. I considered, as I would guess all mothers do, that Tahvi might not be healthy or, even worse, that I'd lose him during birth. My happiness about Tahvi was mixed with the grief I felt for Stefan.

"We had tried for so long to have a baby. It almost seemed cruel that I didn't discover I was pregnant until after he died. I remember looking at his side of the bed and touching his pillow. I would hold it in my arms and cry, thinking about how much I missed him and how much I still loved him.

"When I realized Stefan and I might never be able to have children I thought that would be the most difficult thing I'd ever have to overcome, but I was wrong. Losing Stefan was by far the most difficult thing I'd endured, and some days I wasn't sure how I would live without him. I felt that I was dying of grief until just before you told me I was pregnant. I think I must have known. All that time we had wanted children and were unable to have them. And now there was this miracle, this unexplained, beautiful miracle. Even though I would never see Stefan again I realized I had a piece of him—of us—to love and care for and that gave me more than enough reason to be. Sometimes it's still painful, especially when I think about how Stefan will never get to meet his son."

Sephine listens patiently. She's heard Evangelina share similar reflections before, but rarely.

While Evangelina speaks she continues to frost the sweetened breads, the rhythm of her voice slow and soothing. She talks about how much she cherished the life they had built together. She was a skilled seamstress and Stefan an excellent merchant, and together they had generated a successful tailoring shop, well known by most of the local villages. She thought their life together was charmed.

They had enough currency to care for their home and small farm and support their business, plus more than plenty left to overindulge at times. Many times after delivering orders to another village, Stefan would return home with a beautiful gift for her. During the earlier years, it was just little trinkets, things they could afford. Soon his gifts became more lavish and expensive, beautiful dresses or gowns that she could wear on special occasions. She remembers being playful with him the first time he brought her a dress. She said it was unsuitable to buy things from their competitors and she refused to accept it. They had both laughed as Stefan explained it was the only way to surprise her, as he couldn't possibly ask her to tailor a surprise dress for herself.

She speaks of the trips they took together, and how grateful and blessed she felt to have a man who loved her so much, one who was always so kind and considerate of her needs. When their success far surpassed what they had hoped it would be, he hired townsfolk to help with the shop so they wouldn't have to sacrifice their time together. She was worried that the success of the shop might drive them apart somehow, but it only brought them closer together. Stefan refused to let their work take priority over their union. He would say to her, "What we have means nothing if we don't have each other. We must always remember that." They had enough money to help other families in the village, and they did so. Because of it, they gained much respect and devotion from many of the villagers.

As she speaks about Stefan and describes what a good man he was, the tears come. She tries to hold them back but can't.

The happy memories that fill her heart always shift to the one that almost destroyed it. She tells Sephine of their last morning together. She had been crying because she'd dreamed of the children she was sure they would never have. Stefan encouraged her to have hope. She had 26 years then and they had tried for so long. She knew time was running out. Most women in the village had already birthed several children by the time they were her age and she had not even begun. Stefan, always supportive, had told her not to worry. He said children were certain. But even if they weren't, that if the stars did not bless them with children, then that just gave him more time to have her to himself. But he was always sure they would have a child someday, and she wondered how he could be so confident. She loved how much he had loved her and how reassuring he always was.

She tells Sephine how she remembers kissing him goodbye and waving as he drove away in their larger wagon to deliver a shipment. She recalls the day those from another village had come to see her. She remembers seeing Stefan's horse and wagon and the looks in their eyes. She had felt cold and sick to her stomach. They told her that Stefan happened upon thieves trying to steal from travelers from another village. These thieves were not trying to steal goods or coin, but children. The villagers saw Stefan disengage one of his horses from his wagon and confront the thieves, badly injuring one and then pursuing the others. Several of the villagers waited hours for him to return, but he never did. The villagers knew who Stephan was and felt indebted to him for saving their children, so they were kind enough to return the other horse and wagon to her when they brought the mournful news. She remembers panicking, asking them to show her exactly where the attack had happened. She hired several men to help her look for him, and some of the villagers helped as well. But when they found his horse not far from where he'd disappeared, it was slaughtered. She knew then that he was never coming home.

Sephine hands Evangelina a handkerchief to wipe her eyes. She also gives her some water and Evangelina thanks her. After a moment, she continues.

"I remember the grief, the unbelievable grief I felt over that next month, until you told me about the baby. I loved him before he was ever conceived. And I know this may sound strange, but from the moment he was born it was as though Stefan was with me again. I have never shared this with anyone until now, but I remember several times I could feel his presence in the room with Tahvi and me."

Sephine stares at her and Evangelina senses she is worried, maybe even frightened.

"I *know* he is not with us and I *know* he is gone, but what I'm trying to explain is that I still feel his love is here, with Tahvi and me. I can still feel his presence, his goodness, his … strength. Other than his body not lying beside mine when I sleep at night, it often feels as though he never left."

"Is this why you haven't considered another?" Sephine asks.

"Yes. In the beginning it was because of Tahvi. With all his complications, I wanted to give him as much attention and time as I could. But later, when I realized he didn't require nearly as much caregiving as I thought he would, I believed I'd naturally want another companion. But I didn't and don't feel the need. What I had when I was with Stefan—I feel as though it's still here. The grief I felt when Stefan died, it seems as though it dissipated once Tahvi was born. And unless I think very hard about our memories together or about the day he died, I remain content. I've heard people say that when you lose a companion it changes you. And I believe it did change me but somehow when Tahvi was born I know I was changed again. I can understand why that might not seem sensible to you or anyone else and it's likely the reason I don't speak of it. But it is what I feel and therefore what I believe."

"I don't doubt you, Eva. You are one of the most sound and reasonable people I know. I think it's wonderful that you feel this way."

They stare at each other with kind eyes and soft smiles. Then a look of solemnness appears on Evangelina's face.

"Are you feeling ill?" Sephine asks.

Evangelina hesitates a moment before speaking.

"I want to share something with you, something I haven't told anyone. Several nights after Stefan's death I went outside to look at the moon. Stefan and I used to do this together as often as we could. It was very cold, and I am sure that night I was still in shock. I had not eaten in days and I missed him terribly. I could not stop thinking about the children we would never have. The night was strikingly quiet, so quiet that the silence was much like it is when it snows, like someone had put a blanket over the world.

"It was so eerie that it made me feel alone and more detached than I was before. I realized later that I had left the house without a coat. I think it was because I felt so numb I was hoping the cold air would help me feel something, even if it was painful. I was starting to slip away from life and wanted to feel connected, feel something that made me remember I was alive, but there was a part of me that also wanted to be with Stefan and in that moment I was not sure which part would overcome me. I was about to return to bed when I saw it."

"Saw what?"

"It was a falling star. At least I believed it to be. It looked like it was heading straight for the house. I couldn't bring myself to move.

I'd never seen one so close. I remember believing that I could hear it. I felt the ground rumbling under my feet and pressure against my body, as though the force of the star was pushing against the air around it. I watched it race across the sky, directly over me, and then disappear."

"Why didn't you—"

"But that's not all. As I saw the star disappear, I noticed everything had a green hue, as though the moonlight had changed color. It took me a moment to realize it was raining—or something like rain. It was like dust, like a powder but cold, like flakes of snow just before they turn to water. It's difficult to explain. But this dust, it … it fell all around me, on my gown, on my skin, in my hair. And then it was gone, as though it never happened."

"Are you sure it wasn't a dream?" Sephine asks in a skeptical but sensitive tone.

"I've considered that, but it seemed very real. And because of Tahvi's disfigurement, I've wondered if, maybe, well … "

"Maybe what?"

"Do you believe it's possible that the dust from this star was, somehow, an enchantment that caused Tahvi's disfigurement?"

"Oh, I don't think so. I believe it's more possible that you were dreaming. You were grieving. Grief can cause troublesome things. I'm not claiming that what you say happened did not. But grief can twist the mind. It's even been known to cause visions. It's a very powerful emotion."

Evangelina puts her hand on her chest, without realizing she's done it, then looks away from Sephine.

Sephine realizes Evangelina is holding something back. "Is there something else?" she asks.

"I would agree with you, except that there is—"

Evangelina is interrupted by cheers and shouting from outside, followed by a boisterous greeting from a male voice.

"I will wager all your frosted sweetened breads that Jabneh is here," Sephine says.

"I would lose that wager."

"Let's welcome him, but then we shall continue, yes?" Sephine asks.

Evangelina nods.

They walk outside to receive Jabneh, the toymaker. He's

surrounded by many of the children. In his left hand he has a long wooden box that's been stained a dark brown and polished to a lovely shine. He also carries a large bag in his right hand. The long wooden box contains Tahvi's day of birth gift, but the bag holds small toys for all the other children. After many of the children have accepted their gifts, Evangelina greets him with a long embrace.

"Evangelina, good day and good health to you!"

"Welcome Jabneh, good day and good health to you."

He and Sephine exchange greetings as well and then he leans in closer to Evangelina, speaking in a lower voice.

"Where is Tahvi?" Jabneh asks.

Evangelina and Sephine look over the courtyard for the boy, then Sephine says, "He is there, playing with some of the other children."

"Ah. Do you have a moment? I've a surprise for you and Tahvi, but I'd like to show you first if I may."

"Sephine ... " Evangelina begins, but she doesn't need to finish.

"Of course." Sephine smiles. "Let me know when you're ready. I am going to walk a bit."

Evangelina nods and she and Jabneh walk toward the house, her left arm linked in his right.

Sephine makes her way around the courtyard. Everyone looks busy enjoying the celebration. As she checks with guests to see if anyone needs anything, she sees the magician again and makes a point of avoiding him. She notices Tahvi with her twins and several other children in a far corner of the courtyard playing a game, evidently not having seen the toymaker make his entrance.

She watches Tahvi as he plays with the children and notices something different about him. At first, she thinks maybe it's his gait: despite his false limb it seems graceful, though really it's always been that way. Even when Tahvi first began using the limbs he seemed to adjust quickly. Over time, with practice, he had gotten better with them, so today was like any other day. Then she thinks maybe his clothing is the reason. He is wearing an eggshell-colored tunic that Evangelina hand-embroidered, with a black intricate decoration that lines the tunic at the wrists, around the neckline and circling the bottom, with small black stones down the middle to serve as clasps. He wears leg coverings of a black color with it. Together, it's a handsome ensemble that fits him comfortably but loosely, and it sways as he moves, giving him a refined and poised appearance.

*No, it's not his gracefulness. What is it that's different?* she thinks. As they continue to play the game she observes his interactions with the other children. Though Humbul seems to be leading the game, the other children are crowded around Tahvi. They're playing ring peg, the object of the game being to get wooden rings looped onto a peg in the ground. They're nearly three meters from the peg and each child has three chances to get the rings onto the peg before the next child takes a turn. When it's Tahvi's turn, she notices the children paying close attention to what he's doing. When it's someone else's turn they watch that person, but also look to Tahvi. For what, she's not sure. *Is it guidance or approval?* she wonders.

She moves close enough to get a better view of who's getting the rings on the peg but not so close that they notice her. As others take their turn she watches Tahvi guide each of them, his hand moving in a motion that shows them how to try to get the ring onto the peg. As each child takes their turn, when they miss, Tahvi comforts them or encourages them to try again. Several times the rings land far from the peg and laughter ensues from everyone, even the current player.

Then it's Tahvi's turn again. He throws the first ring and from the moment it leaves his hand, it seems sure to catch the peg—and does. Then he throws the second ring and it catches the peg as well. The other children smile and cheer and jump. Some pat him on the back. As he's about to throw the third ring he stops. Instead of using his last turn he gives it to the child who had a turn before him, who couldn't manage to get any of his rings on the peg.

Tahvi hands him the ring and then has the child practice moving his arm and wrist in a way that might improve his chances. When he seems ready Tahvi whispers something in his ear, points at the peg and then takes a step backwards to give the child some space. The boy throws the ring. As it nears the peg Sephine is sure it's not going to catch it, but remarkably it changes direction. It barely catches the peg by the tip and spins wildly around the top of it before it settles on the ground.

Sephine flinches and shakes her head in surprise. She doesn't notice her mouth is agape or that she's taken a step forward. Clutching her dress with both hands, she realizes she's holding it so tight that her wrists are starting to ache. She releases her dress and tries to relax her hands. She watches as the children cheer and congratulate the boy. She's having difficulty grasping what she's just seen. It looked to her as if the ring were pushed while still in the air. *But how is that possible?* she thinks. The children drop the rings and toddle in her direction like a herd of sheep, moving on to another game. Despite the limp Tahvi leads the way, with Sheree and Humbul on either side of him. As they approach the card table where children can play the memory game, Sephine asks Tahvi if he will speak with her.

He comes to her and greets her with a hug.

"Are you enjoying your celebration?" she asks.

"Very much so, Sephine."

"Good. It always makes me happy to see you happy, Tahvi."

"Thank you for helping to make everything wonderful."

"It's my pleasure." She pauses. "Tahvi, will you answer a question for me?"

"Yes."

She kneels to meet him at eye level. "I was watching your game of ring peg and I saw Mabud catch his ring with your last turn."

The look on Tahvi's face shifts to another look, so brief that Sephine thinks maybe she's imagined it. She has enough time to wonder if it was a look of guilt or maybe sadness, but then Tahvi smiles and she can't remember what she saw on his face.

"Wasn't that amazing? I was very impressed!"

"Yes, I was as well. I was wondering … what did you say to him before he threw the ring?"

"Oh," Tahvi says, sounding surprised. The other children call to Tahvi, beckoning him to join them at the card table.

"I told him to sharpen his attention. To believe in the ring catching the peg. To close his eyes and see it in his mind before throwing it."

"Well," she stands up, "I would say that worked."

"Me too." He turns to walk back to the other children when Sephine stops him.

"Wait!"

"Yes?"

"What did you think I was going to ask you?" she asks kindly.

Tahvi pretends to be confused and doesn't answer her right away.

"I didn't know. May I play now?"

"Yes. Thank you, Tahvi."

"You're most welcome, Sephine."

Sephine watches Tahvi join the other children. This time Sheree leads the game. Like before, the children assemble near Tahvi. She feels that feeling again—that something seems different about him.

One of the guests walks over to Sephine and they speak for a short time about their welfare and their families. Sephine has difficulty staying present during their conversation. Once they're done Sephine notices Evangelina has finished her conversation with Jabneh and is standing at the entrance of the house. As Sephine is walking there to join her, a realization strikes her.

She stops, not even realizing that she's done it, and nearly trips on her own foot. She turns around and looks at Tahvi and the group of children. She was having trouble recognizing it, because she was looking for a *change*, something specific to Tahvi that has shifted.

*But there's nothing different about Tahvi. I just didn't see it until now. How could I not see it?* she thinks. What is different, what has always been different, is Tahvi's relationship with the children. In all her years and her experience with children, there is one thing all children had in common: they all had conflict.

As a midwife and herbalist, she knows at some point in a child's early years, their guardians have to begin acting as peacemakers. She learned that conflict always begins at an early age because children are too young to understand anything but their own importance. As they grow older, nearer to Tahvi's age, they become more aware of their differences. They learn more about how important it is to behave like those around them. Some of them can't help but tease or insult each other for even the smallest variations in behavior or appearance. It's something that always begins at that age and it happens with even the most docile children. It's a natural part of a child's manner to at times be rude, cruel or even violent. In those times it can be difficult to help them get hold of their emotions or reactions towards other children.

Sephine is aware Evangelina had made it known that Tahvi has a *lame* arm and leg rather than a missing arm and leg. Evangelina did this to spare him from exactly this type of ridicule or cruelty. As he grew older children noticed he didn't have the stamina they possessed. He didn't attend as many village gatherings as others his age. And of course, there are his spells, which he is having more frequently now. There had been several times when he had nearly lost consciousness while he was in the company of people not of his family. Tahvi was very different, so different that he should have been a target for other children's enmity.

As Sephine watches Tahvi playing with the children she notices it's the fellowship that's different. There seems to be an energy that surrounds them. It is almost tangible, as though they're all living in a bubble of exhilaration mixed with tranquility. As she watches them she thinks of memories and events where Tahvi was present with three or more children. For a moment she is convinced her memory is mistaken, or maybe her affection for Tahvi is clouding it. But she knows neither of these things is true.

She stares intensely at Tahvi and the children that surround him. Her eyes look upon a familiar scene of enthusiastic laughter and numerous smiles. It is nearly identical to the many scenes she has seen Tahvi in before. She thinks of his relationship with Sheree and Humbul. They're enamored with him, so much so that he is often the first thing on their minds when they awake in the morning. She knows then that it is not an error with her memory or how much she cares for Tahvi.

What she knows feels unmistakable. What is different about him, what has always been different, is that she has never seen another child in conflict with Tahvi.

She thinks about the conversation she and Evangelina had begun and finds herself eager to get back to it.

# THE TOYMAKER

Two months before Tahvi's day of birth, the village had celebrated Evangelina's expected motherhood by gathering for food and festivities. They had given her many gifts, which she looked forward to sharing with Tahvi. But when Tahvi was born with missing limbs, she was sure it was a sign that the infant would not live long. She was convinced that what she saw on the outer parts of his body was an indication of something gravely wrong with the inner parts of his body. She couldn't help but believe that he might not live past his first year, if even that. She coped with this uncertainty by living for the day and trying to enjoy every moment with him. She avoided thinking of days that likely would never come and tried her best to think of ways to make his life as full as possible. After sorting through all the gifts she'd been given, if the gift was not something Tahvi could use within the first year of his life she packed it away. Her thought, as much as she hated to think it, was that maybe she would give it to another mother in need once she had the strength to do so. She wasn't sure if this approach was mournful or positive. What she did know was that spending her days being with Tahvi, loving him and enjoying him, made her happy now. It made him happy, too.

It wasn't long before Evangelina forgot to worry about the years to come. Her perspective changed. She felt more hope and began to believe that there was nothing wrong with his inner body. Evangelina found herself frequently thinking of Stefan's opinions about having children. He had been sure that someday they would have them, and though he did not live to see the birth of his son, he had been right: Tahvi was born just as he said he would be. She remembered how hopeful Stefan had been. This hope, even though he could not possibly have known what the coming years would hold, brought him such happiness and joy. Though there were many days when Evangelina wanted to stop trying, she realized that Stefan's hope had also brought her hope and joy as well. It was because of that hope she could continue to enjoy life as much as she did even without children. So, when Tahvi had six months she decided it was time to change her approach.

"Sephine?" Evangelina had called.

"Yes?" Sephine was folding Tahvi's clothes and putting them in his dresser.

Evangelina was holding Tahvi, swaying from side to side. Each time she briefly increased the motion of her rocking he would smile at her. She smiled back while gently stroking his head.

"I've decided to make Tahvi an arm and a leg to replace the ones he doesn't have. I think it's important that his body become familiar with the weight of them."

Sephine had stopped what she was doing and looked at Evangelina. She took a moment to gather her thoughts before saying them. She decided to phrase them as a question instead.

"What prompted you to decide this?"

"I've thought on this very much lately. As Tahvi gets older he'll need to look more like other boys. I don't know how his condition will affect him as he grows older, but I believe it could cause more difficulties with his body than he has now. I'd like to prevent that if we can. I also don't want him to be uncomfortable around other children. If he doesn't have both legs he won't be able to walk and he'll feel strange around them. I don't want that for him. No one needs to know just how different he is."

"Eva." Sephine had a troubled expression on her face when she said her name.

Evangelina's eyes met Sephine's and she knew what Sephine was thinking. She saw the sorrow, the doubt, and what she perceived as disappointment. She knew what Sephine was going to say before she said it.

"I thought the plan was to think day by day with the boy?"

"It was. But haven't you observed?"

"Observed what?"

"Tahvi is strong and healthy. Other than his missing limbs, his health isn't different from that of other babies."

Sephine sighed. She was about to speak when Evangelina spoke first.

"He hasn't had any other special needs that we thought he might have. He hasn't even been ill."

"Eva, he has only—"

"I'm aware of his age. Still, I believed we would have seen other complications by now, but we haven't."

"Yes, it's good that we haven't seen signs, but it doesn't mean that his inner body is not affected. It could be too early to—"

"No." Evangelina stopped rocking Tahvi. She stood very still. "I know he is young and I understand that he ... is not completely healthy. But I will no longer live my life as though I could lose him at any moment. If I do ... lose him ... the pain will be great. But I ... I can't possibly plan for that, and I've been a fool to believe I could."

Sephine didn't speak. She walked closer to Evangelina and reached for baby Tahvi. Evangelina passed him to her and Sephine rocked him and kissed him gently on the forehead. Evangelina's eyes filled with lingering tears.

"My dear boy," Evangelina said to Tahvi as she cupped her hand over the top of his head, "you will have a long and healthy life, and we will not see your condition as something that limits you. It will be a possibility, a chance to see how clever your mother and her dear friend can be."

Sephine smiled as tears rolled down her own cheeks. She wanted to believe that Tahvi would be healthy. She didn't want Evangelina to have false hope, but she saw that her friend was resolute in her decision.

Evangelina was aware Sephine felt this way but hoped it would change. She believed her own hope would become contagious to Tahvi and Sephine the way that Stefan's hope had for her. For a moment, Evangelina had considered telling Sephine the one thing that only she knew about Tahvi, but she remained silent instead. Every instinct told her that this one thing should remain a secret, and besides, she was not ready to truly consider its significance.

Within days the women unpacked all the gifts given to Tahvi. They displayed the ones fitted for his age in areas throughout his room. They also began to fashion clothes and shoes in sizes that would fit him rightly over the next year.

The town was aware that the baby was unwell. When Tahvi was newly born, Evangelina had allowed only a few trusted people to see him, and she kept him secluded as much as possible to shield him from the heartless parts of humanity. During the first few months of his life, rumors circulated that he was deformed. It was only the reports of regular visits from one of the town's herbalist that gave villagers the idea that Tahvi was still alive.

Evangelina's home rested on the outskirts of Padhraig. Shortly before Tahvi was born and for nearly the first six months after, she had performed much of her tailoring work there. She preferred to work at home instead of at the shop, which stood in the central part of the small village. Now she decided it was time to begin working in the shop again and thought it best to take Tahvi with her as often as possible. She knew people would be curious about him, so she had to decide which parts of his condition she could be open about and which parts she should keep hidden. She also knew the story had to be believable yet unremarkable—her aim was to subdue their curiosity, not entice it.

What was most important was to make his missing limbs less obvious. She wanted to do as much as she could to keep Tahvi from being ridiculed or pitied. Evangelina spent much time trying to determine if and how she could give the boy limbs that made him seem complete without appearing more awkward than he might look without them. She kept a set of tools in her home that closely mirrored the set of tools she kept in the shop, including a scale that they used to weigh fabrics and other materials, so she had the essential items at home to make what was needed before she returned to working in the village shop again.

She began by weighing Tahvi's left arm and right leg, as best she could, to get a better idea of how much the fake limbs should weigh. Then she had to determine how natural she wanted Tahvi's limbs to appear. She decided she would try to duplicate only the weight and general feeling of his limbs—Tahvi was still an infant, so it was more the appearance that mattered, though she knew it would not be long before she'd have to consider what alterations to make for movement.

She decided the best way to imitate the limbs was to use small sacks sewn in the shape of an arm and a leg. She made the stitching a little tighter where the joints would normally appear, at the wrist and knee and so forth, hoping to give them the appearance of bendability. She sewed smaller pouches to fit inside the sacks and filled these with rice to match the weight of his limbs. Then she wrapped those pouches with cotton before stuffing them into the larger sacks to give the limbs a soft and slightly malleable feeling, similar to that of an infant's skin. Finally, she made a pair of gloves and slippers that would cover the boy's entire hand and foot. For the missing hand and foot, she simply overfilled these with cotton, which to the touch might not feel real but at a glance would do the trick. She realized that although she was an excellent tailor she didn't have skills in arts such as carving or sculpting, so she didn't plan to attempt fashioning anything that appeared to be real fingers or toes. Finally, she fastened delicate but durable fabric straps to each limb to enable her to attach them onto his body easily and comfortably underneath his clothes.

She and Sephine were surprised by the change they saw. The attachments were far from genuine but they were convincing enough to give the appearance, at least at a glance, that all his limbs were real. Tahvi resisted them initially but grew used to them in time. Both Evangelina and Sephine were extremely pleased with the outcome, and not even a month had passed before Evangelina was able to work in the shop again.

When she did return to work she brought Tahvi with her, so she could be with him throughout the day. She spent most of her time overseeing what went on in the shop rather than directly handling buyers' requests; she only worked on the tailoring jobs that were very intricate or important custom jobs. Sephine helped in any way she could, including watching Tahvi when Evangelina was busy. The village was growing, and so the shop was accepting more business than ever.

When villagers noticed Evangelina had returned they would come by to visit, almost always asking to see the baby. Evangelina was very open with them, and those who asked she told about his condition, sharing that his right arm and left leg were lame. She had said it was possible he might not have use of them, but only time would tell. Evangelina tried to appear overly protective to discourage anyone from requesting to hold him, but most people tried to be close to him and asked to hold him anyway. There were only a few who seemed nervous to be around him and made attempts at excuses or reasons why they could not be closer to him. Evangelina was not offended. Overall the response she received was overwhelmingly pleasant in comparison to what she expected. She often wondered if word had gotten out about Tahvi's true condition, and if pity or curiosity about that had played any part in their behavior.

One day while Evangelina was working in the shop, when Tahvi had nearly seven months of age, she was handling the accounting for the shop's inventory. She heard Tahvi laughing from the shop's sitting room, where he was with Sephine and Sheree. It was such a sweet sound, a high-pitched, squeaky giggle that filled her heart with joy and brought a smile to her face. She left the workroom and headed toward them to better hear her son's laughter and to see what it was that was making him so happy.

As Evangelina walked into the room she noticed Sephine sitting on the floor, cross-legged, holding Tahvi on her lap. He was facing away from Sephine and watching Sheree. She was entertaining him with one of the dolls Sephine had given Evangelina at the celebration before Tahvi's birth. It was very intricately made, and something a child would likely not find entertaining until they were much older. Until recently it had been packed away for that very reason. He laughed again and Evangelina smiled. Sheree made the doll dance, making the doll's legs and arms move as she hummed. Then Sheree moved it into a backwards flip. This time Tahvi's laugh was louder and more boisterous. He kicked with his leg and moved his arm up and down all the while. Then all the women were laughing.

Evangelina put one hand over her mouth, not wanting her laughter to distract Tahvi. As she watched him smile and laugh, she became curious about what he could possibly find so amusing. She looked at Sheree and then the doll. The doll was wearing a light blue dress with a material that looked smooth and glossy. Lace lined the bottom of the dress as well as the cuffs and the neckline, and she had dark hair that ended at her waist.

Evangelina thought the doll had an eerie realness to it. Because of its authentic figure and Sheree's maneuvering of it, it seemed to be dancing of its own volition. Evangelina stopped smiling. She looked at Tahvi. Then she looked at the doll. She looked at Tahvi again and once more at the doll. Sheree was still making it dance, but this time she was holding it by only its hands. Evangelina looked closer at the doll's arms. They were bending. And the doll was bouncing when Sheree made it touch the ground.

Evangelina rushed into the room, nearly tripping over her own feet. She dropped to her knees in front of Sheree and Sephine, startling both of them.

"Sheree, give me that doll!" she said loudly.

Sheree handed it to her without question and moved to her mother's side, fearful of Evangelina's unusual reaction.

"Eva, is something wrong?" Sephine asked.

Evangelina checked the doll's arms first to make sure they were bendable—they were, at both the wrists and elbows. Then she lifted the dress to verify what she *thought* she had seen. She pressed against the foot with her hand and felt the pressure of the foot press back. When she released the pressure, the foot advanced slightly toward her hand.

"Oh my stars and heaven," she said, almost inaudibly.

"Mother … " Sheree said as she cupped her hands together and brought them close to her chest.

"All is well, Sheree. There's no need for worry." Sephine held her daughter close and rubbed her arm. Sephine was still holding Tahvi in her lap. "Eva—"

"It *bends*, Sephine." Evangelina spoke before Sephine could finish. She kept the doll's dress lifted so she could demonstrate what its legs could do. "You see? It *bends* and it *locks* and it … it springs back!"

Sephine only stared at her for a moment, looking confused, and then her eyes grew wide.

"Oh. Ohhhh!" Sephine said.

"I can't believe I didn't think of this until now. How simple. How unbelievably silly of me! A toy! A doll! Where did you get it?"

"I … I had it made, by someone known for this type of work."

"Of course. Of course! Who is he? What's his name?"

"Umm, uh … something like … " She paused. "I'm sorry, Eva, but I can't remember. I know he lives in Violetta, or at least he did when I employed him."

Sephine looked at the doll and then at Evangelina.

"Do you think … maybe … ?" Evangelina started.

Sephine was already nodding, knowing what Evangelina was going to ask.

"If he can do this for a doll, then why not for Tahvi? Is that what you're thinking?

"Exactly. I must meet him."

Sheree had moved even closer to her mother. She was biting her nails and watching Evangelina closely. When Evangelina's eyes met Sheree's she realized she had frightened her.

"Oh dear. Oh, Sheree, I am very sorry. I frightened you?"

Sheree nodded. "Are you angry with me?" she asked.

"Absolutely not, my precious girl." Evangelina reached for Sheree and embraced her. "I'm happy and it's because of you."

"Me?"

"Yes, my dear. You've shown your mother and me a way to help Tahvi. And when he's older I will be able to tell him that you're the reason he's able to walk like all the other boys."

Sheree smiled. She didn't understand how she'd helped, but she felt happy nonetheless. Evangelina returned the doll to her and then moved a chair next to Sephine. She sat next to her, took Tahvi and held him in her arms. He was starting to fall asleep.

"Now," she whispered to Sephine, as she moved her index finger up and down the bridge of his nose, "Tell me everything you remember about this doll maker."

* * *

Within days of speaking with a few of the other merchants Evangelina discovered the doll maker's name was Jabneh. He was well known for both the quality and originality of his work. He was a general toymaker as well as a doll maker, and he ran a fruitful business making exceptional dolls and toys, including some that were custom made for people who wanted and could afford them. The success of his business very much mirrored that of Tahvi's parents.

Evangelina learned he was a widower who had lost his wife several years ago, and even more ill fated, had also lost his daughter at the same time. They'd been traveling to the town where his wife was born so that her parents could meet their granddaughter. It was very far from the village of Violetta. They could not afford to both be gone for the time it would take to complete the journey, so his wife's brother agreed to accompany them. Unfortunately, they had to pass through dangerous territories to get there. They never made it back. His daughter had only four years. After his family was gone it was said that Jabneh spent all his time on his work. It was known by many that he no longer lived in the home he had shared with his wife; he slept in a room in the back of his shop, in the central part of the village.

Except for the hours when the shop was open he spent much of his time as a recluse. He was known to be decent to all, but he rarely attended village functions or festivities. The only exception was when he had agreed to deliver a special toy or toys for a child's celebration of age or a similar momentous occasion. But even so, on those days he would not stay or participate in events—he simply made his delivery and would quickly be on his way.

The more Evangelina learned about him, the more empathetic she felt. She began to feel a sense of connection with him. She wondered if he felt lonely spending so much time by himself or if he felt lonelier when he was around people. She wondered if being with others made him think of his family and how much he loved and missed them. She thought about what it must feel like to lose a child, and then thought about losing Tahvi, but she quickly put the thought out of her mind. It was too much to tolerate.

It worried her that he was so secluded. Even if he were able to make limbs for Tahvi that could pass as real, she wasn't sure how long it would take to make them or what would be involved. Knowing what she knew about him now she also was not sure she could trust him with the knowledge of Tahvi's condition, but she knew she had to try. She was grateful that the trip to his village could be completed in less than a waking day. If she left in the early morning she could arrive there in the later part of the afternoon and see him before supper.

Less than a week after having her wonderful realization about Tahvi's doll, Evangelina decided to make the trip. She used her own smaller wagon but hired a driver, and asked Sephine if she would watch over the shop and her home while she was gone. Sephine, as usual, had agreed.

* * *

Evangelina left much later than she had expected to, and when she arrived in Violetta it was after dusk. It was a small village like that of Padhraig and most of the shops were closed. The few that Evangelina could see open held no interest for a mother and child. She paid for a room in the only boarding house with rooms available. After quickly settling in, she relieved her driver for the evening and asked the boarding house's caretaker about the toymaker, Jabneh. He advised her to walk outside, turn left and pass five other shops on the same side of the road. He said the shop was closed but if she was there to pick up an item, and had arranged this with Jabneh ahead of time, she could go around back. She nodded and thanked him for the information.

She wasn't sure if seeing him at night was a sensible idea and she was certainly tired from traveling. Also, since he didn't know of her arrival, there was a possibility he might be out making a delivery. Still, she found herself already walking in the direction of his shop. Tahvi had been sleeping in her arms since they'd arrived but now he was beginning to stir.

As she walked toward the shop, her fear, anticipation and hope all quickly amplified to the point where she felt nearly overwhelmed. She took several deep breaths and realized her hands were shaking. She sat down on a wooden bench and considered what she was about to do. Though she had heard nothing that gave her the impression she should be extra cautious, she had no personal experience with this man's character. It unnerved her that she was about to share one of her and Tahvi's most sacred secrets. If it turned out that he wasn't a man of good character not only could things go horribly wrong, but she would've revealed Tahvi's secrets to someone she couldn't trust. She began to cry as a sense of hopelessness enveloped her. She'd cried only a few tears when Tahvi awoke and spoke without warning.

"Mama."

Evangelina looked at him. Her first thought was that she had imagined it. Her next thought was that maybe she was more tired than she realized. Before she could consider a third possibility he spoke again.

"Mama."

She was looking right at him and she saw his lips move.

"You said Mama! You said Mama! Oh, my dear boy, your first word! Seph—" she started and then remembered she was in Violetta and Sephine was home in Padhraig. She looked around herself, as if to find someone to share this moment with, but it was only she and Tahvi.

"Mama," he said again.

This time Evangelina laughed aloud.

"Oh, it is like muuusic!" She held him to her chest and then gave him kisses on both cheeks. She wanted desperately to skip and dance, to release some of her joyous energy, but she didn't want to shake him. The nervousness and hopelessness she was feeling continued to melt away every time she heard him speak.

After her euphoria subsided, she realized she was more than happy—she was surprised. *What is the normal age for a baby to begin speaking?* she thought. But she couldn't remember. Because of Tahvi's condition she'd made the presumption that he might be slow to learn. However, his first word sounded like the most perfect one she had ever heard.

"We'll have to ask Sephine when we return," she said to him.

He smiled at her as if in agreement. Then his eyes took on that vacant look that babies often get, as if they know nothing about the world and are still awed by everything in it.

Evangelina looked forward and realized she was standing in front of the toymaker's shop. At least she assumed it was his shop, because it read 'Teresa's Toys and Trinkets' on the window. She thought it funny that she forgot to ask about the shop's name. There was a candle lamp outside the shop that was just bright enough to let her clearly see the lettering in the shop's window, but it was not bright enough to see inside it. She put her face against the glass and noticed curtains had been drawn so she was unable to see inside. There was a sign on the door that read CLOSED. Still, Evangelina found herself turning the doorknob to see if it was locked. When the door would not open, she decided to circle around to the back.

She had forgotten all the uncomfortable feelings she'd just experienced. Suddenly all that mattered was to find out if the toymaker would be able to help her. She walked around the shop until she could see the back entry, then stopped when she was several meters away from the back door. There was a small window in the door, covered by a shade on the inside. She could see a twinkle of light coming from inside the room. Then she heard a squeaking noise that sounded familiar and she was sure that the toymaker was inside.

She knocked on the door and waited.

She knocked several more times before she heard a response. "Who's there?"

He had a deep voice and spoke with a harsh tone. Evangelina tried to speak, but when she opened her mouth the only thing that came out of it was air.

And once again, Tahvi spoke. "Mama."

Evangelina giggled; she couldn't help it. She felt exhausted and emotionally drained. What exactly was she going to say to him? She realized it would've been best for her to wait until morning.

Just then she heard a click. The shade on the window flipped up and the window in the door opened. It was big enough for her to see what she assumed was the toymaker's face, as well as part of the lantern he was carrying. He looked at Evangelina, and though she couldn't read his face, she thought maybe he was confused or angry. He closed the window and a few moments later he opened the door.

"Who are you?"

"Good evening and good health to you, sir, I—"

The man sighed and leaned against the door. "My lady … it is not evening. It's well past evening. It's night. You see?" He pointed at the sky. "Now who are you?" This time, he said it slowly as if she were slow to think. "I don't have any orders scheduled to be picked up this evening."

"I'm not here for an order, sir. I'm looking for Jabneh, the toymaker."

"I am the toymaker," he said, "but as you can see, my shop is closed. Come back in the morning." As he started to close the door Evangelina put her hand against it.

"Wait! Sir, this is very important. I've traveled here from Padhraig. I had hoped I would arrive sooner. I saw your sign showing the shop was closed and I planned to wait until morning, but … but I've a shop as well and I have to get back to it. I was hoping maybe we could just … just talk about what I need and you could tell me if you will agree to make it. If you can't, I can be on my way."

"My lady, I can make almost anything, but I can't discuss almost anything when my shop is closed. Come back in the morning. I open shortly after dawn."

"Mama." Tahvi uttered.

When Tahvi said her name again Evangelina was looking at the toymaker and she tried to stifle her laughter. The situation suddenly seemed ridiculously absurd. Her restraint failed her and she laughed uncontrollably until she began to cry from laughing so hard. The toymaker watched her. He couldn't help but be amused.

Once she regained her composure, Evangelina said, "I'm very sorry to have bothered you. You're right. It was rude of me to ask to speak with you while your shop is closed. You must excuse my behavior. We have been travelling for much of the day and … well, my son Tahvi said his first word just a few minutes before I knocked on your door. And he's said it several times since then." She was still occasionally laughing as she spoke but she did her best to suppress the laughter. She wanted him to know she was sincere.

The look on the toymaker's face changed from amusement to something Evangelina could not quite place, but it was clear that he was considering something.

"Did you say your son's name is Tahvi?" he asked.

"Yes."

"And this is Tahvi?" He pointed at the baby.

"Yes."

He pushed the door open further with such force that the hinges squeaked and it banged against a bucket that was leaning against the wall. He looked behind the door to make sure the bucket hadn't toppled over. Then he stepped outside to get a better look at her. He was still holding the lantern.

"What is your name?"

"I am Evangelina of Phillip and Katherine."

"Oh my. Are you … Stefan's wife?"

Evangelina stared blankly at Jabneh. At first she didn't understand the question.

"Yes, I am. I mean … I was. No … wait." She stayed silent, trying to gather her thoughts.

"Oh dear, come in. Please come in."

He leaned against the door to hold it open for her and waved his hand to usher her in. He guided her to a room where he lit several lanterns, making it bright enough for her to see that it was a working room. There were two large tables with various tools on them, as well as what could only be toy parts. He told her she could sit where she liked and offered her some tea, which she accepted.

Now that she was able to see him in better light, his appearance astounded her. He was easily two meters tall, with a lanky frame. He had dark brown hair, a moustache and beard that had grown to the middle of his torso. His eyes were a darker brown, with dark circles under them to match. He was so thin that his clothes looked like they were meant for someone two sizes bigger than he was. Looking at him made Evangelina think of a walking cane with hair.

"You knew my husband," she said softly.

"Yes, I did," Jabneh replied.

"He never mentioned you. How is it that you knew him?"

"I am a customer of sorts," he said with a smile. "Your husband has been ... I'm sorry." The toymaker looked towards his feet and then rubbed his chin, feeling embarrassed. "He had been here every several months or so to sell your shop's fabrics and clothes."

Evangelina nodded.

"When my wife and I decided to try this business, it was slow at first as you can imagine. We made countless sacrifices and were not sure it would succeed. I had to borrow money many times and barter my skills for supplies or any other thing we needed. It was an arduous time for us. I met your husband in our village's fabric store, where I now buy all my material, since they buy much of their fabrics from you."

Evangelina nodded again and smiled. She remembered how she'd been nervous when Stefan wanted to venture into business. He'd believed in her much more than she had believed in herself and to her, his ideas had seemed nearly impossible. But they all worked out just like he'd said they would.

"I met Stefan, or he met me rather, in the store trying to barter for fabric. Unfortunately, there was nothing they needed at the time. Stefan overheard our conversation and asked if we could have a meal together. He offered to pay."

"Stefan would do that."

The toymaker nodded.

"We talked for a long time and when we were finished we came to an agreement. He said he would give me the fabric I needed in exchange for two things. First, I had to tell as many people as I could about your shop. Second, I had to agree to make a special toy for his son or daughter once he or she was born, something one-of-a-kind that no other child possessed."

Tahvi was sleeping again and Evangelina switched his position to put most of his weight on her opposite arm. When she looked at the toymaker again, she was crying.

"Should I stop speaking about your husband? I would understand if you wanted that."

She shook her head.

"Perhaps over a meal. Have you eaten supper?"

Evangelina realized she hadn't eaten in hours. She didn't even feel hungry, but she knew because of Tahvi she had to eat.

The toymaker gave her some bread to eat before the meal, then he began preparing a meal for them both. While he was cooking he continued to tell her about Stefan. He explained that Stefan would visit the shop each time he was in the village and sometimes, if they both had the time to do so, they would share a meal together. He said that over the past year before Stefan had died, Stefan became more and more convinced that he and Evangelina were going to have a child. Stefan told him the names they had picked. When the toymaker heard Stefan had died, he planned to keep his promise but he had also heard rumors that the child was stillborn, so he was unsure of what to do.

The toymaker spoke of his wife, daughter and brother, and how distraught he was over their deaths. Evangelina told him she'd heard about what happened to his family and they exchanged condolences.

The toymaker explained that in his grief he nearly ran his business into the ground from drinking and negligence, but he managed to save himself before that happened—barely. It took him over a year, and he still didn't feel like he was completely whole again, but maybe he never would be. What was important to him was the success of their shop because it was all he had left of their life together. He shared how despondent and broken he had felt and that he was sure Evangelina must have felt the same way. So he decided he would wait and after a year or so he would go to her, let her know what he promised to do for Stefan and see if there was anything else he might do to fulfill that promise.

"It was when you mentioned your son's name—that is when I knew it was you. I remembered the name *Tahvi*. Stefan talked about it a lot. I thought it a very good name for a boy and a man. Obviously, the rumors I've heard about the baby are not true. Thank the stars."

Evangelina gave him a brief smile. She was no longer crying but he thought her eyes seemed sad.

"I must apologize for my temperament. I am not normally this … demonstrative," she said.

"It's more than understandable, my lady. And I feel it is I who must apologize to you. Being a woman with a child who has travelled so far to see me, I should've offered you a few minutes. It was rude of me not to extend you an invitation."

"I believe you made up for that with the meal. It was delicious and I was famished."

Jabneh gave an odd look of concentration. "You said before that Tahvi said his first word today, yes?"

"That's right," Evangelina replied. "It was very unexpected. I didn't think he would speak until he had more months."

"How many months does he have?" the toymaker asked.

"Seven."

"That's a bit early, I think. He seems to have no trouble sleeping."

"That's right, he doesn't. And he sleeps often. But when he's awake he's more than a handful."

"Most are." A look of sadness fell over his eyes and he turned away from her. He waited a moment before speaking again.

"I presume you already know my name and lineage, yes?"

"Yes. I was told you are Jabneh of Sarah and Fahvyl."

"That is true. I am happy to meet you properly."

"And I you."

"On behalf of your husband, whom I am gratefully indebted to, I am eager to pay my debt," he said grandly. "What is it you would like for me to make for you?"

Rather than explaining to Jabneh what she wanted, she began to tell him about the doll Sephine had purchased from him. She recalled the first time she saw the doll in her shop with Sephine and Sheree.

"What fascinated me about the doll was that its arms and legs bent, like those of a real child. And its feet—when I pushed them against the ground or against my hand, they seemed to push back, as if they reacted to the strength of it."

"It sounds like one of the dolls I make with spring-loaded joints. Pressure placed against the feet in those dolls will cause them to recoil. It helps make the doll seem more real and it extends the doll's life because it prevents damage from the constant banging and thrashing that children—"

"Have you ever made one for a child?" Evangelina interrupted.

"All the dolls I make are for children," he said, sounding confused.

Evangelina shook her head. "No, have you ever made one for a child to wear?"

Jabneh stared at her and said nothing, still trying to comprehend the meaning of her question.

"From the moment I decided to meet you, I've been very nervous. I was not sure if you would be able or willing to help me. Obviously, both your friendship with Stefan and your promise to him were unknown to me. But now that I know of them I am very excited. I also feel at ease trusting you with what I am about to share and must ask that you share it with no one else without my permission. Do you give me your word?"

"I do."

Evangelina took a deep breath. "Thank you. You promised my husband that you would make something that's one-of-a-kind?"

Jabneh nodded his head slowly.

"It's time to fulfill that promise." She stood up and walked over to Jabneh. "I would like you to hold Tahvi. Will you?"

"I ... I think I'd rather not." He gently pulled at his beard. He looked at Tahvi and then looked away.

"But it—" she began to say. Then she stopped as she remembered the story about his daughter. Her cheeks took on a reddish color and she felt heat on her face and ears.

"I am so sorry. It's important that you get a good look at him. May I come closer to you?"

"Of course." When Evangelina brought the baby closer, Jabneh put both hands behind his back.

She stood in front of Jabneh and was so close that her forearms were nearly touching his stomach. Tahvi was still sleeping.

"Can you tell me if you notice anything ... different about him?"

It had been years since he'd allowed himself to be this close to an infant. At first, he felt touched when looking at the baby. Tahvi looked tiny, vulnerable and peaceful in his mother's arms. But soon, watching the baby sleep made Jabneh think of his daughter. He was reminded that he would never see her again. He felt a sinking, empty feeling that nearly overcame him ... until the baby opened his eyes. Jabneh looked into them and saw they were a dark brown, almost black. Before Jabneh realized it, he was speaking to those eyes.

"Hello, little one."

Tahvi giggled when he heard his voice, and Jabneh felt a sense of joy he had not felt since he had been with his family. Jabneh smiled and reached for him. This surprised Evangelina, but she handed him over. Jabneh rocked him in his arms and spoke to him, asking him how he liked travelling and if he was enjoying being in their village. His tone was gentle and loving. Evangelina imagined that he must have been a wonderful father. Each time Jabneh spoke, the baby smiled. Jabneh seemed to have forgotten Evangelina was there.

"Jabneh?"

"Yes? Oh, forgive me."

"Do you notice anything … different about him?"

"He seems more delightful than most babies I've seen, but nothing else."

"Good. Then my work is better than I believed it to be."

"I do not understand?"

Evangelina took Tahvi from Jabneh and set him on a clear area of the worktable. He was still wearing his day clothes and had a blanket wrapped around him. She unwrapped the blanket and as she did Tahvi moved only one arm and one leg, trying to stretch them. Jabneh noticed immediately that there was almost no movement in the other limbs. He stared at Tahvi, waiting for them to move but they remained nearly still.

"Is he … ?"

"People in our village believe he's lame. That's what I've told them. But he is not lame. At least, not in the way he appears to be."

"I don't understand."

"The promise you've made to me is to keep Tahvi's condition a secret. You will tell no one what I'm about to show you." Evangelina undressed her child and removed everything except his loincloth. Jabneh could see the delicate straps laced around his shoulder and waist. Evangelina began to untie the straps for his right arm. When she was finished she gently removed the false limb and placed it on the table next to him.

Jabneh gasped and then gripped his beard as if he were afraid it might fall off. Evangelina then removed the false leg. Once she did, Jabneh could not take his eyes off the boy.

"My stars," he said under his breath. "May I?"

He motioned toward the boy, implying he wanted to touch the

limbs. Evangelina nodded to let confirm her consent.

"What happened to him? These couldn't have been severed? He couldn't have healed so quickly or so ... "

"He was born this way."

"Born this ... but ... the ends of his limbs, they look ... almost ... "

"Carved?"

"Well ... yes, I suppose that's the best way to put it." Jabneh touched the stumps on the boy's leg and arm. They were smooth, like the appendage had been cut or severed by a sharp instrument, and there were no marks or imperfections in the skin. Just under the skin of each limb the surface felt hard. There were flat, round bones where the joints should have been.

Jabneh looked at Evangelina.

"I know. It is very unusual, but it *is* how he was born."

Evangelina placed her hand on his arm and said, "Jabneh, I don't know what his coming days hold. I don't know if he has other ailments that we have yet to see, but I want to make sure he enjoys life as much as he can. I don't want the world to be any harder for him than his destiny has already determined. I don't want other children to be cruel to him or try to hurt him because he's different. Life is already hard enough for children, even without the added difficulties. I want to make him look common and I want no one, save the few people who must be involved in his care, to ever know about his condition. Will you help me? Please?"

"Yes," he said almost immediately. "It would be my honor."

# VERTIMUS

He is a tall, strong and highly intimidating-looking man. Handsome, with black eyes and black hair, his overall appearance makes most men keep their distance and most women careful yet curious. It was rumored that even his horses had shied away from him the day he procured them.

He brings with him a fellow strong but odd-looking man. Odd because his face resembles stone, as his expressions rarely change. He is often deep in thought and his eyes have an empty look, as though he lives somewhere else and his body is just a shell he occasionally comes home to. He doesn't speak much, though the other man finds this doesn't matter because when he does, it is always stimulating. He is older and slightly shorter than his companion who brings him to this place. He looks forward to meeting the young boy that he's heard so much about.

"Take the wagon behind the barn and wait for me there. I'll signal you when it's time," the tall one says.

The shorter man nods and rides off with the wagon.

The tall one smiles as he approaches the house from the rear. Trees and spring bushes surround the yard, so the tall man knows he will be well hidden until he comes closer to the house. Evangelina's barn and stables stand about five meters away from the main house. If he walks between the main house and the barn, but closer to the house, this will give him enough opportunity to get closer to the courtyard. He won't be seen by any of the guests until it is too late.

He sneaks along the side of the main house. The laughter and chatting grow louder as he approaches the courtyard. He peers around the edge of the house to get a full view of the festivities and he scans the courtyard until he finds who he is looking for—there is the boy, playing a card game with his friends not far from the home's front entry. Most of the adults are occupied in other areas of the yard as he had hoped. No one will see him until he is nearly upon the boy. *This will be far too easy*, he thinks.

He moves away from the side of the house, abandoning his cover, and creeps slowly toward the children. Tahvi and most of the other children have their backs to him. Sheree, who is leading the game, is standing opposite them. When he is about four meters away he grows his speed to a running pace. Sheree looks up from the table and sees a large dark figure heading straight for them. She runs to Tahvi and stands in front of him, her back to him and her arms outstretched.

"Outsider!" she yells and points in the man's direction. The other children scatter. Some of them run to their parents and some stand behind Tahvi and Humbul. Only a few, who either have not registered the warning or are too frightened to move, stay where they are.

It all happens very quickly. Humbul turns in the direction Sheree is pointing and quickly moves by her side, as does Tahvi. They form a line, with several children still standing behind them. The boys are both frightened until they see the dark figure and realize he is not an outsider at all. Then Sheree realizes it too. The tall man had been running with the sun star behind him, making it hard to see his face. Now that he's been spotted, he is no longer running but standing and waiting with his hands in the air, to show he has no intention of harming them.

"All is well," Sheree yells. "He is not an outsider!"

"Uncle!" Tahvi shouts and limps toward him.

"Blast it! I meant to scare you," Vertimus says. He drops to one knee and embraces his nephew.

"I'm so happy you're here. Did you bring me a gift?" Tahvi asks.

He nods. "I have it right here." He pats his pocket to confirm it.

Some of the children hesitate before coming back to the card table. Several parents had stopped what they were doing, but once they see it's Tahvi's uncle, they return to their activities and advise their children to continue their play.

Sheree and Humbul approach Vertimus as he stands next to Tahvi. He places his hand on Tahvi's shoulder.

"Good day and good health to you, Sheree. And to you, Humbul," Vertimus says.

"Good day and good health to you, sir," Humbul replies.

Sheree stares at Vertimus, her arms crossed and her stare firm.

When she doesn't receive his greeting Vertimus asks, "Is all well with you, Sheree?"

"No. Sir, you are my elder and Tahvi's uncle, and therefore I respect you, but I must tell you that what you did wasn't very kind."

"Oh?" Vertimus says, smiling and crossing his own arms.

Sheree holds her stare. The muscles in her throat work as she swallows air. She looks nervous but she continues. "This is Tahvi's celebration, where many children are present, and as you can see you gave them quite a scare."

Vertimus leans forward, stares into her eyes and says kindly but firmly, "That certainly wasn't my intention, young one."

This time when Sheree speaks she holds her resolve but just barely.

"Yes, well ... because of this, one of the children could have been hurt ... in a panic. It's lucky that ... that the village is familiar with you ... or you could've been hurt as well ... if our elders hadn't ... recognized you."

Vertimus holds his stare, waiting to see if she's finished. He smiles, impressed by her tenacity and directness.

"You are right, young one. It was irresponsible of me to not first consider my actions."

"That is all I ask. That you consider what you do in the presence of the children."

"And I thank you for the reminder, Sheree. I must say that each time I see you, you seem to grow lovelier and more refined."

Sheree's cheeks turn a bright pink and she smiles. "Thank you. We um ... should be getting back to our game."

"I'd like to visit with my nephew for a bit, if he will permit it and if you all can spare him?"

"Of course," Sheree says with a relieved smile.

Vertimus leads Tahvi to a table where they can be away from most of the guests.

"Have you missed your uncle as much as I've missed you?"

"I have. I wondered if you would be here. The celebration wouldn't be the same without your attendance."

"I absolutely agree," he laughs.

They speak a while about the recent trip that had kept his uncle away from home for almost a month. Vertimus has a talent for bartering and this is how he makes his living. Unfortunately, this means he sometimes has to travel for a considerable amount of time. But the first thing he always does upon his return is to visit Evangelina and Tahvi. He asks the boy how his mother has fared over the past few weeks and Tahvi shares his thoughts. He is remarkably perceptive for a boy his age. His uncle understands why so he is not surprised.

"And how is Kaco?"

"He's wonderful. He's always been such a smart creature who's able to learn so much. He seems bored if I do not continue to teach him new tricks."

"And *where* is Kaco?"

"Don't you remember, Uncle? He is a nightwalker. He prefers to sleep mostly during the daytime."

"I see. And how are *you* doing, my boy?"

Tahvi speaks about how well his wooden limbs are working. He tells him how Jabneh has to keep adjusting them because he is growing so fast. He speaks about the lessons he's learning from his mother, how he's been helping at their shop on some days and how much he enjoys seeing and speaking to the other villagers. He also speaks about how difficult it sometimes is to hide his limbs from others.

Vertimus listens patiently and then moves closer to Tahvi. In a quieter voice he asks, "And how are the *other things* coming along?"

"Very well."

"Well, let's hear about your talents, then! Any new ones?" Vertimus gently nudges Tahvi's arm.

Tahvi smiles and puts his hand on his uncle's arm. "My mind has grown very strong, Uncle. I understand things much faster than before. I also know things that I haven't had lessons about. I can read beyond the books that mother wants me to read. And when I ... well, sometimes when I touch something, a tree, an animal or even a rock, I understand it better. I can learn its history, sometimes from its beginning." He pauses, then speaks in a quieter voice. "And of late,

I've learned that if I focus on something happening, I can make it come about."

Tahvi shares some of the things he's tried, including how he was able to start and stop a fire that morning. He mentions that Humbul and Sheree were present at the time.

"I believe I can trust them with anything, Uncle. Do you believe that's naive?"

"No, you can trust them with anything."

"How can I know?"

"You have very good instincts, my boy. I doubt those two will ever betray you in any way."

Tahvi smiles. He's always pleased when his uncle compliments him.

"Are my instincts the only reason you believe that?"

"Well, I'd say my instincts are pretty sharp as well. They tell me those twins are the likes of which you'll want to keep by your side."

Tahvi looks down at his feet. Vertimus thinks it's the first time the boy looks his age on this occasion.

"What troubles you, Tahvi?"

"This morning ... the fire ... it burned unexpectedly. I tried to make only a small flame but it escaped the fire pit and burned a spring bush nearby. If Sheree had been standing closer to it, she might have been burned. I felt ... "

"Ashamed?" Vertimus asks.

"Yes," Tahvi whispers.

"And guilty, or reckless maybe?"

Tahvi nods.

"That is reasonable."

Tahvi tilts his head. He studies his uncle's face and decides his uncle is being honest and not playful. "I don't understand."

Vertimus moves closer to Tahvi and gently puts his hand over his nephew's. "Tahvi, what you are able to do, the talents you've been given—they're not a child's game. I know you understand this now, but it's most important that you never allow yourself to forget it. You must continue to cultivate your gifts but never misuse them. Only use them in ways that are worthy of your character. Do whatever you can to avoid using them maliciously. And above all else, be careful that you never intentionally hurt anyone. Do you understand?"

"Yes."

"You look unsure."

"I was considering … what if someone tries to hurt us, like what happened to father or Jabneh's family?"

Vertimus sighs. It's a sigh of consideration and sadness. He thinks about Stefan, his only brother. As he considers Jabneh's family, it frightens him to think of Evangelina and Tahvi in harm's way. "I believe it's important to protect yourself and the people you love. In your case you'll need to learn to attune your abilities so that you don't ever use more than what's necessary."

"Are you disappointed in me, then?"

"Whatever for?"

"For nearly hurting Sheree."

"But you didn't hurt Sheree. If you feel regret about nearly hurting her, it's because you understand that you must be careful. One who commands such a gift must also be capable of the compassion and accountability needed to manage it. Your learning of that responsibility is required when you have abilities such as these. It's a valuable lesson that most men take decades to understand, yet you are learning it at a young age. I'm not disappointed. I am in awe of you."

Tahvi embraces his uncle. Vertimus returns his affection.

"Now," he says, "about the spells … let's speak of what's happening with them."

# JABNEH'S GIFT

As Evangelina and Jabneh walk into the house she asks, "How was your trip?"

"Fair. I made several stops to stretch my legs and back but I regret not stopping a few more times."

When they enter the cooking room she offers him water and he accepts it. He sets the box down on a part of the table that is not littered by sweetened breads.

"I've been thinking of moving here, to Padhraig," Jabneh says.

"Is it because the trip is not convenient?"

"No, it's not that. I often wish that our villages were closer, of course. The time it takes to travel here is not easy on the backside." Jabneh rubs his hip to emphasize his point and they both laugh.

"I'm thinking of expanding my business. I've even hired an apprentice. Did I mention that in my last letter?"

"No, but that's good to hear. Is he very helpful?"

"Surely. I've placed him in charge of shop maintenance and taking new orders. He's done well with these tasks. He is friendly and respectful, and he was raised in Violetta so the residents are very comfortable with him. Now I can focus all my time on building toys, accounting and Tahvi's needs. Those are the things I prefer most anyway. But I've been thinking ... I am renowned in Violetta. People know me there and trust my work. From what I understand they rarely go outside the village to buy toys. And Padhraig is growing. Do you know how many villagers live here now?"

"No, but I think it's nearly double the size it was before Tahvi was born."

"112 people according to the last resident count, much bigger than it used to be when I first began to visit. Since I'm visiting more often, it seems like a sensible choice to open another shop here."

"I agree it is a sensible choice."

Jabneh lowers his head, looking solemn.

"Is something worrying you?" Evangelina asks.

"There is another reason." He pauses, trying to find the best way to articulate what he wishes to say. "As I made the trip today I realized that this place feels more like my home than my own village. I no longer have any land there except the store. Since my wife and daughter died ... well, you and Tahvi ... it's as though you're my only family. You're both such a big part of my life that I ... I ... "

Evangelina moves close to him and takes one of his hands in hers. "I understand. I hope you know we feel the same way about you. You have built a special place for yourself in our family. I'm excited and joyful to hear that you might soon make Padhraig your home."

They both remain silent for a moment. Their eyes say more to each other than they have just shared with words. Their shared glance speaks of relief, comfort and friendship.

They hug briefly. It's then Jabneh who breaks the silence.

"How is Tahvi getting along with other children? Are all still ignorant to his condition?"

"Yes, all except Sheree and Humbul, of course. Remarkably enough, no one has questioned it. He doesn't play with the other children for long periods of time except on social occasions such as today. That's likely made it easier. Children are still very curious about him when he's in the shop with me. They ask lots of questions about how he gets along with his limitations. They seem instantly drawn to him. Then again, my shop is full of fabric and not toys; I suppose to the children Tahvi is the most interesting thing in it."

Jabneh nods.

"Though there is a young boy who seems uncomfortable around Tahvi," she continues. "When I consider it, I believe he's uncomfortable around most villagers. His parents aren't very warm. I suppose he's inherited that behavior from them."

"Is it Aahil of Rebecca and Onym?" Jabneh asks.

"You know him?"

"I believe everyone knows him, or of him. He seems a very

unpleasant child. Is he here today?"

"We invited him but I've seen neither him nor his parents. I doubt they'll be in attendance. I believe they avoid social gatherings unless they have business to be done."

"I've heard this as well."

"They've only lived in the village for a few months, though. Maybe as time passes they will make more appearances."

Evangelina moves her hand over the box on the table. It feels hard and smooth, and she smells fresh wood and polish. It's so beautiful it could be a gift in itself.

"Do you want to know what's in it or do you want to *see* what's in it?"

She considers this for a moment and then says, "I want to know what's in it. But I prefer to *see* it with Tahvi. Is that fitting?"

"Of course." Jabneh places his hands over the box so that now both he and Evangelina are touching it at opposite ends. He slowly moves his hand over the top of it, back and forth, as if it's an animal to which he wants to show affection. "What is in this box is something I've never made before and something I believe will make Tahvi very happy. It's also perhaps my finest work ever. In this box is a new arm … with a moveable hand and fingers."

"Movable?" Evangelina nearly whispers.

"Yes. I know it's hard to believe. I could barely believe it myself when I discovered how to do it but let me assure you that it will work for Tahvi. I know because I've already tested it with one of my dolls. Tahvi will be able to use two hands—not with the freedom of a real hand, of course, but it will be much more helpful than the lame hand he has now.

"There are two pieces to the device. There is the section that fits to the elbow and extends to a wrist. Then there is a hand, which he can manipulate using small levers, though he'll need to use his other hand to make them move. The wrist has adjustable joints in it. These will allow him more flexibility. I'm excited to see what he'll be able to accomplish with it."

Evangelina pulls the box toward her and begins to pull at the latch that keeps it closed.

Jabneh pulls the box back toward himself.

"I thought you preferred to wait for Tahvi?"

Evangelina removes her hands from the box as if it's grown hot to the touch. She sits back in her chair and sighs deeply, feeling grateful. "I knew that this was something special, but I had no idea that … that you'd be giving him a gift such as this today."

"Would you still like to wait?" He taps the top of the box and waits patiently for an answer. Then with a smile he says, "It really is quite remarkable."

"No!" Evangelina says quickly, and then just as fast, "I mean yes! I will wait for Tahvi."

They laugh together. It's joyous laughter, but for Evangelina it's also relief. Tahvi is a brilliant child. What he lacks in physical ability he seems to make up for in resourcefulness. He manages exceptionally well, all things considered. But at times she has noticed him watching the other children running or playing a game that requires much physical skill. In those times she believed the look in his eyes had seemed sad. Tahvi is rarely sad, and it is hard for Evangelina to see him that way, his eyes coveting something he doesn't have. She can't help but think of how much more normal he might feel with this new arm.

Evangelina stands and picks up the box. It's remarkably light. She moves the box to confirm the weight and then looks at Jabneh.

"You're thinking about how light it is?" he asks.

"Yes."

"It's nearly the exact weight of Tahvi's other arm."

She rubs the box once more. "I'm taking it to my room. Tahvi can open it after the other guests leave. Thank you for … for making this for my son."

"Let's see how it works and then you can thank me."

"It will work. It will work just as you say it will. Everything you make does."

When she returns from her room Jabneh is standing. "Sephine came by and said the play is about to begin," he says.

"I've heard great things about their act and have been looking forward to this since I hired them. Come. I would like it very much if you sat by me."

Evangelina links her arm in his and they walk outside together, both excited about the play.

Many chairs have already been arranged in front of a large stage. A rug has been laid out in front of the chairs for the younger children. There are several people helping arrange the chairs that remain, including Tahvi, Sheree and Humbul. Tahvi is dragging one with his functional arm and moving a little slower than the others, but they don't seem to notice. Evangelina goes to Tahvi to help him. When he sees her, he drops the chair and limps toward her, embracing her waist.

"Mother, I'm enjoying this so much! My uncle said there will be magic!"

"I'm happy that you're enjoying your celebration, and what your uncle told you is true, there will be magic. Would you like help with your chair?"

He nods and they grab the chair together, carrying it toward the other rows.

"Where is your uncle?" she asks Tahvi.

Tahvi looks up at her and smiles. When she turns to look for him she finds him standing right behind her. She drops the chair in surprise.

"Heavens, Vertimus! How long have you been here?"

He embraces her and lifts her off the ground. "Not nearly long enough. Good evening to you, Eva. How are you?"

"I'm well. But I've been on my feet most of the day, so I'm grateful for the chance to sit and be entertained. How are you?"

"Glorious. You look amazing, and so does my nephew."

They look to Tahvi and see he has resumed dragging the chair. Sheree is now helping him.

"Thank you. Care to sit with us?"

"Yes."

They help the others finish setting up the chairs and then sit together. Other guests have started seating themselves and many of the children are still trying to find their places on the rug, chatting all the while, eager with anticipation. They look like busy little ants.

Tahvi is sitting in front of Evangelina, with Sheree and Humbul on either side of him. Jabneh takes a seat on Evangelina's left and Vertimus takes a seat on her right. Before Sephine sits next to Jabneh she gently hugs her son from behind.

Sephine looks over at Evangelina and asks, "Eva, did you finish frosting the sweetened breads?"

"Oh, the sweetened breads, I forgot!" Evangelina stands, intent on walking inside but Sephine makes a motion with her hand, urging her to sit down.

"Not to worry, I'll finish them, there aren't many left. I insist. Please sit down."

Evangelina smiles and sits back in her chair. "Thank you. If you change your mind—"

"Nonsense, I will be finished before the play begins."

She gives a welcoming smile to Vertimus, whom she had not had a chance to greet yet, and then takes her leave.

"Does Tahvi know what this performance is about?" Vertimus asks.

"He knows of the magic thanks to you." She nudges him gently in the gut with her elbow. "But he doesn't know the subject of the play. It's a threaded theme. The magic and the theme are meant to complement each other."

"I see."

Evangelina sighs. "We've missed you, Vertimus. I'm so glad you are able to be here. And I know this day is more special for Tahvi because of it. It doesn't surprise me that you were able to come, though, since you've made it a point to never miss special occasions."

Vertimus places a hand over hers. "I will always try to be here when you need me ... and even when it's merely a want." He winks at her and she jokingly pushes his hand away.

"I've a favor to ask. May I ask it?

"Please do."

"I've brought a friend with me for this trip."

"And this friend is?" she asks, waiting for a name.

"This friend is resting in his wagon. I wanted to speak with you before inviting him. I believe he would enjoy the play and was hoping he could join us."

"Of course. A guest of yours is always welcome in my home."

"Very well, I will return with him."

"I will make sure your seats are not occupied. Be quick, though. They're about to begin."

Vertimus nods. As he walks to the carriage, he admires Evangelina's home. It is quite lovely and looking at it brings up memories of when he had helped his brother build it. He misses Stefan very much and he still carries guilt for not being here when he died. He's convinced his presence could have made a difference.

As he walks past the house sadness overcomes him and he has to look away. It's best for him to focus on what he can influence now rather than what was meant to be lost.

# PLAYERS AND MAGIC

The wayfarers break through the noise in the crowd, announcing the show will begin within minutes. Almost everyone is seated now. A few of the guests are straggling in from the yard, still making conversation.

It's nearly evening by this time. The sun star is low, painting the clouds on the horizon with a dark pink and purple glow. The contrast with the gray clouds in the dark part of the sky gives it an ominous look, like something wonderful but scary is about to happen. The sky has yet to cry rain but the air feels moist, as though rain is on its way.

The wayfarers' stage is made of solid, dark brown wooden panels and easily measures six meters wide by four meters deep. It's surrounded by large stakes placed in the ground at the four corners of the stage, each holding a torch that burns extremely bright against the overcast sky. The stakes in the background of the stage are wider than the stakes in the foreground, and nearly a meter taller. This, coupled with the dark red curtain used to conceal the back section, gives the stage an impressive appearance.

Sheree and Humbul are the first to notice them: figures garbed in black masks and robes, so covered that not even their faces are visible, approach each of the torches with a long wooden stick tipped with a glossy substance. In unison, they place the glossy ends atop the torches, which simultaneously burst into larger flames with a loud POP. Some of the smaller children applaud while others gasp. Several parents laugh nervously. Humbul pulls lightly but rapidly on Sheree's sleeve and begins rocking back and forth with excitement. The act has already won his approval.

The robed figures slowly walk backwards and disappear behind the stage. Then the curtains part and a wayfarer dressed in a simple dark blue tunic walks to the forefront of the stage. He reads from a scroll. "Welcome, all. This evening you will hear a narration about the origin of magic and see one of the greatest magicians in all the lands. Don't leave, don't speak, don't even blink—lest you miss one of the most astonishing tricks anyone has ever seen!"

Music begins to play from flutes and guitars, but the players and their instruments are nowhere to be seen. It's a peaceful yet somewhat haunting tune. The curtains part again and the act begins with a tall, beautiful woman who enters the stage. She has black hair that drapes down past her shoulders and chest and ends just above her stomach. Sections of her hair are braided, some flowing down over her arms and others rolled on top of her head in a round formation. She wears a black dress that shines like satin with dark purple sequins that appear in clustered patterns. The flames from the torches give the appearance that the clusters are moving of their own will. Long intricate feathers run down the length of the back of the dress from her shoulders to her mid-thighs. She wears black, tight, fitted gloves that cover the length of her arms, tied with delicate bows at the end of them. Sheree thinks she looks like some sort of beautiful but dangerous bird.

The woman begins to tell the wayfarers' story of the origin of magic.

"*Magic … is a gift from the gods. The gods, who created the stars and skies, called it their music.*"

As she speaks, the curtains open behind her and figures dressed in dark clothes appear on the stage again. They carry props that represent the characters and objects in the story. They bring them to the foreground of the stage when the woman mentions them.

"*Many moons ago, the gods sent their music to all the worlds that were inhabited by people, in hopes that people would use it as the gods did.*"

As she describes the planets the gods sent magic to, Vertimus returns with his guest and takes a seat next to Evangelina. His guest takes a seat next to Vertimus, then he looks over at Evangelina and greets her.

"I am Exos," he speaks softly.

"I am Evangelina," she whispers.

"Good health to you and thank you for the invitation."

Evangelina nods. Before she turns her attention back to the play, she notices his solid features, which are a strong contrast with his gentle voice.

*"And as the gods had hoped, some of the inhabitants used their music well. Today, these worlds continue to flourish and their people live in harmony, using magic to further the progress of their people and to honor the lives and worlds they were given."*

As she speaks she walks the length of the stage, careful to not stand in front of the actors or props as she does. She makes use of much of its space by opening her arms wide and lifting or waving her staff at the appropriate moments.

Sheree is mesmerized by her beauty and mannerisms. She's never seen anyone like her. As she watches her, she longs to possess the beauty and grace this woman has. It is right then that Sheree decides a player is what she would like to become.

*"However, in some worlds this was not the case. The magic was ill treated and inhabitants used it to dominate, conquer and plunder brazenly. They used it to manipulate and punish in ways the gods had not expected nor intended. This made the gods very angry, and they began desolating entire worlds where people had taken their music and corrupted it—purifying the worlds, they called it.*

*"But in their rage and disappointment the gods had inadvertently destroyed the virtuous as well as the culpable.*

*"There was one man in our world who still possessed the gods' music. He'd heard of the gods' anger and their efforts to purify the worlds, so he tried to hide the magic within himself in hopes the gods would not find it.*

*"The gods did find it. But when they felt the fear within his heart, they were ashamed. They ceased the cleansing that very moment and chose not to take the magic from him. This man later fathered children, and he shared this gift of magic with them. They in turn passed it onto their families and, in some cases, trusted friends.*

*"For many years these people used the magic as the gods intended … until one day, one who was not pure learned how to use this magic. He soon taught others, and our world was at odds with the music of the gods yet again.*

*"The gods discovered this but were not eager to purify any world again, as the last cleansing had taken the lives of so many innocents. The gods also carried remorse over learning that magic, though easily managed by them, could be overwhelming to people and could corrupt their hearts. So the gods decided to leave our world as it was—with a small group of us in possession of magic. Some use magic well, and those the gods leave to themselves. Others use it to taint, and these*

*are the ones the gods hunt for. As they search the stars carrying out their godly duties, like parents watching over their children, they look upon worlds and withdraw their music from those who seek to destroy balance and harmony.*

*"It is for this reason that those who use magic but are dark in their hearts must be cautious and must practice it in secret. They can't wage war and plunder because they would be sighted by the gods. They must hide themselves from the gods or the magic will be taken from them, just as it was from the others long ago."*

As the wayfarer finishes the tale, Sephine returns amid the applause. The introduction has captured their attention completely. She takes her place beside Jabneh, just in time for the play to start.

The characters and props have withdrawn and the woman stands alone on the stage. Her eyes search the audience and then she makes a circular motion with her staff. The end of the staff brightens and the fire in the torches surrounding the stage amplifies. The audience gasps and laughs.

The woman steps to the edge of the stage. As she extends her staff the curtains are drawn open and characters stand motionless, as if stopped in time.

*"Now, a true tale of enchantment, love, deception and retribution, as we present ... The Beckoning of Hadden."*

Sheree watches the beautiful woman descend from the left side of the stage and walk gracefully behind it, as though she is still playing a part. Sheree extends her neck to keep the woman in her view as long as possible. As the woman disappears behind the stage Sheree smiles at the idea of being able to someday wear a costume that looks like hers. She runs her fingers through her hair, imagining what her hair will look and feel like when it's fashioned in the same way. When the characters begin to move she returns her attention to the stage. But from time to time, she looks on either side of the stage hoping to catch another glimpse of the woman.

A narrator, heard but not seen by the audience, tells much of the play. The actors mostly mimic what the narrator is saying but at points critical to the story, they speak their lines. The tale begins with a young boy named Hadden, who lives on a farm with his mother and father. The father is cursing the boy because he has overwatered some of their crops. He explains that the crops are a necessity and that he must learn to tend to them properly. The boy apologizes. The scenes show Hadden growing older, revealing scenarios that all have similar outcomes.

The boy becomes a young man whose life is littered with a series of failures. Long after his father has died he continues to care for the farm with his mother, but just enough to survive. The boy's mother tries to tell him, as she has many times in the past, that life can sometimes be difficult. She encourages him to have faith and believe that life will mend. She tells him he must pray and ask for help from the gods, but he has grown bitter and resentful and refuses to do so.

Feeling humiliated and beaten, Hadden decides he will end his life by jumping from a cliff close to their home.

The wayfarers have created a marvelous illusion to represent the cliff and the sea: as Hadden begins walking across the stage, light blue sheets appear in front of him, moving in a way that gives them the appearance of fluidity. As they rise, Hadden rises in the background. The sheets must be hiding a ladder or platform, Sheree thinks, because he is now nearly two meters above the stage floor. The idea of falling into the sea seems to bring him a sense of peace—his shoulders relax and his body hunches slightly over the edge. As he's about to jump, he hears a man's voice from behind him and nearly falls over the cliff. The audience shares gasps followed by nervous laughter.

Hadden curses the man for scaring him. The man is wearing a cloak of a fine and costly cloth, which does not escape Hadden's attention. The man laughs and tells Hadden he knows he was about to jump and that he should reconsider ending his life. He tells Hadden that he has the power to change fate and he can give Hadden this power. Hadden will become wealthy and will know only success in every area of his life from now until death. Hadden does not believe him. He waves his hand at him in a dismissive gesture, but then wonders how this man knows what he was about to do.

Hadden turns to ask him and the man grabs Hadden's arm forcefully. Hadden tries to pull away but the man pulls him closer and begins to whisper to him the specific details of all his failures ... and furthermore, *his thoughts and feelings* about his failures, things Hadden has not shared with anyone.

Hadden's eyes grow wide and his mouth hangs from his face. He drops to his knees and grabs at the man's cloak, begging for his help. He begins to weep and confesses that everything the man has told him is true. Hadden swears that if the man helps him, he will do anything he asks of him.

The man caresses Hadden's head and smiles. He tells him of the affluence, admiration and even love that he will experience if he accepts this power. Then he tells him it's costly.

Hadden puts his hands over his eyes and shakes his head, feeling defeated and humiliated again. Hadden tells the man he has no means to pay for this power. The man tells Hadden money is not needed— he will pay him with a life.

The man promises Hadden that for the next ten years he will need for nothing. He explains that Hadden's life will be envied by many and he will live like the prince of his kingdom, but at the end of those ten years he must give up a life.

Hadden accepts quickly. Though he has only 19 years he imagines ten years of a life filled with success would make up for all the time he has lived without it. The man smiles and explains they must make an oath to keep this agreement, and if Hadden breaks it, the man will return Hadden to his miserable life and take from him all that has been given. He will also take the use of his arms and legs and will ensure he lives a long life this way, dependent on others to survive. When Hadden agrees to all the terms the man reminds him that they must make an oath. He grabs Hadden forcefully and opens his tunic to reveal his chest. With a smile, he says to him, "This will not be absent of pain."

With the nail of his right index finger, the man burns a strange circular symbol into Hadden's chest. The audience makes sounds of awe as they hear a sizzling sound and smoke appears. Hadden cries out, but the pain lasts only a few moments. Hadden straightens his back and stands tall. He takes a deep breath and lifts his head, smelling the air. The feelings of desperation he felt just moments ago are gone. He feels weightless and hopeful. He looks back at the sea and he is instantly drawn to the beauty of the world and the feeling of wanting to end his life is banished from his spirit. He looks at his hands and arms to see if his body has changed, but it hasn't.

"Remember your oath to me. In ten years … a life."

When Hadden turns to thank him, the man is gone.

Hadden's luck changes that very day. On his way home he finds a bag of lavish clothes, coinage and tools left by the side of the path. It is not placed neatly as though someone had intentionally left it for him; instead it is strewn about as if it had fallen from a carriage unknown to the driver. He rushes home with it eager to begin his new life.

Just as the strange man had predicted, Hadden soon becomes wealthy, prosperous and well liked by all who know him. Within a year he meets a woman he quickly falls in love with, and she follows suit and falls in love with him as well. They have a long courtship that is the envy of everyone in their village. Shortly after they're married, fate blesses them with a girl child.

When Hadden's daughter has five years, he is walking with her through the town, enjoying a pleasant day of shopping and learning. He teaches her the names of many things that she sees in the town. As their driver takes them home in their carriage Hadden sees a man and woman sitting by the side of the road. They're very thin and dressed in rags that are barely clothes. He asks the driver to stop the carriage so he can give them some food and coins, but when he approaches them he notices the man's arms are misshapen. As he reaches toward them to offer his charity, the man looks up at him and Hadden notices his chest: it bears the same mark as his own.

Just then Hadden's daughter calls his name. Hadden drops the fruit and coins and runs back toward the carriage. He can hear the woman thanking him and shouting blessings.

That night Hadden has trouble sleeping. He paces throughout his home as his wife and daughter sleep. He sits on his daughter's bed and rests his hand on her back, thinking about how much he will miss her. Then he goes to his wife and watches her as she sleeps peacefully. He walks outside his home, sits on the floor of the porch and touches the fine, smooth wood. He begins to cry as he thinks about the oath he made. He knows he must keep his promise.

Hadden begins arranging his affairs to ensure his wife, daughter and mother are secure with the wealth he has attained so that when he gives his life to the man, they will want for nothing.

On the last day of the tenth year, Hadden is prepared to say goodbye to this world. He spends the day with his family, knowing the man will soon come for him. They watch the rising of the sun star together, visit the animals on the farm and walk and play games until late in the afternoon. As Hadden is with his family, admiring the sight of the vast property he now owns and contemplating how different it is from what he owned when he was a child, he sees a figure appear in the distance. Hadden watches as it walks toward him.

The man has returned as promised, wearing the same type of cloak, albeit modernized in the latest fashion.

The man smiles when he sees Hadden and congratulates him on his wealth and success. His wife and daughter are not far from Hadden, and his wife notices Hadden speaking to someone she does not recognize.

Hadden expresses his gratitude and thanks the man for giving him the happiness and prosperity he has experienced. He shares that his life has been full of joy just as the man said it would be and that he is ready to honor his oath. He asks if he can wait until he's able to send his wife and daughter away, so they don't have to see him leave.

The man laughs and tells him there's no need for his wife and daughter to leave, as Hadden has to choose which of their lives he will sacrifice. Hadden shakes his head in disbelief and argues with the man. He reminds him of their deal and that he agreed to give his *own* life and not anyone else's.

The man corrects him in a firm and cunning tone. He repeats the exact words of the oath: "You swore to give *a* life."

Hadden is furious. He challenges the man, stating over and over again this was not the deal they made. Then the man points a finger at Hadden's tunic. The audience murmurs and gasps as Hadden's tunic begins to burn. A small hole burns, showing the scar from the oath they made, then the burning stops.

"You owe me a life and you must choose. If you do not choose, I will choose for you." His voice is loud and menacing and suddenly the audience hears the sound of farm animals wailing and howling coming from backstage. Hadden's wife, realizing the animals sense danger, approaches from behind holding their daughter's hand. She asks who this man is and what he wants of them.

Hadden urges them to stop where they are. He stands in front of them to protect them from whatever malevolent magic this man has brought with him.

With tears in his eyes, Hadden says, "You will not take either of them."

"Then you must pay the price."

Hadden remembers the man on the side of the road and the woman with him. He remembers that everything will be taken from him and from his family. He knows he's been tricked but he is trapped by his oath.

The wife curses the man and demands that he depart their land. The man responds by telling her that were it not for him, they would not have any property; that her husband's wealth and fortune has a toll and he has yet to pay it. He tells her about the deal her husband made.

"My lady, your husband promised me the life of you or your child long ago, and I've come here to claim it."

The wife denies that this could ever be true. She holds her daughter close to her and looks to her husband for an explanation. He tells her that he thought it was his own life he had promised. He holds her and kisses her and does the same with their daughter. He tells his wife how much he loves her and they both begin to weep. He apologizes for not telling her about the deal and says he was prepared to sacrifice his life because the years he's spent with her have been filled with joy, and he never expected to have the love he was so blessed to have received.

"You must choose!" the man yells.

Hadden looks at his wife and thinks of the woman on the side of the road.

"You must find another," he tells her at last. "You must marry another and you must take our daughter with you."

Then he turns to the robed man and repeats that he will not give the life of his daughter or child, and he agrees to the consequence.

The robed man becomes infuriated. He was depending on Hadden's weakness and fear to claim his reward. Now he will acquire nothing. In his haste, he strips the farm of all its bounty. The audience makes sounds that convey their excitement and anticipation as the stage floor and setting begin to shake. Animal figures of pigs, chickens and horses placed around the stage slowly fall over, to represent their death. The settings of green rolling hills are removed and replaced by settings of tall weeds and hills overgrown with brush. The house, which the players made to appear far away on one of the hills in the background, begins to fall apart and tiny pieces of wood fall onto the stage.

The audience watches in astonishment as the clothes Hadden, his wife and daughter are wearing begin to darken and rip right before their eyes. As the characters are surrounded by desolation, the man looks at his wife and reminds her that she and his daughter are what have brought him happiness and he will be forever grateful. He clings to them both and tells them to close their eyes. He starts to feel weakness in his legs and collapses. His wife, crying, tries to hold him but his weight carries her to the ground with him.

As he begins losing feeling in his arms he sees a bright light appear, like a star but much larger, slowly crossing the sky. The audience makes awe sounds as they watch a bright light that at first sparkles fiercely over the stage but then quickly becomes a solitary glow. Hadden looks to the sky and says, "Do you hear it? It is the sound of our creators."

The voices speak as one, in a melodic tone that sounds mostly feminine. The evil magician had become careless. He had forgotten to practice his magic in secret and so the gods had found him.

In an instant they separate the magic from the magician and because over the years he had let it consume him, there is nothing left of him when they're done. The robe he had clothed himself in sinks to the ground and the man disappears.

The creators tell Hadden they're touched by the sacrifice he was willing to make for his family, and they are honored by his honesty and courage. They tell him they feel sympathetic and remorseful, as the magic and any result of it are a direct consequence of their actions. In an act of atonement, they restore the farm to its original condition and give life back to the animals. They offer their blessings and assure Hadden and his family that they won't be harmed in this way again.

Before they depart, Hadden thinks of the man and woman he saw on the side of the road and pleads, "Wait! I believe there are others who have been deceived. Will you help them?"

The voices reply, "There are always others. We are always watching."

Then the star disappears.

The actors step forward to bow once the play is over. The audience erupts with applause and whistles. Tahvi, Sheree and Humbul are on their feet. The twins hop up and down while Tahvi claps his hand against his leg.

Tahvi turns to Evangelina, "Mother, that was fantastic!"

"Yes. I thought so, too."

Exos watches the boy from his seat. A look of curiosity appears on his face as he observes the boy speaking with his mother. Exos wishes he had been sitting closer to him.

The actors clear the stage and the woman in blue returns to introduce the final performance, the magician by the name of Aaban. People in the audience gasp as he takes the stage. He has a charismatic and commanding presence: he is a tall, handsome man, with bright blue eyes, chiseled features and long, black hair tied back in a braid. His illusions are as enjoyable as the play. Though he performs a few tricks that one might see in any wayfarer group, he also does several that no one in the audience has seen before.

When he makes fire appear in his palm and passes it from one hand to another, Sheree and Humbul look toward each other at the same time and then look at Tahvi. Sephine happens to notice this and touches Sheree on the shoulder.

Sephine whispers to her, "Is all well?"

Sheree nods and turns her attention back to Aaban.

The audience cheers after every trick. For the final one, the magician asks for a volunteer from the audience. Many of the children raise their hands, including Tahvi, Sheree and Humbul, with Humbul's hand being remarkably high, as he is practically standing.

Then the magician asks, "Where is the boy who has eight years today?"

Tahvi looks back at his mother. He has a smile on his face that shows nearly all his teeth.

"I am! I'm Tahvi!" he shouts.

Sheree and Humbul help Tahvi stand before he moves toward the stage by himself.

As Tahvi ascends a short flight of stairs made up of four steps, Evangelina realizes he is on display. This is the first time, which she can remember, that Tahvi is the center of attention for so many people. She looks around at the audience. Everyone is looking at him. She feels heat in her chest and behind her ears. Her palms feel damp. She starts rubbing the back of her neck and considering what she should do. She had asked that they include him in the performance but had not considered the handling of it. *How could I be so careless?* she thinks.

A sense of panic rises within her as she thinks about what they might ask him to do. Whatever it is, she's not sure he can do it or if it will give the audience an idea about the truth of his condition. She wants to pull him off the stage but doesn't know how without arousing suspicion or encouraging questions. She tries to be calm but her nervousness gets the better of her and she is about to stand up when Vertimus gently grabs her forearm.

He moves closer to her, still looking toward the stage, and whispers, "It will all be well."

She looks at him and sees he's focused on Tahvi. He squeezes her hand to reassure her. She turns back toward the stage. She feels less nervous now. She holds his hand in return, trying to allow herself to relax.

Once Tahvi is on the stage the magician welcomes him. He asks Tahvi what his favorite part of the celebration has been so far. As Tahvi answers two men covered in dark clothes wheel out a large box on the stage. It's big enough for the magician to stand in. Tahvi hears whispers and gasps from the audience as the men move the box behind him. The beautiful woman in the blue dress appears on the stage again. She directs Tahvi to move aside while the magician opens the box.

The magician stands within it and pounds it in various places from the inside to show its solidity. As he does so, the woman crouches next to Tahvi and whispers, "You're very lucky. The magician shares the secret of the illusion with those who volunteer. They must, in turn, promise not to share the secret."

Tahvi smiles, looks at his mother and waves to her. He begins to fidget and tremble with excitement. The woman notices two of his limbs are trembling more than the others and remembers what his mother had told them about his condition. She adjusts her dress so she can gracefully but comfortably kneel next to him and offers her hand. Tahvi takes it but continues to watch the magician as he spins the box and shows that it can only be opened by a door in the front.

The magician asks for another volunteer to test the fortitude and composition of the box. When he chooses Humbul, Humbul nearly steps on one of the children as he runs to the stage.

He nudges Tahvi. "I was picked too!"

Tahvi nudges him in return with equal enthusiasm.

The magician asks Humbul to test the inside and outside of the box just as the magician had. Unfortunately, Humbul is a little more exuberant than the magician expects and while trying to find a door in the side of the box he nearly knocks it over. The audience laughs, as do those on the stage.

While Aaban oversees Humbul testing the box, most of the

audience is watching them. Sheree, though, watches the beautiful woman. Sheree notices her whispering something to Tahvi and that he's not fidgeting as much as he was. She notices an intense look on his face. She's seen him that way before. He's concentrating but he's also captivated by whatever he's thinking about or, in this case, what's being told to him.

It's during this dialogue that the woman quickly explains to Tahvi how he will achieve getting out of and back into the box. "Dear boy, I have something to tell you. Will you hear it?" she asks kindly.

Tahvi nods.

"There is a trap door at the bottom that leads to an opening in the stage. When you hear the magician recite his chant, you are to leave the box quickly. There will be someone there to help you open and close the trap door as it only opens from the outside. When it's time for you to reappear, you will hear the magician chant again but this time he will recite it from end to beginning. This will give you time to climb back into the box. Do you understand?"

Tahvi nods again, trying his best not to smile. He can hardly wait for the trick to begin.

The magician thanks Humbul and directs him back to his seat.

"Is there nothing else I can do? Humbul asks. "I can be a wonderful apprentice!"

Light laughter arises from the audience, and Aaban thanks him again and sends him on his way, looking quite relieved to see him walk off the stage.

Now it's time for the illusion to begin and Aaban extends his hand to Tahvi. The woman guides Tahvi toward him and states, this time loud enough for the audience to hear, "Remember, you have no reason to be afraid, little one. Trust that the master will take care."

She and Aaban exchange a sign that confirms Tahvi was given the proper instructions.

"Are you ready to begin?" he asks Tahvi.

"Yes!" Tahvi shouts.

The magician opens the box and helps Tahvi stand inside it. He tells Tahvi to put his hands firmly on the sides. Tahvi uses his functional hand to move his forged one against the interior wall. As he does so Evangelina tightens her grip on Vertimus' hand. Tahvi smiles and looks directly at her. She smiles and waves to Tahvi, attempting to hide her concern.

All sides of the box are lined with a smooth, black material. It feels soft and comforting on his hand. It reminds him of the material his mother has used to make some of her dresses. He's small inside the box compared to the magician.

Aaban tells him, loud enough so the audience may hear, "You must breathe deeply while you are in the box. Do you understand?"

Tahvi nods.

"You must have complete trust in me or this cannot work. Do you trust me?"

"Yes!" Tahvi shouts and the audience explodes with laughter.

Aaban laughs as well. "Then let us begin!" he exclaims.

Aaban begins to close the door and Tahvi acts like he's biting his nails, pretending to be afraid. The magician sees this and gives him a quick wink before the door closes completely and Tahvi stifles a giggle.

"You are a most charming apprentice," he whispers to Tahvi.

The men dressed in dark clothes help Aaban cover the box with a lightweight black cloth. The magician begins to chant strange words. The audience is already captivated and can't stop looking at the box. Aaban commands the men to turn the box in four full revolutions and then signals them to stop. When the box stops moving, the torches ignite briefly but powerfully, and the same POP sound happens again. Aaban jerks the cloth away from the box and opens the door.

Gasps and sounds of awe arise from the audience when they see only emptiness. This is quickly followed by applause. Sheree and Humbul exchange a swift glance, as though the other's acknowledgment is required to confirm their own reality.

Evangelina's nervousness ignites again when she sees Tahvi isn't there. She tries not to worry but is finding it more difficult to stay seated. Aaban stands in the box to show the emptiness is not an illusion. He then exits and duplicates the same steps. He has the box covered with the cloth and begins to chant. This time the chant seems longer and different from the original recitation. The men in robes turn the box again, this time in five revolutions. When they stop, the torches ignite one last time. Aaban smiles at the audience and jerks the cloth from the box again.

There is silence and a heavy feeling of anticipation from the audience as he delays the opening of the door. In that moment, there is a clear and audible THUD from within the box. Aaban and the woman on stage exchange an apprehensive look. She nearly opens the door but stops herself. Hoping all is well, Aaban yanks open the door with a dramatic gesture.

Aaban is looking towards the audience, sure that something is not right—the applause and nervous chuckling that usually follow the opening of the door is absent, replaced by gasps and looks of concern or shock. Some of the women and children have raised their hands to their faces and he sees a tall man from the audience moving quickly towards the stage.

When Aaban looks into the box he sees Tahvi, not moving. He's collapsed, his body slightly curled, with his eyes closed.

# THE VISITOR

By the time Evangelina reaches the stage Vertimus is there, lifting Tahvi out of the box.

"Is he in good health?" Aaban asks. "I ... I am not sure what's happening. There is nothing in the box that could've harmed him."

Vertimus sees the crowd is growing anxious. He notices the magician and the woman are nervous as well. As wayfarers, he knows they're accustomed to being a target; considered both wanderers and outsiders, wayfarers are often blamed for unfortunate coincidences.

"The boy is well," Vertimus whispers to Evangelina. "Best you take care of this."

Vertimus makes a quick gesture toward the audience and Evangelina knows she must do as he suggests. She puts her hand over Tahvi's lips, feeling the warmth of his breathing.

"Take him to his room. I will see to the guests."

As Vertimus departs the stage with Tahvi, Sheree and Humbul follow him into the house. Everyone is watching them, including Exos.

Their attention returns to the stage when they hear Evangelina's voice.

"All ... if I may have your attention? Tahvi is not hurt. You all know of his condition, but some of you may not know that he sometimes has fainting spells when he is excited or overwhelmed. He's not familiar with this much activity in a single day. With this celebration, he has been playful and restless since this morning. It seems that now he'll need to rest, so unfortunately, we will have to end the evening before he's able to open any gifts."

Evangelina motions to the beautiful woman to call the actors and musicians on stage.

"I'd like to share my gratitude to our guests who have provided the incredible merriment this evening."

Evangelina gives the woman a hug and then begins clapping. The audience quickly follows suit. Evangelina takes a moment to thank each of the wayfarers individually as the audience continues to applaud. Then she turns her attention on the crowd once again.

"Our entertainers will close the evening by playing some music for us and we have sweetened breads for you all to take home with you. I'm honored you were all here to help celebrate Tahvi's day of birth. I regret that Tahvi and I are unable to spend the rest of the evening with you, but I must retire now to care for him. Thank you again for your presence and kindness."

Exos watches Evangelina as a few of the more curious guests try to question her about Tahvi's well being or to thank her for her invitation and hospitality. She is brief but graceful in her responses. He's sure she must be eager to be with Tahvi, tempered with her need to ensure the celebration closes on a positive note. He sees it's important to her that her guests do not direct suspicions or prejudices toward the wayfarers, and Exos admires her diplomatic nature. He considers what a challenge it must be for her to care for someone as special as Tahvi for this long.

Exos allows his gaze to drift over the evening's activity. The wayfarers are playing music now. Some of the guests are gathering near Sephine and Jabneh, who are bringing out the sweetened breads. Others are still lingering, talking about what they enjoyed in the play or trying to figure out how the magician did some of his tricks. Most of all, Exos notices the crowd no longer seems worried. Evangelina doesn't appear to be worried either, but he believes this is merely a ruse. A few of the guests cast quick, distrustful looks at the wayfarers, but then their gazes drift elsewhere.

*They seem highly aware of what a protective mother Evangelina is and how much she loves her son*, he thinks. She wouldn't take the time to thank the wayfarers or even to say goodbye to a number of guests if Tahvi were in danger. She gracefully contained a situation that could have easily become quite dangerous. A small grin appears on his face as he realizes this woman's potential for understanding and empathy.

* * *

Evangelina appears calm when breaking from the crowd, but the moment she walks inside her home she closes the door and rushes to Tahvi's room.

Tahvi is asleep on his bed. Vertimus sits next to him, monitoring the boy's breathing. Tahvi's room is spacious, with large, comfortable pillows lining the wall opposite his bed and several chairs lining the other walls. Sheree and Humbul had dragged a larger chair next to Tahvi's bed so that they can sit together and be closer to him. Kaco is resting in Sheree's lap.

"The boy is warm and his breathing seems slow, even for one who is sleeping. This is a normal reaction with his spells, yes?" Vertimus asks.

Evangelina nods her head and then looks to the twins. She gives them a gentle smile.

"You've seen this before, and you know he'll be well in time?"

The twins nod in unison but both look as concerned as Evangelina feels. They're holding hands. Evangelina kneels in front of them and pets Kaco.

"It would be of great help to me if you both helped your mother and Jabneh pass out the sweetened breads and bid goodbye to our guests. Once they're gone you can come back and be with Tahvi. Would you do that for me?"

Humbul concedes but Sheree is hesitant. After a moment she agrees as well.

"You may take Kaco with you. I'm sure some of the children might enjoy seeing him."

Kaco jumps off of Sheree's lap and onto Tahvi's bed. He lies next to the boy and rests his chin on his arm.

Evangelina grins. "Or maybe he can stay here."

Sheree and Humbul begin to leave the room, with Humbul in the lead. Sheree delays a moment to look at Tahvi. She looks like she's about to walk back to him until Humbul gently takes her hand and guides her out of the room.

Evangelina takes the chair the twins were sitting in and moves it even closer to the bed. Vertimus offers to exchange seats with her, as he is sitting on the bed next to Tahvi. She waves her hand to show it's not necessary.

She rubs Tahvi's head and feels the heat radiating from the boy's body.

"He's never had a spell in front of anyone from town before."

"Never?" Vertimus asks.

"No. Not even the herbalists have seen it happen. There were times when I thought he might, but he never has. Only those closest to him know it's a symptom of his condition."

"The spells don't seem to hurt him, though."

"Not that I know of. But I'm frightened regardless."

"Why is that?"

"Because they're happening more often."

\* \* \*

Most of the guests have left. Sephine and Jabneh are giving sweetened breads to the few who are still lingering, and Humbul is busy throwing scraps away and wrapping the meat that had gone uneaten, but there isn't much. Sheree has brought most of Tahvi's presents inside. She's carrying the last two in when she notices the beautiful woman speaking with Aaban. The other wayfarers are still playing music, but not on the stage, which they have already finished dismantling.

Sheree watches the woman as she speaks, again admiring how graceful and beautiful she is. She stares intensely at the detail of her dress and wonders if Evangelina or her mother could create something that extravagant for her. She thinks that maybe one day she might be able to make one herself. When Sheree's eyes drift back to the woman's face she realizes the woman is staring at her. She smiles at Sheree and it's the only invitation she needs; Sheree walks over to the woman with presents still in hand.

"I think you're so beautiful."

"Another one," Aaban complains. "I need to start wearing a dress. I'm off to help the others, Sabina. I'll leave you to your admirer."

He bows to Sabina and then Sheree, who can barely take her eyes off Sabina long enough to acknowledge him.

"Your name is Sabina?"

"Yes, it is."

"It's as beautiful as you are."

The woman smiles, "What's your name?"

"I'm Sheree of Sephine and Gaelan."

"Sheree is a beautiful name. Did you enjoy the play?"

"Yes. I thought it most creative and well done. And I thought you were fascinating."

"Thank you. I'm humbled by your flattery."

"I'd like to be as you are when I have your years. Does it take many years to learn to be a ... " Sheree hesitates.

"A player, my dear. Or performer, if you prefer. I've been a player since I was a child. I think you would make a good player, if that's truly what you wish to do."

"How can I be as beautiful as you are?"

Sabina laughs. "You are already beautiful. What *we* do, it's all just a veil."

Sabina holds her dress with both hands in a gesture of presentation. "The robes, the hair, the paint—they're all only a costume. It's the person who wears them that gives them real beauty. But they're a necessary part of the illusion. If you want to be as I am you must learn the art of costume and face painting. You must also learn the art of performing. Ask your parents to see many plays. And practice the arts daily whenever you can."

"I will." Sheree's voice is filled with conviction and sincerity as if the words are an oath.

The woman smiles and lifts Sheree's chin with her hand. She has many admirers, but this child is particularly endearing. She wonders at her maturity and candor. Sabina studies her face for a moment. Her features suggest she will be a beautiful woman. Her green eyes are striking and her dark brown hair will look lovely in braids and rolls, as Sabina's does.

Sabina reaches behind her neck and unhooks one of the necklaces she's wearing. It holds a dark blue stone that is about half the size of Sheree's palm. She kneels down to Sheree, places the necklace over her head and closes the clasp around her neck.

Sheree puts Tahvi's presents on the ground so she can touch the stone. The necklace is so long that the stone rests on her abdomen. When she lifts it, it captures light in a way that makes it shimmer in the center, as if many stars are trapped inside.

"This is my gift to you. It's the first piece to your wardrobe of illusion. I hope there are many to follow."

"Thank you! There will be. I promise!"

"I must take my leave now. I hope your friend recovers soon and that he enjoyed the play as much as you did. Farewell, Sheree."

Suddenly remembering Tahvi, Sheree thanks the woman again, picks up the presents and heads back to the house. As she walks, she feels like her feet are gliding over the ground with each step she takes. She shifts the presents, carrying them with her left hand so she can hold the stone in her right.

* * *

"Tahvi mentioned the frequency had increased yet again. He said the change began not long ago and that it was a sudden one," Vertimus says.

"It's true. Not only has the frequency increased but the duration as well. He was in this state for half a day a few weeks ago. I nearly lost my senses and decided to call one of the herbalists, but then he awoke. When he did, same as every time, it's as though nothing's happened. He remembers that it happened but it's like sleep; he has no sense of time. When he does wake, he doesn't know if he's been sleeping for minutes or hours."

"Have any of the village herbalists helped much?"

"No, not with regard to the spells," Evangelina says, frustrated.

"Has Tahvi visited other herbalists who were helpful?"

Evangelina thinks a moment. "No. Sephine advised of an herbalist that we should try, but she is in a village that requires at least a day's travel, which is difficult for Tahvi, as he grows tired easily. I was hoping this change would pass and that the spells would lessen, but we may have to ready ourselves for a trip instead."

Evangelina had placed a bowl of cool water by Tahvi's bed. Now she soaks a small rag in the water and puts it on his forehead to cool him. Kaco is still lying on his arm, occasionally lifting his head when Tahvi's breathing changes and then setting it back down when Tahvi doesn't awaken.

"Maybe that won't be necessary," Vertimus adds.

"What makes you think so?"

"The man I brought with me, Exos—he is an herbalist. I was hoping you'd be open to letting him see Tahvi."

Evangelina's voice is cold. "He knows nothing of his condition. How could he—"

"He knows everything about his condition, including what you keep hidden."

She stands suddenly, dropping the rag in her anger. "Vertimus, he's an outsider! I can't believe you would risk—"

"He's not an outsider, Evangelina."

"He is to us!"

"Evangelina, please hear me. I've known him for almost half my years. Stefan knew him."

Evangelina is crying now, stunned by the revelation that Vertimus has told someone of Tahvi's condition without her permission. "Stefan never spoke the name Exos."

"There was not a reason for him to share it with you."

Evangelina wipes the tears from her eyes. She's about to ask another question when Vertimus speaks.

"Many times he has offered me guidance and resolutions when I didn't know what to do. And you know all herbalists are not equally effective, nor do they all practice the same talents. I've watched him succeed where many herbalists have failed. I trust him. That is why I risked telling him about Tahvi. I believe he may be able to give you the answers you're seeking."

"If you've known him for many years why didn't you mention him before?"

"There didn't seem to be a need until as of late. Now that his spells have begun to increase … it's something I believe you should consider."

Evangelina stares at Vertimus and then at Tahvi.

Vertimus moves closer to her and speaks softly. "Do you have any idea what's happening with the boy? Do you know anyone who does?"

"No."

"What harm can there be if one more person knows, especially if it's someone who might also know how to help him?"

Evangelina tries to remember how much she trusts Vertimus. She knows he would never do anything to harm Tahvi. She is quiet for a long time before she speaks again. "Let him see him."

* * *

When Exos enters the home he sees Jabneh, Sephine and her children cleaning and storing the dishes used for the celebration. They're efficient but quiet, and their concern hangs heavy in the air. They all stop what they're doing to look at him when he walks by. He raises his hand in a greeting, which is returned first by the twins, then the elders, as Vertimus leads him to Tahvi's room.

"Thank you for inviting me into your home. I wish it could be for a different purpose."

"Vertimus tells me he's known you for many years and that you know about Tahvi's condition."

"It's true," Exos says.

"Do you have an understanding of his special circumstances? Have you seen this condition before?"

Exos looks at Vertimus. Vertimus shakes his head and places his forefinger over his mouth. Evangelina is looking at Tahvi and doesn't see this exchange.

"I've worked with many that have had special conditions but I haven't experienced all of these specific ones before. In my history I've helped to ameliorate and sometimes cure some of the strangest of disorders and afflictions. I have the ability to see what the body requires on the inside based on the signs it is showing on the outside. If you allow me, I may be able to tell you why your son is having these spells … and possibly even stop them."

"Do you truly believe it's possible to improve his condition?" Evangelina asks, on the verge of tears again.

"Based on what I've seen, there is much that is possible that I first thought impossible."

"I must be present, and I must ask that you do not share the details of Tahvi's condition with anyone. Do you swear it?"

"I have already sworn it, when Vertimus shared it with me."

"Very well." Evangelina moves away from Tahvi to give Exos room to sit by him. Vertimus stands close to her, aware that she is frightened.

"May I touch him?"

"Yes."

Then Exos asks Tahvi, "May I touch you, Tahvi?"

"He can't hear you," Evangelina answers sharply.

After a brief period of waiting, Exos places his hand on Tahvi's chest for what seems to Evangelina like an uncomfortably long time, but is only a few minutes. Soon, his breathing begins to synchronize with Tahvi's. Occasionally Tahvi makes a noise that sounds like he skips a breath or he takes a deep breath. Each time Tahvi does, Exos does as well.

"What's he doing?" Evangelina whispers to Vertimus.

"I don't know, but I've seen this before. It is part of his method."

While Exos has his hand on Tahvi's chest Tahvi moans and begins to stir. Exos waits a moment before continuing to see if the boy will wake, but he doesn't.

"It's not usual for him to stir during his spells. What are you doing to him?" Evangelina asks.

"Wait … he's nearly finished." Vertimus grabs her gently by the arm but she pulls away from him.

"Tell me what you're doing to him," she says firmly. Vertimus sees her cheeks are flushed. He hears the frustration building in her voice.

Exos removes his hand from Tahvi's chest, lays it flat on his own and takes a deep breath. Evangelina sees what looks like sadness and maybe joy when she looks at his face, but she doesn't know him well enough to read him properly.

"I'm speaking with the boy—with his body and his consciousness."

"I'm not an herbalist. Tell me in words I'll understand."

"I am unfinished, but I've heard enough to know your son carries a greatness within him."

Evangelina curls her hands into fists. Her lips tighten and she exhales a quick breath. "This examining goes no further until I understand what you are doing."

"Evangelina, he—" Vertimus begins, but she interrupts him.

"No! I know you trust him, but I need more than that." She begins to cry as her weariness and confusion overwhelm her. "This is my son and he's not well; he may even be in serious danger and I don't have time for puzzles or cryptic answers. If you know how to help him, then tell me so now. If you don't, then make your farewell."

"Your son will continue to have these spells until he is healed."

Sephine walks into the room and is just about to ask how Tahvi is doing when Evangelina shouts at Exos.

"That confirmation is of absolutely no help to me! When you can tell me *how* he can be healed I'll be interested to hear it. I would thank you for your time, but I fear both yours and mine have been wasted here." Evangelina faces Vertimus before she starts to walk out of the room. "As always, you are welcome to stay but it's better that your guest leaves now."

"Your son is not only incomplete on the outside. He is incomplete on the inside."

Evangelina stops. She turns back to look at Exos. She does it slowly, as though she's afraid to look at him.

"He's missing a lung. I believe this is one of the reasons he often becomes tired and likely why it's happening more often as he is growing older. As he grows, his body is finding it difficult to accommodate his needs. These spells will continue. They could last days, maybe longer, if he's not healed soon."

"Who is this man?" Sephine asks.

"Vertimus brought him here," Evangelina replies.

"How it is that you know all of this by just by sitting next to Tahvi?" Sephine asks.

"This is what I do. A short time is all I need to see inside someone. It's my gift."

"Do you know how to heal him?" Evangelina asks him, now more receptive than angry.

"You must make him whole with the pieces he's missing."

The color suddenly drains from Evangelina's face. She grows quiet and still.

Sephine sees Evangelina's face and decides they've both had more than they can handle for one day. She looks at Vertimus when she speaks.

"I am not sure who this man is or how you know him, Vertimus, but it's time he took his leave. Evangelina looks very tired and I believe she'd rather spend whatever strength she has left this evening focusing on Tahvi. Please escort him out, or I can to do it myself if you prefer."

Vertimus sits calmly and does not respond.

"Shall it be me, then?" Sephine asks.

"He's not just an herbalist," Vertimus corrects. "He's a thaumaturge."

Evangelina sits down so slowly that she looks like an old woman whose muscles have grown stiff. Her gaze is still fixed on Exos.

Sephine looks at Vertimus, shocked. "He's a what? Are you insane? You brought a thaumaturge *here*? For stars' sakes, why? Can you imagine what could happen if anyone were to know of it?"

"No one will know of it," Vertimus says calmly.

"How can you be so bold as to think so? How could you risk the lives of your nephew and us, or even your own?"

"Because my nephew's life is already at risk. As for Exos, the duration of his visit will be a short one. There will not be enough time for others to learn about him."

"That is not acceptable. We are *all* in danger every minute he is here. He must leave this house immediately."

"Wait," Evangelina says to Exos. "Is that really what you are?"

"It is," he says calmly.

"If that's really what you are, then you've worked miracles, haven't you? I've heard that your kind are healers. If this is true then you truly can help him, yes?"

"I can help. Your son is incomplete, but I can't make him whole. Only you can."

"It's not a wonder they're outlawed. They're as crazy as they are useless," Sephine adds before continuing to lecture Vertimus. "You know what Eva has been through. How can you of all people give her this false hope? I'm going to take her outside for a bit. I think the cool air might be helpful to her. Please make sure this man is gone by the time we return."

Sephine helps Evangelina stand up, puts her arm around her waist, and begins to walk her out of the room. Evangelina doesn't seem to notice that she's walking.

"Where is the speared gem?" Exos asks.

Evangelina stops. Sephine feels the stiffness in her body. Her face is still pale and she looks scared.

"What's the matter, Eva?"

"What did you say?" Evangelina asks Exos in nearly a whisper.

"Where is the speared gem?" he repeats.

"How ... how did you know?"

"From Tahvi."

"Eva, what's he speaking of?" Sephine asks.

Evangelina doesn't hear her. To Exos, she says, "What did he say to you."

"When I joined with him I was able to see some of the memories his body has stored. It was part of the memory of his birth. His ... second birth. I saw his memory of when he was born, but I can't see what happened to this gem. I presume you took it and have kept it hidden. That was clever. It's what I would have done."

Evangelina's legs tremble. She looks like's she about to have a spell of her own. She sits on a chair again.

Sephine looks at Evangelina and realizes what Exos said is true. She kneels before Evangelina and gently strokes her arm.

"Eva? What is he speaking of?"

Evangelina doesn't answer. Instead, she crosses her arms and rocks herself gently.

"Eva, please hear me," Sephine pleads, in nearly a whisper.

Evangelina looks at her son. Her eyes peruse his body and she realizes how normal he looks. "Isn't it strange," she says. "Even during these spells he looks like a healthy young boy. It's not at all evident that he's missing two limbs. Those that know him see him as a fairly ordinary, if unlucky, child. The possible nature of his true condition, whatever it may be, has gone unrevealed for eight years. Our efforts and sacrifices have made this possible."

A feeling of immense relief washes over Evangelina and she begins to weep. As she does, her body settles back into the chair and she feels less tense. She feels a release of tightness in her shoulders and neck that she hadn't previously been aware of. Sephine brings her a face cloth and Evangelina continues to cry for a few minutes. She welcomes the tears. It's only now that she realizes just how big this burden was, to keep this secret from everyone she loved.

The others wait patiently. The twins, secretly spying from outside the room, are waiting as well. They move slightly closer to Tahvi's door, anxiously wanting to hear whatever will be said next.

"I was so afraid. When Tahvi was born and I saw his body. I saw that it wasn't the way a baby's body should be. I was terrified. But my love for him ... it was great, great and blinding. I was convinced I could do whatever was necessary to make him well, and that I *would* make him well … somehow."

Evangelina looks at Sephine.

"Then, just after you cut our lifeline, you left the room. I don't remember why, but after you'd gone, I remember holding Tahvi, promising him, swearing to him that I would do whatever was in my power to heal him. Then I heard a crackling noise, like an egg breaking, only … it was louder and sharper, maybe. It's hard to describe."

Evangelina looks to Exos before she continues.

"The noise, it was coming from Tahvi. The part of his lifeline that was still attached to his belly, it broke off by itself, and as I watched it, it … changed. It straightened and began to shimmer and it hardened. When it was finished … it looked like a small, twisted spear, made of stone. Stone that looked like a gem."

Exos holds Evangelina's stare. She sees kindness and understanding in his eyes, as though he feels exactly what she's feeling now.

Evangelina directs her attention back to Sephine.

"I didn't know how to tell you or what to do, so I hid it. It wasn't intentional, just an instinct, for Tahvi's sake. Later I remember thinking I must have dreamed it. But when I went to the place where I kept it hidden and unwrapped the cloth I'd placed it in, it was there. It was a confirmation of my sanity and Tahvi's oddity. There were many times I tried to tell you, I wanted to tell you, and you as well, Vertimus, but I was afraid others might learn of it and that would put Tahvi in danger. Some days I've hoped and prayed that I'd imagined it. I thought if I could convince myself it didn't happen, that somehow Tahvi would be … safer. But I know now I didn't wholly believe this because I never thought to dispose of it or try to destroy it."

"You were right to not do either, my lady. It's instrumental to his protection," Exos says.

Sephine wraps her arms around Evangelina and holds her. "I'm so sorry you had to carry this burden alone. I wish I could have … that there was a way to convey my devotion to you and Tahvi."

"Don't accept blame, Sephine. It was my choice and it was made out of fear, not of mistrust. I love you and would trust you with my life, if need be."

"If you've kept it hidden since the day of his birth that means you know nothing about it? How it can protect him?" Sephine asks.

"No, I know nothing except that it hasn't changed. It's just as it was eight years ago."

"Is it hidden close by?" Exos asks.

"Yes, it is."

Humbul and Sheree are squatting against the wall outside of Tahvi's room, when Humbul turns to Sheree and whispers, "I know where it is!"

Humbul practically launches himself into the room and Sheree gasps.

"Humbul, no!" She reaches for his leg but he's already gone. She makes a grunting sound as she follows her counterpart into the room, knowing she's bound to share whatever punishment he's about to receive.

"It's in the shed, below one of the stalls, isn't it?" Humbul shouts from just inside the doorway. Sheree stands next to him her head hung low, eyes hesitant to make contact with her mother's.

Sephine stands up, crosses her arms over her chest and frowns at her children.

"How long have the two of you been listening?"

"Longer than we should have," Sheree says.

"It's in the shed, yes?" Humbul asks again.

"Child, you *must* learn to restrain yourself," their mother snaps. "What were the two of you thinking, eavesdropping in this way?"

"We have worry for Tahvi, is all. Eva, it wasn't our intention to be disrespectful," Sheree says.

Humbul shakes his head, but he's still preoccupied with knowing where the gemstone is hidden.

Sephine and Evangelina look at the twins, both thinking the same thing. They do not know how to make the twins understand the gravity of the situation and the importance of their discretion.

"Your concerns are of no consequence," Exos says plainly.

"Which concerns would those be?" Evangelina asks, surprised at being so easy to read.

"The ones you have about the children."

"And why is that?" Evangelina asks.

"These two hold many secrets. Don't you, little ones?"

Sheree and Humbul stare at Exos, both wondering how much he

knows.

"What's he speaking of?" Sephine asks the twins, but it's Exos who answers.

"They know more about Tahvi's … uniqueness than anyone else. They've been loyal to him by keeping secret anything that Tahvi has asked them to. Any dishonesty they have precipitated is out of devotion to him and not with intent of wrongdoing. They, like your friend Sephine, can be trusted with his life." Exos looks at the children. "I would've been honored to have friends like you as a child."

Sheree smiles. Humbul is focused on Evangelina, still waiting for a response about the speared gem.

"I presume Tahvi shared this with you as well?" Evangelina asks.

Exos nods.

"It seems he had quite a lot to say."

"That he did."

Evangelina sits by Tahvi's side and feels his forehead again. He no longer feels warm, so she removes the cloth from his forehead. His breathing is still slow, however, so she knows this spell is unfinished.

Humbul tries one final attempt. This time he is uncharacteristically tentative. "Is it in the shed?" he asks softly, with his shoulders hunched to the point where his chin is nearly buried in his neck.

In a harsh tone, Sephine says, "Humbul, we will have not another question from you!"

Vertimus, still in a seat near the corner of the room, can't help but chuckle. Sephine and Evangelina glare at him and he stops abruptly.

"The boy is very, um … determined."

"It's not in the barn," Evangelina says. "But I suppose I'll have to move some of the other precious items I've stored there, won't I?" She looks at Humbul, who responds with a shrug and then looks away, embarrassed.

"I believe it's time Tahvi becomes reacquainted with it. Do you agree?" Exos asks.

Evangelina casts a glance over everyone in the room and then holds her stare when she looks at Exos. She knows he is an outsider but he seems to know more about Tahvi than anyone else. She's about to ask him to promise her something but she doesn't know what promise to ask for. All she wants is for Tahvi to be safe. She's about to speak but Exos speaks before she can.

"There are many things in our world that spawn iniquity but this spear is not one of them."

Evangelina lets out a deep sigh. "I will get it."

# THE BIRTH STONE

Evangelina kneels on the floor in her room. She leans against her bed with one hand and uses the other to lift a loose floorboard. From under the floorboard she pulls out an object wrapped in a piece of cloth that's such a light shade of blue it resembles the sky on a clear day. The cloth is tied loosely with a white velvet ribbon. She returns the floorboard to its original place before she leaves the room.

When she enters Tahvi's room again she sees he is still unconscious. Everyone is waiting anxiously and Evangelina sees the children looking at her hands.

"Should the children leave the room?" Sephine asks.

Before Evangelina can answer Humbul protests, "Surely not! Why must we leave? We've shared nothing about Tahvi's secrets. We've been trustworthy. You didn't even know we had secrets!"

He looks at Sheree, his eyes begging. He shakes his hands at her, a sign that she should plead their argument with him.

"Sheree, don't harvest silence now!"

"Eva, mother, I agree with Humbul. We've kept many of Tahvi's secrets at the risk of consequences to ourselves. We care for him very much and know it's important to keep what we've learned concealed. We would not speak of it to others, or even openly. If this is something that can cure Tahvi, we would like to be here to see it."

"Yes! What Sheree said," Humbul follows.

Vertimus rises from his seat and stands next to Evangelina. "I believe these two are the least of your worries. I see no reason for their complete loyalty to Tahvi to change now. Besides, there are

97

benefits from knowing such a special boy and keeping such important secrets. Am I right, my friends?"

They nod in unison. Though neither of them is exactly sure what he means, they understand the wrong answer might prolong the discussion and potentially cause them to be removed from the room.

"Very well," Evangelina says. "You understand how important it is that you share what you see with no one?" she asks. Everyone in the room nods their agreement, but she continues. "You all must swear an oath to keep silent about all that has happened that evening." Once each of them so swears, she begins to untie the knot. As she does, everyone in the room moves closer to her so that they're standing in a circle.

When she unties the knot and removes the rag, they see a spear-shaped, dark-green object that spans a few centimeters beyond the length of Evangelina's hand, from her wrist to her middle finger. One end is blunt, its width almost a third of her palm, thick and rectangular in shape. The other end is much thinner, coiled and pointed at the end. It looks very much like a short tree branch except for the color and composition. It's shiny and hard like a crystal, but much more beautiful than any crystal they've seen before.

"Did this really come from Tahvi?" Sheree asks.

"Yes," Evangelina answers.

"With your permission?" Exos asks.

Evangelina hands him the speared gem and he inspects it. He sits in the chair and holds it close to a lantern by Tahvi's bed. Everyone circles around Exos now, trying to see what he sees.

The stone is transparent, and is so beautiful that if it were broken into pieces, it could be used as jewelry. It's not as smooth as a gemstone, and is even a little coarse, like newly sanded wood. As he moves it closer to the light, he can see something inside it. It has small fragments trapped within it, spots that look clear like bubbles of air, as if the stone were liquid before it was imprisoned in this form.

"Miraculous," Exos whispers.

"What should we do with it?" Evangelina asks.

"We return it to its owner," he says.

Exos takes the speared gem and lays it gently upon Tahvi's chest. Everyone crowds around Tahvi's bed. The scene makes Kaco stir. He moves into an upright position and leans on his hind legs. He looks at everyone and begins sniffing the air. After deciding there's no cause for alarm, he lies down again and begins cleaning his paws.

Everyone's eyes are firmly planted on the spear except for Evangelina, who is looking at Tahvi's face. She and Exos switch positions, and she sits down and puts her hand on Tahvi's chest. The rate of his breathing has increased, and knowing this she is able to relax more. Her eyes join theirs on the spear as they all anxiously watch and wait. The room is so quiet that they can hear Kaco's little tongue sweeping across the hairs on his paws.

Humbul is the first to notice it.

"There!" He gets closer to the bed and points to the center of the spear. The clear spots are moving inside it. As they pick up speed they suddenly disappear and the spear begins to glow in the middle. Kaco makes a clicking noise and paws at the air around the spear. Slowly but steadily the brightness increases until the entire gem is glowing. A bright-green light erupts at one end of the spear, moving through it to the other end, flashing a beam of light across the room. As it does, a short burst of heat shoots from it, causing a slight increase in the temperature around Tahvi's bed. At first Exos is the only one who notices it. Then, everyone is the room is fanning themselves. Just as quickly, the speared gem returns to its original state.

Everyone's mouths are hanging open, save Vertimus who is smiling and Exos who is half-smiling, which seems to be the only kind of smile he can manage. The others look like they've never learned how to close their lower jaws. Kaco sniffs the spear and whimpers. When he doesn't smell what he seeks, he rests his head on Tahvi's arm again. At that same moment, Tahvi opens his eyes. Everyone looks to him in wonderment, afraid to speak as they take in what just happened.

It takes Tahvi some time before he's lucid enough to speak. Once he is, it's his mother he addresses.

"I was the star of the show."

Evangelina laughs, "Of course you were, my dear." She helps him to sit up and then hugs him for a long time. When she speaks to him, she is crying tears of relief. "Your timing is flawless. You didn't tell me you had planned your own disappearing trick. How are you feeling?"

Before he can answer he notices something feels different about his lap.

Tahvi sees everyone is gathered around the bed. He senses a feeling of uneasiness, like everyone in the room had just heard terrible news. Humbul points to Tahvi's lap and Tahvi looks down and sees the speared gem. He picks it up with his hand and just as Exos did, he holds it to the light. His eyes grow a little wider and a smile crosses his face.

"Do you know what this is, Tahvi?" his mother asks him.

Tahvi looks at Vertimus and Vertimus nods.

"I believe so." Tahvi puts the gem back on his lap, closes his eyes and runs his fingers along the length of it. Then Tahvi wraps his hand around it firmly and sits with the gem without speaking. After several minutes he opens his eyes.

"It's part of me. It's ... vital." He gives Exos a curious look. "I know you."

"Yes."

"I remember you from my dream."

"Tahvi," Evangelina asks, "How do you know it's vital?"

"I was sure that I'd seen it in a memory, but I had to ask it to be certain."

"Ask it?"

"Yes. I asked it to share its history and it did." Tahvi looks at Exos again. "Are you and I the same?"

Exos raises the left side of his mouth, giving Tahvi a half-smile. Tahvi wonders if his smiles are rare.

"We are all the same—we vary only in degrees. But yes, in this area you and I are alike."

"I haven't met anyone like me, but my uncle told me that one day I would."

Evangelina looks at her son in amazement. She feels a mixture of many emotions with confusion lying at the forefront. She knows Tahvi is her son and that she loves him, but hearing him speak this way, she feels like he's an outsider. *Can he speak to other objects like this? How could I not know about this ability? Is it dangerous? Could he hurt himself with it? Could he hurt others? Could it help him? Surely it must be able to ...* The questions come so fast, they begin to tumble over one another in her mind, each absent of an answer.

It's too much to handle at the moment, so she chooses to set them aside as best she can. There is only one question that is important right now.

Evangelina holds Tahvi's head in her hands and kisses him on the forehead. He smiles at her, then she takes the speared gem in her hands and turns to Exos.

"Tell me how this can help my son."

"I don't know."

"But—"

"The process was interrupted. I was able to learn only so much in the time I had."

She looks at Tahvi, "Do you know?"

Tahvi shakes his head. "I asked it only one question."

"If you would allow me to continue," Exos says, "I believe I could—"

"Of course, please." Evangelina interrupts. She moves from the bed and she and Exos change positions again.

Exos sits next to Tahvi and asks his permission to place his hand on his chest, which Tahvi allows. Exos closes his eyes, but Tahvi's remain open. He watches the serious-looking man as he takes deep breaths. As the transference begins, Tahvi's gaze shifts from looking *at* to looking *past* him. He seems to be focusing on something far beyond the room he's in.

His mother notices this immediately and says his name, but he doesn't respond. She brushes his hair from his forehead and he doesn't react. Curious but not alarmed, she continues to watch.

After several minutes, Tahvi lets out a gasp and Exos opens his eyes.

"My stars. Do you remember it all?" Exos asks.

"Yes!" Tahvi exclaims. He grabs the speared gem from his mother and holds it to his chest. His eyes suddenly filled with tears.

"Tahvi, what's the matter?" Evangelina asks.

"Give him a moment," Vertimus says kindly, putting his hand on Evangelina's shoulder.

When they see Tahvi crying, Sheree and Humbul can't help but cry as well. Standing at the foot of the bed, Sheree places her hand on Tahvi's leg to comfort him. She cries freely, though she doesn't understand why, but Humbul has more difficulty accepting this feeling that he doesn't understand. He wipes his tears away as they come. Evangelina is kneeling by the bed now, holding Tahvi's hand. She notices the speared gem is glowing again, but only slightly. She can feel its warmth.

Tahvi puts his head on her chest and continues to weep. Eventually he stops. He looks at her so that she can see his face as he speaks. He holds the speared gem in both hands.

"Mother ... this ... this will help make me whole."

Tahvi's eyes begin to fill with tears again. "I am very tired," he says. Then he closes his eyes and quickly falls asleep.

"Tahvi?" Evangelina says, alarmed. *Is he having another spell already?* She tries gently to wake him.

Exos touches her arm. "I believe he's only sleeping now. The process is very strenuous, and Tahvi is more sensitive to it than others. Most aren't able to see or know what I do. But Tahvi is. He can see and remember everything I learned of his history."

"What did you see?" Evangelina asks.

Exos brings another chair close to the bed and sits directly across from Evangelina.

"I will tell you everything I've learned, but it must be done in a certain way. Will you trust me to give you this knowledge in the way I am accustomed, with no questions asked, at least not at first?"

Evangelina carefully considers his question and then agrees.

"Give me your hands."

Evangelina does as he asks.

"I want you to breathe deeply. Keep breathing this way until I tell you to stop."

As she breathes deeply, Exos matches her pace so that soon their breathing is harmonious. A sense of ease moves through her. It starts in her chest and then spreads to her extremities. She feels tension release in her shoulders and neck as she settles into her chair. She feels so comfortable that if she were to close her eyes, she would easily drift into a deep sleep. But she keeps her eyes open and waits for Exos to tell her what to do next.

"Your son is a sensitive, the likes of which I haven't seen before. He's what I can only call a star-child, as his essence was not born of this world."

Evangelina stares at him with a perplexed look on her face.

"He is your child, one of Evangelina and Stefan, but he is also a gift from the universe."

"I don't understand."

"I don't believe that all can be understood now. Here is what you must know. When Tahvi was born … when his *spirit* was born, it was through a falling star that was sent here, to you. Something went amiss and the star broke apart before it could reach you. What you see with your eyes, his physical constitution—it's a reflection of the fragmentation of his spirit. In the simplest terms, he was born broken because his star shattered."

Exos gives her a minute to take in the information. He can see the muscles in her neck tightening and the look of awe in her eyes. He begins to breathe deeply again and reminds her to do the same. She follows his lead, and soon feels calmer.

She has difficulty accepting his words as truth but then she remembers the night she thought was a dream. She remembers the falling star and she thinks about the night Tahvi was born and how his lifeline changed into a gem right before her eyes. She's not sure what to believe anymore, but she knows she can't look at the world the same. She steels herself to question everything she's believed to be real thus far.

"If this is true, what do I do now? How can I help him?"

"The speared gem will guide you to the missing pieces."

"Missing pieces? He can be made whole again?"

"He can."

Evangelina begins to weep. She is still holding his hands and now she pulls them toward her. She holds them against her cheek and thanks him. She reaches to hug him when Exos stops her.

"Wait."

Sheree and Humbul are sitting at the foot of Tahvi's bed, on top of the chest his mother uses to keep his false limbs in. They look at each other and share a thought. It is Humbul who gives it a voice.

"What if the pieces are broken? Or someone has them?"

"I doubt they're broken. They will be much like this gem: virtually indestructible," Vertimus says.

"Here is the dilemma," Exos says. "The pieces could be anywhere. It's also very possible that someone may have found one or all of them. To find them, you may have to travel a great distance. But—if it hasn't been found—there is one that is not far from here. It looks very close to the red rock canyon where Tahvi's star first touched the ground."

"Do you mean the Tabarak Canyon? That's just short of a two-hour ride from here!" Evangelina says as she stands and takes the gem from Tahvi's bed. It is slightly warm and has a dull but pulsating glow in the center. She stares at it, waiting for it to reveal a clue about how to find the missing pieces.

"How do I use this? What do I do?"

"That I don't know," Exos utters. "I only know that it will act as a guide for you."

"Eva, take it outside," Vertimus suggests.

"What?"

"Take it outside."

"How do you know that will make a difference?"

"I don't know that it will."

Though she doesn't yet know why, the suggestion seems to make sense. She leaves Tahvi's room and walks quickly toward the door to the front yard. When she passes the cooking room, Jabneh is sitting at the table, having tea and reading. He asks if all is well, but she doesn't hear him.

Sephine and the twins follow her outside. Kaco comes, too. It's well into the evening now, and the stars are shining bright in the sky now that the clouds have fled. The full moon lights the night well, and the four of them are able to see each other clearly, but Kaco practically disappears in the grass.

Evangelina holds the spear in her hand with her palm facing upward, the pointed end facing away from her. The glow in the center intensifies and she can hear Kaco making squeaking noises. He scampers over in front of Evangelina, sits on his hind legs and sniffs at the spear. Evangelina waits for what feels like a long time. Then the glow intensifies more. The temperature of the spear does not increase, but it's still warm and she can feel her palm growing slick with perspiration. With the glow, it's easy to see inside the spear and she sees the fragments moving and circling, as though they're looking for a way out. A burst of light emits from the spear, just as it had in Tahvi's room, and the spear's glow intensifies even more, the pointed end begins to glow, slowly pulsating. The spear is pointed northwest, the same direction as the Tabarak Canyon.

Evangelina and the others hear a *clink* from behind them, and they all turn in unison. Standing just outside the doorway, Jabneh's eyes are wide, his jaw agape, his right arm trapped in the air in front of him, his metal cup lying spilled on the stone walkway.

Evangelina looks back at the gemstone and grins. Again, she is overwhelmed by feelings but this time they seem less muddled. Fear, confusion, anxiety swim in her head, but when she feels the energy in the spear, when she sees the glowing, directing her to the red rock canyon, she feels hope. They have a chance, a real chance, to heal her son. This is something she has dreamed of for years but believed could never happen. Now there is a possibility. She puts the gem in her dress pocket and walks quickly to Jabneh.

"Are you well?" she asks him.

"What ... what was that?"

"Try not to be alarmed. If you have any interest in taking a ride with me, I'll explain everything. Would you like to do that?"

"Now?"

Evangelina nods, "Now. You'd be of great help to me if you said yes."

"Then yes."

"Marvelous. Let's prepare."

# BEYOND THE TABARAK CANYON

Everyone helps. Sephine fills three flasks and a small barrel of water while Vertimus gathers two shovels, two pickaxes and several blankets. The weather is chilly outside and they know it will be colder within the canyon. As Vertimus puts the supplies in the wagon, Exos prepares two lanterns and brings enough oil to light the lanterns for double the amount of time they expect to need. Evangelina decides to take the smaller of the two wagons, as it's the more sensible choice for this task: both wagons have a large wooden seat in the front, big enough for at least two people to steer the horses, but the larger wagon is enclosed, with intricate woodwork on the outside, making it look more like a carriage. The smaller wagon is shaped more like the bottom half of a large wooden box, and without an enclosure will be much easier for them to get any supplies in and out of it. Sheree and Humbul ready the horses. Evangelina has six, but two will do for this evening's work. She decides to take Sadie and Baleel.

Sheree picks Sadie to ready because of Evangelina's six horses, she likes Sadie most of all. Sadie is more obedient and is quick to nuzzle when she's given food. Sheree enjoys any opportunity to spend time with her, so she's delighted when asked to help. When Sheree and Humbul are finished Exos helps ensure the horses are hitched to the wagon properly.

They decide that two others should go with Evangelina in case heavy digging is needed. Both Exos and Jabneh volunteer. After eight years there is no telling how deep the stone might be buried now. In watching Tahvi's history Exos learned that the stone was not far from the surface, but with the weather conditions over the years it's possible it could be deeper.

Sheree wants to stay at home with Tahvi but Humbul begs and pleads to go with Evangelina. He offers to help dig, hold the lantern or do whatever is necessary. In the end it's a losing battle and instead of a ride to the canyon his mother gives him a long lecture about the significance of privacy, followed by a reminder that he needs to help clean the cooking room. Although this is a normal chore for him he sees it as punishment for some of his inappropriate outbursts throughout the evening.

Jabneh and Evangelina board the wagon, and Jabneh prepares to lead the horses. Exos and Vertimus walk out of the house together. Exos holds Kaco in his arms and steps onto the wagon with him.

"You're bringing Kaco?" Evangelina asks.

"I am. I don't know how effective the spear will be as you get close to one of Tahvi's … gems, but I believe Kaco may be of some help."

"And what makes you believe that?"

"Because Kaco was with Tahvi when he was born."

"No. Tahvi didn't—" Evangelina stops. She looks at Kaco. She can't remember exactly when it was that she'd noticed Kaco with Tahvi but she knows it's been years. She thinks of the countless times she's seen Kaco and Tahvi together and how close they are. She can't remember ever being worried that the animal might harm Tahvi, which she knows is strange.

"Tell me." Evangelina says to Exos.

"Kaco was the first entity to feel Tahvi's spirit. They will be connected to each other throughout their lives. Tahvi wouldn't have been able to help you understand why an animal such as Kaco would want to be near such a young child, so it makes sense that Tahvi kept this a secret until he was older. Tahvi's memory tells me he knows Kaco is the only one who was present when Tahvi was born. Kaco knows where the star landed and he likely knows exactly where we can find the gem. I don't know how to communicate with Kaco so I can't be sure, but my instincts tell me he knows where to find it and that he might be of help to us."

Evangelina looks at Kaco and asks him, "Do you know where the gem is?" She feels strange doing it but things have been so strange this evening that a little more strangeness doesn't seem to matter. As an answer, he sniffs at the air and paws at it in her direction.

Evangelina feels a hand on hers. It's Vertimus.

"Though it's a mere two-hour ride to the canyon by day, it will likely take longer with you driving at night. And I can't predict how long it will take to find what you're looking for."

"I know this," she says kindly.

"Ride well and watch for sinkholes. If you don't return by dawn I will follow."

"I'm sure we'll be well. Thank you."

When he pulls his hand away Evangelina grabs and holds it firmly.

"Vertimus?"

"Yes?"

"How did you know to go outside?"

She holds his gaze and his eyes tell her he has secrets, possibly an abundance of them. She begins to feel about her husband's brother the same way she felt about Tahvi a short time ago, as though she knows only a part of him and there is a bigger part that she hasn't seen. But she has no doubt that she loves him and that he loves her. She knows he will do whatever he can to help Tahvi.

"We'll speak of this when you return. Will that do?"

"It will." She looks to Jabneh. "Lead the horses, please."

Vertimus watches them ride away. Between the moonlight and the torch they'd lit in the front of the wagon it is easy to see them. As they ride, the light from the torch grows smaller until eventually they look like a firefly in the night.

Vertimus breathes deep the cold air. He can hear only the soft sounds of stirring insects. Other than those sounds the night is quiet. He looks at the stars and then the trees on the edge of Evangelina's property. They're tall and lush, and their leaves look black in the moonlight. His eyes fill with tears. Not from worry about Evangelina or the others—he knows he will not need to follow them this night. They will be back by morning. But he also knows that Evangelina's life, as is it now, will soon meet a harsh end.

* * *

When Vertimus walks into Tahvi's room he finds him awake. Sheree and Humbul have moved all the gifts into his room save the one Jabneh brought. They're helping him to open them and speaking of all that's happened that evening. They've also brought Tahvi some food and he eats with enthusiasm. They stop abruptly when they notice Vertimus in the room.

Tahvi, with a full mouth, says, "Sephine said we could open them."

Vertimus lets out a hearty laugh. He knows Tahvi is different, that he holds a maturity that most children do not. But in many ways he is a child and it gives Vertimus great joy to see him behaving as one.

"I suppose we all have our priorities tonight. Would anyone mind if I joined?"

The children permit it and they continue to open the gifts together as if tonight had been as ordinary as any other night. Though Tahvi enjoys many of the gifts he's been given he is too exhausted to play with any of them.

Once they finish opening the gifts it's well past the time for sleep for all of them. Vertimus is still with them, drinking tea. Humbul is gathering the papery that Tahvi's gifts were wrapped in, after moving all of them to a corner of his room. Sheree has fallen asleep on the bed next to Tahvi, holding her necklace in her hand.

Tahvi notices it and points to the blue stone on Sheree's necklace. "Where did she get this? I haven't seen it before."

Humbul walks over to the bed and peers at it. "That is one of your gifts," he teases. "She decided it would suit her better."

Vertimus and Tahvi chuckle.

"I don't know where she obtained it. It looks familiar," Humbul adds.

"The narrator was wearing it," Vertimus says, then sips his tea.

"This is true. I remember now," Tahvi says.

"She pilfered it!" Humbul jokes.

"I'd venture that she asked for it and based on her assertiveness the woman simply handed it over," Vertimus says playfully. This time, they all laugh.

Humbul looks at Tahvi, who meets his gaze invitingly. Humbul hesitates for a moment before asking the question.

"Do you think they will find it—the gem in the canyon?"

Tahvi smiles. He looks to Vertimus. "Yes, I believe they will."

"What do you think will happen when they find it?" Humbul asks Tahvi.

"I am not sure."

"Are you not excited or curious?"

"I am tired."

"Now that's a good point," Vertimus says. "I think it's time you boys follow Sheree's example and get some sleep."

Humbul is tired and so he doesn't resist. "Promise to wake me when they return?" he asks.

Vertimus agrees and then looks to Tahvi. Vertimus can see that the boy wants to converse but he also knows Tahvi needs sleep. Vertimus suggests that Tahvi try to rest and if he is unable to, then he will consider telling him a tale.

Tahvi nods and closes his eyes. He is asleep within minutes.

* * *

The drive to the canyon takes just over two hours, giving Evangelina plenty of time to tell Jabneh about all that has happened. While she speaks, she finds herself being overwhelmed by emotion and at one point feels so much that she can't continue. Exos picks up where she ends and gives Jabneh the remaining details from the back of the wagon. He has brought a thin rope with him and is making something with it.

Kaco is in her lap now. He had moved there shortly after he felt the emotional energy building up within her. Though over the years Evangelina had learned that Kaco posed no real harm to her son, she hadn't let herself grow attached to him. She had expected that one day he would likely run off back into the woods and never return.

Now that she knows about the special bond between Tahvi and him, her fondness for the animal is growing quickly and she finds it difficult not to show him affection. She rubs his fur and feels comforted by his presence. He's a very agile creature and thought she knows she doesn't need to hold him in order for him to stay out of harm's way, she sporadically keeps one hand on him for his safety regardless.

In the other hand she holds the crystal, which continues to glow and pulsate at the narrow end as they approach the canyon. As it does, Kaco paws at it and does his best to be close to it. He nearly knocks it out of Evangelina's hand until she finally uses a tone stern enough to chasten him. He doesn't attempt to reach it again but he makes a clicking sound from time to time to voice his displeasure.

At one point the trail veers left, considerably far from the center of the red rock canyon, to avoid a large rocky area that is impassible by wagon. As they steer the wagon away, the glow in the crystal fades until Evangelina points it again toward the direction of the center of the red rock canyon, when it quickly resumes its pulsing glow.

"It's as a compass," Evangelina says aloud.

"Will you explain?" Jabneh asks.

"The brightness fades when we move away from the canyon." Evangelina replies.

As they approach the canyon the moonlight makes what appears to be flecks of gold in the red rocks shimmer and twinkle in the night. The rock walls surrounding the canyon are at least thirty meters high. It is truly a magnificent structure. Though the moon is full and brightening the night, the space within the canyon looks dark and unpromising. When they arrive at the entrance they notice that the road has narrowed, and is now just wide enough for the size of the wagon.

The light from the torch coupled with the moonlight gives the atmosphere in the canyon a soft hazy glow that allows them to see fairly well considering they're in the hours of darkness. As they drive through the canyon they're greeted with a strong breeze, causing the fire from the torch to undulate so much so that it nearly extinguishes itself before springing back to life again.

The light casts a shadow of the wagon on the ground. As the wagon moves, its shadow looks like silent dancing creatures creeping up and down along the rock, following them as they ride by. The shadow distorts shapes of the rock still embedded in the ground, making it impossible to tell how deep or long some of the crevices are.

The road is on the left side of the canyon and is the only option for travelling by wagon. Jabneh has the horses pull the wagon along the path at a much slower pace now, for caution's sake. There are at least four areas in the canyon in which small bridges were created to provide stability for areas where the rock has become fissured or unstable, as the separation in the rock makes it too easy for wagon wheels to get caught or broken. No one is assigned to maintain the bridges even though the canyon is occasionally used for a wagon route, so it's always difficult to know what kind of condition they're in. Still, even if one of the bridges happens to be damaged, driving at a slower pace will give them a better chance of jamming a wheel, which they can recover from, instead of breaking one altogether. The rest of the canyon is covered by rock that is so uneven it's too difficult for wagons to pass through, though it's possible to pass on horseback or on foot.

Evangelina looks at the spear and sees it has maintained its brightness and the pulsing light is increasing in frequency. She hopes they're not far now, and just as she is about to voice that, Exos speaks.

"Stop the wagon!"

"Why am I stopping?" Jabneh asks, bringing the horses to a stop as he does.

"We're in a very special place."

"Yes … and in the middle of the night. Maybe you could share more about your reasoning?"

"I believe we're very close to where Tahvi was born."

Evangelina turns to him to correct him, then realizes he's not referring to his physical birth. *My child is mine but not of this world.* The thought makes her disoriented and she has to grab onto the seat of the wagon to steady herself. The thought repeats in her head but she still can't fully grasp it. She's not sure she will ever be able to.

Exos steps out of the wagon and removes the front torch from its post. He walks over to Evangelina and asks her to move the spear closer to the middle of the canyon. She does so, but the intensity and pulsing of the light doesn't change.

"There's no variation. I don't believe this place has what we're looking for."

Exos looked at Kaco, who sits calmly on Evangelina's lap. He pets the animal behind the ears. "And nothing from you, little one?"

Kaco raises his head but gives no indication that he's in any way excited by this area.

Exos walks from the wagon path toward the middle of the canyon while still holding the torch. He puts it near the ground so he can closely watch his footing.

"There's an energy here. When I was connecting with—"

He stops abruptly when he notices a depression in the middle of the canyon.

It's lucky for him that he notices it before falling in. When he brings the torch closer to the ground he sees he's standing by the edge of a massive fissure in a cluster of rock nearly the size of a covered wagon. It has a clean semi-circular opening in its center, as though something has taken a large bite out of it.

Exos gently drops to his knees and puts the torch near the edge. He sees it's not like a bite at all. He moves his hand along the circular edge of the rock and then runs his hand down the inside of the break. There are horizontal grooves in the rock that feel as smooth as newly sanded wood. He is lying on the top of the rock now, with his arm all the way in the opening up to his shoulder, and he can't feel a bottom.

"Exos, what is it?" Evangelina asks.

Exos gets up from the rock and walks quickly back to the wagon. He asks Evangelina to hold the torch while he lights another, smaller one.

"Give me a few minutes and I will explain, yes?"

Evangelina consents.

He takes the larger torch back from her so that now he is carrying one in each hand. He walks back to the broken rock and holds the smaller torch over the edge. He thinks for a moment. He looks at the canyon and sees that trees and other brush are rare and wonders if any might be growing in this hole. He's concerned about starting a fire in the canyon and then realizes that even if foliage is growing in the hole, there's nothing growing around it. Confident in his decision, he drops the smaller torch down the hole. It quickly reaches the bottom, which is closer than he thought—it can't be more than five to seven meters deep. He can't see any brush, at least not in that immediate area. Suddenly the light from the torch reflects off of something in the ground. Whatever the surface is that's reflecting is no bigger than the tip of the torch itself, but it's bright enough to arouse his curiosity.

*This must be Tahvi's birthplace,* he thinks. Just then he notices it's only part of a hole that he is looking at. Exos goes from merely walking along the edge of the opening to nearly running to see how far it continues. He holds the torch close to the ground the way he did when he tried to ensure he didn't lose his footing before. What he's looking at is actually the end of a very long trench. He doesn't have to run far before the trench becomes shallow. Where he's standing now, the trench is only about a meter deep. Exos feels his arms and neck turn to gooseflesh. His heart races. This has to be where Tahvi was born, but there is only one way to be sure.

Exos quickly walks back the way he came and then he walks over to the wagon to tell Evangelina and Jabneh what he's found.

"I believe there is something significant about this place. I feel an energy that I've only felt with Tahvi earlier tonight. This place is connected to him, and I believe if we're able to find the origin of his birth it may help us somehow."

Evangelina looks at the spear.

"But the light hasn't changed. Do you think that matters?"

Exos shakes his head. "I don't believe so. I see something shimmering down there," Exos points toward the trench. "My instincts tell me we should see what it is. I've learned to trust them and I am asking that you trust me. Will you?"

Evangelina thinks about all that has happened tonight. She is tired and anxious but she knows almost nothing about obtaining what they're looking for. She's in a world where she is a child again and it makes sense to let someone else guide her. "We'll do as you think we should."

"How deep do you believe that area is?" Jabneh asks Exos.

"Maybe four or five meters. It's a trench." Exos looks at Evangelina. "Likely created by your son's star when it reached our world."

"What? You believe the gem is here?"

Before Exos has a chance to answer her she has already climbed out of the wagon. She puts the spear securely in her pocket, takes the torch from Exos, and holds it as he'd done while she walks over to the opening in the trench. She peers into the blackness and it takes a moment for her eyes to adjust. The torch below is still lit and it's not long before she sees the shimmering as well.

Exos lights another torch and follows her.

"Let me explain. I don't believe this is where the gem is—you said the light in his spear didn't get any stronger—so maybe nothing is here now, but I believe this is where his star landed," Exos says.

She hears footsteps behind her and soon Jabneh is standing next to them. He is holding Kaco. Kaco's little nose is twitching but it seems to sense nothing of importance.

"I see it," Jabneh says.

"As do I," Evangelina replies. She looks to Exos.

"Do you believe we should take the tools?"

"It might be a good idea."

"Let's take one shovel, one pickaxe, and some water. We can come back if we need more."

"Would you like me to go too?" Jabneh asks.

"I believe it's better for one of us to stay with the horses and Kaco," Evangelina says, rubbing Kaco behind his ear.

Exos grabs the supplies and puts them in one of the carrying bags. He and Evangelina each hold a torch. When they walk to the area where the trench is only half a meter deep Exos puts the bag on the ground. He hands Evangelina his torch and jumps in, then she hands him the bag of supplies and both torches, one at a time. He places one on the ground, keeps one in hand, and offers the other hand to Evangelina. She accepts it and then jumps into the trench as he has.

Again, Exos marvels at what a strong woman she is. He wonders if she might let him learn her history someday—she is quite a remarkable woman, and must have an even more remarkable past.

They walk in the trench together, holding the torches slightly raised in front of them. They can see the light from the torch Exos dropped ahead of them, but they can't see the shimmering they'd seen when they peered over the edge.

"Wait," Evangelina says softly. She stops walking and Exos stops with her. She doesn't say anything else. She only stands very still.

"Are you unwell?" he asks.

He puts the torch closer to her so that he can see her face. She looks very pale and she has one arm placed over her chest. Her breathing has quickened and the expression on her face tells Exos that maybe she's confused or scared.

He drops the bag of supplies and sets his torch on the ground. He grabs the torch from her hand and guides her to a slab of rock that she can sit on.

"Evangelina, what can I do?" he asks.

"I ... I don't know ... " she clutches her chest and tries to take a deep breath. Although she's able to inhale she can't feel the air in her lungs and she feels a great pressure on her chest and stomach. "I don't know ... what is happening."

She starts to sob and this time Exos is sure he sees panic in her eyes.

"I can help you if you let me. May I touch you?"

"Yes!" she nearly yells.

Evangelina is still clutching her chest. Exos puts his hand on top of hers. He closes his eyes and listens to her body. She continues to sob, not understanding what she's feeling and scared that she's not able to control it.

"Evangelina, can you hear me?"

"Yes."

"Your constitution is intact."

She is still sobbing.

"You are overwhelmed with emotion. Your body is experiencing an abundance of fear, sadness and confusion. You have to let it runs its course. You're trying to stop it and that's why you feel this way. If you let it go it will only last a few minutes longer."

Evangelina shakes her head. She is on the verge of panic.

"All is well. I assure you. If you allow your body to feel this you will feel comforted in a few minutes. When you breathe again your body will feel like it's getting air again. The more you give into it the easier it will be. Trust me, Evangelina."

She shakes her head and sobs even more. To her own bewilderment she finds herself reaching for Exos and as she does he holds her. He is a strong man. She can feel the hardness of his arms and chest. His large hand on her back feels comforting and safe. Her face is buried in his tunic and before she realizes it, she has let out a scream and then another. It is muffled but still powerful and during the second scream she feels tension release from her body.

After a few minutes she moves away from Exos. She's still crying but the panic has subsided. She notices she feels like she can breathe again just as he said she would. When she takes a deep breath she feels her stomach and chest expand. The pressure, as intense as it was just moments ago, has disappeared.

"Better?"

"Yes," she says. To her surprise she starts to giggle. Tears are still falling from her eyes but she feels a sense of weightlessness in her body and a feeling that she's spinning. She sits up straight and composes herself by wiping the remaining tears from her face and straightening her dress.

"I must apologize."

"It's not necessary. It's not every day a mother learns her child is born from a falling star."

Evangelina takes a few more deep breaths and thanks him for helping her.

"I suppose we should get back to it," she says.

They pick up the torches and supplies. As they began walking they see light coming from the top of the trench. It's Jabneh, standing over the edge with a torch in one hand and Kaco in the other.

"Are you both well? I thought I heard crying from … someone."

Evangelina chuckles at the implication. She tries to imagine Exos crying in a way that would sound as she did. "I'm sorry if I worried you, Jabneh. I'm feeling better now."

"That's good to hear. I'll go back and wait by the wagon. Just call out if you need anything. I'll be listening for you."

Evangelina and Exos walk to the end of the trench until they reach the place where Exos had dropped the torch, still burning on the ground. Only Evangelina proceeds to try to see what the shimmering is. It's not long before she finds it. The shimmering is coming from a strange rock that's just longer than the size of her hand from her wrist to her middle finger. It's like nothing she has seen before. Its surface looks jagged, bumpy and rough to the touch. She pulls the speared gem out of her pocket and points it directly at the rock.

There is no change in the pulsing of the spear. She's about to put it back in her pocket when she notices the light in the spear is changing. It dims for a moment and then begins to pulse again, but this time in the opposite direction. She stares at it and adjusts it in her hand. She had previously thought only the pointed end would be a guide. Now it appears that both sides act as a guide.

"Exos, look."

He moves closer to her. He sees the spear pulsing more on the blunt side of the spear.

"Both ends work like a compass," she says.

"Magnificent," he replies.

They both move away from the opposite ends of the spear so that nothing is blocking them and they wait a moment. It continues to pulsate in the same direction as it previously was, paying no attention to the rock that is lying on the ground. Evangelina turns it so that the more pointed end is facing away from the shimmering rock. And just as she's sure it will, the brightness and pulsing cease for a moment and then continue to pulse and shine at the pointed end of the spear.

"Should we head in that direction?" Evangelina asks.

"Yes, shortly. I would like to get a better look at this first."

"I would as well, but I'm anxious."

"Try not to worry. I believe we'll know what we are looking for. It can't be far from here."

They both move closer to the rock and Evangelina reaches for it, hesitates and then touches it. It feels just as it looks, smooth in some areas but jagged in others. It's not so sharp that it will tear the skin if she holds it, but she thinks it could easily be used as a weapon.

She looks at Exos. He already knows what she wants to ask.

"I think you can pick it up," he says.

As he moves the torch closer for her she notices the shimmering they're seeing is the light of the torch reflecting off the surface of the rock. It's a metallic-black color. When she tries to pick it up there is great resistance.

"It is very heavy. Too heavy."

"Let me try." Exos moves in closer to her. He tries to pick it up but he can't move it.

"Something feels strange about this rock. Can you move the torch closer?" he asks.

She does as he asks and they both realize they're not looking at the entire rock, but merely a piece of a rock that is protruding from the ground.

"I need a pickaxe. Will you give me the tools, please?"

Evangelina hands him the bag of tools and holds the torch over the bag, enabling him to see it better. Then she holds the torch closer to the rock so Exos can dig around it. As he tries to remove some of the dirt from around the rock he accidentally strikes the rock with the pickaxe. He feels a reverberation through his hand, arm and neck. The blow does not damage the rock.

"This is the strangest rock I've ever seen," he says as he rubs his arm.

"That's because it's not just a rock, is it?" Evangelina says softly, almost mesmerized. "May I?"

She reaches her hand out to him and he gives her the pickaxe. He takes the torch in return. She begins to carve out some of the dirt around the rock. As she continues to remove more dirt, the natural shape of the object becomes more apparent. After some time, she has dug enough dirt out to uncover nearly half of it, and the object begins to reveal an egg-like shape just over half a meter in diameter. When she notices the size and shape she looks at Exos and he gives her a half smile.

"This belongs to my son."

"Yes."

"I ... I can't believe it."

"It's real. I assure you," Exos says, as he gently but briefly squeezes her hand.

She cuts away the dirt from around the outside of the object until she sees a hole in the object that's sealed with more dirt. She uses the pickaxe to begin removing the dirt around the hole. After striking the dirt a second time, a large clump of it falls away from the object, revealing the hole to be an oblong-shaped crack.

Exos moves the torch closer to the rock.

Evangelina stares at the crack so intently that she's startled when she hears Exos speak.

"Evangelina, are you alright?"

"It looks like it cracked just enough for something to get out. Like a bird's egg, just after the young hatched," she says.

Exos nods his head in agreement.

"Can you bring the torch closer to the opening?"

Exos does as she asks.

Evangelina notices the dirt that sealed the rock does not fill the rock. She has enough room to put her hand inside it, which she does—but stops abruptly. She grabs the smaller torch Exos had lit earlier, still burning though the tip is much smaller now. She takes the tip of the torch and puts it inside the hollow rock, moving it back and forth, attempting to graze every part of the inside—she hopes the fire will not damage it. She leaves the torch in only long enough to kill anything that might have taken haven in it. Once she's done, she waits a moment to let the heat escape the inside. In the meantime, she removes more of the dirt on the outside. When she's sure it's safe she puts her hand inside—at first just to test the temperature, then to find out what the inside feels like. She yanks her hand back.

"What's the matter?"

"I ... it feels strange."

She puts her hand back inside and this time she doesn't pull away. Initially, she thought the inside surface was wet because it was cold and it moved when she touched it.

Now, as she's touching it again she realizes it's not wet, but pliable. Firm at first, it then adjusts to the pressure of her fingers, until abruptly there is resistance after her fingers are about a centimeter deep, where she feels a clear stopping point. Each time she retracts her fingers from the inside surface, and then touches it again, she has the same experience.

"You must feel this."

Exos puts his hand inside and does as she had done. She sees from the look on his face that he is experiencing what she was. Exos lets out a brief, almost boyish giggle.

"I've never felt anything like this," he says.

"Nor have I."

Without saying a word about it, they both decide on the same course of action: though this object does not hold the gem they're looking for, they decide not to leave it here. They continue to dig until most of the dirt is removed, but when they have nearly exposed the entire shell, the bottom seems to be attached to part of the red rock embedded in the ground.

"This trench was formed by Tahvi's star," Exos says. "The speed and pressure is what likely made this trench so big. But the star or rock itself is quite small in comparison to the size of the canyon it has formed. This must be its final stopping point. Based on the condition it's in, I would guess it hasn't been moved or even noticed. I would doubt anyone has seen it or even been around it. But here is where it was blocked, the force and hardness of the red rock finally stopping it in its tracks. If you want to take it with you, we're going to have to try to cut through the rock. That could take a long time. Do you want to try?"

"I do."

They decide that Exos and Jabneh will try to separate the shell from the rock. Evangelina agrees to wait with Kaco and the horses.

It takes just over an hour before they're able to dislodge the shell from the rock, after which Exos calls Evangelina from the trench. She walks over with Kaco and sees her son's shell.

"Look," Exos says.

He holds the torch close to the rock and she can see what it looks like completely excavated.

"Is it broken anywhere else?" she asks.

"Not that we can tell," Exos replies.

"We should cover it with a blanket," Jabneh says.

Evangelina nods. Again there is no explanation needed. They haven't seen anything like this before and likely neither has anyone else—it's better that they're as inconspicuous as possible.

She brings a blanket back and drops it below. They lay the blanket on the ground, roll the egg-shaped rock onto it and then lift it with ease. When they realize how light it is Jabneh offers to carry it alone and is easily able to. Exos places the tools in the bag and picks up the smaller, extinguished torch. After swinging the bag of supplies over his shoulder he also gets the larger torches from the ground, carrying one in each hand.

"Is it very heavy?" Evangelina asks.

"No, it's remarkably light," Jabneh responds cheerily.

Exos walks close to Jabneh and guides him with the torch, helping him with his footing.

"Could you drive the wagon near the opening of the trench so … " Jabneh begins.

"So you don't have to walk back?" she finishes.

Jabneh smiles.

Evangelina does as he asks and meets them as they're walking out of the deepened ground that was created by her son. As she watches Jabneh approach the wagon with this blanketed bundle she tries to imagine her son—or her son's essence, she reminds herself—being in that rock. She is overcome with a sense of awe and gratitude that despite Tahvi's limitations he made his way to her and is safe. All of this is so strange and she randomly feels a flux of emotions that seem to rock the ground beneath her, throwing her off balance, when in fact nothing is moving except her mind's perceptions shifting within her.

Jabneh puts the rock in the wagon and Exos puts the supplies in it. After placing the torches back in their holders around the wagon, Jabneh climbs into it. Exos is about to climb into the back when Evangelina asks him to wait. Kaco leaves the comfort of Evangelina's lap and scurries over to the blanketed rock. His nose twitches as he sniffs it, smells nothing interesting, but sits next to it anyway.

"Do you mind if I ride in back?"

"Of course not," Exos answers.

Evangelina sits in the back of the wagon next to the blanketed rock. She puts her hand over the bundle and tries to imagine her son's essence being inside it, whatever that means. She smiles at their decision to bring it home, relieved that it didn't take longer to remove it from the ground.

"Onward?" Jabneh asks.

Evangelina nods. As they drive Evangelina pulls the spear out of her pocket and points it in the direction they're headed. She notices right away that the pulsing is different. It appears to be moving faster than before.

"Exos?" she calls to him and he turns around. "Does the light seem faster to you?"

Exos looks at it. His two eyebrows come together and for a moment it looks like he has only one. "I believe it is." He half smiles again.

"Will you share your thoughts?" she asks.

"Both sides act as a guide. I find it a wonder. No matter what direction you're headed, the brightness will move to the appropriate end and will guide you to the right place. But more than that, it seems the pulsing indicates how *close* you are. Without the pulsing you could be wandering around a general area for all time, not knowing if you have the right place, especially if you don't know what to look for. As we get closer both the brightness and the pulsing should continue to increase."

"Exos?"

"Yes, Evangelina?"

"Do you find it strange – the condition of the trench?"

"In what way?"

"It's a large hole at the bottom of a canyon. And Tahvi has eight years. Why isn't it filled with dirt?"

Exos looks back towards the trench. "I had not considered that but yes, I find it very strange."

"Certainly not any stranger than anything else that's happened this evening," Jabneh says.

Exos looks at Kaco. He's now sitting beside Evangelina, who is petting him on the back of the head.

"Enjoying the trip, my little friend?" Exos asks Kaco.

Kaco sniffs at the air and makes a clicking noise as a response.

Evangelina smiles at the animal and then leans back in the wagon. The spear is in her lap. She watches the light pulsing in it and wonders how much further they have to travel. She feels her eyelids beginning to droop.

As the tension releases in different parts of her body she finds herself drifting into that comfortable place between the waking world and sleep. The stars look blurry as she watches them. She tries to keep her eyes open, but they seem so heavy and the night air feels cool and soothing. The movement of the wagon only helps to lull her. Her eyelids close again but this time she doesn't resist.

Seconds after they close, Kaco climbs into her lap and sits next to the spear. He paws at it and is finally able to touch it. He falls asleep within minutes with his front paws wrapped around the spear.

* * *

Evangelina dreams of falling stars lighting up the sky. There are hundreds upon hundreds of them. As they fall to the ground they explode and each one releases a baby bird with large wings. They burst into flight the moment they escape their star pods. It's lovely at first, but then something goes terribly wrong. One by one they begin to fall out of the sky. Some start to twitch in mid-air and then drop to their death. Others look as though they're being shot out of the sky from below. She is standing amidst all of this, birds dropping dead from the sky. She reaches her hands out to try to catch them but each time they escape her grasp. She begins running, trying desperately to save just one and also protect herself from the falling death, and then she feels something pull at her leg. It doesn't stop her, but the pulling becomes stronger until she's unable to resist it and she trips.

In her dream she falls slowly, as though time is her friend and wants to break her fall, toward a pile of bird bodies. Some of them look like they're peacefully sleeping; others lie with broken necks and bones protruding from their bodies. She lands in the gruesome but soft graveyard. She's repulsed knowing they're all dead, yet comforted because their feathers feel smooth against her body. Then she feels the pulling again and when she looks back there is nothing, only darkness trying to envelop her. She opens her mouth to scream, and then she awakes.

"Evangelina?" Jabneh whispers, trying not to startle her.

"What? What is it?" She rubs her eyes and sits up in the wagon.

"We're here."

"Here? Where?" She had slept heavily indeed, so much so that she has forgotten where she was.

She looks at the spear. It's still in her lap but the pulsing has changed. It's moving rapidly, faster than she's seen thus far.

"Are you sure?"

"Yes. We're sure."

She notices Jabneh has the bag of tools looped over his shoulder. He's holding a torch with the other hand.

"This is where it's pulsing the strongest. We tested it to be sure by driving past this location and noticed the pulsing started to slow again so we doubled back. And Kaco is behaving as if he's lost his mind." Jabneh points at him.

Evangelina sees Exos near the front of the wagon. He's barely able to hold Kaco in his arms. Kaco is restlessly kicking and pawing at him, sniffing the air constantly and making clicking and high-pitched squeaking noises. He's clearly in some sort of distress.

"It might have been a mistake to bring him," Jabneh declares.

"Jabneh, would you hold a torch closer to me?" Exos requests, "Not too close, I don't want to upset him any more than he already is."

"What's the matter with him?" Evangelina asks.

Exos does not answer her. Instead he shushes and pets Kaco until he is calmer. He then places his hands on either side of Kaco's torso and closes his eyes. The animal continues to stir, and then his body relaxes and the fidgeting and whimpering stops.

"What are you doing to him?" Jabneh asks.

"Wait," Evangelina says kindly, "let him finish."

Minutes later, Exos removes his hands from Kaco's torso and thanks the animal out loud. Then he reaches into the back of the wagon and grabs the rope he'd been fiddling with earlier. He has made a harness with it.

"You believe he knows where it is," Evangelina says.

"Yes, I believe that's what he is trying to tell us," Exos responds. "As we get closer he might grow more anxious and agitated, and he's likely to run off into the darkness. I get a sense that he wants to help us, but it's difficult for him to control himself. He wants desperately to follow his instincts."

# Broken

"And his instincts in this case … ?" Jabneh asks.

"His instinct is to be near the gem. He's drawn to it as he was drawn to Tahvi when his essence was born and as he continues to be drawn to him now."

"But Kaco doesn't behave this way now. He is not overly excited around Tahvi," Evangelina protests.

"But it's not Tahvi that Kaco senses now. It's his *essence*. What Kaco is sensing is the purity of Tahvi's spirit, much like … " Exos takes a moment to find the right words. "It's what you might feel if you were in a desert with no water for days and then suddenly you saw water."

Jabneh stares at him blankly.

"It's difficult to explain."

While he speaks Exos continues fitting the rope onto Kaco. The animal is a bit squirmy but he does his best to accommodate the harness. It doesn't take Exos long to make sure the harness is adjusted properly.

"This should secure him, and it should help him to be our guide. It will keep him from running too far ahead of us and since the animal seems to be in an overly sensitive state, if what we're looking for happens to be in an area that is too dangerous to approach, it should keep him from hurting himself as well. I'm sure the gem will continue to guide us well, but Kaco might help save us some time fiddling around in the night for the exact location. I tried to communicate with him to ask for his help but I don't know to what extent he understands."

"I believe he understands quite a bit," Evangelina says.

"I do as well," Exos agrees.

Exos holds the end of Kaco's harness in his hand and the others see he's also formed a loop that he has tied loosely around his wrist. Kaco jumps off of the wagon and begins running away from it. He runs into a clearing in front of them until he is abruptly stopped and yanked back as he reaches the end of the harness, which is about six meters long.

"It seems he doesn't understand how a harness works," Jabneh says.

Evangelina watches Kaco pull with all his force to move forward. He even begins clawing at the harness until Exos asks him to be calm and promises him they will soon be on their way. Evangelina thinks

125

of when she tried to escape the something or someone that was pulling her leg in her dream.

"Where exactly are we?" she asks.

"We are less than an hour's ride away from the red rock canyon. This area is mostly flatlands and brush. I'm hoping if we have to dig this time, we will not meet more rock," Exos says.

"Do you have all the tools?" Evangelina asks Jabneh.

"Yes, and the water."

"Would you like me to take Kaco?" she asks Exos.

"No, I believe I should lead him. All we need is another torch and someone to anchor the wagon."

Evangelina steps out of the wagon and uses the mallet they have in the back to drive a small stake into the ground. She ties the end of the reins to the stake, pets the horses and then grabs a torch from the front of the wagon. She walks to Exos and Jabneh and takes a deep breath. She takes the spear out of her pocket and sees that the pulsing is just as intense. The direction is straight ahead. They all begin walking, Kaco still pulling at his harness in front.

They walk for only a few meters before the pulsing in the speared gem begins to grow more intense with every step. Evangelina begins walking faster. Before she realizes it she's running. The others begin to run with her and Kaco no longer has to pull at the harness. He is running just ahead of Exos and Evangelina while Jabneh is trailing at the end.

Exos had been correct: because the area is a flatland there is almost no rock. It is mostly patches of sand and dirt, random trees and other brush. The plants they have seen thus far are a murky green and brown, looking like they're on the edge of life, so it surprises her when they run head-on into a lavish bush that is bursting with wildflowers. It's larger than most plants in the area, nearly half the size of the wagon.

When Exos and Evangelina reach the bush, they almost topple over. The bush is growing in a depressed area in the ground, but they can't immediately see the change in elevation with the light provided by the torches and moonlight. It takes Jabneh a minute to catch up so they're able to warn him about his footing. Out of breath, they stand in awe. What they had thought to be one bush is actually a cluster of them.

They have seen nothing like them before. The flowers growing from the bushes look much too exotic for a flatland area such as this. What is even stranger is that they're not only one type of flower— different types grow from the same bushes. Some have short, rounded petals and others have long, loping petals like a donkey's ears. Others have petals that curl around each other like braided twine. There is a mixture of different colors and shapes but each is as rich and stunning as the next.

Kaco reaches the bushes just before Evangelina, Exos and Jabneh do. Veering directly for the bottom of one he begins to dig furiously. He digs with such speed that sprays of dirt fly through the air on either side of him.

Evangelina looks at the spear to confirm what she already knows: its intensity is brighter, and it's pulsing faster than before.

"We will be digging here?" Jabneh asks.

"Yes," Evangelina replies.

"I thought we were looking for a trench, like we found in the canyon." Jabneh says.

Evangelina walks around the bushes while holding a torch. After circling almost half the area she realizes that the bushes are growing in the center of a small crater.

"No. Not a trench. You said the star broke?" Evangelina looks to Exos.

"Yes."

"Then this piece fell straight to the ground," she says.

She looks up at the sky. Her mind returns to her dream and the image of the falling stars. She wonders how beautiful it must have looked when Tahvi's star flew into the world. She thinks that even when it was breaking it must have looked fantastic. She remembers the night she was standing outside in the moonlight, not long after Stefan died. *Is that what I saw that night? Was that you, Tahvi?* she thinks. She looks at the bushes and wonders how deeply this part of his star is buried.

Exos and Evangelina exchange a quick glance and then simultaneously turn to Jabneh, reaching for the tools. He helps them open the bag and everyone takes a tool to dig. Jabneh holds the shovel and Evangelina watches him walk toward the bushes. The moment she hears the shovel sink into the ground she stops him.

"Wait!"

Jabneh nearly falls over, startled.

"What is it?" Exos asks.

She looks at the shovel and the bushes and can't quite say what she wants to. She shares the closest thing she can think of. "I'm wondering ... should we be careful with the tools? So we don't damage the buried gem?"

"I don't believe that's necessary," Exos answers. "I would guess that the gem is going to be nearly indestructible, much like the speared gem you hold in your hand. But we can be careful with the tools if you'd like."

She doesn't respond.

"Is that your only concern?" Exos asks.

She tries to bring herself to say what she can't say. She's not sure they will understand. She's not sure she understands.

"I ... I would like to make sure we don't harm the flowers, if it can be helped."

"Evangelina, I'm sure they'll grow back," Jabneh says.

Evangelina looks at the cluster of bushes. In that look Jabneh realizes the mistake he's made. What they're looking for is a piece of *Tahvi,* and that piece of Tahvi buried under these bushes is what gave them life—what gives them life now. What they're looking at is Tahvi in a different form and she can't bear the idea of harming any part of him.

Evangelina's eyes begin to tear as she struggles to put this into words but can't. Jabneh walks over to her and puts the shovel down.

"I am so sorry. I believe I understand." He looks at the cluster of bushes and then back at Evangelina. "This is your son."

She begins to cry and Jabneh holds her. She returns his embrace. He knows she is a strong woman but she feels like a child in his arms.

"We can do our best to find it without damaging the flowers and we can make sure any soil that is disrupted is returned to its normal state, as best as we can."

"Thank you. Where do you think we should start?" she asks Exos.

"Kaco has started for us. I think we should follow his lead."

It turns out they don't need the tools. When they start to dig they notice the soil is so delicate and moist that they're able to remove it with only their hands. Jabneh and Evangelina dig while Exos holds a torch for them. It amazes them to see such robust, beautiful flowers in an area that would not normally sustain them. They do their best to dig around the roots and try not to damage any of them until they have almost exposed the entire shrub that Kaco had initially started digging under. After they remove it entirely, they set it aside and are surprised to find that the soil continues to be moist and fertile for almost half a meter below them.

Jabneh and Evangelina have similar reactions after having their hands in the soil. They start to giggle and laugh. They become playful with each other, digging like it's a race they're both trying to win. They pitch the soil at each other and this makes them laugh more. They stop digging to smell it. It smells like it's been watered with the juices of different fruits: oranges, berries and apples. They're tempted to see what it feels like on the rest of their skin, so they rub it on their arms and face, giggling all the while. Exos stares at them. He smiles, amused by their behavior but confused by it too.

Then Kaco does something very strange. He stops digging and begins rolling around in the soil. He rubs his fur on it. He sniffs at it and claws at it, his body writhing in sensual pleasure that looks like he's in agony. He tries eating it, but as magnificent as it apparently feels, it seems he doesn't like the taste of it and he spits it out. He continues to roll around in it while they dig and it's not long before he falls asleep in the soil. As he sleeps, he's occasionally dashed with soil from their digging.

It's Jabneh who feels it first—the soil is so soft and moist that he recognizes the difference immediately.

"I think I found something," he says, through giggles. Exos and Evangelina both move closer to him.

What he's found is hard and rough, very different from the texture of the soil, and he continues to dig around it. As soon as Exos moves the torch over it, they all can see that it's the same type of metallic rock they have just dug out of the canyon. Jabneh continues to dig but Evangelina stops. She's still kneeling in the soil but now she looks confused.

She pulls the spear out of her pocket. The moment it is pointed at the part of the rock that is showing, the entire spear lights up. It's much brighter than the light from both the torch and the moonlight combined, giving the night an ominous green glow. The heat increases and the change in temperature is so sudden that it surprises Evangelina. She accidentally drops it in the soil.

The moment it touches the ground it ceases to glow fully. Its brightness and pulsing continue, the pulsing moving at a rate that is so fast now it's almost imperceptible. She lightly touches the spear to feel its temperature. It's very warm, but not too hot to touch. She picks it up and points it toward the rock again so there is nothing in between the two. Again the spear lights up entirely, and after a moment they notice the metallic rock starting to glow. Thin and thick beams of green light, the same color as the spear, suddenly erupt from the rock. They're not as bright as the light from the spear but they're still impressive.

"My … stars!" Jabneh gasps.

"My stars indeed," Exos agrees.

At that moment Kaco wakes from his nap, feeling the energy from the glowing rock in the ground. He makes a squeaking noise and before the others realize what he was doing, he has his paws on the rock. There is a surge of energy as the light intensifies for a moment and then returns to the level of brightness it was before. Kaco lies next to the rock, looking like he's ready to sleep again.

With her free hand, Evangelina reaches for the rock and she's able to easily pull it out of the ground. It's no bigger than the size of her hand, and like the other rock it's very light. The moment that it's in her hands she feels a sense of comfort that she's sure she's never known. The muscles in her body loosen and she drops both the rock and the spear. Her eyes are still on the rock but they look as though they're looking through it, beyond it to somewhere else.

Exos has been leaning over them with the torch. As he stands up to stretch he realizes the glow from the spear is lighting up much of the area. He looks around to see if there are any other travelers, even though he does not sense any. He listens for the noise of a horse or horses that might be close.

"Evangelina?"

"Yes?" she says, stunned to hear his voice.

"Cover the spear."

"What? Why?" she asks without taking her eyes off the rock."

"Look up," he replies.

She does as he asks and notices the brightness. There won't be a way to explain this to a passing traveler.

She puts the spear back in her pocket and the rock stops glowing the moment it loses contact with it. The overwhelming sense of ease leaves her as well. She turns the rock over in her hands, noticing how similar and different it looks from the rock in the back of the wagon:

the texture is exactly the same, but none of the surface of the rock is cracked or appears damaged in any way. In the torchlight, she's able to see that this rock is not exactly like the one they found in the canyon. It's still metallic-black in most places but it's also green, as if a large emerald is trapped inside it. The green coloring in the rock is exactly the same shade as the color of the speared gem. Though it's not glowing now, the way it did when the spear interacted with it. She inspects it thoroughly, focusing on the composition of its surface and its weight.

"You look confused," Exos says.

"It's not what I expected."

"What did you expect?"

"To find something like the spear, the gemstone we have now."

"I see. I wasn't sure what we would find," Exos shares.

"It makes sense," Jabneh says.

"How does it make sense?" Evangelina asks.

"You said he was born of a falling star, yes?"

Exos nods.

Jabneh points to Evangelina. "And you said that this spear, this was actually a part of Tahvi when he was born?"

"Yes."

"The rock that is sitting in the back of the wagon … if that is his star, then the crack we found in it must have been where Tahvi or his essence escaped or hatched or whatnot. But if Tahvi is not complete, if there are other pieces of this star, then this is how we will find them. Not as gems but rocks, with Tahvi's essence completely unscathed and sheathed in the stone."

Evangelina looks at the rock again. She realizes how much of what Jabneh says makes sense. Looking at Exos, she can see that he believes the same. What she should be looking for are these metallic rocks. This brings her comfort, to know that she now has a better idea of what they should be looking for.

Before they pack their tools and head back to the wagon they place the plants back in their original place and return the soil to how they found it.

"Do you think they will continue to flourish without the stone's influence?" Jabneh asks Exos.

"I don't know. The soil seems rich enough."

Evangelina hadn't considered this and realizes she feels some sadness leaving the plants behind. She wonders what the future will hold for them and if Tahvi will ever get to see them.

Jabneh asks Exos for the torch and walks around to the other side of the bushes, the opposite side of where they were digging.

"Oh … my," he says.

"What is it?" Exos asks.

"Look." Jabneh points down, toward his feet.

Exos walks over to him. Because of the darkness they hadn't noticed that the area these bushes are in is actually the top of a small ridge that descends just over the other side. Exos looks down the slope and sees it's covered in these same bushes. The slope looks like it could be at least two meters high.

"Evangelina, you should see this," Jabneh says.

Evangelina joins Exos and Jabneh near the edge of the ridge. "There's so many," she marvels.

"Yes. I think they will continue to grow on their own. I hope they will," Exos says.

Evangelina asks Jabneh and Exos for some time alone at the site and they agree to wait for her at the wagon. Exos pulls at Kaco's harness but the animal doesn't want to leave. He claws at the soil and holds some of it with his front paws, seemingly wanting to take it with him.

"Come, little one. Tahvi is waiting for you at home." Exos picks him up and carries him to the wagon.

Not long after Exos and Jabneh are settled in the wagon they hear Evangelina approaching. When they look at her they see she is carrying a spray of wild flowers with her.

Jabneh hadn't noticed before, but the flowers have a radiant quality to the petals, shimmering like the rocks in the red rock canyon. It strikes him that Evangelina looks beautiful holding them in the moonlight. A feeling of grief sweeps through him as he thinks of the wife and daughter he will never see again. He turns away from her and pretends to adjust the reins on the horses.

Evangelina sets the flowers down, wraps the rock in a cloth and places it safely in a corner in the back of the wagon. She then begins arranging a comfortable spot with the blankets they have. Kaco scampers over and sits in the middle of it once she's done.

"Jabneh?" Evangelina asks.

"Yes?"

"I will drive home. You should rest."

"I am actually quite—"

"I insist that you try. Besides, I feel very much awake and would enjoy driving. I promise to let you know if I tire."

Jabneh looks at Exos, who speaks before Jabneh can. "I too am not tired," he shares.

"Very well," Jabneh says. He moves into the back of the wagon.

Evangelina takes the reins and directs Sadie and Baleel to turn back in the direction from which they came. They've travelled quite a bit and she knows she has a long drive ahead of her. But she feels well rested and is grateful for the time to think.

Exos looks at the flowers in the back of the wagon.

"Tahvi will be happy to see what he's helped to create," Exos shares.

Evangelina smiles. She drives the horses at a slightly faster pace. Searching will not slow them, now that they have the stone. As she drives, the night air brushes against her face, cool and invigorating. She begins to think of what will happen when she brings this rock back to Tahvi. *How will it rejoin with him? What part of him will it fulfill?* she thinks.

She imagines what it will be like when they find all the pieces. He can wake in the mornings and not have to attach his limbs. He will have two hands to hold and build things with. He can run and play, like any other boy. These thoughts bring tears to her eyes and a smile to her face. She's happy to be going home and eager to see her son.

# THE VERTIMUS FORETELL

Tahvi's nightmare at first had seemed like a dream. The sky is filled with falling stars exploding into arcs and streams of light. He flies amongst them and then he begins to fall. It's not the fall that he fears but what he sees rushing towards him: his mother, lying in a pile of feathers. She is kicking and screaming at something that is trying to overcome her. Tahvi can't see what it is, but sees only darkness. He calls her name but she doesn't hear him. He reaches for her but she doesn't see him. When he is nearly to her, the darkness abruptly turns on him and takes the shape of a man. Tahvi thinks he can see his face but it's too dark and muddled. Before he can get a clear look at it he wakes, gasping. He's clawing at his blanket with his one hand, covered in beads of sweat.

"Tahvi, calm yourself." Vertimus tries to soothe him by moving his fingers through Tahvi's hair. "You're safe. You're home, in your bed. There's no need for fear."

"Mother ... she's in peril. She is ... "

"She's well. She's likely in the Tabarak Canyon now."

"But I saw her, covered in ... something. She was ... I don't remember."

"You were dreaming. Your body was shaking and you're sweating. It must have been very frightening. Are you warm?"

"Yes."

Vertimus dips a towel in the bowl of cool water next to it. He wrings it out and gives it to Tahvi.

"Put this on your head and I will get you some water, yes?"

Tahvi agrees, then Vertimus returns with water for Tahvi and tea for himself.

In the time it takes to wipe the sweat from his face and neck, most of the details of the dream have faded. By the time he drinks the cup of water Vertimus had brought him, he has trouble remembering why it was that he was so scared.

"I don't remember what it was I dreamed."

"That's as it should be. It doesn't seem like the type of dream I'd want to remember."

"I think my mother was in danger. But I don't know why."

"Dreams of parents in distress are always frightening. I remember having many of them as a young boy."

Tahvi looks at his uncle, drops his eyes to his cup and then looks at his uncle again.

Vertimus smiles at him. "What a very serious look for such a young boy."

"I was thinking about you." Tahvi's eyes meet his uncle's.

"Yes?"

"I was wondering … about what you haven't told me."

Vertimus adjusts his position in the chair and sets his tea on the small table by Tahvi's bed. "I had a feeling this subject would surface tonight."

"You felt it, or you *knew* it?" Tahvi asks bluntly.

Vertimus does not answer right away. He's had many conversations with Tahvi when Tahvi is like this—when he doesn't sound or seem at all like a young boy. During these conversations, Vertimus knows he needs to be truthful and sincere with Tahvi, but he also needs to be sensitive. No matter how knowing Tahvi is, no matter how gifted, he is still a child.

"It's practicality, Tahvi. A boy's mind wanders when his feet and hands can't."

"You said you're special like me?"

"Yes."

"That I am not the only one?"

"This is true."

"Are we special in the same way?"

"No. I don't have the connection with matter that you do. I can't tell you the history of an object or manipulate its momentum."

"How *are* you special, then?"

"How do *you* think I'm special?"

Tahvi looks at the doorway to his room. It's late and it's likely everyone is asleep, but he can't be sure. "Should we close the door?"

Tahvi asks.

"No, but we should keep our voices low. You must also promise to share this with no one, not even your mother or the twins. Your word?"

Tahvi gives his word and agrees to keep his voice low. They spend the rest of the conversation whispering.

"You said my mother is well. You said she's in the Tabarak Canyon?"

"I believe I said *likely* she's in the Tabarak Canyon."

"Do you know that's where she is now?"

"No."

Tahvi looks at his cup again and gently bites his lower lip. "But you know she's coming home and that she'll be well when she does?"

Vertimus smiles. "Yes, I do."

Tahvi's thoughts turn to the strange man who had come into his life that night. "You brought Exos here tonight."

"Yes."

"Not by chance?"

"No."

"You travel very much but mother says you often return when you are wanted or needed, even when it's too soon to send a messenger to you."

Vertimus nods.

"Do you know when you're wanted or needed?"

Vertimus smiles and nods again.

"You can see our destinies! That is your gift?"

Vertimus laughs, shaking his head. "That's an admirable guess, boy. But not exactly."

"But it must be. You said—"

"I said not *exactly*. In many ways I can't see your destiny, and yet in some ways I can."

"Is this a riddle?"

"No, maybe a poor explanation." Vertimus moves his chair closer to his nephew's bed. "Like you, Tahvi, I am what's called a sensitive. My skill, the gift given to me, is that of foretell. It's like seeing a painting of what is to come. I get a picture in my mind of a scene or story, of something that hasn't yet happened. More importantly, I get a sense of exactly when and where it will happen."

Tahvi's eyes widen. "That's amazing!"

"It can be, yes."

"Is it always something that hasn't yet passed?"

"Yes."

Tahvi thinks about this for a moment. "If you can always see what has yet to happen, then can you endlessly make good fortune?"

"Not exactly."

"I don't understand."

"I can't *always* see what is to happen. The impressions come to me of their own volition. I've no control over them. Your mother, for instance: I believe she's well because I've foreseen a conversation with her that has yet to take place. During this conversation she looks to be in good health and uninjured. I also know the conversation will take place soon. From these facts, I can deduce she must currently be in good health."

"You can't choose what you see?"

"No."

"But there are opportunities in what you *do* see?"

"Yes."

Tahvi is quiet again.

"I ... " he pauses and looks at his uncle. "Am I asking too many questions?"

"Of course not."

Tahvi thinks for a moment of what he wants to ask next and then it comes to him.

"Can you ... *change* what you see happen?"

"Ah ... a marvelous question. I would say that I can *influence* what happens, but most often, the end result is the same."

"What? I don't understand."

"It's difficult to explain. Let me try to give you an example. Let's say that I get an impression that a war will occur, and the war is between a peaceful village and a violent one and the peaceful village is outnumbered. If I choose to, I could—"

"You could bring reinforcements!"

He smiles. "I was about to say 'bring more soldiers,' but you are correct and more eloquent in this case."

"So you *can* change what happens."

"Not always, but sometimes. But in this case, the war would happen nonetheless."

"But the victor might change?"

"This is true."

"And have you? Changed what has happened before?"

Vertimus smiles.

"You have!" Tahvi exclaims.

Vertimus gently shushes Tahvi, casting his eyes to the doorway.

"You have!" Tahvi repeats, whispering again.

"When I believed it morally right to do so, yes."

"Is that all?"

Vertimus laughs, "Is that not enough?"

"No ... um ... that's not what I suggest."

"I'm just teasing you, boy."

"When was it morally right?"

"I would say much like in the example I gave you: when someone or something was in danger and the odds were not in their favor."

Tahvi looks down at his cup again.

"Is something the matter?"

Tahvi does not speak for a long time and Vertimus does not push him to.

"You said you can't choose what you see?" the boy asks at last.

"That's correct."

"Is that why you didn't help my father?"

Vertimus leans back in the chair. He closes his eyes and puts his hand over them. This time it's his turn to be silent.

Tahvi watches his uncle and stifles a yawn. He wants to hear the answer to his question but he's still very tired. He closes his eyes, wondering if the conversation is over for now. Just when he's about to decide that it is, Vertimus speaks.

"I didn't foresee my brother's death ... and it's hard to not curse my gift because of it. I did see your mother in pain and in need, but I couldn't see why. By the time I returned home, it was known that your father had passed. I loved him very much and I miss him very much. If I had foreseen it, I would've had no choice but to stop it, even if it had meant giving my life. He was not only my brother but also my friend and a great man. All who knew him believe it still."

"And my father, he had a gift too?"

"Yes."

"What was it?"

Vertimus smiles, wanting Tahvi to think through it.

"My mother said fortune welcomed him."

"That's fitting. Your father could find promise is nearly any situation. He was a man who could make endless good fortune. I believe that was his gift. If an opportunity presented itself, he knew when it would and would not work. He would have an idea and know instantly if it would be profitable and if time should be invested in it. Maybe his gift was that he was fortunate and the money was secondary, because not only could he turn any situation into an opportunity, it was that opportunity frequently presented itself to him. Regardless, I think we can say good fortune was his gift, because it was so prevalent."

"Did his gift begin early, like mine?"

"It did—for the both of us, in fact. Due to the nature of it Stefan's was more obvious. To those around us, he seemed to be the most fortuitous boy in the village."

"Can you tell me a story about him? About when he was lucky?"

"There are so many that it may take me a moment to … " He scratches his chin as he thinks about when they were boys. Suddenly his eyes smile as he remembers one of his favorites.

"Has your mother told you about your father's first work?"

Tahvi shakes his head.

"Good."

Vertimus gives a hearty laugh and then claps his hands together loudly. Both he and Tahvi look at the doorway waiting to see if he has woken anyone, but no one comes calling. When they're sure no one has heard them, Vertimus continues.

"Your father had twelve years when he met the only woman he thought he would ever love. Of course, then she was just a girl. Her name was … umm, something that sounded like Jana. No, it was Hannah. Hannah! That was it.

"He thought her the most beautiful girl in the village and he would spend every spare moment he had watching her or helping her with chores. He would do anything he could do to spend time with her. It wasn't long before he confessed his feelings to her and told her he intended to marry her when they were older."

"Marry her? He had only four more years than I do now!"

"This is true, but so many things change when you have twelve years. You'll see." Vertimus nudges Tahvi's arm.

"But yes, with only twelve years he announced his intention to marry her. And he meant it at the time—this was long before he met your mother. He wanted Hannah to know that he was firm, determined. He wanted to do something special for her, so he began picking flowers for her each time he expected to see her. He saw her at least three times a week, and each time he would try to pick different flowers. He would arrange them in a way that presented them well, tying them with different colored braided ropes or ribbons. Well it was not long before Hannah told her mother that your father had proposed marriage."

Tahvi's eyes grow wide and he covers his mouth with his hand.

"Hannah's mother told Hannah's father, who did not take kindly to the information. He decided to have a talk with your father. It was my mother who answered the door. Your father shared nearly everything with me, so when she called to Stefan, saying that Hannah's father was at the door, it wasn't long before I was at the door too. As a boy with only nine years, I was always curious and desperate for excitement. I was eager to see if Hannah's father planned on being less than a gentleman. I arrived just after Stefan did and was surprised to see that Hannah's father seemed remarkably calm, considering the circumstances.

"My mother invited him in and she, your grandfather, your father and Hannah's father sat at the table in the cooking room. They sent me to my room but I didn't stay there.

"Hannah's father had much to say about Stefan's inappropriate behavior. And though I clearly remember the man being angry, there was a tone of respect and humility in his voice. They had a very polite discussion that ended with Stefan promising not to confess marriage or love to his daughter again until she had at least sixteen years. Everyone agreed and it seemed that the matter was settled, but before he left, Hannah's father had one more thing on his mind.

"Hannah's father wanted to know if it was your grandmother who had prepared the flowers for Hannah. Stefan explained it was he who had prepared the flowers on his own. In the most respectful way he knew how, Hannah's father confessed he couldn't believe that your father could arrange the ribbons, braids or even the flower arrangement on his own, as they seemed too artful and skillfully done for a boy of his years. Your father asked to be excused, left the table and walked past me to his room. On his way back he urged me to come along and I knew he wanted me to see whatever was to happen next. Anticipating that our mother might not approve, instead of following him I stayed where I was but continued to listen. As he passed me again he was holding a bundle of flowers, dark blue and green ropes and a piece of mesh in the shape of a half circle. I could hear rustling but no one was speaking. The near silence was too interesting to me, so I moved close enough to peek in, and before I knew it, I was in the room with them. In what seemed like no time at all, he had arranged the flowers so that they were spread out like a fan. Your father used the ropes to create a braid that tied the flowers together. He interwove and tied the braid to the mesh in such a way that enabled the flowers to keep their form while easily carrying them at the same time."

Tahvi smiled, enjoying the idea of his father proving his talents. "What did Hannah's father do then?"

"Nothing at first. He was very quiet. Then he scratched his chin and looked at my mother and father and said, 'It seems your boy is the artful one,' to which my mother simply replied, 'Yes.' What was fortuitous is that Hannah's father had a farmer's shop and flowers were one of the many things he sold. He offered your father temporary work on the spot. He had to haggle about wage a bit, because your father was uninterested. When he raised his offer to twice the wage he offered initially your father accepted. That trial week turned into a lasting position when flower profits showed a significant increase after Stefan was hired. He worked there for nearly a year before moving on to his next work."

Tahvi was trying to picture the scene: his father as a young boy, arranging items in the shop in a creative way that would make others want to purchase them, while villagers greeted him and made light conversation.

"Did you fall asleep with your eyes open?"

"No." Tahvi gives a quick smile. "I just wish … I wish I had met my father. I know what he looked like, as an adult and a young boy. When I've touched things he has touched, I see his experiences with them and I get the sense he was a loving and kind man."

"That's true. Do you sense anything else about him?"

Tahvi considers it. "He was quick to wit and slow to anger. He loved my mother very much."

"That he was, and that he did."

"But it's not real. It's as though I'm seeing a play of a play. I can't touch or feel him … He doesn't know I see him, and I can't speak to him … It makes me very sad."

Vertimus stays silent.

"I also know he loved you."

Vertimus sits forward in his chair.

"I've seen the two of you, as you raised this house. When I've touch parts of the wood or stone, I've felt some of the joy and closeness they felt when you were together, building it. It's like what I feel for Sheree and Humbul. It is wonderful and sometimes frightening. But I feel less scared knowing they feel the same as I do. Was it like that for you with my father?"

Vertimus gives Tahvi a crooked smile, his eyes gathering tears that have yet to touch his face, "It was."

Tahvi holds out his hand and Vertimus takes it. They both sit in silence for a while. It's Tahvi who drifts into sleep first. Vertimus eventually follows, dreaming of things to come.

# THE FIRST AMALGAMATION

It's just before dawn when they return. Sheree is in the cooking room preparing to break her fast. As she's slicing an apple she hears horses approaching outside. She turns to the window, hoping it will be Evangelina and the others and is delighted to see that it is. She drops both the knife and fruit and runs to her mother's room, where she is sleeping.

"Mother! They've returned!"

Sheree shakes her mother's arm as she says it but there is no need; Sheree's voice is enough to wake her mother, and before Sephine can sit up Sheree has already run out of the room. She runs into one of the guest rooms, where Humbul is sleeping. She nearly pushes him out of bed when she uses the same amount of force to shake him.

"Humbul! Rise! Awake! They've returned! AWAKE!"

"What?" he groans. Then recognition sets in and he almost falls out of bed when he tries to rise to his feet before putting them on the floor.

The only room she doesn't burst into is Tahvi's. His door is open, and when she enters she sees he's still sleeping. Vertimus is asleep in the chair by his bed. She leaves them be, knowing they likely had less sleep than the others. She had heard them whispering in the night.

The air is crisp and cool and the sun star is close to appearing on the horizon. Evangelina veers Sadie and Baleel toward the barn. She, Jabneh and Exos work to unhitch the wagon, care for the horses and store Tahvi's rock safely in the barn. When they begin walking back to the house they carry only the small metallic rock and flowers Evangelina had picked. The latter look healthy and unaffected by the air and the lack of soil, but Evangelina decides to put them in water right away.

When the three of them walk in the house they're pleasantly surprised to see Sephine, Humbul and Sheree waiting for them.

Humbul is the first to speak.

"What happened? Did you find it? What does it look like? Is it—"

Evangelina interrupts him by shushing him gently. "Sephine, can you please put these in water and then meet us in Tahvi's room?"

As Evangelina and Exos head to Tahvi's room, Sheree and Humbul follow them. Sephine follows shortly after, noticing Jabneh is staying behind.

"Are you coming?" she asks him.

"Are you sure I wouldn't be intruding?"

"Jabneh, you spent the entire night helping her. I'm sure she would want you to be there." She offers her hand to lead him. He hesitates at first, but he takes it anyway and walks with her to the room.

When Evangelina walks into Tahvi's room, Vertimus is stirring in his chair though his eyes are still closed. She puts her hand on his shoulder and kneels down beside him. When he opens his eyes he finds her holding his hand.

"Good day to you," Vertimus says through a yawn.

"And to you."

"You look exhausted."

"I am. May I sit here for a moment?"

"Yes, of course."

Vertimus and Evangelina switch places so that he's now standing and she's sitting in the chair.

"Did he sleep well?"

"He was restless but he slept through most of the night. Did you find it?"

Evangelina smiles at Vertimus but doesn't answer him. She caresses Tahvi's forehead and his cheek, trying to gently wake him, and before long he opens his eyes. He hoists himself up into a sitting position and looks at his mother.

"Good day, my dear boy," she whispers.

"You found it!"

"I did."

In her hand he sees something wrapped in cloth. She removes it and he sees a metallic rock, mostly black but some parts are also a deep, dark green. Everyone was standing around the bed when Evangelina removed the cloth. Now, they all move in a little closer.

Evangelina takes the speared gem out of her pocket and like

before, once it interacts with the rock, the full length of the gem lights up. The green color in the rock lights up as well, sending streams of light from itself.

Gasps come from the children and Sephine. Tahvi stares at it as if he expects nothing different.

Vertimus holds his hand up and lets the light from the rock show on his fingers.

"Magnificent!" It's Humbul who speaks.

"Yes, it is," Vertimus agrees.

"That happened when we first found the rock as well," Exos says.

"As bright as it is now?" Vertimus asks.

"It seemed brighter. But that may be because it was so dark."

Evangelina puts the speared gem back in her pocket and the light in the rock stops glowing. She puts the rock in Tahvi's lap. "This is a part of you."

"Yes."

"I don't know what to do now. Do you know?"

Tahvi adjusts his body so he's leaning against the headboard. He wraps his fingers around the rock and closes his eyes. The room is silent. Several minutes later, Tahvi opens his eyes again.

"I'm supposed to be with it," he tells his mother.

"Be with it?"

"Yes."

"Do you know what that means?"

"I believe so." Tahvi puts the rock back in his lap and lies flat on his bed. He places the rock on his chest and puts his hand over it. "This feels right." He looks up. "Mother?"

"Yes?"

"Will you stay with me?"

"Of course I will, Tahvi."

Tahvi sighs and tries to relax. He begins taking long, slow, deep breaths. After several minutes, his body sinks more into the bed as though all his muscles have relaxed at once. Everyone is very quiet and they wait patiently for whatever is going to happen next. Humbul and Sheree both stare at the rock, but nothing changes that they can see. They continue to wait.

After only a quarter of an hour the twins become restless and start fidgeting. Leaning against the foot of the bed, they try their best to stay focused on the rock, but their eyes wander to other things.

Humbul looks at Tahvi's new toys and wonders how soon they'll be able to play together. Sheree looks at the stone in her necklace and thinks about how beautiful it is. Humbul grows anxious to speak— this may be the longest amount of time he's ever been silent while awake.

"How are you feeling?" Evangelina asks Tahvi.

He doesn't respond to her.

"Tahvi, are you well?" She moves quickly to him and puts her hand on his, which is still on the rock. He's very warm. She feels his head and it's warm as well. She takes the washcloth that's still by the bed from the night before, places it in the bowl of cool water and then wrings it out.

"Is he having another spell?" Sephine asks.

"I am not sure. He's very warm. I will get him—" Evangelina begins to say when she hears Tahvi's breathing become more rapid. She notices something has changed in the room.

"Do you feel that?" Evangelina asks.

"I do," Sephine says. "It feels warmer."

"And heavier. Like the air is heavier in the room. More pressure," Vertimus adds.

"Yes. I feel it too," Jabneh agrees.

It's Humbul who notices it first. "Look!" he yells.

The black sections of the metallic rock have turned green, and they begin to glow and then to move. They appear to become fluid, moving like thick water inside the rock, slowly at first but quickly increasing. As the fluid moves faster, Tahvi's breathing increases as well. Beads of sweat grow on his forehead, neck and chest. Evangelina puts her hand on his head and pulls it away because it's so hot. She looks at his nightshirt and notices it's getting soaked.

"Something is not right," she says.

"No. All is well," Vertimus replies calmly.

"He's burning to the touch." She reaches for the rock. "I've got to stop—"

"No!" he grabs her arm firmly but doesn't hurt her. "You shouldn't interrupt this."

"Vertimus, he's as hot as a flame. And look at his bed!" They can see steam beginning to rise from all around Tahvi as his sweat covers his sheets."

"This is going to kill him."

"Look at me." He turns her toward him so that his eyes meet hers. She is starting to cry.

"Evangelina, he's not hurt and he's not in danger. Do you see any blisters or burns?"

She looks, then shakes her head.

"Listen to his breathing. He's in a different state. He's here but he is not aware. He can't even feel what's happening. He said he knew what he had to do. Trust him, Evangelina. He is … he is more than a boy."

"Not to me."

Vertimus holds her. There is nothing she can do but wait. She feels frustrated and trapped. Every instinct tells her to take the rock away from her son, but what exactly was she expecting? Did she think this would be effortless for Tahvi? That they would come home and he would hold the rock and wish it to be part of his body and then it would be? She promised her son that she would stay with him, but now she feels if she doesn't leave she might interfere with the very process that is supposed to be helping him. Vertimus tries to calm her.

"He will be fine," Vertimus says.

Just then, there is a crackling noise, like something burning or popping in a fire. They hear a loud CRACK as the rock splits open beneath Tahvi's fingers and the green liquid inside transforms into a smoky substance. Unlike smoke, though, it does not dissipate or separate—it gathers above his stomach where Tahvi previously held it and floats there for a moment, as if it's considering where it wants to go next. Then it slowly enters his chest. As it does, it makes a hole in his nightclothes before it disappears. The cloth does not burn or tear, but simply vanishes as though it was never supposed to be there at all. The exterior of the rock quickly crumbles into tiny metallic black grains.

"Tahvi!" Evangelina yells. His mother reaches for him. This time when Vertimus tries to grip her she pulls away. Tahvi's breathing is rapid, but he still seems unharmed. She puts her hands on his incomplete arm and he is still very hot, so she removes them.

"Tahvi?" Evangelina says, this time nearly in a whisper.

Evangelina looks at Sephine. "Please bring me a bucket of cool water." Sephine goes to the cooking room, where they have plenty of water stored in large jugs.

The green substance begins to reappear at the bottom of his incomplete arm. It moves through the sleeve, making a new hole appear there as well. It forms a translucent shell around the stub of his arm, filled with specks of light that look like stars in a green sky. The twins move closer and the adults follow their lead. Some are fanning themselves as the air around Tahvi gets warmer.

When Sephine returns with the bucket Evangelina thanks her. She soaks a towel in the water and then places it on Tahvi's head. Then she pours some of the water on his chest, on his arm and some of it falls over the translucent shell. The water soaks into his clothes and the bed, but it drips away from the translucent shell, unable to penetrate it.

"He's hot like he has a high fever, but he doesn't seem hurt," Evangelina says to Vertimus.

"I don't believe he's in pain or that this is hurting him in any way," he replied. "But I believe pouring the water over his clothes and the bed is a good idea."

No one can see exactly what's happening inside the shell, but there are odd noises coming from inside. There is a squishy sound that reminds Jabneh of a time he had been fishing and the fish flopped around in the bucket after he'd caught them.

There is a soft crunching noise that makes Exos think of the sound he makes when walking on gravel.

Then the shell begins to move. It's so slow that only Evangelina notices it at first. "My ... stars," she says under her breath.

Her son's arm had previously stopped before the joint. She remembers being in awe over how the end of his arm had always looked like it had been severed in a clean cut. She remembers feeling the flatness there and feeling a small, round plate-shaped bone just beneath the skin. Now, as the shell moves she can see the forming of an elbow joint.

"What do you see?" Humbul asks, moving closer to her heedless of the heat.

"It's ... making an arm for him. Look!" she grabs Vertimus by his wrist and yanks him closer so he can see. "He has an elbow. Do you see it?"

"I do."

Evangelina yells and begins to hug everyone in the room. Then they all begin to hug each other. Humbul tries desperately to stay focused on the shell over Tahvi's arm so he lightly hugs those that hug him but moves his head to look around them. Sheree notices this and smiles. After everyone settles they return to watching and waiting.

Tahvi is still sleeping when the translucent shell disappears from his new arm, which now extends almost to the wrist. Like before, it doesn't form a stubby or irregular end but a very smooth and flat surface. Evangelina takes the arm carefully in her hands and moves her fingers along it, gently applying pressure and feeling for the two bones inside the arm. They're both present along with the elbow joint, but at the end of his arm she can also feel an additional bone holding the other two bones in place. She gently twists the arm and it has just as much flexibility as the boy's other arm. The bony plate at the end has sockets that allow him to move the bones just as they would with a hand on the end of them.

The entire process takes just over an hour. The moment it's complete, Tahvi's breathing returns to normal almost immediately. So does his temperature.

Exos uses a bowl to gather the sand-like metallic grains that still sit on Tahvi's nightshirt. He puts the bowl on the table by the side of the bed.

"In case the boy wants them," he says.

While everyone is still looking at this new part of Tahvi's arm, Evangelina realizes that no one has eaten. She's exhausted and hungry and wonders if everyone else feels the same way.

"I haven't broken my fast. Has anyone else?" Evangelina asks.

Everyone is hungry except Sheree, so Sephine and Jabneh go to the cooking room to help prepare food for everyone. The twins help too even though they'd prefer to stay with Tahvi. Vertimus, Exos and Evangelina stay in the room.

"Is it the same with his leg?" Exos asks.

"Is what the same?" Evangelina asks.

"His leg, does it have the same strange bone?"

"Yes. Just as the arm used to be without the elbow."

Exos gives a half smile.

"Do you know what it means?"

"It seems sensible. The bones are able to twist and move just as they would if they were not missing a hand. That will keep him from having other problems. I've seen people with incomplete limbs that aren't like your son's. They aren't flat at the end, and they have many problems with the skin. They have to use medicines and oils to keep it from getting too dry and rough. They have infections that occur again and again and their use of the limb is limited because of the sensitivity and fragility of the stump. They also have problems with muscles and sensing. What typically happens is that the muscles weaken and the limb becomes less useful, sometimes unworkable, which causes more issues."

"Placeholders." Vertimus says.

Evangelina looks at him. She almost asks a question before realizing she already knows the answer.

Vertimus continues to speak. "Tahvi's body knows these things are missing. It knows it's not complete. The flat bony plates—it's his body's way of designing a method to protect the limbs until he joins with their missing parts."

"Yes," Exos agrees.

"It's remarkable," Vertimus says.

Evangelina sits in the chair by the bed. She watches her son sleeping and silently thanks the universe for him. "Exos?" she asks, sounding very tired.

"Yes?"

"Would you do me a kindness and let Sephine know Vertimus and I will eat in here when the food is ready? And would you give us some time alone, please?"

"I will." Exos leaves the room.

Vertimus brings another chair near the bed and sits next to her. She doesn't talk for several minutes. Vertimus thinks she's fallen asleep until she speaks.

"My son is more than a boy, you said." Her voice is soft, almost a whisper.

"Yes."

"He is different from other children in more ways than I ever imagined."

She'd been watching Tahvi and now she turns to face Vertimus. She looks him directly in the eyes. "That is what you meant, isn't it? When you said he was more than a boy?"

"Yes."

"And you're different as well?"

"Yes."

"As was my husband?"

"Yes."

Evangelina sighs. Now she's craving sleep as much as food and isn't sure which she wants first.

"I want you to tell me everything you know about my son that I don't."

"I will."

Evangelina gives him a brief smile and then she lies on the bed next to Tahvi. She puts an arm underneath his head, coddling him and then holds his new arm with her other hand.

"After I wake," she adds.

After she falls asleep Vertimus watches over her and Tahvi until Sheree comes into the room to let him know the food is ready.

After Vertimus breaks fast, he leaves the room to eat and helps everyone clean and store any food that wasn't eaten. He speaks with Exos for some time. Exos tells him about what happened during the night. Then Vertimus shows Exos where he can rest. It's the room Vertimus uses every time he visits. Vertimus suggests he sleep before riding back to his village. He then walks out to the barn to see the larger rock that Exos had told them about. He returns to Tahvi's room when he's done. He wants to be with his nephew when he discovers his new arm.

# THE CIRCLE OF STONES

When Evangelina awakes her son is not lying next to her. He's sitting upright on the edge of the bed, feeling his new forearm with the fingers on his other hand. She watches him as he repeatedly bends it. As he does this he moves his forearm back and forth to the opposite sides of his face, trying to get a better look at how the elbow is moving. Then he spends a long time feeling the elbow itself. He caresses it over and over again like it's the last time he'll ever see it. Finally he moves on to the stump and touches it much like the way Evangelina did earlier. He puts his hand on top of the flat, smooth stump and feels the bone there. He then twists his forearm left to right to feel the way his new forearm moves and flexes under the unique plate of bone.

"Does it feel different?" she asks.

"Not very ... and yet very much." Tahvi stays silent for several minutes while continuing to feel his new arm.

"What doesn't feel different?"

"I have another arm, so this one feels just like that one in a way. But ... "

"But what?"

"It's difficult to explain. It feels like I've always had it. I know that doesn't sound rational."

"Honestly, Tahvi, I'm not sure that I know what's rational anymore."

Tahvi sighs wistfully. "Mother, have you ever known that something was going to happen, but when it did you couldn't believe it?"

"Yes I have. Did you know this would happen to you one day? That you'd ... that your limbs would be ... that you'd be complete?"

"I knew it was possible. And that I would need to find them."

"How long have you known this?"

"From the day I was born."

"You … you remember when you were born?"

"Yes."

"But how?" Evangelina asks, confused and frightened.

"I can remember many things. And if I forget them, I can find them in my memory."

Tahvi touches his new arm again. "I'm sorry I couldn't tell you. We thought it was better if you didn't know until … until you had to know."

"We?"

"He and I." It's Vertimus who speaks. He is sitting on a chair on the opposite side of the room with a scroll in his lap.

"Uncle!"

Tahvi pushes himself off the bed and hops over to the chair where Vertimus is sitting. His false leg is not attached, so instead of leaning on anything he pinwheels both arms to keep his balance. Vertimus lifts him on his lap and holds him.

"Do you see it?" Tahvi holds his arm in front of his uncle's face so close that he almost hits him with it. His uncle laughs and gently blocks the arm before it strikes him in the nose.

"I do. I also saw your body make it."

"You did?"

"Yes, as did everyone else."

"You saw it too, Mother?"

Evangelina nods and sits upright on the bed.

"Do you remember anything? Did you feel anything?" She asks.

Tahvi shakes his head. "I remember seeing the rock. I remember when I held it, it told me I had to be with it."

"It *told* you?"

Tahvi looks at his uncle for guidance. Then he hears his stomach moan.

"You must be starving, boy," Vertimus says.

"Yes."

"Should we put your leg on?" Vertimus asks.

Tahvi nods.

"Good. It will give your mother and I time to talk."

Vertimus and Evangelina spend the next few hours of the afternoon together. Vertimus tells her as much as he feels comfortable revealing about Tahvi's abilities. He's discreet with certain things when he knows it is important to be. Evangelina learns that Tahvi is able to have a special relationship with almost anything or anyone he encounters: he's able to learn the history of it simply by touching it, as long as the thing or person is open to sharing it. He's also able to manipulate matter and energy if they are willing to be manipulated. He shares examples of experiences Tahvi has shared with him. Tahvi also has the ability to store an unlimited amount of information and recall that information at will.

Vertimus then shares that he is a sensitive—as was her husband, as is Tahvi. He tells her of his own abilities and her husband's. She listens patiently and asks many questions, most of which he answers freely. He feels guilt over the ones he doesn't answer, knowing he's being dishonest with Evangelina when claiming ignorance. But there are certain things that he knows he must not reveal to her yet.

Though Evangelina trusts Vertimus, she would've never believed such a fantastic story if things had not happened as they did over the past day. She is relieved to have a better understanding of her son and of what is happening to him, but she still feels somewhat overwhelmed.

"Tahvi says he knew he was incomplete from the day he was born," Evangelina says.

Vertimus nods, noting that she is less emotional today, and is more focused on what they should do going forward.

"So he knew that his ... his star broke?"

"Yes. Because he has the ability to learn the history of all objects, he's able to know and understand his own as well."

"How much of the history?"

"From their creation, as I understand it."

"Then ... " She stops, thinking through what she wants to say.

"What are you thinking?"

"If he knows his own history, wouldn't he know where the other pieces are?"

"I ... I don't know. But I would think he would have shared that with us."

"When?"

"I don't understand your question."

"When would he have shared it with us? With you advising him to keep so many secrets and his doing so, when would he have had time to mention it?"

"Last night? He could have—"

"But he didn't, unless he told you something that you haven't shared with me," Evangelina interrupts.

"No. He didn't."

"And he said nothing of it this morning."

Vertimus thinks about this. He tries to recall the many conversations he's had with Tahvi. He can't remember if he's ever asked this question. *Ridiculous considering how important this information is.* He scratches his chin, concentrating harder, but nothing comes of it.

"We should ask Tahvi," Vertimus says, and they both walk quickly to the house.

It's been some time since Tahvi finished his lunch and he's now sitting with Sheree and Humbul, still talking about all that's happened. Sephine listens while working on a pattern for new slip-shoes for Sheree. Jabneh and Exos are napping.

Evangelina kneels beside her son.

"Tahvi, your uncle and I talked for a long time and I understand now that you have special gifts. I'm going to ask you a very important question and I need you to answer it for me."

"Yes, I will if I'm able."

"Your uncle says that you can tell the history of ... things. Is that right?"

It's Humbul who answers. "It's true! Once we were by the river and Tahvi picked up a—"

Evangelina gently but quickly puts her hand over Humbul's mouth. He murmurs briefly before stopping.

"I so often want to do that," Sheree says. Humbul glares at his sister as Evangelina's moves her hand from his mouth.

Tahvi giggles. "Yes, that's right."

"How much of their history?"

Tahvi thinks about this for a moment. "All of it, I believe."

"By all of it, do you mean from its youth?"

"I mean from its origination."

"Does that include you, Tahvi?"

"Uh-huh."

"Can you tell me the first thing you remember about your origin?"

As Tahvi takes a moment to recall the information, Vertimus grows nervous.

"I remember flying, floating ... like I was connected to everything.

I felt calm. That's the first thing I remember."

"And after?"

"Disconnected and sad, like something was stolen from me."

"And after that?"

"Feeling warm and cradled inside your body."

"What? You remember being inside ... here?" Evangelina puts her hand on her belly.

Tahvi nods.

"I felt warm, safe, loved."

She hugs him. "I love you more than anything."

"I love you, too."

"I suppose it was too much to hope for," Evangelina sighs.

"What was too much to hope for?" Tahvi asks.

"I thought because you knew your own history you might be able to tell us where the other pieces had fallen."

"I'm sorry. I can't."

"There is no reason for an apology." She looks at Vertimus. "But now we need to decide what the next step should be." She kisses Tahvi on the head and begins to walk away.

"Maybe if I held one of the pieces."

Evangelina stops. "What?"

"I could hold one of the pieces. They might be able to tell me the part of my history that I can't see."

"Any piece?"

Tahvi looks at her and tilts his head. Then his eyes open wide up as he realizes what she's trying to do.

"Mother! I didn't think of that. I should have asked to do that with the piece you brought me. But now it's gone and it's too late."

"It's not too late. We brought your star or ... shell ... or something. I don't know what to call it, but we brought it back with us. It's here. In the barn!"

"My star?"

"Your shell that your essence travelled in. They found it last night and brought it with them," Vertimus says.

Tahvi looks at Sheree, who makes a high-pitch squeaking sound that she often makes when she's excited. They all abandon their chairs at the table and start heading towards the barn.

* * *

Evangelina, Vertimus and Sephine walk quickly to the barn, the children running just ahead. Humbul and Sheree each have an arm linked under Tahvi's shoulders and Tahvi's arms are propped on the tops of their shoulders. Tahvi giggles at the thought of being reunited with his star shell and from the pleasure of feeling weightless. His foot and limb are not touching the ground, his other leg bent, and he can see them passing underneath him. Sheree and Humbul are giggling as well. Tahvi's jubilance is often contagious.

"Hurry, hurry!" Tahvi yells.

The twins run faster, and as their speed increases so does their giggling.

Vertimus smiles as he watches the children.

When they reach the barn, Humbul hauls the door open and begins searching immediately. "Where is it?" Humbul asks.

"It's in the last stall on the left," Evangelina responds.

When the children reach the last stall they're disappointed to see it's empty.

"There is nothing here!" Humbul yells, though the adults are already at the barn door.

"Look closer. In the corner."

When the children scan the stall they see that the hay is higher in one corner, heaped in a more rounded shape. As they move closer, they notice a blanket showing under a very thin layer of hay. Tahvi stands beside it. Sheree and Humbul are at either side of him. He pulls the blanket and the hay spills off easily. Underneath it he sees the black glimmering surface of the star shell.

"Heavens!" Humbul exclaims. He reaches for it and Sheree grabs his hand.

"Humbul, wait." She looks at Tahvi and asks, "Is it safe to touch it?"

"I believe so. Why do you ask?"

"It was covered with a blanket," Sheree says bluntly.

"That was just to keep it hidden, dear," Evangelina says.

Sheree turns to look at her. She had not noticed that they entered the stall, and neither had the others.

"It's safe to touch if you're careful. Parts of the surface are

157

spiked."

Humbul falls to his knees and begins touching the outside of it. He puts his head near the opening where the shell is cracked and tries to peer inside.

"It's so small. I don't see how you could fit in something this size."

"He wasn't the size he is now, Humbul," Sheree teases.

"That wasn't my meaning." Humbul slaps her arm playfully.

"Children, I know you're both excited but Tahvi and I have something important to do. When we are finished I promise you can play with this rock, or shell, as much as you would like to as long as Tahvi is agreeable. Does that sound like a bargain?"

Sheree and Humbul nod simultaneously. They each take several steps back when Evangelina moves closer to Tahvi.

"Are you ready?"

Tahvi nods. He places his hand gently on the star shell. He closes his eyes and takes several long and slow deep breaths. After some time passes, his body twitches and then jerks. Then he's still again. When he opens his eyes he reaches out to his mother and holds her with a smile.

"Mother, you're brilliant."

"What did you see?"

"I know where they are."

"Oh my stars! Can you tell me?"

"Yes."

She lifts her son from the ground and holds him tightly in her arms.

"You're the brilliant one! Come. Let's—"

"Look!" Sheree yells.

The shell begins to collapse and disintegrate just as the piece had on Tahvi's chest. Everything dissipates except the black metallic grains that are now on the floor of the barn.

"Aww! We were going to play with it!" Humbul exclaims.

Tahvi walks over to where Humbul is standing.

"I'm very sorry, Humbul."

Humbul sighs.

"I have to gather these grains. Would you be willing to help?"

"Yes," Humbul says with a disheartened tone.

"Do we have a jar large enough to hold these grains?" he asks his mother.

She goes to the area in the barn where they keep supplies and brings a jar back for Tahvi. "Why do you have to keep the grains?" Evangelina asks.

"I don't know. I know only that they're important."

He thanks his mother when she hands him the jar and then gives it to Humbul.

"I just need you to hold it still. Can you do that?"

Humbul nods.

Tahvi focuses on the grains. Within seconds they all hear rustling in the hay, like small animals are moving through it. Everyone feels a shift of energy in the area. The air seems thicker and more potent, as it does just before a thunderstorm. They all feel more *alive*. Everyone can see the hay as it begins to move and separate from the grains. Then, all the grains slowly and simultaneously lift approximately one meter above the ground. Sephine gasps and Evangelina watches in amazement as they witness Tahvi's abilities for the first time.

"Yay!" Humbul yells.

Tahvi holds his focus on the grains. Focus and concentration are all he really needs: once he establishes a connection with the object, he asks its permission to do what he wants it to do and the object gives it or denies it. The process doesn't take long and it only requires that Tahvi maintain the focus regardless of what's happening around him. Because Humbul's disappointment was so great, however, Tahvi wants to make a show for him. Once he begins to manipulate the grains' movement he also moves his arms as though this action is required to make the grains move.

Tahvi separates the grains so that they're clearly four arrays bundled in the air. One at a time he transforms them into different creatures. He turns the first one into a stinging fly and makes it fly into the jar, and it loses its form once inside. He takes two of the other sets of grains and makes them into small birds that fly in circles around each other and then over the others in the stall before they dive toward the jar. The adults gasp and watch with admiration while Sheree claps and giggles. Just before they approach the opening of the jar they turn into a stream of grains allowing them to fit inside. Humbul flinches as they fly toward him but he tries his best not to move the jar.

Tahvi turns the last bundle into a butterfly and asks it to fly through the air slowly. Then he does something that surprises even himself: he asks the grains to manipulate their color. The center of the butterfly remains a metallic black but the wings begin to change color. At first, they're a dark red, then a dark blue, and then waves of both colors move through its wings as the butterfly roams in the air. Tahvi manipulates some of the grains to stay behind the butterfly as it moves so that it looks like it's leaving a trail of its flight in mid-air. It slowly flies in a circular pattern several more times before heading toward the jar. There, it separates into five different butterflies, all with different colored wings, and then each slowly flies into the jar where they disassemble entirely. The jar, which is thin, but almost as tall as Humbul's head, is nearly filled to the opening.

Tahvi looks back at his mother and gives her an ear-to-ear smile.

"That was amazing!" Humbul says.

"Thank you."

"It really was, Tahvi. Better than any trick we've seen thus far, I think," Sheree says.

Evangelina believed Tahvi and Vertimus when they explained what Tahvi could do, but it is different to actually witness it. She looks at her son, trying to gather her thoughts. "I can't believe what just happened. I didn't realize how ... I didn't ... Tahvi," she says at last, "I didn't realize you had the ability to move things so easily."

"Oh no, I can't."

"But you just did."

"Not everything is that easy. It takes much focus and concentration to move the things I've tried to move. These were different. They were easy to move. And it's the only instance where I've had any influence over their color or shape. I've never moved anything in this way before."

"It is still very impressive."

Tahvi smiles at his mother and then asks Humbul for the jar.

"Can you do it again?" Humbul asks.

"Maybe later. But now I must draw a map."

"A map?" Evangelina asks.

"Yes. How will you find them if you don't have a map to guide you?"

"I—" Evangelina is not sure what else to say. She's stunned by Tahvi's indication that it's even possible for him to draw a map to the location of each of the stones.

"—will get some papery," she finishes.

"I'll help you look for some," Sephine says.

"Yes. Tahvi, meet us in the cooking room, will you?"

Tahvi nods. As the women leave Tahvi covers the jar with the lid.

"Sheree and Humbul, would you go into the house?" Vertimus asks. "I need to speak with Tahvi alone."

Sheree nods but Humbul hesitates, his eyes on the jar of grains that Tahvi is holding.

"Let's take leave, Humbul. There will be more tricks later." She links arms with him and they walk out of the stall together.

"That was quite the display," Vertimus says.

"It was."

"You sound surprised."

"I am very much surprised."

"Why?"

"I didn't know the grains would move that way."

"I thought you manipulated them as such?"

Tahvi shakes his head. "I ... umm." He pauses as he tries to think of a clear explanation. "Every attempt begins with me asking an object to move and the object approves."

"Yes, you've shared that."

"I asked the grains to lift and enter the jar. Then I just *thought* about changing them into different shapes and colors, and once I did it happened."

"Are you saying that you didn't actually ask their permission to change color?"

"Yes. All I did was think it."

"May I hold the jar?"

Tahvi hands it over to him. "What do you think it means?"

Vertimus opens the jar and holds some of the grains in his hand. He lets them sift through his fingers. They're light in weight, feeling very much like sand.

"I have no ideas yet, but you must keep these in a safe place. We'll have to talk more about this later."

Vertimus puts the lid on the jar and gives it back to Tahvi.

"I agree," Tahvi says. "Is that what you wanted to speak to me about?"

"Partly. The talk that your mother and I had ... I—"

"You didn't tell her everything."

"Is that a question?"

Tahvi shakes his head. "No, a guess."

"You guessed right, clever boy. She can't know everything at once. She's overwhelmed as it is."

"So I should continue to be careful about what I share?"

"Yes. Only what's absolutely necessary, Tahvi. The time will come when she'll know everything. For now, try to remember that she's not like us. She doesn't have the capacity for understanding and emotions that we do. Knowing too much could frighten her or impede her judgment. Maybe even paralyze it. Do you understand?"

"Yes."

"I knew you would. Let's join the others."

As they walk back to the house Vertimus offers to carry the jar for Tahvi.

"Should I also be careful what I share with Sheree and Humbul?"

"You should be careful what you share with anyone, but those two … those are the ones you can be the least careful with, for at least two reasons that I can think of."

"One is because they are children, isn't it?"

"Yes. Do you know what's significant about them being children?

"They're minds are more flexible, more imaginative, so they don't … they're not scared by the things I tell them. They're excited."

"Very good, Tahvi."

"The other reason?"

"Those two will always be loyal to you. They love you like a brother, and love makes friendships strong."

"That makes me happy."

"It makes me happy as well."

They walk into the house together and find Sheree and Humbul in the cooking room. They sit together waiting for Sephine and Evangelina.

* * *

The women return with papery, ink and a writing brush. Evangelina gives them to Tahvi and watches as he begins creating a map. He's quick about it, and while he draws Sheree and Humbul are very quiet. He labels the villages of Padhraig and Violetta, the Tabarak Canyon and other locations that he's learned from his lessons. Then he draws more locations, areas he hasn't visited or learned about during time with tutors. He draws markings in some areas to indicate landscape changes. The map includes mountain ranges, bodies of water, forested areas, circles to designate villages and so forth, all represented in impressive detail. When Tahvi is finished he places four Xs, telling them that each represents one of the stones they haven't found. Then he places two Xs by the Tabarak Canyon, representing the stone and the shell that Evangelina and the others brought home with them. These Xs are the closest to Padhraig. The location of the stones forms an oblong shape around the shell that landed in the canyon.

Tahvi pushes the map over to his mother when he's done.

"Tahvi, how do you know this is where they are? How could you possibly … "

She's not sure exactly how to finish her question. She knows only that she wants to understand, but no matter how many questions he answers, she's not sure that she will.

"It's not difficult. But papery alone makes it … I don't know the words. I can try to explain it."

"I would like to know how you know," Humbul says.

"I would as well," Sheree says.

"I think we all would," Sephine adds.

"Please continue, Tahvi," Evangelina says.

Tahvi moves the map so that it lies in front of him.

"My star showed me our history from the time it entered our planet's surroundings. I was not able to see anything before that moment, and there's a part shortly after it entered where its memory is not clear. What I could see was that something caused my star to veer off course. It was just after when it split apart and the smaller pieces flew in separate directions."

"You saw all of that? Like you see us now?" Humbul asks.

Tahvi takes some time to think about the best way to explain what he wants to say next.

"It is like I could see it from far away. I could see the path the falling pieces took in relationship to the planet and the stars. Were it not for the stars I don't believe I would be able to show the general area where they've fallen."

"It's like sea navigation," Vertimus says.

"That's a much clearer way to explain it," Tahvi responds.

Everyone looks at Vertimus.

"What does that mean?" Evangelina asks.

"It's how ships maintain navigation when travelling in a large body of water. They use the stars as a method to chart where they're going. Without the stars they would be lost at sea. Tahvi, are you saying you know the coordinates of these stones?"

"I don't know what 'coordinates' are.'"

"It's a fixed set of numbers that tells us where a specific location is. It's a lesson for another time."

Vertimus now speaks directly to Evangelina. "I believe whatever method he's using is following the same principles, so I've no doubt that these stones are in the area where he's marked them. Look at the ones in the red rock canyon. Aren't these exactly where you said you found them?"

Evangelina looks at the map and notices he's right: the X Tahvi has drawn is just outside of the Tabarak Canyon, in the flatlands where they found the first stone. There's also a mark on the map at the far end of the red rock canyon to indicate where the star shell had landed. Assuming the map is drawn to scale, and she would guess it is, these locations are exactly where they found both.

"Mother, this is where they are."

"These circles are supposed to be villages?" Evangelina asks.

"Yes."

"How do you know about these?"

"I don't. But in the memory I can see that they're inhabited, or were. I've added tick marks to show areas where there are structures that might be dwellings."

Evangelina points to the map. "I know this one and these two, but the others I don't know. I've not travelled this far before. I don't know that Stefan did either."

"I have," Vertimus says.

Vertimus looks at the map. He knows of all the villages and surrounding areas that Tahvi has drawn on it. The one near the forested area gives him pause, but he's careful not to reveal his concern to anyone. Tahvi has marked an X just beyond this location.

Vertimus asks, "This furthest one is at least a month's ride from here, if not more. And these marks, are they a collection of mountains?"

"Yes," Tahvi answers.

"These would be the Gadarine Mountains, then. There isn't a solid path through them that's large enough for a wagon to travel, so we would have to go around it. And the two crosswise from it, they're each about a two weeks' ride from one another, but that's by horse alone."

Evangelina moves the map closer. She bends toward it to get a better look at the locations of the Xs and of the map itself.

"Evangelina?" Vertimus asks.

She doesn't respond.

"Eva?" Sephine calls.

Again Evangelina doesn't respond. She moves her finger from X to X. Her lips are moving, but words are not escaping her mouth. Each stone's location is revealed before her—this map represents her son's future in more ways than one.

Then she looks at Vertimus and says, "Assuming I'm able to find each of the stones as quickly as we found the first one, this still looks to be a very long journey. Two of these locations are quite close. Not as close as the red rock canyon, but close enough to travel to and bring each one back separately. Since they're on opposite sides of Padhraig it would make sense to do it this way. Once I obtain those two I would search for all the ones located in the farthest areas last and then bring them back to Tahvi all at once. If both the universe and good fortune are on our side I could collect them and be back in less than half a year, but I would need a guide for the last of these."

"I don't believe that's a wise idea," Vertimus says bluntly.

"Employing a guide?"

"Yes. Have you thought of what your explanation will be as to why you need one? And what will you do when the guide discovers the true reason for your travel?"

"I won't have to explain anything. The guide I plan to hire is in this house. It can only be one of you three."

"Which three?"

"You, Jabneh or your companion, Exos."

"Jabneh? Has he ever been to villages other than the ones surrounding Padhraig and Violetta?"

"I don't know, but these are my options. And if you or Exos can't go then I will ask Jabneh. If he can't go I will go alone."

"That would be foolish," Vertimus says sternly.

"Eva, you can't possibly—" Sephine begins.

Evangelina interrupts, "You think I don't know it's foolish? Of course I know. But what is my alternative? I can't allow a stranger to learn about Tahvi. Vertimus, just because I've led a blessed life it does not mean I'm naive to all that's in this world. I've heard the same stories that you have about what happens to those who are said to use magic. I've seen how sensitives are mistreated and accursed. And I know there are other dangers in this world. Have you forgotten that I know what happened to Stefan and why it happened?"

Now she looks to Tahvi as she speaks. "And I've no doubt that you've shared some of this with my son, seeing as how he's done such a remarkable job of keeping his gifts a secret. I'm sure he's well aware of how important it is to be discreet with this information, probably more so than I."

Tahvi's eyes meet hers and she touches him gently on the head.

"I'm not trying to force anyone to do anything they don't want to. I am being forthcoming and practical, Vertimus. We're the only ones who know about Tahvi, and it *must* remain that way. But you're under no obligation to aid me."

"Evangelina, I didn't mean to convey that I wouldn't—"

"I'm aware of what you meant. Again, I'm merely trying to save time. These are the options as I see them. I'm willing to hear any thoughts about an easier plan."

It's Jabneh who speaks next as he enters the room. He hadn't been awake long, judging by his yawning and disheveled hair.

"What if we alternated in helping? Maybe I can go with you to the closest villages and Vertimus and Exos can go with you to the furthest—ones that Vertimus is more familiar with. I've been to several villages near Padhraig, but if the other villages are beyond the Gadarine Mountains then I can tell you with certainty I haven't been there."

"Did you rest well?" Evangelina asks.

"I did. Thank you."

"How long have you been awake?"

"Long enough to hear your proposal, which I accept. I'll help in any way I can."

Evangelina gives him a gentle smile.

"May I see the map you've been speaking of?" Jabneh asks. Jabneh moves closer to the table and Tahvi hands him the map.

"I see you're an artist as well. I think it's unfair that the universe has given so many gifts to one boy. I'm jealous." Jabneh winks at him.

"Jabneh, I meant no offense about—" Vertimus begins.

"I heard no offense," Jabneh says sincerely before Vertimus can finish.

"What do you think of my proposed plan?" Evangelina asks Vertimus.

"It's a solid plan."

"You will help, then?"

"Yes. I'll speak with Exos when he wakes."

Evangelina embraces Vertimus. He puts his arms around her and whispers something to her that the others can't hear.

"He's awake. Has been for some time," Jabneh says.

"Still in bed?" Vertimus asks.

"No, he's outside. Speaking to rocks or something of that sort."

Tahvi's head snaps towards his mother. "May I go to him?"

"Is he really speaking to rocks?" Evangelina asks Vertimus.

"It wouldn't be a surprise. If you approve I'm sure Exos wouldn't mind Tahvi's company."

Evangelina gives Tahvi her blessing and he limps out of the house. Sheree and Humbul follow him.

Evangelina pours herself a cup of tea. It's still hot, as Sephine had recently put a kettle on. She offers some to Vertimus and Jabneh. They both accept.

"We should pack the wagon and leave tonight," Evangelina says.

Jabneh nods, looking at the map. "Where we're headed is just beyond my village, so I should go home first and let my apprentice know that I'll not be back for some time. He was expecting me back today. While I'm there I can get any supplies I'll need. I want to stay with you for as long as you need my help."

"Evangelina, it's better that you rest and leave in the morning," Vertimus says.

"I don't see a reason to leave in the morning. Jabneh is well rested and I'm not tired. If I grow tired I can sleep in the wagon, just as I did when we went to the red rock canyon."

"It's best that neither you nor Jabneh rest in the wagon."

Evangelina stares at Vertimus, frustrated.

"Let me explain," he says patiently. "Based on Tahvi's map, it makes sense for you to rest now and travel in the morning. Padhraig to Violetta on horseback takes at least several hours and that's only if you're riding at a brisk pace. Travelling by wagon, a large wagon in this case, which you will need, could make that time two fold. Then you will need to stop in Violetta so that Jabneh may get his affairs together, which I'm assuming will take a few hours, does that sound right?" Vertimus looks to Jabneh for confirmation.

"That's right," Jabneh says.

"Then from Violetta to *this* village—and it's not even a village really. It's more of an encampment they call Baldric. If it continues to attract travelers, it may be a small village in a year or two."

"I know what it's called," Evangelina responds flatly.

Sephine and Jabneh exchange a nervous glance.

Vertimus waits to see if Evangelina has anything else to say before he continues. "It's practically another day's ride from Violetta to Baldric, by wagon. That's at least sixteen hours riding the wagon. Have you ridden a wagon for that long before?"

"No."

"It's a hardship. It's exhausting and difficult. It affects your mood and your decision-making. You must be well rested, and you must be willing to rest during the day to stretch your legs and back or you will have pain. If you leave in the morning you'd be well rested. Then after the drive to Violetta you can rest there as well. If you leave Violetta early the next morning you will have time to rest properly and then arrive at Baldric by evening. Shortly after dawn you can begin looking for the stone."

"But if we leave after the wagon is packed, shorten our trip to Violetta, and take turns sleeping in the wagon, we can be there the following morning," Evangelina says.

"Eva ... we still need to prepare the wagon, and you don't know how hard it will be to search for the stone at—"

Evangelina interrupts him, raising her voice. "What does that matter? We'll have to search for the stone regardless!"

When Vertimus responds his tone is direct, speaking slowly in an effort to be patient with her. "In the red rock canyon the chance that you would encounter anyone was slight. You were travelling at night, on a road that's not often occupied, and in a place that's not inhabited. You could have probably dug for hours without being disturbed. The circumstances are exactly the opposite here. How do you intend to explain what you're doing? What's your plan to search for the stone in clear daylight and then dig for it? What will be your explanation to anyone who sees you?"

Evangelina hasn't considered this. Frustrated that it's something they must work around, she paces back and forth in the cooking room, wringing her hands.

"I'm not trying to hinder or delay you. I know you're not a stranger to travelling to areas that take less than a day but extended travels are different. You have to consider things you normally wouldn't. A trip that's expected to last several days could last longer and you don't want to be stranded in a strange place without the supplies you need. It could cost you a great deal, in time and coin, if you haven't prepared for this. You must pack extra of everything you need, most importantly food and water. You must be well rested, and that's not merely a suggestion, it's necessary. Both you and Jabneh will have to be alert because getting there and back are not your only considerations. You must know your surrounding area well enough to have an alternate plan in case you run into serious trouble, like thievery or something worse. You—"

"Stop!" Evangelina pleads.

Vertimus holds his tongue.

The silence weighs heavily on the occupants of the room. Sephine has been watching Evangelina closely. She knows her behavior is unusual. She's not sure when she will speak to her about it but knows that now is not a good time.

Jabneh, meanwhile, is thinking about everything Vertimus has said. He knows Jabneh doesn't have the skill and experience that he does. He thinks of his brother, his wife and daughter, and how he lost them. He thinks about what happened to Stefan and he knows that what Vertimus is saying is true. Though he would do anything to protect Evangelina, he may not be skilled enough to take care of both of them. It's important that they're both awake and alert when they travel so they can protect each other.

At last Evangelina says, "I know you're well versed in extended travelling and I concede to hearing you. And I do want to follow your advice. I hate the idea of the stones being anywhere but here, and I know that may be contributing to me wanting to make a …

hurried decision. I want to get them to Tahvi as quickly as we can, and the longer I have to wait, the more … the more helpless I feel."

Vertimus approaches Evangelina. When he speaks, his voice is comforting and sympathetic. "I understand and I would likely react the same way if he were my boy. It's difficult even for me to not react that way now. You must believe me when I say my objective is the same and that Tahvi's safety is my utmost concern. But your safety is just as important. What will the stones matter to Tahvi if you're not able to get them back to him? And you're not waiting, you're planning. There's a difference. Planning is a major factor in the success or failure of any venture, and I can help ensure our plan is as safe as possible. Will you trust me to help you do that?"

Evangelina takes a minute to think about everything Vertimus shared. Finally she says, "Yes, as long as it's *quickly* as well."

"It will be. And thank you … for your trust."

"What should we do now?" Evangelina asks.

Vertimus walks through the entire plan for them. Exos is not present, but Vertimus says he will inform him later, and he explains that he's confident Exos will agree to travel with them to obtain the last three stones.

They'll start by preparing Evangelina's small wagon for the trip to Baldric. They will stock it with extra supplies, coin and anything else they might need for the extended trip. They'll also take the tools they need to dig for the stone, and weapons in case they encounter travelers of an undesirable nature.

Vertimus tells Evangelina that she must also take samples of her cloths and embroideries with her and Jabneh should take some of the toys he's made with him. With these items, they can tell anyone they speak with that they're travelling wayfarers looking for work or barter. He advises that though she has plenty of coinage, she should spend it sparingly as this will help support the falsehood that she and Jabneh are wayfarers.

While Evangelina and Jabneh travel to Baldric, Vertimus will stay with Sephine and the children and prepare the larger wagon, this one stocked with supplies for a much longer trip. The goal is to have it ready and waiting by the time Evangelina and Jabneh return from Baldric, though Evangelina and Jabneh will still first need to go to Encarta, the second closest location on the map.

Encarta is an established village that Evangelina had visited previously and many times with Stefan. It is larger and more populated than Padhraig. Evangelina hasn't been there in years but she remembers finding it beautiful and exciting. It's becoming what people call a metropolis, which is a much larger village with more centralized events and activities. She's also heard people describe a metropolis as a breeding ground for bad elements, but it's hard for her to imagine Encarta being much different that when she experienced it with Stefan.

Then they touch upon the subject of Tahvi—can he be brought with them? If they're to gather the stones quickly they can move faster without having to worry about Tahvi's safety or supervision, surely, but it quickly becomes clear there are other factors to consider as well.

Though no one wants to talk about it, they discuss what must be done if while they are away Tahvi has a spell that presents a new symptom while travelling. So far, his spells have seemed almost harmless, but when they have happened it was important that he was watched and cared for in case something more serious occurred.

Because the spells are growing in frequency and intensity, they need to be sure there is someone with them to help with healing, if healing is needed. Evangelina's knowledge with healing is more informed than most parents, but it's not as vast as Sephine's, so Tahvi would need to stay with Sephine or they would have to bring her with them, and Sephine cannot go without the twins.

Though neither of them knows of it, Evangelina and Sephine begin thinking about the same thing at the same time as it occurs to them that Tahvi has never been wounded. Even with the complications that his condition presents, he's managed to never have an incident or accident that caused him to hurt himself. Their thoughts progress similarly in their minds: they each question their memories and think there must be an event that they've forgotten. They search through the periods in which they've attended to him. They also consider when they took him to other herbalists but recalled that the reason for the visit was always about how to improve his condition and not due to an injury or illness.

Then Sephine is reminded of what she had noticed at Tahvi's celebration. She had planned to speak to Evangelina about it but the world she knows has changed in a day and the discussion suddenly seems less urgent.

Evangelina decides not to mention what she's thinking. They have more pressing things to discuss.

Vertimus doesn't mention his hidden motive for wanting Tahvi to remain at home, which is to never allow Tahvi into the village in which the farthest stone is located on the map. This is a metropolis called Telracs, and it's unlike any place Vertimus has ever seen or wants to see again. When it's necessary, he resolves he'll tell Evangelina that this area is no place for civilized people, though he fears if the map shows a stone there he can't keep her from it.

Finally, they decide that Tahvi will stay with Sephine and the twins while Evangelina is gone. While at the two closest villages, if searching for the stones becomes so time consuming that they have to stay longer than three days, Evangelina agrees she will go to a message post and send a messenger or carrier bird to let them know that she and Jabneh are safe and still searching. While travelling to the areas that are further away they agree to continue to send messages each time they arrive at a village or metropolis that has a message post, then another message every day after that until they leave the village they're searching.

Somberly, the talk turns to what they must do if Evangelina and Jabneh don't return. It's Evangelina's wish that Tahvi stay with Sephine and when he has thirteen years, he can live with his uncle Vertimus if that's what he chooses. Vertimus is more than willing to accept this responsibility. Evangelina will leave Sephine in charge of the shop while she is gone as well. Sephine has accepted this role many times in the past when Evangelina visited different villages in hopes of finding an herbalist that could help with Tahvi.

Once everyone has a solid understanding of the details they've covered so far, Vertimus wants to discuss one last item.

"I know you've all heard stories of sensitives and wayfarers, many of which are unfavorable. I will tell you the truth of the matter now. In my experiences, most of the sensitives and wayfarers I've met are good-natured and respectable people, much like Exos and I. Many have special gifts or talents. We call these people Gentians. It's a term of affection that kind sensitives and wayfarers use between one another."

"I thought Gentians were a mythical army?" Sephine says.

"The Gentian army was real, but it doesn't exist anymore. I will explain more later if you have questions, but what's most important for you to know is that unfortunately there's another type that frequents these groups. We call them troglodytes."

"I've heard my husband use that term before. What does it mean?" Sephine asks.

"It's a different term for wayfarer really, but we only use it to describe those who are ill-willed and self-seeking. Some of them are extremely dangerous. They've even been known to prey on other wayfarers and sensitives. Many troglodytes are sensitives also, but not all. Most people don't identify them until it's too late because they're so skilled at hiding their intentions.

"This being said, other than your names and what you do, neither of you should mention your home village or history. Say that you've been travelling for a long time, so long that you don't even remember where you're from. It's not uncommon for wayfarers to say this and anyone who's not of a suspicious nature will accept it as an answer about your past. Be wary of anyone who is overly friendly or asks many questions. If they press, try to avoid them without arousing suspicion. Keep to yourselves as much as you can, except during meal times or attempting to earn a wage or trade. And even during these times, try not to share too much about yourself. If you must, act as though you are tired or ill, anything that keeps you from wanting to speak too much or too often. I know this may seem rude or unfriendly, but you must do it for your own safety. The doors to the wagon should always remain locked unless one of you is with it. Finally, if either of you meet someone you have a familiarity with, speak to that person privately and ask that they not reveal where you're from. Are we agreed?"

Evangelina and Jabneh agree, and Vertimus asks them to share their understanding of what they've heard. Once they do, he gives them examples of phrasing they can use and they go over the recommendations he's given them a few more times. Vertimus suggests that they continue to practice the phrasing while on the road.

This last item brings their conversation to an end and when they're done speaking there is an uncomfortable silence that blankets the room. In the silence, there exists a mutual understanding that what Evangelina is undertaking is more dangerous than anyone has acknowledged with words. What they all understand is this; anyone who agrees to help her may be in danger as well.

Sephine is the one who breaks the silence by saying, "I will pack the food."

# 15 PRAYERS AND PREPARATIONS

Everything is set for the morning. The larger wagon is prepped along with the horses. Evangelina and Jabneh need only hitch the horses to the wagon and they can be on their way. They packed enough water, bread and dried meat for ten days. This is more than twice what they needed but Vertimus had suggested that they pack extra meat to be used for bartering, if necessary.

Vertimus has spoken to Exos about what happened with the star shell and the map Tahvi drew. He also told him of Evangelina's suggestion and Exos agreed to act as a guide for her and help search for the stones. He feels honored that Evangelina trusts him enough to make the request. When Vertimus mentions the furthest location on the map, Exos stares at him blankly.

"The only occupied area in that forsaken space is Telracs," Exos says.

"The boy confirmed this is where one of the stones is," Vertimus says.

"Are you certain? He marked it south of the Silver Forest?"

"Yes. And the Gadarine Mountains. The boy drew an X in the heart of it."

Exos is quiet for a long time and then says, "Telracs is no place for women."

"All things considered, it's no place for men either."

"It would be foolish to go there without weapons and something valuable to trade. And we must look like we belong. Can she do that?"

"For Tahvi she'll do what is necessary."

"Does she know about Telracs?"

"No. But I will explain it to her. And if we can't find the proper attire, she can fashion nearly anything if she's supplied with the right materials."

"Your thoughts on how to proceed?"

"I can arrange something valuable to trade. And I believe the closest village with the kind of weaponry we need is Tadgh. They may also have the fabric we need."

"She has none here?"

"No. I will ask her but I'm almost certain she doesn't. Let me know what you believe it will cost and I'll give you the coin for it."

"When will we leave?"

"If we're fortunate, ten days, fourteen at the most. Evangelina said you're welcome to stay here until then. It would be better than staying in the town's boarding house. More discreet."

"I agree. I will leave for Tadgh tonight."

"Very well," Vertimus says as he begins to walk away.

"Is everyone familiar with using weapons?"

"No."

"Best to get them acquainted, then. Even those not travelling. Do you agree?

"Unfortunately, yes."

"The children as well."

Vertimus nods.

\* \* \*

Evangelina and Tahvi sit on the deck behind the house, discussing what she plans to do. Tahvi is sad that he can't go with her and asks repeatedly if there is any other way. At one point she asks if he has any suggestions but he has no ideas to offer. The plan they devised seems to be the best solution.

She holds Tahvi the entire time she explains it to him. He sits across her lap on a large rocking chair that Stefan had made for her. When Tahvi begins to cry she cries with him. The idea of being apart for more than a few days, on an errand that could turn out to be very dangerous, overwhelms them both. Evangelina realizes the trip to the red rock canyon was likely the longest time she spent away from him and she is suddenly not sure she can be away for months at a time. Not a day has gone by since the day he was born that she was not with Tahvi to bid him good night or wish him good day.

Evangelina again tries to soothe him with her words.

"We still have time before the longest journey. Tomorrow I will leave for Baldric and Encarta but I will return within several days. And when I do, who knows what new pieces you will have next?"

"I hope one will be for my hand. I can't wait to feel what it is like to have two hands."

"I noticed you opened your gifts. Do you like them?"

"Yes, all of them."

"But you didn't open all of them, did you?"

Tahvi has been facing away from her. Now he turns toward her, straightens his back, and gives her an incredulous look. "But I did!"

"Do you remember opening one from Jabneh?"

"No! I have another?

"One he wanted us to see together. Shall we open it?"

"Yes!"

Evangelina asks Tahvi to wait at the table in the cooking room. When she returns from her room she is holding a long wooden box. Tahvi smiles as he moves back and forth in the chair. Sheree and Humbul come in just then and sit at the table with him.

"I asked them to be here."

"I know." Evangelina says.

She lets Tahvi open the box and when he does, he sees something surrounded by a black velvet cloth. He unwraps the cloth and his jaw drops.

"It's an arm!"

Sheree and Humbul make similar exclamations while they hold down the velvet wrapping so Tahvi can remove the arm from the box. Evangelina is stunned as well. The arm is much like the forged arm that Tahvi already has, but the difference is the hand, which has switches and adjustments that allow the fingers to be moved and manipulated so they can be used like a real hand. The fingers are wooden but have false joints inserted to make them more bendable and moveable. Each piece is carved to match the size and shape of the fingers on Tahvi's opposite hand. There is also a lever that connects to all sections of the entire hand. When Tahvi moves the lever back and forth it allows the hand to change from its natural open position to a fisted position and then back again. The craftsmanship is extraordinary: it does not look bulky or complicated, but simple and elegant. The switches are unpainted metal and the wood is stained a deep dark brown, much like the color of the box Jabneh had made for it.

It is obvious that it is made for private use only as it would need to be exposed in order for Tahvi to use it; he would need to use the other hand to manipulate it and the small levers and switches would likely get tangled up in any cloth or material he tried to place over it. The purpose of this new arm is to improve function: Jabneh wanted to give Tahvi the gift of dexterity.

As Evangelina and the children admire the hand, they do not hear Jabneh approach.

"It will not work now," Jabneh says sadly.

Evangelina gasps when she hears his voice.

"Jabneh! I hope you're not going to make a habit of that," she says with relief.

He gives her a smile but his eyes show disappointment.

"I am sorry, Tahvi. I made this for you before we knew ... well, everything we know now."

Tahvi places the arm gently on the table and gives Jabneh a hug. "I am honored. It's amazing."

Vertimus and Sephine walk in the room, toting water to drink with supper.

"Uncle, look at my gift!" Tahvi grabs the arm from the table and takes it to his uncle.

"Where did you get this?" Vertimus asks.

"It was a gift from Jabneh," Evangelina says.

Tahvi nods enthusiastically.

Vertimus inspects it, "This is fine work, Jabneh. I had no idea you were so skilled in this area."

"Thank you. It's a shame that it will not work now."

"Why will it not work?"

"It is meant for a boy who is missing part of his arm. Tahvi is not missing that anymore. He is missing only a hand, so now I must alter it before it can work properly. And I had hoped to give Tahvi a gift he could use without delay."

"The forearm has to be removed and the wrist adjusted to fit Tahvi's new stump?" Vertimus asks.

"Yes."

"I could help you do that when you return. Unless there is

something special you need, I believe Evangelina has all the tools we need here."

Jabneh tugs at his beard, thinking. "With the help of another, it should take no more than a few hours to complete."

"Then let it be done!" Vertimus says with excitement.

"I will be able to use it then?" Tahvi asks.

"You will. And I believe it will make life much easier for you until we can find the hand that truly belongs there—if that's not one of the pieces your mother returns with," Vertimus replies.

Tahvi reluctantly puts the arm back in the box.

That evening they all eat supper together. In comparison to the topics covered during the day the supper is light-hearted and festive. The conversation includes nothing of Evangelina's upcoming journey. The only mention of the stones is when Sephine brings Tahvi's flowers to the table, using them as a centerpiece. Evangelina explains how they came to find them and that they had to dig them up to get to his stone. She also explains that she had never seen different flowers grow from the same roots as these ones had. She told him of the flower bushes they left behind and that when their journey is complete, she will take him to see them.

They eat well and they enjoy each other's company as much as the food. There is an enchanting energy in the room and their connection is stronger than usual, although no one speaks of it. Sheree and Humbul are sitting much closer to Tahvi than they usually do, so close that if he needs to leave the table he will have to ask one of them to move a chair. Sephine and Evangelina hold hands several times throughout supper and each time their touch lingers before one of them lets go. Jabneh and Vertimus chat like old friends, even though they had only met a handful of times in the past. Though Exos is quiet through most of the meal, he is comfortable and grateful to spend time with a family that is so kind to one another.

When all have finished eating and the dialogue dwindles, everyone helps with cleaning. Though the pleasant energy remains, the talking is replaced by near silence. Everyone is emotionally drunk from the company, laughter and food. The adults are beginning to tire, partly because it has been such an eventful day but also because they drank much wine with supper. Evangelina is the only one who didn't partake, preoccupied as she is with tomorrow's journey.

The children don't resist when they're reminded that they must take to their beds. Sheree asks if she can sleep with Tahvi and Humbul follows suit. Evangelina says as long as Tahvi is agreeable then she will consent, so into his bed they go.

Evangelina stays in Tahvi's room long enough to tell him a story that calms his mind and helps him drift into sleep. She tells him of when she and Stefan first met—one of his favorites. Sheree and Humbul are fast asleep not long after she begins but Tahvi stays awake until nearly the end. She kisses him on his forehead and bids him goodnight. When she walks away she hears him whisper.

"My heart is with you."

"And mine with you."

* * *

Evangelina stands outside and looks at the stars. It is chilly, and she is not wearing a weather coat, but she hardly notices. She pulls the spear from her pocket and holds it in front of her. She points it toward Violetta and after a moment the spear brightens. It pulses slowly toward the direction it is pointed in, confirming that the stone is where Tahvi's map shows it should be. She puts it back in her pocket and looks up at the stars. She feels small and unsure. Tears fall from her eyes and silently she prays to the universe. She asks that her journey be undemanding and swift so that she and Tahvi will not be separated for long.

As she prays, she hears the sound of something moving in the grass behind her. When she turns she sees Vertimus standing there. He sees the tears in her eyes and offers his hand to her. She takes it and continues to look up at the stars.

"What if we can't find them? I don't want to think of it, but it is a possibility, is it not?"

"Eva, we will find them."

"But what if we do not? What will happen to Tahvi?"

"I suppose he will live as he does today."

"That is unacceptable."

"Why?"

"Because he does not have to."

Vertimus considers this and knows she is right.

"Swear to me that you will continue looking for the stones, should I fail," she says.

"We are one in this. If you fail, I fail."

She looks into his eyes, pleading. He knows this look and knows what she needs to hear.

"Nothing is going to happen to you," he tells her somberly.

"Can you guarantee it?"

His eyes reveal that he can't.

"Swear to me that you will continue."

"I swear it."

Evangelina begins to weep. She does not fear for her own safety. She only fears what it will do to Tahvi if she can't be there to protect him or help him become whole again.

"Eva ... "

"Yes?" She is sniffling, tears continuing to fall from her eyes.

"I've foreseen Tahvi with a new part of his leg. You were with him when I saw this."

She pulls him to her. He accepts her embrace and allows her to cry soundlessly in his arms.

"Thank you," she whispers.

He holds her a little longer and is relieved that he can console her in this way. He suspects there will be many times in the future when that might not be possible.

When Evangelina retires for the night Vertimus stays outside a while longer. He looks at the stars and can't help but think of his brother, Stefan. He misses him dearly. He thinks of his nephew—what an exceptional boy he is and what he will be like as a man. He feels fear settle in his stomach because he can only imagine it. In all the foretells he has had thus far, he has seen nothing of Tahvi as a man.

Vertimus sleeps deeply that night, but before he does, he says a few prayers of his own.

# THE LONELY ROAD

Evangelina sleeps for only a few hours. When she wakes, it's from a nightmare that she can barely remember. In the nightmare, someone had stolen Tahvi's stones and they were destroying them. She tries to go back to sleep but can't. She is anxious about tomorrow and she remembers that she had slept several hours earlier in the day. Emotionally she feels exhausted but physically she is not tired. She lies in her bed wondering what she can do with her time. The wagon is packed and all preparations made. There is nothing to do but sleep. She feels frustrated again knowing that she has to wait.

Then she recalls what Vertimus said. *I've foreseen Tahvi with a new part of his leg. You were with him when I saw this.*

Vertimus said he wanted her to wait because he was worried for her safety. But if he had foreseen her with Tahvi this way, then that meant she must have acquired at least one more stone.

Evangelina examines his words carefully, ensuring she did not misunderstand something. She decides that if Vertimus had foreseen her with her son, then her safety could not possibly be in jeopardy, at least not yet. The more she considers this logic the more it makes sense to her. She tries to think of a reason that she should not go but can't find one. It takes her less than a minute to make up her mind. She dresses quickly and decides to leave a letter for the others.

She makes her bed tidy. When she finishes the letter, she places it on her pillow, so they will find it easily. She knows if they realize she is gone, they will come looking for her, but it likely won't be until sometime the next morning. By that time she will have enough of a head start that she will have passed Violetta and it would be senseless to ask her to turn back if they were to catch up with her. If they choose to ride with her after Violetta she would certainly welcome that.

She goes to Tahvi's room to check on him and he is sleeping soundly. Tahvi is in the middle of the bed, with Sheree and Humbul lying on either side of him. She kisses each of them on the forehead, kissing Tahvi last.

She walks through the house, worrying that someone might still be awake but everyone is sleeping. She leaves the house and walks quickly to the barn. After she hitches Sadie and Baleel to the wagon, she drives it slowly out of the stable and then closes the stable doors. The horses nicker but she does her best to calm them. She rubs the sides of their necks and lets them smell her scent.

Once she has lit the lanterns on the front of the wagon she climbs onto the wooden seat. She drives as slow as possible, hoping the horses and the wagon will make less noise. She thinks she will be warm in the extra layers she is wearing but it is colder than she expected and her wardrobe turns out to be just right. Once she is far enough away, she flicks the reins so the horses will pick up speed. She smiles at the thought of her son being reacquainted with the next stone.

Riding in this wagon always makes her think of her Stefan. He built it years before he died and custom-made it in a style Evangelina had not seen before, but she still thinks it is very beautiful. She imagines driving at a speed that's faster than she ever has before, but though it is strong and built well, the wagon is still only wood and bolts, and she must be careful not to push it or the horses beyond their limits.

The moon is full so the night is well lit. She uses the light to her advantage and rides as fast as she can. She has learned she is quite good at gauging the right speed. She focuses on the road, watching for anything that might damage the wheels. She hears laughing and realizes it is her own. The laughter makes her feel alive and vigilant. Every noise she hears is magnified and the stars and moon seem brighter than normal. As she continues to laugh she notices she feels more relaxed. Her shoulders drop and the tightness in her stomach, which she had not previously noticed, releases.

The only thing Evangelina is not aware of is the guest in the back of the wagon.

\* \* \*

Evangelina drives for over an hour before she stops to stretch her legs. The moment she stands up to dismount from the driver's seat she knows she's waited too long; her legs and back are stiff and it takes her several minutes to relax them enough to walk normally. Frustrated, she tells herself she will make more frequent stops during the rest of the trip.

After driving and breaking for a few more hours, Evangelina is beginning to tire but she's pleased to know she is able to drive through the night quite well. She hasn't encountered any other wagons on the road, and wonders if she will. She didn't expect to see anyone in the red rock canyon when they went searching for Tahvi's first stone, but because this is a busier road she thought maybe she might see at least one or two riders.

After another four hours she passes the wagon road that leads to Violetta. At about the same time the sun star begins to appear on the horizon. Now she knows she's making good time. Her horses are doing well with hauling both her and the wagon. After breaking fast by eating some dried meat and bread, she drives to a small patch of trees behind which she ties the wagon. She handles a few other necessary morning rituals, then removes the spear from her pocket to check the pulsing and direction of the light. She is definitely headed in the right direction.

It occurs to her that as much as she needs access to the spear she should consider a way to carry it and keep it hidden at the same time. The weather is chilly enough so that it will not look conspicuous if she wears her weather coat when she is outside, even in the middle of the day, so she decides to sew a hidden, reinforced pouch in the breast of her coat. She makes it a deep one, keeping it close to her center and making it harder for her to accidentally drop or lose the spear while making it easy to expose to the stars but quickly conceal it if needed.

With the new pouch complete, she climbs into the back of the wagon and locks all the doors from the inside. She lies down on the blankets and pillows Sephine packed for her. She can't remember the last time she was so tired and wonders how it is that some people can travel so often by wagon. She is asleep within minutes.

As she sleeps, her guest climbs on to the bedding. In his paws he holds dried berries, which he fished out of one of the food baskets stored in the wagon. When he finishes eating them he lies down next to her feet and falls asleep. Kaco is indeed a night walker, and he is tired from being bounced around in the wagon.

* * *

When Evangelina wakes she is slick with sweat. She can feel it on her neck and forehead. There are tears on her face as well. She knows she must have had a nightmare but can't remember what it was about. She sits up and opens one of the wagon doors to see how bright it is outside. She doesn't know how long she was sleeping but she feels ready to drive again. She reaches for her washbasin next to the bedding and drops it when she notices the ball of fur.

"Kaco! Where did you come from?"

His eyes are open but his eyelids are drooping. In that moment she's suddenly aware that she's been lonely. She had remained focused, but the drive has taken a toll on her and she misses Tahvi dearly. She pets Kaco's fur as he stretches his legs but does not move from a reclined position. She smiles, excited to see him and happy to have company. She finds herself wishing she had done as Vertimus suggested and waited until the morning to leave. But it is too late for that now as she is closer to Baldric—another seven or eight hours and she should be at the encampment.

She thinks briefly about driving straight there without breaks but then remembers the stiffness in her legs after the first couple of hours of riding, like someone had stabbed her legs and back with tiny knives. She prefers not to feel that again. She might even be able to make better time while driving in the daylight.

"If we start soon, we could be there just after nightfall," she says to Kaco.

Kaco's eyelids are partially open and his eyes are glossy and unfocused. Evangelina is almost sure that he is asleep again. She moves her hand in front of his eyes to see if they will follow it but they do not.

"I wonder if Tahvi knows where you are. I hope he doesn't have worry for you." She pets him again and soon his eyelids are closed.

Based on where the sun star is in the sky, it must be close to midday. She could not have slept more than four or five hours. She washes and then begins driving the wagon again. She is not hungry but she is thirsty, so she keeps a flask of water by her side.

She encounters travelers on the road during the day. Some are friendlier, returning her wave when they pass. Others ignore her. At those moments she prefers the night's loneliness to their inconsiderate nature.

When evening comes and the sun star settles over the horizon, Kaco moves from the back of the wagon to the front. Evangelina is happy to have him join her. After some time, he moves to her lap pawing at the pouch with the spear in it, and she has to remind him to settle or she will move him to the back of the wagon. He does as she asks, but he also occasionally whimpers and whines to show his dissatisfaction.

Evangelina reaches the outskirts of Baldric in the late evening. The encampment is just over a small hill and she can see the glow of light behind it. She hears faint noises that sound like music mixed with boisterous laughter. She takes the spear out of her pocket and checks its response. The light is brighter and the pulse stronger. Evangelina feels the excitement and fear rise within her again.

"We are almost there, Kaco. Can you believe it?"

Kaco looks at her, licks his paw then scrubs the back of his ear with it. She drives toward the hill, eager to learn what she will see when she reaches the other side.

# SEWING AND SECRETS

Sheree wakes feeling hot and finds that the sleeve of her nightshirt and parts of her hair are soaked in sweat. But it is not her own. It is Tahvi's—he is having another spell.

She walks to Evangelina's room and knocks on the door. When there is no answer she checks to see if it is unlocked. She is about to open it when she remembers that Evangelina is leaving that morning. She lets go of the door handle and makes way to fetch her mother.

Sheree tells her mother that Tahvi might have a fever, that Evangelina is still sleeping, and asks if she should follow their normal course. Sephine tells her yes and that she will meet her in Tahvi's room as soon as she is dressed. Sheree goes into the cooking room, where Jabneh and Vertimus are discussing the adjustments needed for Tahvi's arm. When she walks in they both greet her.

"Good day, Sheree."

"Good day," she replies. She notices the arm on the table and asks how they are going to alter it. She is intrigued but has to interrupt their explanation, because she must leave to get the kettle of cool water back to Tahvi's room. She pours the cool water in the bowl they keep next to his bed, wakes Humbul and asks him to move so she can reach Tahvi easier. He manages to get to the foot of the bed, where he quickly falls back to sleep.

Sheree soaks a washcloth in the water, wrings it out and begins wiping Tahvi's face and neck to help cool him. When Sephine enters the room, she switches places with her daughter.

"Do you know when it began?"

Sheree shakes her head.

"He was already warm when you woke?"

Sheree nods. "Should I try to wake Evangelina?"

"No, she needs her rest. There is no need to wake her unless we see something different."

"I understand."

"Are you hungry?"

Sheree nods.

"I am hungry," Humbul murmurs in a muffled voice, his face pressed against the blanket.

"I will make food to break our fast. Call to me if you see anything unusual."

"I will." Sephine kisses her daughter on the forehead and walks towards the cooking room.

"Humbul," Sheree says. "Humbul, wake up. Will you watch Tahvi?"

"I am tired," he mumbles.

"It's important."

Humbul drags himself off the bed, still half asleep. He sits in the chair next to Tahvi and lazily waves his arm at Sheree, giving his consent for her to leave the room. She kisses him on the cheek, then she follows her mother into the cooking room.

Vertimus greets Sephine first and then Jabneh follows.

"Good day to you both," Sephine replies.

"How is Tahvi?" Vertimus asks.

"He is having a spell."

"Another?" Jabneh asks.

"Yes, they've been more frequent as of late."

"Is Evangelina with him?" Vertimus asks.

"No, she is not awake yet. I see no need to wake her unless Tahvi reacts differently to this spell. I thought I heard her awake late in the evening. It would not surprise me if she sleeps in later than usual this morning."

"Do you think she'll sleep in for long?" Vertimus asks.

"I am uncertain. Why do you ask?"

Vertimus and Jabneh exchange a glance.

"Do you think we could complete it before she wakes?" Vertimus asks.

"Provided she sleeps for a few more hours," Jabneh responds.

"Where are you off to?" Sephine asks.

"We will be in the shop room. We need Eva's work table," Vertimus replies.

"Very well. I will have food ready soon if you would like to break fast."

"Can I go with you?" Sheree asks.

"With us?" Vertimus asks, surprised at the girl's appearance.

"You will be working on Tahvi's hand, yes?"

"Sheree, you are supposed to be with Tahvi," Sephine says.

"Humbul is watching him."

"With his eyes closed?"

"I woke him before I left."

"I've no issue with it," Vertimus says.

"Nor do I," Jabneh says. "If your mother does not mind it."

"Yes, go on then," Sephine agrees.

"Please let us know if you need help with Tahvi," Vertimus says. Sephine nods in response.

Vertimus, Jabneh and Sheree walk downstairs to the workroom, the large underground room that Evangelina uses for work and storage. It is the largest room in the house. The walls are lined with shelves, many of which are filled with different types of material like tools for crafting and woodworking and there is a long worktable in the center of the room, with two wooden benches and chairs on either side of it. Jabneh and Vertimus do a quick inventory check and are able to find all the tools they need. Once they're assembled on the worktable they take the arm out of the box.

Jabneh built the arm in two sections, so it's easy for them to detach the forearm. Once they disconnect the forearm the hand is free to be altered, then they simply need to fit a fastener to it by attaching it to the area acting as the wrist. The metal pins Jabneh previously used to connect the forearm can now be used to attach the new fastening device. Vertimus removes the leather fastenings from Tahvi's forged arm, then cuts and adjusts them as needed to fit Tahvi's wrist. Vertimus is good with a needle and thread, but he is out of practice so Sheree helps where she can. With the three of them working together, it takes less time than they expected to complete the hand that can now be buckled to and supported by Tahvi's forearm.

Though Jabneh is happy that Tahvi will get to be complete again, he sighs at the thought that the hand will not have much use. He thinks maybe another boy might be able to use it someday, but it does not seem right to ask Tahvi to give this gift to someone else. Either way, Tahvi may at least have use for it until then.

When they're finished they're excited to see how it fits Tahvi. Vertimus thinks it's an amazing creation and he's impressed by Jabneh's skill and creativity. They both praise Sheree for her help and then go into Tahvi's room. He is still sleeping.

Sephine is sitting by the bed but Humbul is no longer in the room.

"Where is Humbul?" Sheree asks.

"He is outside looking for Kaco."

"Oh," Sheree replies. Then she crawls on the bed next to Tahvi.

It's hard for Sheree not to worry when Tahvi has his spells. But she does her best, and when she feels scared she prays. Sometimes she calms herself by doing something else, as she did today, but most of the time she finds it comforting to stay by his side.

Vertimus and Jabneh ask Sephine if they may see how the new hand fits the boy. Sephine says that they can and then moves to the foot of the bed, Jabneh taking her place in the chair. Now that Sephine is closer to her daughter she notices Sheree is holding something in her hands.

"What do you have in your hands?"

Sephine shows her mother the stone. Though Sheree has been wearing it since yesterday, it is the first time Sephine notices it.

"Where did you get this?"

"The woman in the play gave it to me. Her name is Sabina. She said I could have it as the first piece of my wardrobe."

"Your wardrobe?"

"Yes, I want to be a player as she is!" she says excitedly.

"I see. And did she want to trade anything for it?"

Sheree shakes her head. "No. It was a gift. She was very kind. She said I would make a fine player someday."

"I agree that you would make a fine player. It's a very beautiful gift."

"I think so, too."

"Look!" Jabneh says, "It fits perfectly!" He holds the boy's arm up so that Vertimus can see it. It is a perfect fit. The men finished the alterations in less than two hours. Sephine looks at the stitching on the fastener, especially around the reinforced holes.

"Who is responsible for this?" She points to the stitching.

"Sheree is," Vertimus says proudly.

"And Vertimus helped," Sheree quickly follows.

"That is very good work from both of you. I think I could hardly do better myself."

"That is a fine compliment coming from you, Sephine." Vertimus winks at Sheree.

"He will need a small rice bag to place against the frame of the wrist, so his stump does not become moist or uncomfortable," Jabneh says.

"I've all the supplies to do that, and it would take less than a quarter of an hour," Sephine says.

"Could you do it now?" Jabneh asks.

"I suppose, if one of you will stay with Tahvi and the children."

Jabneh looks at Tahvi with compassion. "How long do his spells normally last?"

"They can last minutes or hours. They seem to be lasting longer each time, as of late."

"But do they hurt him? He doesn't seem harmed when he awakens from them."

"No. The symptoms have not changed. It's as though he's in a deep sleep, and he gets very warm. Sometimes he moans as though he's dreaming, but mostly he's soundless."

"Do you think Evangelina would want to see this?" Vertimus asks, speaking of the hand.

"I think she would enjoy that. I will go wake her and then I will work on the rice bag so that Tahvi can wear it when he feels better."

* * *

Jabneh and Vertimus are sitting quietly with Tahvi and Sheree when Sephine rushes back into the room frantically.

"Evangelina's gone! When I went to wake her, I found this." She hands the letter to Vertimus as he rises from the chair.

As he reads it silently he quickly becomes angry. "Damn!"

"What is the matter?" Jabneh asks.

"She left for Baldric," Vertimus says stonily. "I don't know when, the letter doesn't tell."

"Alone?" Jabneh asks incredulously.

"Apparently."

"Oh my stars," Sephine says. "I hope she took the wagon and not just a horse."

They go to the barn and see that the larger wagon is gone. "At least she is not completely senseless," Vertimus says.

Jabneh and Sephine are quiet, simmering in anger and worry, as Vertimus curses himself for mentioning his foretell. "How could I be so naïve?" he shouts.

"That fault is not yours, Vertimus. You told her it was dangerous to leave on her own," Sephine says.

"We must leave immediately. I don't know how much of a lead she has. Jabneh, are you free to travel directly there or is it necessary that you stop in your home village first?" Vertimus asks.

"I can ride with you. I will stop at my home village on the way back. I do not value the idea of Evangelina travelling alone."

"Nor do I," Vertimus says. "Sephine, we are going to prep the horses. Can you pack enough food and water for four days?"

"Only four?"

"Yes. We will ration our supplies along the way and get more food from Violetta when we return, if necessary. But we must leave as soon as possible."

"Say no more."

Sephine goes back to the house to do as Vertimus asked. She has the twins help her. When they're finished they help Vertimus and Jabneh pack the supplies in the saddlebags.

"We are going to ride near the main road; it's the only way her wagon can travel. I can't imagine a reason we would not cross paths, even if she were already on her way home before we were able to reach Baldric. But if we don't happen upon her, and returns before us, do not let her leave. Can you do that?" Vertimus speaks with an angry tone, but Sephine hears fear in his voice as well. His fear arouses a fear in her and she grows more concerned.

"I promise to do everything I can to keep her here," she says.

Vertimus nods. "Be well."

As they ride away on the horses Sephine hopes they will make good time and she prays for the safety of her friend.

* * *

Tahvi sits up in his bed. It is nearly too dark to see anything at first. He assumes it's night because of the lack of light in the room and he can see the stars and the moon, illuminating a small patch of wood on the floor. The light makes him feel peaceful and humble. He gets up from his bed and straps on his leg so that he can walk. As he begins walking it does not feel as though he is walking with a forged leg but with a real one. The movement feels relaxed and comfortable. There is rhythm in his gait, unhindered by the pause that his limp typically presents. Then he realizes that the rhythm is exceptionally slow, as though he is walking underwater. He's not sure if he is dreaming or if he's awake.

He continues to walk until he is standing outside, his left foot bare on the cool grass. He looks up in the sky and sees what he had seen earlier, before he drew the map, but this time the details are more elaborate as if it's happening now instead of in the past. He sees his star try to adjust its direction and then hears a loud thunderous noise as it splits apart sending pieces of itself everywhere. The planet becomes smaller, enabling him to see all the settings of where the star pieces fall in his view. He becomes much larger and seems to be almost floating near the stars, overlooking the planet and the pieces as they strike the ground. They all light up at once, as though communicating with each other, and then all is dark and he is plunged back to his ordinary size.

He feels a shift in his body as if he had been outside of it and was abruptly thrown back into it without warning. His eyes grow wide as the realization comes to him and he looks down at the ground, wondering if it could be. He impulsively drops to his knees and as he does, he feels the forged leg break underneath himself, sending his body forward so that his face strikes the ground on its right side. He places his hands flat on the ground and concentrates as best as he can. He senses nothing. He clutches the ground harder; collecting dirt under his fingernails, demanding that it comply, but there is no response. The elements are difficult to manage. He flails and thrashes until his energy is depleted and then begins to weep as he realizes that the map he drew might be useless. He does not know if he's dreaming or awake.

# BALDRIC

Evangelina is pleased to know she was right. When she reaches the encampment she discovers that laughter and music are what she had heard, and the music is very pleasant. It sounds fun and exciting and it makes her want to join the festivities.

She parks the wagon in an open lot and is surprised but delighted to find that what she thought was a festival is merely supper. Her mouth waters at the smell of chicken and lamb and a variety of spices and seasonings. She also smells pumpkin and cinnamon and wonders if they have different types of sweetened breads

Kaco sniffs the air as well and begins to fidget and whine.

"I can take you with me if you promise to be good."

As he continues to whine, she realizes again that she's not sure if he really understands her. It seems like he does, but the animal being her only company, she might be overestimating his ability to comprehend what she's saying. What she does know is that Tahvi will be heartbroken if she loses him so she decides to not leave it to chance.

"Very well. You can come with me but not as you are."

Evangelina goes into the wagon and begins looking for something to make a restraint. They had packed rope as part of the supplies and she has scissors in her sewing kit to cut the pieces she needs. She remembers the one that Exos had made for him at the Tabarak Canyon and tries to mirror it as best she can. When she is nearly finished with the restraint, she puts her scissors back in the box and sees the various fittings. In addition to many different spools of thread, the box has a variety of different accessories—buttons, clasps and other things—but her eyes fix on the jingles, small metal square ornaments that have tiny hollow spheres inside. The spheres make a chiming noise when the metal square is moved. Evangelina had used them on hats, gloves and bracelets. She picks one up and shakes it. She's always surprised by how loud such a small thing is.

She attaches a small metal ring to three of the jingles and then attaches the ring to the area of the rope that she'll wrap around Kaco's neck. She shakes it and as she suspects, the noise is louder with three jingles instead of one.

"Perfect," she says.

She places the restraint on Kaco and tests the restraint by pulling and tugging in different areas to see if it's tight enough so that Kaco can't escape it but also sufficiently comfortable enough so that it will not hurt him. Then she ties a knot in the loop made to fit around her wrist. When she is satisfied, she puts her weather coat on, removes the spear from her dress pocket and puts it inside the pocket she had sewn inside the coat. She locks the wagon before she leaves it and carries Kaco with her to the center of the encampment where the supper is being served.

She has to pass several rows of wagons to get there, but torches have been placed around the area so that the wagon roads can be distinguished from the walking trails. It is dark, but the torches are large and do a good job of lighting the area. As she passes the wagons, she notices they're very much like her own: the stain that Stefan used to dye the wood, the style in which he used to carve the designs, and even the colors and decorations that he used on the wagon cover look like the ones she sees now. She feels a sense of belonging and relief.

Some of the wagon doors are open and some have occupants inside, preparing goods for trade the next morning, she suspects. Some are relaxing or preparing to retire for the night. One or two greet her when they see her but the others keep to themselves. She remembers what Vertimus said about this being customary. Most of the wagons are empty, as nearly everyone seems to be at supper. When she finally makes it through the last row of the wagons she comes upon a scene that makes her feel as though she fell asleep and slipped into an exotic but calming dream.

The area she walks into is covered by a large tent. There are sixteen long tables set up in a rectangular formation, but only a fourth of them are occupied. At the east side of the tables is a stage where a band of wayfarers are playing a jovial song with a fast tempo. The area on the inside of the tables is flatland covered in grass. The grass, cut short, is trampled and compressed from the many feet dancing upon it. Evangelina watches as they move quickly to the music. The light under the tent is a crimson color, and Evangelina notices the lanterns posted along the inside of the tent are covered in glass windows, stained a dark but transparent red. It gives the dancing area, and those dancing within it, a mysterious look.

Laughter explodes from one of the tables and conversation is plentiful among the others. She looks from table to table to get a better idea of the menu and sees a food bar stationed at the opposite end of the stage. Just before she arrived in Baldric, she thought her appetite would have been satisfied with the dried meat and bread packed in the wagon, but the smell of the food here is overwhelming and she feels an urge to try everything. She also thinks it might be a good idea to eat here, even if it is only so that she can sit near some of the occupants and try to learn a little more about the activity around the encampment.

As she walks toward the food bar, she notices two dancers passing her. She looks toward them briefly, continues walking and then stops unexpectedly. Kaco whimpers from the abruptness of her movement. When she looks back at the dancers, she notices they're wearing dresses that do not cover their shoulders or part of their upper back, and only barely cover their breasts. Evangelina's eyes widen a bit as she notices these are not the only people dressed this way—many of the wayfarers look as though they're wearing nightclothes. Evangelina watches with curiosity and though the sight shocks her a bit at first, she does not find it indecent. The dancing seems harmless enough and they seem to be enjoying themselves. As she watches them move across the floor, she feels a feeling of freedom and nostalgia, like she is a child again. The scene is warm and oddly familiar, even though she has never been to an encampment such as this one before.

She walks to the food bar and orders something to eat. Kaco's nose begins sniffing wildly while she picks the items she wants. She brings some fresh berries for him. Carrying Kaco and her food, she walks over to a table with a full group and asks if she may join them. A few of them give her strange or suspicious looks and she wonders if she's made her first mistake by asking instead of claiming a seat.

Then a woman speaks to her.

"Yes, we have many seats!"

She smiles warmly but does not say thank you, not wanting to seem overly grateful.

"I am Maggie," the woman says. "I've been here for several weeks now. I don't recognize you. Did you arrive today?"

"Yes," Evangelina says.

"Is that your dog?" An obnoxious man at the same table shouts, pointing to Kaco. The man looks scruffy and unpleasant. "He is very small for a dog."

"Shut up, Orbis," Maggie says. "Orbis has had much wine tonight."

"Orbis has much wine every night," another woman at the table says. Nearly everyone at the table laughs, including Orbis.

"So which direction did you ride from?" Maggie asks.

"West," Evangelina says.

"Are you travelling with a companion, or is it just you and your dog?" Maggie asks jokingly.

Evangelina feels nervous about the questions. She wants to look around and see if anyone is looking at her, but she doesn't want to arouse suspicion. Unsure that she wants anyone to know she is travelling alone, she decides to lie. "I am with a companion, but he is not with me now. He stopped in Violetta to see a friend and will be joining me tomorrow."

"I see. And you have items to trade, I suppose?"

That is the fourth question this woman has asked her. The woman seems nice enough but she recalled what Vertimus said. Evangelina is not sure if she should be rude or answer the question, so instead she begins to eat her food—what the merchant called a meat pie. She had never tried one before but he described what it was made of and said that it was his most purchased meal. It tastes fantastic. She takes another bite and forgets about Maggie for a moment.

"I am so sorry," Maggie says. "You must forgive me. I am not a wayfarer—I mean, I've not been for long. I just started travelling a few months ago and I only got as far as one stop before I settled here. I liked it here so much that I decided to take a job organizing the trader exchange. That is why I asked you if you had items to trade."

Evangelina smiles. This woman is almost as unversed with

wayfarer dialogue as she is, but her job is to make sure she keeps track of what everyone is trading in the encampment. Still, Evangelina is not absolutely sure this is the case and she can't ask without appearing unfamiliar with the practice, but she thinks if she lets this woman talk enough she will probably explain it.

"I am a seamstress. I also make and trade my own fabric," Evangelina says at last.

"Oh good! We have only two others skilled at sewing but they are not fabric weavers, so I believe you may do well here. How long do you plan to stay? Ah! Never mind. You can answer all of that tomorrow. I am at the east end of the village—we are trying to call it a *village* more often in hopes that others will begin seeing it that way. I awaken shortly after dawn. You can come by and let me know how long you're staying and what you and your companion have to trade, and I will add it to our purchase and exchange log. We send the log out to the surrounding villages too, to draw in more buyers. We get most of our buyers near the end of each week."

"I will come and see you in the morning then. That's usually when I prefer to meet," Evangelina says, trying to behave as though this isn't the first time she's done this.

Maggie smiles and then turns her attention to the group.

"May I ask you a question?" Evangelina asks.

"Of course," Maggie says.

"In other places that I've traded, they start very early, I would say just after dawn. What time do you start trading here?"

"Oh, that is very early. We do not get started nearly as early here. The merchant's exchange opens at midday. You can purchase, sell or barter. It remains open until just after nightfall. There are no food merchants available to break fast or to eat at midday, but they have supper available every night. And judging by the way you are eating that meat pie, I would say you already know it is well worth the price. With supper being served so late in the evening you can see why many are still stirring. You will find the band often plays late into the night and there are still souls wandering the encampment around that time. But many are asleep not long after the supper bar closes so they can prepare for the next day's trade."

Evangelina thanks her and acts grateful, but she is frustrated at this news. It means she may have to wait longer than she'd hoped before she can begin looking for the stone. And once she does, how can she be sure that no one will be watching her?

She finishes her meal and thinks on buying dessert but then decides against it. Kaco finished his berries long before she finished the meat pie. She sits with him, petting him and trying to decide what she should do next. She wishes Vertimus were here to tell her and curses herself for leaving without him. She wishes Maggie good evening and returns her wooden tray and mug to the food merchant. As she begins walking back to her wagon, she hears cheering and clapping as a woman approaches the stage. Evangelina thinks that she must be well known because everyone seems happy that she is about to perform. The moment she opens her mouth, Evangelina feels happy too.

The woman begins singing before the band joins in. Her voice sounds like an instrument all its own. The song she sings is in a language that Evangelina does not understand but it touches her nonetheless. It is a slow melody that makes her immediately think of Stefan and Tahvi. Without realizing it, she begins walking toward the stage. People are still dancing, but slowly, holding each other tightly and gently swaying back and forth. She moves through the dancers to get closer to that sweet sound, still holding Kaco in her arms. To Evangelina, the song sounds like an intimate yet haunting lullaby. She feels a sense of loss and peace all at once. Not all the band plays with her. Only the stringed instruments and a flute can be heard accompanying her voice. Evangelina feels eager and happy at just the thought of being closer to the sweet sound until those that are dancing move from her path, and give her the opportunity to do so. She nearly gasps when she sees the woman's face clearly. She stops for a moment and then nonchalantly changes direction as though she never intended to stand near the staging area. Evangelina turns her head slightly so the woman will not see her, as Evangelina is now close enough to be recognized.

She looks over her surroundings to see if anyone notices her but everyone is watching the woman on stage. She passes the tabled areas and walks several feet over the gravel that surrounds them before she turns back to see the woman on stage again.

Evangelina is standing in an area that allows her to see the woman's profile but is far enough away that she is sure the woman would have no reason to look in her direction. Evangelina stares intently, though there is really no reason. She is sure the woman on the stage is Sabina—she remembers her from the play at Tahvi's celebration. Suddenly she is anxious to get back to her wagon. She knew there was a risk of seeing someone she knew but she presumed it would be someone from another village whom she could speak to discreetly. She is not sure how to handle being recognized by this woman. She walks toward her wagon, feeling uncertain and scared.

When Evangelina is almost to her wagon she decides to test the spear. She can still hear the woman singing from the stage. There is a striking echo that makes the melody sound eerie. She puts Kaco on the ground and looks around to make sure no one is watching her before she opens her coat. She pulls the spear from the hidden pocket just enough to reveal the tip to the stars. It lights up immediately and begins pulsing quickly. She turns in different directions to see where the pulsing is stronger—to her left. She walks quickly in that direction.

"Come, Kaco!"

She holds the restraint and allows him to scamper on the ground. His bells are chiming but the music nearly masks the sound. Because there is no one around her, she continues to check the spear every few steps until she reaches an area directly in front of another wagon where the pulsing is strongest. There is a lantern on in the wagon and the selling doors are still open, allowing her to see the merchandise inside. There is a variety of jewelry and what she thinks must be herbs or maybe perfumed spices because the inside of the wagon has an assortment of odors coming from it, mostly pleasant but a few that are overwhelming. The wagon is fairly large, nearly twice the size of her own, and though the selling window is open she does not see anyone inside.

When she walks past the wagon on several different paths, the pulse slows and the direction of the light switches to the opposite end of the spear each time. She moves back in front of the wagon where the pulsing is the strongest. She looks around again, to see if anyone is nearby and when she sees no one she risks taking it out of her coat, and bends downward to get close to the ground. The spear is lit and pulsing as much as it can be without having direct contact. *The stone must be buried directly under this wagon,* she thinks with dismay.

She stands back from the wagon to look around it and realizes that she feels unsure but doesn't know why. Then she sees there is no trench, no crater and no flowers or anything else for that matter, not even a patch of grass. Kaco had been sniffing around the area as well but he soon lost interest. Then she remembers the maintenance needed for any village. *They likely park and move the wagons here frequently,* she thinks. *Years of doing so probably keeps anything from growing.* But even as she thinks it, Evangelina does not believe it.

Suddenly, Kaco begins squeaking and trying to climb the wheel of the wagon, his jingles sounding louder with the erratic movement.

"Kaco, shhhhhh!" She pulls on the restraint trying to quiet him but he can't be pacified. She curses herself for putting the squares on his collar. She is finally able to calm him by holding and petting him, as she does so he fishes the spear out of her pocket. She quickly grabs it to force it back in, but before she can do so, it lights up entirely for a moment, sending a stream of green light into the air, but it only reaches as far as the wagon that she's standing in front of. She also notices a green light in her peripheral vision, coming from inside the wagon. She puts Kaco on the ground again, and again he begins clawing at the wheels.

"Kaco, you must be quiet. Please be quiet!"

Kaco looks in her direction and whimpers. Again, she's not sure if he understands her words but he must have understood her tone because he stops clawing at the wheels and begins to whimper, though he does so quietly.

Evangelina looks around again. Seeing no one around her or inside the wagon, she takes the spear out only for a moment, but it's long enough to see a stone glowing on a shelf inside the wagon. She shoves the spear back in her pocket immediately and looks at the stone. It is with two other rocks that look unique, but not nearly as beautiful as Tahvi's. She'll have to find some way to get inside the wagon.

She begins circling the wagon to look for another opening. The wagon is anchored to the ground. There are no horses present so Evangelina can't tell which side is the front and which side is the back, but if it's like her wagon there should be doors on either side. She moves to the right of the wagon and is surprised to see that the door is slightly ajar. There are three steps leading to the door. She looks through the crack of the doors and can see the stone from here. All she need do is walk up the steps, go into the wagon and take it.

Just then a woman swings the door open and looks at Evangelina.

Evangelina, quick as a whip, says, "I am sorry if I disturbed you. I was trying to get my ... pet."

"Pet?" the woman asks bluntly.

The first thing Evangelina notices is how pretty the woman is. She has dark hair, skin the color of dark amber and strikingly dark eyes. She looks to have as many years as Evangelina.

"Yes. Come here, Kaco," Evangelina pulls at Kaco's restraint, acting as though he's resisting until she's able to hold him. "He is especially drawn to the area under your wagon."

The woman looks at Evangelina and smiles. Evangelina does not want to leave but she has no idea what to say. Going back to her wagon seems to be the only thing she can do until she thinks of a plan.

"Again, I am sorry. I hope we did not wake you."

"You are not here because your pet likes it under my wagon," the woman says.

"I'm not?" Evangelina's face turns bright red. She feels guilty knowing she just lied to this woman and even guiltier that the woman is clever enough to know. She is nearly prepared to confess her wrongdoing and beg for this woman's forgiveness when the woman speaks again.

"No. But I know why you are here."

"I—" Evangelina begins but the woman interrupts her.

"You are seeking something and you know I might be able to help you find it."

Evangelina has been holding her breath and now she releases it with nervous laughter, relieved that the woman didn't say, *You want to break into my home and steal my pretty rock.* A saleswoman herself, Evangelina recognizes the welcoming smile, the tone, even the mysterious line—maybe the woman is using this as an opportunity to sell her merchandise. "We are all seeking something, are we not?"

"Indeed. Please ... come in," the woman opens the door for her and steps back so she can enter. The minute Evangelina tries, Kaco becomes erratic. He jumps out of her arms but gets tangled in the rope. Evangelina remembers what he was like in the flatlands outside the red rock canyon—Exos could barely contain him and he had nearly the same reaction when they found the flowerbed. He was likely going to continue behaving this way until he was able to get to the stone.

The woman steps back, frightened, "Control your animal, please," she says in a stern voice.

"My apologies again, he is tired and irritable. I will take him to my wagon. It's not far. I will be back in a moment."

"Very well," the woman says, looking distressed.

Evangelina takes Kaco back to the wagon and puts him inside it.

"I am sorry, little one, but you will have to remain here. I can't risk your behavior causing me to lose the very thing we came for. I will be back soon."

Evangelina locks her wagon and heads back the way she came. She can hear Kaco whimpering and scratching at the wagon door as she walks away.

When Evangelina returns, the door is open but she doesn't see the woman.

"Hello?" she calls.

"Come in. You may sit anywhere."

Evangelina steps into the wagon. It is littered with things she's heard of but never seen up close. There are two glass orbs resting in nestled frames on a shelf, one completely transparent and one black as night. There are different types of jewelry displayed and ready for sale including necklaces, bracelets, rings and pendants. There is a variety of spices, scents and rubbing oils, as well as a collection of exotic rocks. When Evangelina sees Tahvi's stone she does her best to keep her eyes moving about all the other items to prevent the woman from sensing how eager she is to obtain it.

"You have many beautiful things. Are you a wayfarer? Is that how you've acquired so many beautiful things?" Evangelina asks.

"It would be true to say that, though I am also a sensitive." The woman watches Evangelina's face closely, waiting to see what it will reveal–fear, acceptance, intrigue? But Evangelina's face reveals nothing. "My name is Kallima. What is your name?"

"I am Eva."

"Well, Eva, let us sit so we may begin."

Evangelina sits on a stool that allows her to see Tahvi's rock—she doesn't want to let it out of her sight. She notices Kallima has several large trunks, but the designs seem too beautiful and intricate to be regular carrying cases and she is curious to know if Kallima has more merchandise inside them.

"Your items are intriguing. Do they trade well?" Evangelina asks.

"They sell well. I rarely participate in trade."

"I sell fabric and embroidery myself. I'm also a skilled seamstress."

"Well now we know what you're not looking for."

Evangelina smiles, almost giddy. Kallima seems charming and she feels herself wanting to stay in her wagon and spend more time with her. She doesn't usually feel this comfortable with people so soon and the feelings surprise her.

"Shall I take your coat?" Kallima asks.

"No thank you."

"I burn several lanterns so that it stays warm in the wagon," Kallima reaches to take Evangelina's coat and Evangelina pulls away, trying to look casual as she does so.

"I am always cold so it's better that I keep it on."

"As you wish," Kallima replies. "I think we should do a reading. It will be quicker that way."

"A reading?" Evangelina asks.

Kallima looks at her curiously and Evangelina wonders if she's made a mistake.

"You are a wayfarer who has never had a reading?" Kallima asks.

Evangelina senses the suspicion in her tone.

"I've seen it done but did not know that was its name. The companion I travel with … he is the one who mostly does the bargaining. I prefer to spend my time in the wagon, working on my fabric as I enjoy it so much." Evangelina thinks the explanation sounds suspicious but it's the best she can do.

"I see. A reading will tell me about you. You put your hands in mine and then … well, you have already seen it done so I need not explain that part. As we hold hands I learn more about who you are, what you have encountered on your life path and what you are wanting for in it. It will help me understand your needs so that you can procure something that suits you instead of something needless."

Evangelina begins to sweat. If what this woman says is true she will be able to learn many things about her and that includes Tahvi, the spear and her journey. She curses herself again for coming alone.

"A reading is not what I am looking for. Though it sounds intriguing and I might like to try it before my companion and I leave the camp."

"You don't have plans to stay in Baldric?"

Evangelina casually stands up and begins looking around the wagon, acting as though she's inspecting the merchandise again. Kallima's eyes follow her every movement.

"No. One of my relatives is very ill and I've promised her that I would return soon. I've been searching for anything that can help soothe her ailment."

"Oh. What is it that ails her?"

"It's unknown. She has seen many herbalists but none were helpful. I recently met with another sensitive, like yourself, who said that surrounding her with healing stones, crystals and scents would help her."

Evangelina continues to move about the wagon. "I've purchased every scent I can think of. Lavender and mint seem to do well to lift her spirits, but she has responded best to stones and crystals, and that is what I seek the most."

When Evangelina turns to look at Kallima, she notices she is watching her intensely. It makes Evangelina uncomfortable. Without knowing it, she wraps her coat tighter around herself. Her eyes meet Kallima's and it seems Kallima is not looking at her but *through* her, and she is not sure that Kallima heard anything she said. But when Kallima responds, it is clear she heard everything.

"Certain stones can be very powerful for healing. I've seen them ease those who suffer many times, and I've even seen them help purge an ailment completely."

Evangelina wonders if maybe she imagined the look because after Kallima speaks she feels comforted again.

"This rock here, the one that looks like it has … green stone? On the inside?" She points to Tahvi's rock. "I think I would like to buy this one. I've not seen anything like it before."

"Ah, that one. That is a very powerful healing stone. I've used it many times."

"What is the cost of it?"

"This one is not meant to be sold." Kallima keeps her eyes on Evangelina as she says it. She sees the slightest tightening of her lips, and more noticeably, her hands tighten around her coat.

"I thought all of these were items for sale."

"Not all. I am still preparing for tomorrow, so I've not finished separating all my goods." Kallima reaches for one of the trunks that Evangelina was staring at earlier, turning away from Evangelina to do so.

"I've some other lovely stones in—" Kallima begins.

"I am not interested in other stones," Evangelina says sharply.

Kallima smiles. It's the reaction she expected. When Kallima turns to face Evangelina, her smile is gone and she looks genuinely concerned.

"I am interested in rare stones," Evangelina tries to explain. "The last sensitive said that's what I should search for. She said the elements of the planet are very powerful and if I see a stone I've not seen before then I should purchase it. And I've not seen this one before."

"I truly wish I could help you, but I use that stone for healing. It has become very important to me. I've used it in many charms for those who were ill, when all else did not work. Though you want to buy it to help someone, I use it to help many. I don't see how I could part with it."

"What if I could pay you the worth of one horse?"

"I've not even thought to consider its value in coin."

"What about the worth of two horses?"

Kallima pretends to be surprised. "Two horses! I had no idea fabric making could be so profitable."

"It's nearly everything I have. As I said, I've seen no stone like it before and I've a rather good feeling about it. Unless maybe … "

"Yes?" Kallima says, hiding her amusement.

"Unless maybe you have another stone like it? Then I could buy this one and you could use the other for healing."

Kallima shakes her head. "I am afraid not. I found this stone here in Baldric and it is the only one I know to exist. I looked for others once I realized how potent its ability for healing was but to no avail. I even tried to break it apart. I thought maybe I could use the pieces for jewelry … "

Evangelina flinches when she hears the words *break it apart*.

" … but I couldn't," Kallima finishes.

Kallima reaches for Tahvi's stone and holds it in her hand. It's almost the same size as the first piece Evangelina had found.

"Sometimes I find that I feel better just holding it."

Evangelina stares at Tahvi's stone. It's less than a meter from her—she could grab it and run but she knows she will never escape with it. She will likely be caught and punished for thievery instead.

Her feelings finally overcome her. Her eyes fill with tears and she cries soundlessly in Kallima's wagon.

"Oh dear, do not despair. I am sure that your kin will be ... " she stops, faking a look of concern and deliberation. She hands Evangelina a cloth for her tears. It looks old and ragged, but it is clean and has a pleasant scent.

"Thank you," Evangelina says.

"I've an idea. Maybe you and I could come to an agreement that suits us both. This stone is very important to me, as I've said, but I know that you must love this relative dearly. I will think it over tonight and maybe you can think about how much you are truly willing to pay for it. Does that sound fair?"

"You think my previous offer is not a fair price?"

Kallima gives her a firm look. "It's clear to me that this stone is important to both of us. I don't want to part with it unless I can match what I stand to lose for selling it. I believe that is more than fair."

Evangelina hears a sense of finality in Kallima's tone that makes her nervous and excited at the same time. She realizes that the only thing this woman wants is more coin. To her discredit and despite her best attempts, Evangelina has revealed how badly she wants the stone, and now this woman has the advantage. But money is not a problem. She is irritated that the woman wants so much, but she has more than enough to pay her. Though she has to be careful that it not appear this way; otherwise, this woman might want Evangelina to turn over everything but her name.

"I will do my best to think of an offer that will serve us both."

"We have a deal. Come back shortly after dawn and we can speak then," Kallima says.

"I appreciate your willingness to part with it despite how important it is to you." Evangelina tries to sound polite and grateful without sounding desperate.

"Good night." Kallima says politely. She shows Evangelina out of the wagon and sees Evangelina look back one last time before she closes the door.

Kallima's heart is beating quickly and she feels the temperature rise in her body. She looks at the stone and thinks about when she first found it. She recalls taking it to the Emperor, thinking it would bring her great fortune, but it did not. She had kept it merely because her instincts told her to. And now it seems her instincts are about to bring her prosperity. There is no telling how much fortune it might bring her now.

Kallima snatches her carrying bag, places the stone inside along with a large flask and some other necessary items, and then dresses to prepare for the cold weather. She steps outside her wagon. Evangelina is nowhere in sight, but Kallima continues to look over her shoulder as she walks to the stables to get her horse. She is going for a long ride.

# MAEZON

Kallima ties the reins of her horse to the post outside the inn. She is happy to be off her horse and on the ground. The long and hasty ride takes just over three hours for any regular horse, but her horse can make the ride in two. Though it was a shorter ride for her, it was still hard on her legs and back. She took several breaks but they were quick – only long enough to let her horse, Maddox, drink water. She pets him and gives him just enough water to ease his thirst.

Maddox is an obscenely large horse that Kallima is proud to own. Bred and trained only to work hard, ride fast and protect his master, Maddox is a warrior horse that previously belonged to a soldier in the Gentian army. He is so large that he's equipped with a double saddle, which was included with the animal when she acquired him. Gaining Maddox was one of the few times Kallima had ever partaken in barter and to this day she's sure she got the better end of the deal. She continues to pet him and shower him with praise, when she hears footsteps coming from the back entrance of the inn. She also hears what sounds like sobbing. Two men in light armor are rolling a large wheelbarrow to the structure north of the inn. The sobbing is coming from a bulge inside the barrow. She turns away immediately, grabs her carrying bag from her horse and quickly goes inside the inn.

The Inn of Maezon is one of only four structures in the settlement. There is the inn, a separate structure with a large furnace inside, a stable and a large shed that remains locked when no one is watching over it. It is not apparent to any travelers what this shed is for. The stable is a large structure that seems unnecessary for a settlement that has hardly any occupants, but it is used frequently.

Kallima opens the door to the inn. It is empty except for the innkeeper, who is pouring himself wine at the bar. He is a serious-looking man: tall, muscular, slender, having forty years of age. He has a rough voice with an unfriendly tone that makes him sound displeased each time he speaks.

"I need to see the Emperor," Kallima says, without a greeting.

"I am aware," the innkeeper replies.

"Right this moment," Kallima says. This time she is more direct.

"I assumed. He is occupied. I've let him know you are here and he will ring when he is ready for you." He begins to pour Kallima a cup of warm tea.

"It is very important," Kallima says rudely.

The innkeeper stops pouring the tea and looks her in the eyes. "Maybe you would like to tell him that personally. I'm sure he won't mind being interrupted."

Kallima cringes in response and then says, "I will wait."

She doesn't have to wait very long. She's nearly finished with her cup of warm tea when she hears a bell clang and the innkeeper returns to the bar room. He tells her the Emperor will see her now.

He gives her the signal to wait by the hearth and she does so. She hears a familiar mechanical sound and steps back as the floor in the fireplace moves backward, exposing an entrance to the Emperor's underground kingdom. She walks toward the top of the stairs and sees the large door swing open. A man dressed in light armor, similar to the ones she had seen outside, clears the way so that she may pass. Once she does, she can hear his footsteps as he follows her. She walks down the stairs cautiously, resisting the need to look over her shoulder. The soldier doesn't speak. He walks behind her until they reach the level leading to the Emperor's home and then they switch places as he takes the lead.

The underground kingdom, called Ascuns Loc by the people who know of it, encompasses a large area that contains the same types of structures seen in a regular village. The major difference, other than the fact that it's underground, is that the kingdom has a series of sky tubes with mirrors built into them to allow light to reflect into deep subterranean areas. This piped-in light from the outside world makes its way to the underground corridors and structures, allowing the kingdom to experience much of the daylight that one sees in the world above ground. It's an impressive underground structure, of an architecture that rivals those of any that exist above ground. Dark and ornate, the kingdom is quite lovely for such a secluded and secretive place. Its melancholic beauty always stays in Kallima's mind long after each time she makes a visit. But no matter how beautiful she thinks it is, she is happy she doesn't have to live there.

When they arrive at the corridor that leads to the Emperor's palace Kallima's fear begins to swell. She is excited about her encounter with Evangelina and knows it will help her rise in the ranks of his favor. She also knows she will be paid for her service, and when the Emperor decides to expand his kingdom she may even get her own land, but that is a consideration for another time.

The solider bangs the knocker against the door and Kallima takes a deep breath.

A boy servant quickly appears as though he's been waiting by the door. He looks to have fifteen years, maybe sixteen at most. The boy greets her with sad eyes and holds the door open for her to enter. As she does, she looks over her shoulder and sees the soldier take position outside the door. She knows he will be waiting there for her once she's done.

The boy begins leading her down the hall. From the direction he's going, she presumes he's leading her to the library. The Emperor is often in the library when Kallima comes to meet him. The boy is different than the one she had seen the last time ... but then, she had not been here for some time. She tries not to think of what may have happened to the last one.

This boy is dressed well, as all the Emperor's servants always are. He is confined by the Emperor's signature chains, which are black as night. They begin with a thick metal collar that surrounds the neck, connected to sleek but strong chain links extending down his back where they reattach with bonds that form around the wrists, the waist and the ankles. These chains allow for plenty of movement, so they don't keep the servants confined. It's rumored that these chains are more of a symbol that the slaves no longer belong to themselves, a mocking of the freedom they no longer have.

The boy is very handsome. His skin is of a light color, much like the ivory-colored crystals she uses in some of her healing spells. He has eyes as blue as the color of a river when the sky is clear. She thinks he will make a handsome man when he is older. *If he is permitted to become a man,* she thinks and then quickly pushes the thought away.

The boy directs her to the Emperor's private library as she thought he would. He opens the door and holds it for her, then he enters the room and closes the door behind them. The boy points in the direction of where the Emperor is sitting. Kallima thanks him and walks towards the Emperor with trepidation.

The Emperor's study is palatial, like the rest of his home. He is sitting at a large ornate table surrounded by equally ornate high-backed chairs. Each chair is decorated with a sculpted head of an animal or creature, some mythical and some real.

Emperor Zaavan sits in a chair with a lion's head atop it. He doesn't turn to look at Kallima as she approaches the table from behind him. When she gets close enough she notices several things on the table: the open book he's focused on, piles of parchment and a few sheets lying randomly about. Then she notices drops and smears of what can only be blood on the parchment and on the table itself. They look fresh. She stops moving and holds her breath.

The Emperor, highly vigilant, feels her presence as she approaches and also detects the change in her breathing pattern. A smirk appears on his face, though he does away with it before he speaks to her.

He stands up and turns to face her. He is a handsome man. His height, skin and build suggest that he has no more than forty-five years, though no one truly knows how old he is. It is said that the underground kingdom was built over seventy years ago and there are rumors that the kingdom had been built specifically for this emperor. Kallima, having only twenty-eight years, has no idea if this is true. She only knows that his eyes seem much older than his body and every time she looks at them she feels hypnotized and violated at the same time. She always makes eye contact briefly as a sign of respect, but then she quickly averts her eyes and keeps them averted as much as possible.

"Kallima," he says in a welcoming tone.

The Emperor is wearing a black glove on his right hand. He reaches out to her, holds her right hand in his, and then places the stump of his left wrist over her right hand. She could not now and has never seen the actual stump, which is covered by a beautifully embroidered shroud, custom-tailored to fasten to the end of his sleeve. Her hand is trembling badly, but the Emperor does not appear to mind.

"As always, I am pleased to see you. What brings you to Maezon so late in the night?"

"And I you, Emperor. I had an encounter. I thought it most important to get your guidance on it."

"I see. Please ... sit." He directs her to a chair away from the table, one that will allow him to sit opposite her. She feels nervous having to sit directly across from him while she recounts the events. She has to frequently remind herself of the treasures that she stands to gain from this.

"I met a woman this evening, looking for a stone. She was quite persistent about buying the one that I found in Baldric years ago. The one I brought to you but did not serve you any purpose. Do you remember it?"

The Emperor nods with a movement that is slow and confident. He has green eyes of a color so rich that just looking at them makes her feel dizzy. He smiles gently as he nods and the look on his face seems almost loving but it also seems deceitful, as though it's covering up a secret he doesn't want her to know. She finds herself struggling with not wanting to say anything and wanting to tell him everything.

"She was very persistent. I offered her other stones and she seemed insistent on buying this one. She offered me the worth of two horses."

"Two horses?" the Emperor says, amused.

"Yes. She said—or rather, she implied that she was a wayfarer. But she didn't know what a reading was. And when I explained it to her she didn't want to participate. She shied away from it. I believe she didn't want me to know her history."

She waits a moment to see if the Emperor has anything else to offer but he merely stares at her. She accepts this as her cue to continue.

"Then when I attempted to examine her intentions, I received nothing. I could not read her thoughts or feelings. She was ... a blank."

"A blank?"

"It was obscure; I received something but I didn't know what to make of it. It felt strange. But what was clear is that what I was picking up was not clear. It was as if she knew how to block my attempts."

"Do you believe it was intentional?"

"My instincts tell me it was not."

"Your instincts are better than most."

"Thank you, Emperor."

"Did you try to persuade her to give you the information with your … unique methods?"

"No. Being that I could not read her, I presumed my methods would not work."

"I would have presumed the same. Did she explain the reason she wanted it?"

"For a sick relative, she said."

"Whose ailment is?"

"She didn't say. She said it was unknown."

"And you believed her?"

"No."

"What was your answer?"

"I told her I would consider it overnight and that she should make me an offer that would make it worth my interest. I gave her the impression that coin was my concern."

The Emperor smiles, pleased. He is quite fascinated with Kallima. She is one of the strongest sensitives he has ever encountered, and her ability to capture knowledge from and influence others serves him well. She is more calculating than most beings he has met, and she might make a worthy advisor once she acquires more years.

"Well done, Kallima."

"Thank you, Emperor. I am to meet her shortly after dawn. What are your wishes?"

The Emperor thinks on it for a few minutes. While he does, Kallima waits patiently.

Kallima looks around the room at the beautiful treasures and sculptures. Some are so well sculpted that they seem almost real. Her eyes almost completely pass over the boy servant before realizing that he's not one of them. She looks back at him and sees that his eyes, blue as they are, look empty and lifeless. She looks away immediately and finds herself thinking about the blood on the Emperor's table. She decides it would be best if she keeps her eyes in her lap. It is not long before Emperor Zaavan speaks again.

"I am going to give you a stone. It's very rare and very beautiful. It's unlikely that she's seen one like it before, even if she's being truthful about searching for healing stones. I want you to try to sell it to her. Tell her it has been known to cure many ailments."

"Do you believe she will want this one instead of the other?"

"No. I believe she will want the other. But try to sell it to her regardless. If I am wrong and she does take it, it will not matter. If I am right, keep it with you for now. Either way, I will want it returned to me."

"Yes, Emperor."

"One other thing, Kallima."

"Yes, Emperor?"

"If she doesn't take the stone I give you, I want you to follow her."

"For what reason?"

Kallima regrets the words the moment they leave her mouth. She's confused by the Emperor's direction and afraid that her question has come across as insolent. The Emperor's face does not reveal any sign that he has taken it this way, but it doesn't matter. He has always treated her with kindness and respect … but then, she has consistently shown the utmost humility and reverence. And she, like many, has heard the tales of what can happen when the Emperor is not pleased.

"I humbly apologize, Emperor, I misspoke. I am confused by what I should do, and I want to ensure I serve you well. What is my purpose for following her? Should I merely observe?"

"No. Follow her and watch for anything strange. If you see even the slightest deviation from normal demeanor I want you to detain her and bring her back to Maezon. I am aware that you can't do this on your own. I will give you monies so that you may employ men to help you. I believe two men will be enough. Is she travelling alone?"

"She said she was travelling with a companion but he was nowhere to be seen."

"It's likely a lie, then."

"And if she does nothing strange?"

"I doubt that will be the outcome, but if that is the case then you need not detain her. Just keep me informed of her actions. Send a carrier bird so you can continue to follow her. And make sure no one, save those that you hire, is aware of what you are doing."

The Emperor walks to the table and writes something on a piece of parchment. Then he gives the parchment to the servant boy, whose eyes reveal fear and sadness as the Emperor touches him. The

Emperor does not seem to mind.

"Gabbirrel, follow these instructions and obtain this stone for me. I've written the chamber number and its location for you."

Gabbirrel nods and leaves the room quickly. The Emperor watches him walk away with a look on his face that Kallima can only associate with pride. While he is gone the Emperor asks about Kallima's livelihood and if she is selling many items. She tells him she is doing well but that she feels tired from travelling as of late and she is considering settling in a village near Maezon. The Emperor explains that she is much too young to truly enjoy settling and that she will likely be more prosperous if she stays in Baldric or travels to other wayfarer encampments. It is clear the Emperor doesn't want her settling any time soon, so she agrees that she should stay in Baldric. He is pleased by this; Kallima's abilities will be of little use to him if she doesn't have constant interaction with others.

Gabbirrel returns with a box no bigger than the Emperor's hand and gives it to the Emperor. When he opens it, it reveals a stone that is nearly the same size as the one Evangelina wants to purchase. It has a metallic raven-colored surface on the outside but it doesn't seem to have any color within. When Zaavan removes it from the box and gives it to Kallima, the light from the oil lamps strikes it and she can see that it's not colorless as she previously thought: the color on the inside of the stone is dark rouge. It reminds her of the blood she saw on the table just a short while ago. When she accepts it, she is surprised to see that much like the stone she has, it's deceptively light in weight.

"This is the stone you will attempt to sell her. Remember: if she does not buy it, keep it with you. I will want it returned to me."

"I understand, Emperor."

"Go then and may fortune be in your favor."

When Kallima stands up to leave, the Emperor does not rise with her. He seems deep in thought. She walks toward the door with Gabbirrel. The boy servant has already opened it for her when it occurs to her that she needs clarity.

"A question, Emperor?" She makes it clear that the question itself is a request and does not assume he will be available to answer one for her.

"Yes," he permits, without looking in her direction.

"If she does not buy the green stone, should I follow her

regardless?"

"No. There is no need to follow her if she takes the one I gave you. If that is the case, you can deliver a message to inform me or come back to see me. A visit from you is always a pleasure."

Kallima cringes when hearing him use the word *pleasure*. "The pleasure is mine, Emperor. I will be on my way."

She waits briefly for a response. The Emperor sits in the chair staring at nothing. He rubs his stump with his gloved hand, as though doing so brings him great satisfaction.

When she realizes he does not intend to respond, she quickly leaves the room.

The guard is outside waiting to escort her back to the inn. She feels relieved to be away from the Emperor but is surprised when a feeling of sadness creeps over her as well. She puts the stone in her carrying bag and walks back with the guard the same way she came. The further away she is from the Emperor, the more eager she feels to be away from Maezon.

# THE BARGAIN

Evangelina returns to the wagon expecting a sleepless night. Kaco is almost hysterical and it takes her some time to calm him. He is still wearing the restraint and she uses it to take him outside so he can relieve himself, but then brings him back to the wagon so he won't wander or get lost. She remembers that Kaco sleeps mostly in the daytime and she thinks it must be difficult for him to remain in the wagon at night. The only thing that calms him is the spear, so she allows him to lie with it. The spear doesn't pulse or brighten, as it's not exposed to the sky. But Kaco seems to be comforted by it anyway. She locks the wagon for the night so there will be no surprise entrances and no chance of Kaco escaping.

Though Kaco is settled, Evangelina has difficulty being comfortable. She finds it difficult to sleep knowing she is only wagons away from where her son's stone lay waiting for him. Angry that she must wait until the morning, she considers going back to Kallima's wagon and letting her know that she had decided on an offer—three times what a good horse is worth. She thinks that offer more than fair, but then remembers she has to make it seem as though she spent the evening contemplating it.

At one point she considers thievery again, but it's much too dangerous to risk it in this encampment, and besides, she's not sure she can reconcile stealing from someone. After Kaco is sleeping soundly, she takes the spear and leaves the wagon for a short time. She hopes a short walk in the cold will help make her sleepy. But when she returns she feels even more awake. Once she finally falls asleep it is only a few hours before dawn and she has a disturbing dream.

When the dream begins she finds herself calmed because she and Tahvi are together. They're in a wagon, travelling to a place she does not know. When they arrive, she realizes it's a metropolis. Tahvi is very excited as he has the opportunity to see things he hasn't seen thus far. It's a brand-new world to him and his mother is overjoyed to see him smiling. In her dream, Tahvi's body is as it had been before she had found the first stone and returned it to him—both his leg and his arm are not complete. As they're walking through the crowded dirt roads, Tahvi falls and a man is kind enough to help him up. When the man grabs Tahvi he does so by his left arm and accidentally yanks the forged arm from his body. He holds the arm up in the air with an incredulous look on his face and then he begins to laugh. Evangelina tries to grab the arm from him but he holds it away from her. Tahvi stands up, tries to help, and the man shoves him down.

Everyone is watching and then another person approaches Tahvi and begins to pull at his forged leg. Evangelina abandons her effort for the arm as her son screams her name. She goes to him quickly and tries to push the person away that has gripped his leg. The person's entire head is featureless, with only a blur where the face should be. She pulls Tahvi as hard as she can but the person's efforts exceed her own, and the false leg is torn away from Tahvi.

Evangelina kneels on the ground, crying. Tahvi is screaming and before she can do anything to help him, the crowd surrounds them and pulls them away from each other. Then they begin to pull at Tahvi's real arm and leg and Evangelina panics. She fights as hard as she can to reach her son but they're too strong. Tahvi cries and screams but he is powerless and Evangelina feels like she is dying inside.

His scream is the last thing she remembers when she awakes, crying and in a panic. She is sweating and her breathing is rapid. When she realizes it was a dream she is somewhat relieved, but it doesn't replace the sadness she's feeling. She continues to weep for a long time and then refuses to go back to sleep. She wonders how Tahvi is feeling and curses the stars for being in a position where she had to leave him.

Once she composes herself, she takes out her sewing and embroidery baskets and begins to work on a project. She is angry and hurt, so she works quickly and soon her mind is distracted and she's able to focus on the sewing. But Tahvi stays in the distant part of her mind and every so often she thinks of how much she misses him and must push back the thought to continue. It has been less than two days that she's been away from him. She doesn't know how she is going to survive being away from him for months at a time.

Shortly after dawn Evangelina hears a knocking on the back of her wagon. Evangelina gathers the bag she had placed the coin in, one nearly as big as Kaco. She exits through the front of the wagon, as that entrance is not blocked by supplies, and then walks around to the back. Expecting to see Kallima, she holds the bag out in front of her. She's surprised when she sees it's Maggie.

"Good day to you, Evangelina."

"Good day Maggie." Evangelina brings the bag close to her chest and the coins makes a clinking sound.

"I came to—oh my stars, what is that for?" she says as she points to the bag of monies Evangelina is holding.

Evangelina is not sure if she should lie, but before she can decide she finds the truth spilling from her lips. "I am buying a healing stone from one of the other sellers."

"A healing stone? For the coin in that bag? The stone must be bigger than your wagon!"

"It's a unique stone and my friend is very ill. She might perish and I've a feeling that this stone might help her."

"Who are you buying it from?" Maggie asks.

"A woman named Kallima."

Maggie gives Evangelina an irritated look. "Kallima? The woman with all the jewelry and the crazy horse?"

"Yes, she has jewelry. But I haven't seen a crazy horse."

"I believe Kallima might be taking you for a ride," Maggie says.

"No. She didn't take me anywhere."

Maggie laughs boisterously, "My, you are a sheltered one, are you not? It's an expression, dear. Have you not heard it?"

"I'm afraid not," Evangelina says, curious but not embarrassed.

"It means she's trying to trick you. She's known for selling items that are not worth their value in barter. When are you to purchase this stone?"

"I should be on my way to her wagon now. I believed she was the one knocking then I remembered she doesn't know where my wagon is."

"Evangelina, you seem like a very pleasant person and I'm not supposed to interfere with trade as long as the trade or purchase is legitimate and accepted by both parties. The difficulty is, there is not a way to establish the legitimacy of a stone. So, I've an idea. Do you have a moment to hear it?"

Evangelina nods.

* * *

Evangelina knocks on the wagon. She has to knock several times before Kallima comes to the door. Her hair is rustled and she looks as though she has been asleep.

"Good day to you," Evangelina says.

"Good day. Forgive my appearance. My night was long and … hectic."

"Are you ready to discuss our deal?" Evangelina holds the bag of coin up just enough so that Kallima can see how big it is. Kallima does not attempt to conceal her excitement.

"I am, give me a moment!"

When Kallima steps out of the wagon she holds a stone in a small bag made of a dark-brown colored material. It has a drawstring at the top.

"Is that the stone?" Evangelina asks.

"Well, yes and no. After our meeting last night, I met with someone I know to talk about your dilemma. I discovered she had a very rare stone as well that has a much better history of healing than the one I have. She is not a healer anymore, so she no longer needs it, but she said it has aided with many ailments in a way that can't be explained."

Kallima takes the rock out of the bag and for a brief second Evangelina thinks it might be another piece of Tahvi's star. The outside is very similar, but when she gets a closer look at it she notices the stone on the inside is different from Tahvi's. She gives Kallima an annoyed look.

"This is not what we discussed," Evangelina says.

"Of course not. You said you were looking for rare healing stones, so I just thought—"

"No," Evangelina says sternly. "In this bag I have three times what a good horse is worth. But it is only for that stone which I saw last night."

Kallima smiles. "I believe the offer is worthy of my acceptance. If it's the other rock you want, then you shall have it. Give me another moment."

Kallima walks back into the wagon to retrieve the stone. When she exits the wagon the second time, Maggie is standing outside next to Evangelina.

"What are you doing here?" Kallima asks. Her anger is obvious.

"I see you met our new resident," Maggie says with a mocking smile. "She is a seamstress and a weaver."

"I know what she is," Kallima replies. "We are about to make an exchange and you are interrupting."

"An exchange? This early? Is it because you've finally found someone who wants one of those rocks you've been unable to sell?"

Kallima looks at her with contempt.

Evangelina acts surprised. "I thought you said the rock you plan to sell is a healing stone?"

"Did she say that?" Maggie asks, acting genuinely curious.

"Yes, she said she's used it many times," Evangelina says.

"It is a healing stone," Kallima says. "You have no business here, Maggie. You are the trade organizer and not the trade master, so if you will leave then we can continue our—"

"I've never seen it used as a healing stone," Maggie says.

"I could injure you and then show you how it works," Kallima says sharply.

"Kallima, you know the rules. The selling and trading must be legitimate," Maggie says.

"I am not sure if I'm interested in the stone anymore," Evangelina says. Just saying the words makes her stomach turn and she thinks she might vomit.

"Do not challenge me, Evangelina. I know this stone is what you want," Kallima snaps.

"I'm sure you are right," Maggie says, "And a deal can still be made here if it is a fair one. Or we can go to the trade master's wagon and he can help sort this out. Which one would you prefer, Kallima?"

"I am prepared to offer a quarter of the initial price I offered you," Evangelina says as convincingly as she can.

"A quarter!" Kallima exclaims.

"It's apparent that you've been dishonest with me. How can I trust that the stone will do what you say it can?"

Evangelina tries not to let her fear show. The coin does not matter, but she doesn't want Kallima to know that, and she doesn't want her to know how important the stone really is to her, especially now that she knows she is dealing with someone so full of greed.

"I will sell it for no less than half the original price you offered. Regardless of what Maggie has to say, it has been used as a healing stone. I may not be able to prove it, but you can't disprove it. And though I won't be there to see it, I'm sure you'll be more than appeased with the outcome."

Evangelina separates the coin and gives it to Kallima, who forcefully gives her the stone.

"Now everyone is happy," Maggie chirps.

Kallima glares at Evangelina and then directs her frustration at Maggie.

"If you ever interfere with another of my exchanges I will ensure you are barred from Baldric as a trade organizer," Kallima snaps as she walks back into her wagon.

"If you try another illegitimate exchange I will report you to the trade master!" Maggie shouts, but Kallima has already closed and locked the door on her wagon.

As Maggie and Evangelina walk back to Evangelina's wagon she offers Maggie some coin as a token of her thanks, but Maggie explains she is not permitted to take it. Evangelina insists on offering to buy her a meal to break fast, but Maggie reminds her that the food bar does not open until suppertime. Maggie has access to fresh eggs, butter, milk and bread, so she agrees to let Evangelina cook a meal for her.

Excited to return home to Tahvi with another stone in hand, Evangelina leaves as soon as they finish eating and Maggie says she hopes to see her again in Baldric one day.

Kallima watches her ride out of the encampment. After Evangelina has ridden past the large hill just outside of Baldric, Kallima sees the two men she hired follow her. She had partly hoped the woman would purchase the dark stone so she could turn a worthy profit and not have to track her. But she feels cheated after this morning's exchange and is glad that the woman decided to purchase the green stone instead. Kallima is looking forward to dragging her back to Maezon.

# THE BUSY ROAD TO VIOLETTA

Evangelina is only two hours away from Baldric when she suddenly grows very tired. Having hardly slept the previous night, she's not sure how much longer she can continue without sleep. She looks at the sky and believes it's sometime between dawn and midday—if she sleeps now she will not make it home until long after nightfall, and that's only if she doesn't stop to sleep again—but she feels if she doesn't rest now the ride might take twice as long due to her weariness. Her muscles make the choice for her when she feels the exhaustion in them and it takes only a moment for her to surrender.

She sees a patch of trees ahead and rides on for a bit until she reaches them. She parks the wagon in the shade, not too far from the road. On her way to Baldric, when she drove fairly far from the road to park the wagon, she barely missed a hole that might have tipped it or at the least broken a wheel, so she learned it was better to stay as close as possible to the wagon trail.

Kaco is fast asleep despite not being able to roam or be active the previous night. Evangelina's plan is to park the wagon, leave him be and step outside momentarily to stretch her legs before going to sleep. But after parking the wagon she dozes off instantly.

When she awakes, she is slumped in the driving seat, still holding the reins. She gets out of the driver's seat and begins to stretch as she planned, not knowing there is a hooded figure lying only meters away from where she stands.

When she's done stretching she looks at the road in both directions and sees no one approaching. Believing it's safe, she removes the spear from her coat and the newly acquired stone, which she carries in her dress pocket. The moment they're exposed to each other, the spear lights up completely and the second stone reacts just as the first one had. A smile crosses Evangelina's face. It's a beautiful sight and she's in awe each time she sees it. She puts the spear back in her pocket, even though she sees no one approaching. It's important to be careful.

As she heads back to board the wagon, she wonders if she has made a grave mistake. She thinks about the other stone that Kallima had showed her. Except for the fact that the color of the stone inside is different, the stone is very much like Tahvi's stone. She tries to remember if the outside was exactly like the metallic black surface that was on the outside of Tahvi's stone and his birth star. But she was so focused on making sure she obtained Tahvi's stone that she didn't take the time to inspect the one Kallima was trying to give her instead. And she is so tired, too tired to remember. Then she thinks of the map.

She goes to the front of the wagon and pulls Tahvi's map out of the travelling bag that she carries on the seat with her. She unfolds it and looks at all the locations of the stones. None of the others is in the direction of Baldric. *Fantastic,* she thinks. She places the map back in the bag and moves away from the tree, just in case it obstructs her access to the stars. She looks in both directions of the road again and still there is no one to be seen. She removes the spear and points it in the direction of Baldric. The spear begins to brighten and pulse, but it's too early to tell which direction it's indicating. Then the pulse begins to move faster and Evangelina grows nervous. It seems that the direction it's showing is toward Baldric, but it quickly decides its course and begins pulsing stronger in a different direction. The light is strongest toward Encarta. She takes a deep breath and exhales with relief. She can't imagine having to deal with Kallima again.

She puts the spear back in her pocket and then the image of the map runs through her head. She recalls that three of the locations are somewhat lined up in the same bearing. *What would happen if I were standing in the middle of two pieces of Tahvi's star?* she thinks. It's a question she had yet to consider, but not one she could even begin to try to answer without a few hours of sleep.

She notices how quiet and peaceful the day is. There's a soft wind, which occasionally turns to a strong breeze, and she is surrounded by grass nearly a meter tall. As the wind blows it makes a constant *whiiiiiiisp whiiiiiiiiisp* sound that she's heard since the moment she stopped the horses to depart the wagon. She closes her eyes, enjoying the feeling of the wind moving across her face and through her hair for what feels like a long time. The last thing she remembers is feeling the grass on her fingertips before she's jerked awake.

She stumbles forward and regains her balance before she falls. *I must have fallen asleep standing*, she thinks. She laughs nervously, checks for the spear and finds it's still in her pocket. Just then, she hears a noise behind her. Seeing nothing, she decides it's due to her lack of sleep when she hears it a second time. She hears the *whiiiiiiiisp whiiiiiiiisp* sound again but this time it's different. It's faster, like a *whisp-whisp-whisp-whisp*.

She feels a surge of fear race through her that sharpens all her senses at once, helping her understand what she failed to realize a moment before. The first sound is the wind as it blows through the grass. The second sound is of someone or something moving through the grass.

Evangelina feels in her coat for the dagger that Vertimus packed and then remembers it's in her travelling bag. She's defenseless.

She can think of only two options: she can wait until the figure approaches her and then use the element of surprise to attack. This doesn't seem to be a good idea because the man (she assumes it's a man at first and then considers the idea that Kallima has followed her) could have the advantage of strength or a weapon, or both. She can also run. She is not far from the wagon, and she may not be able to get the horses moving before the person catches up with her, but she may be able to reach the dagger. She believes this is her best option so she casually closes her hand over the dress pocket carrying the stone, and then does so on the other side as well, getting ready to lift her dress just enough so that she will not trip over it. Then she begins to run as fast as she can.

She thinks she hears her name but she dismisses it. When she hears it the second time, she is still running. When she hears it the third time she realizes the voice yelling it sounds familiar.

She has just mounted the front of the wagon when she turns around to see who's calling her name. Standing less than twenty meters from her is Vertimus. In the distance she sees another figure riding a horse and pulling the reins of another behind him.

Evangelina hops off the wagon with too much force, nearly falling backward into the grass, though she manages to balance herself just in time. She runs to Vertimus. She can hear herself laughing as she does so. When she reaches him she throws her arms around him and holds him.

"My stars, am I happy to see you!"

"You and I will need to have words about trust," he says, not yet returning her embrace.

Her laughter becomes more boisterous and then quickly turns to tears. She lets herself cry while she holds him and then he returns her embrace. The lecture Vertimus planned to give her is obviously unnecessary; whatever experience she had in Baldric is likely one she will not want to repeat. He feels great empathy for her and can't help but be impressed by her tenacity and dedication to her son. His brother had chosen an exceptional wife.

Evangelina had eaten recently so she's not hungry but Vertimus and Jabneh are famished. They explain that they had adjusted their schedule to ride as often as they could and they had yet to break fast from the last time they slept. They eat dried meat, bread and some fruit that Evangelina had brought with her from Baldric, and while they do she tells them about her experience there. They're both entertained and impressed by how her negotiations with Kallima ended. They declare it sad but unfortunately all too common that this woman tried to take advantage of Evangelina in such a way.

By the time Evangelina finishes telling her tale her exhaustion has returned. They discuss letting Evangelina sleep while they drive the wagon, but finally decide to let Evangelina rest in the parked wagon, which will allow time to snare something other than dried meat for their next meal. Vertimus knows of a stream that is not far from them and they all agree that fresh fish would be an excellent idea. Vertimus decides to fish alone so Jabneh can stay with Evangelina and keep watch while she sleeps. Evangelina makes no protest about resting or taking their time getting back home, and she's grateful to have their company and support.

\* \* \*

Balfor has grown tired of lying in the grass and he's itching in places he can't reach. He's relieved when he sees the tall, masculine man ride off in the direction opposite himself. The man doesn't look like someone he wants to squabble with, even with the aid of his riding companion.

The plan to apprehend the woman is spoiled the moment both men appear but Balfor stays in the grass, watching to see what the trio will do next. It's apparent they're planning to rest but he can't guess the duration. He crawls backwards on his belly to report to his fellow tracker and riding companion, Pandarus, what he has seen.

Once he's sure he's out of their line of sight, he stands up and hurries back to the place where Pandarus waits with the horses. He's sitting on the ground, eating a piece of fruit.

"Is she sleeping yet?" Pandarus asks.

Balfor nods his head and crouches slightly, his hands resting on his knees, trying to catch his breath.

"Then we should acquire her," Pandarus replies, as he stands up.

Balfor shakes his head furiously.

"You're confusing me."

Balfor holds one of his hands up to Pandarus, signaling him that he needs a moment. He drinks some water from his flask but still is not ready to speak. Pandarus looks at him impatiently.

"She is no longer alone," Balfor says, his breathing struggling to return to normal.

"How did that happen?"

"Two men—came to her just after she took out a wand that glowed."

"What?"

"Two men came to her just after—" he begins but Pandarus interrupts him.

"I heard you the first time. Let us start again. Tell me what you saw in the order it happened. Start with when you came upon the wagon."

Balfor does as he is asked; he is good at following directions if the directions are specific. He explains that he saw the woman take out a wand that glowed and with that wand she made a rock glow. Then she headed back to her wagon, he thought to sleep, but she pulled out something that he could not see and then took the wand out again. Balfor said it did not glow as brightly as it did before but it was bright enough for him to see it from where he lay. And then he tells the rest of his encounter very quickly. "At first I was scared because it seemed she was pointing it at me and I didn't know if she planned to curse me. But then she put the wand away. Then one of the men, a very big one, appeared and at first the woman didn't seem to know who he was but then she did and then she hugged him and then the other man came, tall but not big, and he had two horses and she hugged him too. Then they talked and then the really big man left and the other man stayed with her and it looked like she was sleeping in the wagon. I could not hear what they were speaking of but it seemed as if the other man was coming back."

Pandarus stares at him, trying to filter what's important.

"You said she had a wand?"

"Yes. It was green."

"Hmm."

"But we can't take her with those two men."

"No, we can't."

"But that is strange, yes? A green wand … that is strange?"

"Yes, Balfor. It's strange."

"And she said we had to take her if she did anything strange."

"Yes."

"So what do we do?"

Pandarus considers their options. Normally he wouldn't be worried, but Kallima said this is an errand for the Emperor. He is not about to fail the Emperor.

"You must ride back to Baldric. Tell Kallima she must meet us here because we were unable to acquire the woman. That is all I know to do."

"Do you think she will be angry?"

"It doesn't matter. It's our only option. Now hurry. We don't know how long they'll be here, but the woman is travelling by wagon and she is the one we are supposed to follow. If she leaves before you return with Kallima I will continue to track her. Regardless of what happens, I will leave many signs close to the road so you can easily see them, understand?"

Balfor nods.

"Good. Now ride quickly. We may not have much time."

* * *

Kallima is sleeping when she hears someone pounding on the door of her wagon. She is surprised when Balfor states his name.

Kallima opens her wagon door and finds that Balfor has not dismounted his horse. It's noisy and busy outside, as the selling and trading had already begun for the day. Kallima looks around her wagon to make sure no one can hear her.

"Do you have the woman?"

"No," Balfor says nervously.

"Then what are you doing here? You should be following the woman you were paid to follow!"

"Pandarus is with her. He sent me here to tell you that you have to meet us."

"Balfor, come closer to me."

"Did you employ me?"

Balfor looks confused but he answers nonetheless. "No."

"Then I do not have to do anything."

"I think Pandarus wanted you to meet us because we are outnumbered."

"Explain."

"We could not take the woman because she is no longer alone. She is with two men, two hours south of here."

"So she was speaking the truth about her companion in Violetta."

"I don't understand."

"It does not matter. Pandarus was right to send you. We can't risk losing track of the woman and you may not be able to handle both men. Do they look strong, like soldiers?"

"One does," Balfor says nervously. "I would not want to quarrel with him over anything."

"They're likely both hired hands."

"That is not all, Kallima."

"Tell me the rest then and be quick about it."

"I think she's an enchantress of sorts."

"What makes you think so?"

"She had a wand. It glowed."

"Glowed?"

"Yes. It glowed a bright green. It was like nothing I had seen before. And she used the wand to make a stone glow also."

Kallima is intrigued. This woman could not be a sensitive, as Kallima would have sensed that, but then remembered that she was hardly able to sense anything about Evangelina. Whoever she is and whatever her secret, she's sure it will be valuable to the Emperor.

"I need to pack. Get my horse and then I will come with you. Say my name before you give him any command and he will obey you. Wait for me on the outskirts of the encampment in the direction from which you came."

"You want me to wait for you?"

"That was the command I expressed."

"And get your horse?"

"Balfor, are you partly deaf?"

"No."

"Are my instructions not clear?"

"No."

"Then what is your distress?"

"I'm afraid of your horse."

Kallima smirks at this. "That is as it should be, but he will not hurt you unless I tell him to. Now meet me where I advised. I will need only a few minutes."

* * *

Vertimus does not return from fishing for several hours but when he does he has many fish hanging from his saddlebag. Jabneh wakes Evangelina when Vertimus returns ... or rather, he tries to but she's sleeping soundly. Jabneh and Vertimus decide Jabneh will drive the wagon to allow her to continue to sleep and Vertimus will ride his horse beside the wagon, with Jabneh's horse tied to the back of it.

As they depart for Violetta with Evangelina tucked away safely in the wagon, they feel the tiredness trying to overcome them. They prefer to not rest until they reach Violetta so they do their best to entertain their minds with conversation. It's not difficult; they discovered on the ride from Padhraig that they enjoy each other's company.

"Did you see Kaco is with her?" Jabneh asks.

"Tahvi's Kaco?"

"Do you know of another Kaco?"

"Hah, I suppose not. When did you see him?"

"Shortly before we left when I tried to wake Evangelina. He's asleep in the back of the wagon with her."

"I wonder whose idea that was," Vertimus says.

"Do you think it was Tahvi's?"

"I believe that's a possibility."

"Maybe Tahvi sent him so she would not be alone."

"But how could he? No one knew she was leaving."

"Are you sure? The boy seems to know much more than we thought he did," Jabneh responds.

"I understand your point. My point is that I don't think Tahvi would have allowed it. I think he would have told someone."

"I see. I wonder if anyone noticed Kaco missing." After several minutes, Jabneh speaks again. "I can't tell you how relieved I am to find Evangelina well."

"Yes, as am I."

"Truthfully?"

"Of course. Why wouldn't I be relieved?"

"That's not my meaning. I thought you *knew* we would find her well?"

"What made you believe that?"

"I read her note before we left."

Vertimus is silent.

"You are a sensitive, are you not? That's how you know what is imminent?"

"I don't always know what is imminent. But yes, I am a sensitive. Does that frighten you?"

"No. The dried meat we ate this morning ... *that* frightens me."

Vertimus laughs. He's surprised to find that Jabneh has quite the sense of humor, which does not match what he perceived as a frequently sullen disposition.

"If you don't always know what's imminent, how did you know she would be free from harm?"

"It's difficult to explain. But Evangelina misunderstood; I explained to her that I had a foretell in which Tahvi had acquired another piece of his star and she was with him. That was all I knew, and I only told her because she was so unhappy. But that foretell did not guarantee her safety. The foretell could have represented a time weeks or even months from today. She could have been hurt in Baldric and then healed long before that premonition. She should never have interpreted it as an assurance of safety."

"So your concern was genuine."

"Yes."

Jabneh smiles softly. "You are a worthy kinsman, Vertimus, and a remarkable uncle at that. Your brother would be proud of how well you have cared for his family."

The compliment makes Vertimus emotional, which is not an easy thing to do. "Thank you, Jabneh."

"You are most welcome," Jabneh says sincerely.

Further down the road the conversation returns to their earlier subject. "Do you think Evangelina will attempt such a thing again?" Jabneh asks.

"Leaving on her own?"

"Yes."

"I am doubtful of it," Vertimus answers. "She was very scared when we arrived."

"I noticed that."

"If it had been merely a matter of finding the rock and digging for it, it may have been different. But her experience with that woman ... Kallima, was it?"

Jabneh nods.

"That really shook her, believing that she might not be able to acquire it."

"It would certainly shake me."

"I could have been a great help in that situation. She would not have even had to speak to Kallima. In my experience, women, even wayfarers, are much more cautious of men than they are of other women. That could have worked in our favor in this situation."

"I believe that."

"Though I'm not sure why it is that way. I've met a wagon full of women that I would sooner avoid crossing if it meant bargaining with a man instead."

"Praise to that declaration!" Jabneh says.

Then they both have a long and hard laugh about it. They're silent for a while until Jabneh feels himself growing bored again and decides to make more conversation.

"I do not know what I'd have done if something had befallen her," Jabneh says. His tone is serious and Vertimus can hear the sadness in it.

"You are not alone in that sentiment," Vertimus says kindly.

"Vertimus, you said you do not always know what is imminent?"

"That is correct."

"Will you share what you do know?"

"Of course."

The men spend time discussing the gifts that both he and Tahvi's father possessed as sensitives. They also speak of times that Vertimus has used the gift throughout his life. Vertimus learns much about Jabneh and his experiences, including the loss of his family. He knew of the death of his family, but he had never heard it from Jabneh's tongue. They spend short periods in silence but always began speaking again in an attempt to keep the exhaustion and boredom at bay. They both look forward to resting when they arrive in Violetta, oblivious to the three riders that trail not far behind them.

# SENTINELS

It's late in the evening when Vertimus and Jabneh guide the wagon into Violetta. There are a few people walking the roads of the village and each one waves to Jabneh as they see him.

Kallima and her hired men keep a safe distance and watch with great interest as the two men with Evangelina drive the wagon near the rear side of a row of shops. Shortly after that, Evangelina exits the wagon and speaks with them briefly before she enters the back door of the thin man's shop. Another man exits the back door of the shop a moment later and they watch as the thin man introduces him to the bigger man. They all help to remove some of the belongings from the wagon, which include two trunks and *that oversized rat*, as Kallima thinks of it. After helping Evangelina carry the trunks inside, the men who have been traveling with her guide the wagon and the horses to the nearest stable.

"It appears they all reside here," Kallima says, concerned.

"It's going to be more difficult to take her with so much movement," Pandarus says.

"I was thinking that as well. However … no, this can't be their home. These shops are in the center of town. They must be dropping off supplies or merchandise or something of similar value. They will likely be going somewhere else after stopping here, which might make things easier for us. Hopefully they will leave during the night and we can take her then, when we have the element of surprise to our advantage."

"I am in favor of any plan that does not reveal us," Balfor says, thinking of the large man.

"Very well. We should make camp safely outside of town, where we can rest undisturbed. We can sleep in shifts. Pandarus, you can take the first watch and make sure to follow them when they move on to their home. Once they do, come back for us and we will capture her together, under the cover of darkness."

"And the men?" Pandarus asks.

"What of them?" Kallima responds.

"What shall we do with them?"

"The Emperor wants no one to know what we're doing. So we should be discreet and avoid their attention as much as possible. If it can't be avoided, then we will do what we must."

Both men nod, requiring no further explanation. Kallima lets Pandarus know the direction she and Balfor are heading. Then they depart together to set up camp. Pandarus stays behind to find a location that makes it easier to watch the shop without appearing suspicious to anyone who might see him.

* * *

Evangelina sits at a small table in Jabneh's attached living quarters. Vertimus and Jabneh are exhausted and so they're quick to sleep. Evangelina feeds and waters their horses and removes the saddles so they may rest in the stables. She leaves the wagon and horses as they are, knowing she will be leaving in a few hours at most. Then she helps Nahele, Jabneh's assistant, with tasks in the shop. They make light conversation and speak about their trades. Afterward, she makes herself some tea and decides to cook the fish Vertimus caught. She has just finished cooking when Vertimus and Jabneh awaken. They all eat together, including Nahele, when Evangelina insists that he join them.

"Will you be spending the night here? I can make up another bed in the workroom," Nahele says.

Jabneh opens his mouth to answer, but Evangelina interrupts him. "No, I am returning to Padhraig this evening."

Jabneh puts his hand on hers and asks, "Would you rather we all ride together?"

"No thank you. I miss Tahvi very much, and I ... " She stops because Nahele is still in the room. She looks at Jabneh and he assumes what she's thinking.

"Nahele, would you give us some time alone, please?" The young man does as he's asked and walks toward the display room in the forefront of the store.

"I want to get the stone to him," Evangelina continues. "I am well rested—very well rested, many thanks to the two of you—and I am eager to see him. I don't feel like myself when we are not together."

"I understand. I have worry for you. You have had some adventurous days and I thought we might decrease any further chance of adventure by travelling together."

Nahele reenters the room. "I apologize for the intrusion, but shall I bring the wagon around, since you will be leaving this night?"

"Yes. Thank you, Nahele," Evangelina says.

"As you wish." Nahele leaves the room again.

"I think it safe for Evangelina to ride home. This is a road she's taken many times before. She knows it well. Besides, I understand needing to be close to my family, and I plan to help Jabneh with a few things before we return," Vertimus says.

Evangelina gives him a warm smile. She's glad to hear him give his blessing.

"I feel honored that you continue to trust me, despite my recent error in judgment."

"I am curious about something, though," Vertimus says. "What you said about not being the same when you're not around Tahvi … "

"Yes?"

"What was your meaning?"

"It's difficult to explain. It feels like I am missing a piece of myself."

"I believe that's quite normal," Jabneh says. Then he rises from the table and begins to clean his dishes. He seems to have lost his appetite.

"I don't know that I believe that. I've been away from Tahvi before, for short durations of time and felt something similar. But this is more intense. It feels as though … as though my mind and body are going to come apart, like the seams of a dress. As though Tahvi is what holds me together. It is very strong, nearly overwhelming. I honestly don't know how I am going to get along without him for weeks at a … " Evangelina stops when she realizes Jabneh is facing the other direction, still as stone. She hears light sniffling.

"Jabneh! Oh, my friend, I am truly sorry," she says emphatically. She walks over to him and holds him. He returns her embrace and allows himself the comfort of a few tears before regaining his composure.

"It is I who must apologize. I didn't mean to interrupt you."

"Sometimes I forget what you've been through."

"I would like to forget what I've been through."

They hold each other again for a few minutes. Vertimus can't tell which of them needs it more, but he supposes it doesn't matter.

When both their meal and conversation are concluded, Evangelina is ready to board her wagon again. Nahele has already brought the wagon and horses to the back of the shop. Jabneh and Vertimus help her reload the trunks and she walks Kaco on his restraint. He is obviously tired and grumpy, with his sleep pattern having been disrupted for the last few days.

"I was surprised to see Kaco with you," Jabneh says.

"I was surprised as well. When I awoke that first time in the wagon, he was lying next to me."

"Do you think Tahvi knows?" Jabneh asks.

"I'm unsure. But I'll be happy to ask him when I arrive home."

She gives Vertimus and Jabneh a long embrace. She thanks Nahele again for his help and then she boards the wagon. It is late in the night, with the moon showing just over the horizon.

"Evangelina, are you sure you do not want Jabneh or I to accompany you?" Vertimus asks.

"No, truly I am comfortable taking the wagon home alone. You agreed that you would help Jabneh ready his supplies and I see no reason why that plan should change. I plan to stop only to water the horses so I hope to be home before dawn."

"I don't suppose there is too much trouble you could encounter on a road in which you have travelled more than many times."

"I agree. You two will be close behind, yes?"

"Yes, we will likely arrive there by midday. We should take the remainder of tomorrow to rest, and then you and Jabneh can leave the following day to Encarta."

"Very well."

"Ride safe and have a good journey, Eva," Vertimus says. Jabneh repeats this sentiment.

"Yes, the same to both of you. I look forward to seeing you both at home soon."

Evangelina smiles and rides away in the wagon.

The two men stay outside for a few minutes watching the wagon drive away and then return to the shop.

Evangelina guides her wagon out of town and right past the point where the trio who are following her had entered the small patch of woods to make their hidden encampment.

Kallima and Balfor are sleeping and do not hear the wagon ride by. Unbeknownst to them, Pandarus is sleeping soundly at his watch point as well.

* * *

Pandarus curses himself for having fallen asleep. There is no activity outside the back of the store and it's deep into the night. He can see the moon, which was not previously in the sky when he began his watch. He walks around to the front and passes the store window several times, trying to look inconspicuous as he does so. He can see both men who were on the road, and the younger man who they saw earlier, moving around inside the store. But he doesn't see the woman. He can only assume she has left for the evening, which means he missed the opportunity to follow her. The thought of having to relay this news to Kallima makes him feel weak in his stomach, but he knows he must. He goes directly to their camp and explains what he's seen.

Kallima is furious but she does not lecture him.

"Ready the horses," she orders. "I will find out where she lives."

Kallima walks quickly to the shop. She is growing irritable over the difficulties. She was exhausted when she returned from Maezon so she hired the men not to *assist* her but to do the job *for* her. She thought it would be simple enough but didn't count on the woman having help. Then she left Pandarus as sentry, and he had failed her.

Fortune is not on her side in this endeavor. She decides it doesn't matter, because from this moment she will ensure the outcome by taking the lead. She knows that the woman is able to block her somehow, but she refuses to believe the same will happen with the men, and she plans to use her gift of influence to find out where their home is.

The entire center of town is empty and quiet. She stands in front of the shop's window. She can see two men moving about in the far back of the store. She doesn't see the brawny man. *Teresa's Toys and Trinkets* displays on a sign in front. As with most shops, she can see the door has a bell atop of it so that the merchant is aware when someone walks into it. She moves the handle on the shop's door and opens it slowly so that the bell does not ring. She gently nudges her way through the door and then slowly releases it, without closing it, behind her. She moves through the shop as quickly and soundlessly as she can, to get close to the men before they see her, and then she hears them speaking.

"How long do you expect to be gone?" Nahele asks.

"I would say at the least a few weeks but not longer than six months. I'm taking some of my tools with me so that I can work from there. If we get any special orders you may send them by messenger. And I can't think of any issue that would need my urgent attention but should one arise, you can send a carrier bird. Please send me the inventory and account totals once a week, understand?"

Nahele nods. "Once a week. Will you be staying with Evangelina?"

"Yes, and the rest of her family. She has a lovely home on the outskirts of the village."

"She seems a very pleasant woman."

"She is a lovely woman," Jabneh says. "I've been lucky to know her."

"I've never been to Padhraig. Is it a welcoming village?"

"Very much so. As friendly as is it here. Though it is larger than Violetta and the centermost part of town has more shops than ours."

"Do you ever consider … moving there?"

There is something about the way Nahele asks the question that makes Jabneh realize Nahele possibly has the wrong impression of his relationship with Evangelina. It's a fair assumption though, and Jabneh sees no maliciousness in it.

"I do, but it would be for business reasons and not personal ones. Though I think I would enjoy living close to Evangelina and her family. I've grown very fond of them and she is a dear friend to me."

"I see. I was thinking—" Nahele begins but is interrupted when they hear the bell ring from the front door. They walk to the front of the store to see who has come in but the door is closed.

"Vertimus?" Jabneh calls, but no one answers.

Jabneh walks to the door, opens it and looks outside. There is no one near the shop and the dirt road that runs through the center of town, facing all the shops, is deserted. He shuts it, locks it, and then walks back to Nahele.

"Let us hurry, shall we? I'd like to leave as soon as Vertimus returns with the horses."

Nahele nods and continues packing.

*  *  *

When Kallima hears the man close and lock the shop door, she waits another minute to be sure he's inside. When she's certain he is gone, she steps out from the post she's hiding behind and quickly walks back toward the horses with a smirk on her face.

Pandarus and Balfor are already on their horses and Pandarus is holding the reins for Maddox, who is so large he makes their horses look like ponies. Balfor's fear is obvious by the distance he tries to keep from him.

"You discovered where their home is?" Pandarus asks.

"Yes. It was simpler than I expected."

"Which part of town are we headed to then?"

"None—at least not this one. I don't know when the woman left but I know where she's going. We are riding to Padhraig."

"Padhraig? Are you sure she doesn't live here?" Balfor asks.

"Yes. And that's lucky for us because she's travelling alone. If we're fortunate we'll catch her on the road, but it matters not: she has a home on the outskirts of the village. That should make it easy to take her without anyone knowing. Apparently she has a family but we will deal with that when we arrive."

"You learned all of that in just the last few minutes?" Balfor asks.

"I've many gifts, all of which the two of you should be cautious of. There will be no more faults from here on out, am I heard?"

Balfor looks at the ground embarrassed, but Pandarus looks her in the eyes.

"Do not forget that we're here on the Emperor's behalf," she says sternly. "I can ensure success, but not without your complete obedience. Now acknowledge me."

"Yes, Kallima," they say simultaneously.

She looks at them with disdain. "Then we ride. My horse moves very fast so you must ride at your best speed."

Balfor and Pandarus exchange a concerned glance. Their payment seemed substantial when they accepted it, but now they both wonder if taking this work is an error in judgment. Still, mistake or not, they're hired trackers and will not be able to leave until the job is done successfully. Both of them have heard that the Emperor has neither the skill nor disposition for forgiveness. They follow Kallima into the night, trying their hardest to match her horse's speed.

# THE CHASE BEGINS

Evangelina is less than an hour from home when something goes dreadfully wrong. The horses are galloping at top speed when they hit a trench in the middle of the road. Baleel, the horse on the left, makes an unearthly screeching noise and moves erratically, attempting to throw himself off balance, which threatens to take the wagon with him. His behavior induces panic in Sadie, the horse on the right. The timing and circumstances happen in just the right order to create a disaster.

When Baleel panics and Sadie follows, they both pull in opposite directions at the same time. Evangelina hears several loud snaps at once and realizes it's the yoke breaking. Baleel breaks away from his restraints completely, veers left off the path and quickly goes tumbling to the ground. Eva pulls on the reins as hard as she can, but Sadie continues in a panic until Evangelina's pulling and the weight of the wagon slow her down. Evangelina turns the wagon around to get as close as she can to where Baleel has fallen but she positions the wagon in the opposite direction so that Sadie cannot see him. There's no place to tie the reins so Evangelina has to hammer a stake into the ground and tie Sadie's reins around it. Though Sadie cannot see Baleel she can hear him and his neighing is causing her distress. Evangelina strokes her main twice, trying to calm her. "Shhhhh, girl. All will be well."

She takes one of the lanterns and begins walking toward Baleel. As she passes the wagon, she hears a clicking noise and sees Kaco's face poking out of the wagon's small wooden door that serves as a window. She's not sure if he's just watching or contemplating escape.

"I've no time for this now little one," she closes the door so he can't get out. The sound Baleel is making indicates he's in great pain. Once she reaches him she holds the lantern over his legs and can see why.

"Oh my stars," she says. "Baleel … "

She can see that his front leg is broken in two places. He is neighing and shuddering from the pain. She begins petting his mane and then stops abruptly. It's disrespectful to let him lie in pain this way. She knows what has to be done, so she quickly walks back to her wagon. She grabs the dagger from her travelling bag and hesitantly walks back to Baleel. She kneels beside the horse and prays. She asks the universe for forgiveness for having to take the life of such a beautiful and kind animal, and she asks that his death be quick and painless. She grabs his mane and holds it tight in case he struggles. Then she places the dagger at his throat but she can't cut it. She stands up and steps back. For a moment and considers leaving him this way, but the thought overwhelms her with guilt and sadness.

She turns from Baleel and begins to cry. She shakes her head furiously and then suddenly starts walking along the road, looking for the place where Baleel first became erratic. She looks closely at the ground, trying to find whatever is it that could have hurt him. Then she hears him neighing again and realizes she's trying to change what has already happened. She looks at Baleel and knows that she loves him. But she also knows he's in pain.

She wipes her face and takes a deep breath. Now her eyes look sharp and focused. She has stopped crying. She walks over to him, grabs his mane tight, places the dagger at his throat and pulls across it as hard as she can. The dagger is very sharp and she has applied more pressure than was needed, but she prefers it be too much instead of not enough. That would mean more pain for Baleel and that she might have to cut him a second time. She can barely stand to do it once.

Baleel whimpers but he doesn't resist her. His blood spills from his neck and creates a mist as the warmth from it greets the cold night air. Evangelina gently strokes his mane, trying to soothe him the best she can. The horse twitches several times before he is silent. Though his eyes are open, there is no life left in them. He lies still, but continues to bleed.

Evangelina stands and looks at what she's done. She is overcome with grief but she doesn't cry again. She staggers several steps back from the horse, dizzy, feeling her last meal rising within her. She bends over and vomits in the grass.

She has no time to bury him, though she knows Vertimus and Jabneh might see him along the way and if they do they will recognize him. As she walks back to the wagon, she begins to cry again.

She does her best to mend what's left of the wagon's harness to reattach it to Sadie. Having only one horse is going to slow her down but she's not far from home. She will have to drive slower so that Sadie does not overwork herself, but it could have been much worse; she could have easily lost both horses.

She brings Kaco out of the wagon so he can sit up front with her. He lies in her lap as usual and senses her anguish. Evangelina continues to cry on her way home. She feels sad and guilty thinking of Baleel lying by the side of the trail and is certain that this will be the last time she intentionally travels alone.

* * *

The three ride as quick as they can, though Kallima has to slow her horse several times so that Pandarus and Balfor can keep up. She makes sure she combines the stops with breaks to give Maddox water. After the third stop, Balfor is exhausted.

"If we don't know when she left, and we know where she lives, why are we rushing to catch her?" Balfor asks.

"Balfor, let's hold questions for now, shall we?" It's Pandarus who speaks.

Kallima is pleased by the fear and understanding that Pandarus's question implies. She wonders if this is what the Emperor often feels and thinks of how satisfying that must be.

"Is it no matter. I do not mind explaining." Kallima looks at Balfor and speaks slowly, "Balfor—I don't know when she left, but I do know that the men we saw with her were readying themselves to join her. They also mentioned she has a family. Now, the fewer people we have to encounter the easier it will be for us to take her. Do you understand?"

Balfor nods.

"Then let us be off again," Kallima orders.

"I think my horse needs to rest a little longer," Balfor says.

"Your horse is suffering because you are heavier than us. You will ride with me and Pandarus will bring your horse, so he can move faster," Kallima says. Balfor is about to object when Pandarus interrupts him.

"Balfor, get on the blasted horse."

Balfor hands the reins of his horse to Pandarus before Kallima helps him mount Maddox. Maddox is taller than his horse so he feels nervous being further from the ground.

"I suggest you hold tight if you don't want to fall off."

"Yes, Kallima," Balfor says, his voice trembling a bit.

They head for Padhraig, hoping to catch Evangelina before dawn.

* * *

"Vertimus?" Jabneh asks as they finish securing the bags to the horses. He looks concerned.

"You look distressed," Vertimus replies. "Are you concerned about the time?"

"Yes—I mean, no. What I mean is … have you had any foretells since we found Evangelina?"

"No, why?"

"I am worried about her."

"Is it a common worry or something more specific?"

"I don't know. It's just a feeling."

"Are you sure it's worry?"

Jabneh frowns. "What's your implication?"

"Is it possible that you miss her?"

"Oh, I see. No—that's not the issue. I've a strange feeling and I can't explain it. I had the same feeling when … when my family did not return when they should have."

Vertimus considers this for a moment. "I'm not one to disregard instincts. How are you feeling—about riding?"

"I believe I'm anxious to ride."

"As am I."

"I believe it's only been a few hours since she left."

"Are you able to ride at a faster speed?"

"I am."

"Then we shall."

Jabneh retrieves the last few items he needs from the shop and bids goodbye to Nahele. Once he's finished, he and Vertimus ride toward Padhraig, both eager to reunite with Evangelina.

\* \* \*

It's just before dawn when Evangelina pulls the wagon into the path toward the stable. The final hour of her trip took nearly two because she had to brake often to let Sadie rest, but she was impressed with the horse's stamina. She stays and pets her for a while before putting her away. She gives her apple pieces as well and thanks her for getting them both home safely. She passes Baleel's stable and sees his water and food bucket. She feels heartbroken at the thought of having to tell everyone.

She opens the wagon doors to move only the things she will be taking with her on the next trip—her coin, the meat and bread and so forth—when she realizes it's not urgent that it be done now. She leaves the wagon and all its contents in the stable and locks the wagon doors but she leaves the stable doors unlocked. She remembers that Kaco is in the wagon, so she opens the small door that acts as a window and calls to him. She decides she will ask Vertimus or Jabneh to help her empty the wagon later.

The only things she takes with her are her travelling bag that holds the speared gem, the stone and the dagger. She removes Kaco's harness and sets him on the ground. He immediately runs toward the house and waits for her impatiently by the front door.

When Evangelina unlocks her door she is surprised to see everyone is awake.

"Mother!" Tahvi shouts and limps toward her as fast as he can. He hugs her furiously, and when she hugs him back they both begin to cry.

Kaco runs in ahead of Evangelina. It's Sheree who sees him first.

"Kaco!"

He runs to her and she picks him up and begins petting him. "We've been searching for you, little one."

"I didn't know he was in the wagon when I left," Evangelina explains, still holding Tahvi.

"You left without telling anyone!" he cries. He is nearly panic-stricken. She has never seen him like this before.

"I am sorry, Tahvi. I promise to never do it again."

"I had a dream that told me I might be wrong about the stones!" he says, speaking loudly. "They might not be buried or where I thought they were. The map shows their origin, but they could have been taken, or ... " Tahvi stops when he realizes his mother is nodding. "You know?"

"Yes."

"But how?"

Evangelina reaches into her pocket and shows him the second stone.

"You found it!" Humbul says excitedly.

"Was it in the ground?" Tahvi asks.

"No. A wayfarer had it, a very unpleasant woman. But it's ours now."

Tahvi holds her again. He seems to not notice the stone.

"Are you not overjoyed to see it?" she asks.

"I am overjoyed to see you."

To her surprise, Tahvi asks to hear about her trip before being reunited with his stone.

Sephine explains that he had several spells while she was gone and so he spent more time than usual sleeping.

Everyone's sleep schedule has been slightly disrupted since the day they celebrated Tahvi's birth and they have been keeping strange hours since then. So they sit and break fast and Evangelina tells the story about Baldric. Kaco moves from Sheree's lap to Tahvi's while Evangelina recounts the events.

When Evangelina mentions that she had seen Sabina and had to avoid her, this saddens Sheree, who shares that she wishes she had been there to see Sabina perform. But it makes Sheree happy to hear about Sabina.

Evangelina is honest about Baleel being injured but because the children are present, she tells them that she had to leave him in

Violetta because his injury was too serious for him to return home. Though the children seem confused, they believe her. But Tahvi and Sephine know Evangelina is not being completely honest and the way Tahvi looks at her makes her feel like he may have guessed the truth. There is a look of sadness in his eyes that matches what she's feeling. It makes her feel scared yet strangely comforted.

Then Tahvi shows her the hand that Vertimus and Jabneh adjusted for him. He has used it for several tasks and its functionality is quite impressive. He tells his mother about some of the things he has already learned to do with it and that sometimes everyone laughs when it doesn't work. It will take Tahvi some time to become familiar with how to work the levers and switches.

"Well, you may not get the chance to use it much longer. Are you ready to begin?" Evangelina asks.

"Almost," Tahvi says. He puts Kaco on the ground and then opens the door to let him outside. "He needs time to wander. He is unsettled from being trapped in the wagon for so long."

She walks with Tahvi to his room and he sits on his bed, ready to be joined with the stone.

\* \* \*

Kallima, Balfor and Pandarus are making good time. They do not have to stay directly on the wagon trail as they're riding horseback, so they avoid the curvatures of the trail as often as possible. Because of this they do not see Baleel by the side of the road. At this rate they're on track to be in Padhraig shortly before dawn. Kallima plans to visit any house on the outskirts of the village until she finds the one that belongs to Evangelina.

\* \* \*

Jabneh and Vertimus are also making good time. Like the trio pursuing Evangelina, they don't follow all the curvatures in the trail but they still stick closely by it, to lessen the risk of injury to themselves and their horses. When they're nearly halfway to Padhraig, Jabneh spots something near the trail.

"Did you see that?" he asks Vertimus.

"See what?"

Jabneh forces his horse to stop. Vertimus follows suit. "There was a dark pile back there, by the side of the trail."

"And you want to stop to examine it?"

"Yes."

"Why?"

Jabneh knows this is a reasonable question, but does not have a reasonable answer. "It's just a feeling. A feeling that tells me I should check."

"I understand. Do you need my help?"

"No, I would just like to look quickly."

"I will wait here then."

Jabneh rides back the way they had come. They passed it by maybe thirty meters so it doesn't take long to reach it. He gets off his horse and is sure he knows what it is before he approaches it.

"Whoa," he says to his horse. He lights a small torch and holds it in one hand as he holds his horse's reins in the other. He walks closer to the pile and sees that it's indeed a dead horse. As he moves the torch closer he recognizes it as one of Evangelina's. He is almost sure it's Baleel. The harness used to connect the horse to the wagon is gone. He moves the torch over the horse's body and sees that Baleel's leg is broken. Then he moves the torch further up the body near its head and sees his throat has been cut.

"Vertimus!" he shouts.

Vertimus rides back quickly to meet him. Jabneh holds the torch up and looks around. Though the moonlight illuminates the night well enough for him to see a short distance in front of him, it's no match for the darkness beyond that space. He sees no indication that Evangelina's wagon or her other horse are anywhere to be found, and he wonders if this is reason for joy or despair.

\* \* \*

Kallima has stopped at two homes since arriving at Padhraig and neither is Evangelina's. She is frustrated and tired but her spirits lift when she arrives at the third house. She doesn't even need to dismount her horse to know she's at the right place; there is an energy here that she has never felt before. She is having difficulty absorbing and translating it. But when she sees the house, she is convinced, as it has a design similar to Evangelina's wagon. She remembers admiring the intricate craftsmanship when she saw it previously. The same intricate designs show on different parts of the house. As strange as this is, it's a wayfarer style of woodwork. *Evangelina is not a true wayfarer, but someone in her family must be*, she thinks.

"There," Kallima points toward the stable. "We should tie the horses there."

"We won't be making a camp here?" Balfor asks.

"We won't be staying that long," Kallima replies.

They ride quietly to the stable and tie their horses securely on the side facing away from the house. It's just after dawn. Kallima peeks inside the door of the stable and is relieved to see Evangelina's wagon inside.

"This is definitely the house," she says to Balfor and Pandarus, who both peek through the barn to see the wagon.

"She must be readying for another trip," Balfor says.

"It's good we caught up with her before she left again," Pandarus replies.

"She is leaving again sooner than she realizes," Kallima says with a wicked smirk.

# UNINVITED GUESTS

"Are you comfortable?" Evangelina asks.

"Yes," Tahvi replies with a smile.

His mother helps him remove his new hand and the forged leg he still has attached to his body. She also removes his tunic, anticipating that the garment may burn as it did before. He lies flat on his back and his mother places the rock on his chest. Tahvi puts his hand over it and looks at his mother.

"We will stay with you while you ... be," she says softly.

"You remembered what it wants me to do."

"Are you impressed?"

"I am," Tahvi says through laughter.

Tahvi doesn't say anything further. He just smiles at her, looking as though he feels very safe and content, then closes his eyes. Several minutes pass and then his breathing becomes slower and deeper. He takes long inhales and exhales. Evangelina feels relief just watching him. Humbul and Sheree, anticipating the process will last a long time as it did the previous time, have brought chairs of their own, and Tahvi's bed resembles a stage more than a place for rest.

Evangelina can see the muscles in his body become less tense as his shoulders drop closer to the bed. His real foot is relaxed so much that his little toe is touching the bed as well—she does not remember seeing this reaction when he was reunited with his first stone. Except for Tahvi's breathing, there is a heavy silence in the room until Humbul speaks to offer an observation.

"It seems to be happening much faster this time."

"I remember it being just as slow," Sheree said. She is holding her necklace in one hand and feeling the stone with the other, but her eyes are focused on Tahvi.

"But it's hot and Tahvi's breathing is already different."

Sephine and Evangelina look at each other. "Do you think it means anything?" Evangelina asks her.

"I don't know. Maybe the more pieces he has, the better his body will function. But if that's true then I'm not sure why he's had more spells."

"You were right, Humbul. It is happening again. Look!" Sheree says emphatically but not loudly.

The green flecks in the stone begin to glow and move. They begin swirling around the inside of the stone, like fish caught in an underwater net. Tahvi's breathing increases in speed as the green specks inside the mass swirl faster. Sweat starts to soak through the clothing on the lower half of Tahvi's body and spreads to his sheets. Evangelina promptly soaks a towel in a bowl of cool water and puts it on Tahvi's sweat-beaded forehead. The four of them wait with grave anticipation and it's not long before the crackling noise comes and the stone splits open. Like before, the green liquid inside turns into a smoke-like substance and vanishes within him, leaving only the familiar tiny metallic black grains on his sweat-soaked chest. Everyone holds their breath, waiting to see where the crystal chamber will form. They stare at the stump where the wrist should be but nothing appears there. Sephine notices the translucent crystal cocoon begin forming on his stump of a leg and points at it.

"There!" she says excitedly.

Everyone's gaze follows her finger to the mass as it grows from Tahvi's lower thigh down to what would be his ankle. The swirling storm continues inside the translucent mass.

"Do you hear it?" Sephine asks as the unusual sound of squishing and crunching start again. Evangelina recalls how in awe she was when Tahvi grew his elbow and lower arm, and now she can hardly believe that he's going to have a second leg. Tears begin forming in her eyes.

"I thought it would be easier to believe seeing it a second time, but it seems even more unreal," Evangelina says.

"I wish I could touch it. Just to see what it feels like," Humbul says.

"I would advise against it, Humbul. We have no stones to replace your fingers," Evangelina says.

Her comment surprises and frightens him just a bit, but when he looks at her she gives him a wink and then holds him close to her. They all continue to watch as Tahvi's leg forms right in front of them.

Humbul is indeed correct: the process began faster this time, though the entire process lasts a little longer. No one can avert their eyes, and each person is able to notice something different. Evangelina notices how calm Tahvi is despite his labored breathing and his temperature. She remembers being scared before that the process might injure him and now she is not afraid. Sephine notices the metallic grains are twinkling. They express several different colors and they seem almost alive, like fireflies instead of metallic dust. Humbul notices that the swirling is not random, as he previously believed. It's very hazy, making it hard to see the pattern, but after looking closely and long enough he sees that the swirls are forming a series of elongated eights. They vary in size each time but there is a definite pattern in them. Sheree notices the heat has a specific direction. The whole room is warmer of course, but there are certain areas that are hotter than others. She asks Evangelina if she can feel the area around Tahvi as long as she doesn't touch the cocoon around his leg, and Evangelina gives her permission to do so. Sheree feels the heat increase in specific areas around Tahvi.

When the process is finished, the cocoon dissipates, and underneath is Tahvi's new leg. He has a knee and a leg that extends nearly to the ankle, where it forms a flat surface just as his arm had. Evangelina puts her hand on it. It's still very warm to the touch. Like his arm, the bones in his leg are fully formed and are held in a socket right above what she assumes is a bony plate. *A placeholder for the next piece,* she thinks. Tahvi is still sleeping and Evangelina can hardly wait for him to awaken.

Suddenly the light in the room changes and they realize the sun star is higher in the sky.

"Vertimus and Jabneh should be here soon. They'll be amazed when they see this. I'm amazed to see this," Evangelina says.

"They'll likely be famished. I'll prepare more food for them to break fast. Is your wagon in the stable?"

"Yes, and some personal things that I will need to transport to the other wagon but it doesn't have to be done now. I'll be resting so that Jabneh and I are on the same schedule before we leave."

"Very well. Humbul, I'll need your help in the cooking room."

"But I want to stay until Tahvi awakens," Humbul pleads. Before he can continue to protest his mother gives him a look that makes it clear protesting is not a good idea.

"Sheree, please stay with Evangelina in case she needs anything."

Sheree nods.

Sephine enters the cooking room followed by a reluctant Humbul.

"Can I sit with Tahvi after I'm done helping?"

"Not right away. I'll need your help clearing out the wagon and ensuring they have everything they need for their next trip. It's mostly done but it's a good idea to check inventory one last time."

"Evangelina is leaving again?"

"Yes, and Jabneh."

"But she just came back!"

"I'm aware, but they're leaving tomorrow regardless and we will help to ensure they're prepared."

Humbul scoffs but he does as he's told. Occasionally, he continues to look back toward Tahvi's room, wondering if the boy is awake yet.

* * *

Sheree asks if she can feel the bony plate at the bottom of Tahvi's new leg and Evangelina permits it.

"Are we to take his old leg apart now as we did with his arm?"

Evangelina looks at her curiously. "Take it apart?"

"That's how we were able to fix Tahvi's hand: the limb that Jabneh brought for Tahvi's gift was adjustable. We were able to take it apart and make it a different size so that it would fit his new arm better. I'll show you."

Sheree walks to the trunk near Tahvi's bed and removes the forged arm that used to be attached to Tahvi's new forged hand. Evangelina notices that some of the strapping has been removed.

"How did you know how to do this?" Evangelina asks.

"Oh, it wasn't me. Vertimus and Jabneh did it. I helped but mostly I watched."

"Can you bring me his leg from atop the trunk?"

Sheree brings Evangelina the leg so she can examine it. "We'll have to take it apart," Sheree says, "He's going to need a new foot since the old leg will not work for him anymore."

Tahvi begins to stir in his bed and both of them notice immediately. Evangelina wets the towel again and brushes his face with it. She's pleased to see his temperature is nearly back to normal. Once he's completely awake, he begins examining his new limb with great fascination. With his real hand, he carefully probes the surface of the new part of his leg. He is able to feel sensation in every area and his skin responds by turning to gooseflesh everywhere he touches.

Tahvi giggles and like before, his eyes begin to tear when he realizes he's witnessing a miracle. Suddenly he remembers he's not alone and looks up and smiles at his mother and Sheree.

"I can feel everything," he says.

"It's wonderful, Tahvi," Sheree says. Her heart filled with happiness for him.

"Now I need to learn how to wear a slip-shoe on the end of it."

They all laugh at this and then Evangelina adds, "Sheree and I were just speaking about this. We are planning to take your forged leg apart and adjust the foot portion, the same way it was done to make just a hand from your old arm."

"There is no reason we can't. Jabneh said we have all the tools we need in your workroom," Sheree says.

"May we work on it now?" Tahvi asks.

"Do you feel well enough?" Evangelina replies.

"Yes, although I am very thirsty. And hungry."

"You can eat in the workroom. Can you ask your mother for some food and drink and bring it back with you?"

Sheree nods and leaves the room immediately.

As soon as Tahvi sits up the metallic grains fall off his body and onto his bed. Everyone had forgotten about those. His mother helps him gather as many as she can and then puts them in the jar with the others by his bed. He looks around to see if any are missing and realizes that he doesn't have to search for them. He opens the lid again and concentrates. There are many left on the bed and a few had fallen on the floor. At Tahvi's request, they allow him to lift them into the air and then glide into the jar. His mother watches him as he closes the lid but she doesn't speak. She merely smiles.

Evangelina hands Tahvi his forged leg and then lifts him so that he doesn't have to walk on the stump of his new one. She carries Tahvi to her underground workroom, sits him on one of the chairs, then sets his leg on the table.

When Sheree reaches the cooking room she is very excited. She mentions Evangelina's request for food and drink, and Sephine gives her some fresh bread, juice, water and meat.

"Tahvi is awake, then?" Humbul asks.

"Yes. They're in the workroom. We are to fashion him a new foot the way that Vertimus and Jabneh fashioned him a new hand. And she's trusting me to help!"

Sheree disappears back the way she came and Humbul looks up at his mother, the disappointment showing clearly on his face.

"I know that you desperately want to be with them."

Humbul nods.

"We must finish quickly, then, so that you can." Humbul smiles and begins to work faster.

In the workroom Evangelina, Tahvi and Sheree work diligently to remove the pieces they need from the forged leg. They remove the leather straps and clasps that will be used to keep the foot attached to the leg but they still have to remove only the forged foot from the rest of the leg. Evangelina tries gently to pry the bolts off.

"You will need more pressure than that," Sheree tells her. "Jabneh built it well so they're very secure."

Evangelina reluctantly applies more pressure until finally the bolts break free and the foot comes loose.

"You see?" Sheree says. "More pressure."

"I was afraid to damage it," Evangelina says kindly.

"Now we need to see how many panels we have to take away to make it the right size for his calf, punch new holes in the straps, attach the foot and we can buckle it on."

Evangelina kneels to measure the diameter of the area around his ankle. As she does the crystal spear in her pocket pokes her in the leg. She stands up, removes it from her pocket and lays it on the table next to the oil lamp. Then she kneels again and puts what was previously the thigh cup around Tahvi's calf and discovers that they need to remove three panels. After some adjustments they're able to cut it to the right size to make it fit perfectly. Then they measure the straps to determine where to punch them so that the cup will buckle securely to Tahvi's leg. Sheree gets the punch and the hammer.

"I will punch the holes!" Sheree says excitedly.

* * *

Kallima approaches the front door of Evangelina's home. She orders Balfor and Pandarus to stand on either side of the door, with their backs flat against the wall of the house. She asks in a whisper if they're ready and each responds with a quick nod. Then she knocks on the door and waits patiently.

Sephine is on her way to the workroom when she hears the knocking at the door. She tells Humbul to answer it, knowing it's likely Vertimus and Jabneh. When she walks into the workroom Tahvi's forged leg is in pieces on the worktable.

"That doesn't look like progress, but I'm sure it is," Sephine says.

"It is. We are nearly finished!" Sheree responds.

Evangelina is concentrating so hard that she doesn't look up.

"Do you ladies need anything?"

"Are you thirsty, Evangelina?" Sheree asks.

Evangelina says yes but she doesn't take her eyes off her work.

"I will bring more water. I think Jabneh and Vertimus have returned." As Sephine speaks she finds herself moving closer to the worktable. After several minutes, instead of fetching water, she is just as focused on Tahvi's forged foot as Evangelina is.

* * *

Humbul opens the door and sees a beautiful woman standing in front of it.

She speaks before he's able to say anything. "Hello, handsome boy."

Humbul hears her voice and instantly becomes drowsy.

"What's your name?" the woman asks.

"Humbul," he says, surprised to feel his lips moving.

"Will you step outside so that I may speak with you, Humbul?"

Humbul feels his body begin to move as if something is pulling him towards the woman. He wants to go outside but he doesn't know why. As he walks he keeps stopping. He thinks about turning back, but as he continues to see the woman he feels happy and eager to obey her.

"My name is Kallima," she says.

Humbul hears the last vowel sound trail off, *Kallimaaaaaaaa*. Then he hears the name as an echo and looks around to see who else has said it.

Kallima looks at Pandarus and says, "The children are always much easier."

"Humbul, how many people are in the house?" Kallima asks.

"Four," he answers flatly.

"Does that include you?"

"No. Five. Five people."

"Thank you, Humbul. You're doing very well. You're a good boy." Humbul tries to smile but has trouble controlling the muscles in his face.

"Can you tell me who they are?"

"My mother, sister ... Evangelina, Tahvi."

"Who is Tahvi?"

"My friend."

"Is he a man?"

"No, a boy."

"A boy like you?"

"Yes ... no ... smaller."

"Is this Evangelina's house?"

"Yes."

Kallima is pleased. This is going to be easier than she'd hoped.

"Can you tell me where everyone is in the house?" Kallima asks.

"Mother is in cooking room. Evangelina, Tahvi, sister in ... workroom, making foot."

"Making foot?" Kallima looks at Pandarus.

"Maybe you should lower the flame on the spell," Pandarus says in a low voice.

"Quiet!" Kallima snaps at him. "I need to know where these rooms are in the house."

Humbul covers his mouth with both hands.

"Oh, not you, Humbul. I don't want you to be quiet."

Suddenly they hear a woman's voice from inside the house. The door is open but she sounds far away.

"Humbul, who's at the door?" Sephine yells from the doorway of the workroom.

He opens his mouth to answer his mother and Kallima covers it before he can. "You will sleep now," Kallima whispers in Humbul's ear. His body relaxes into a deep sleep immediately. She lays him down on the ground and moves closer to the door.

"Humbul, can you hear me calling to you?" Sephine walks toward the door at the front of the house and sees that Humbul has left it open. She reaches the doorway and sees Kallima standing just on the other side of it. Then she sees Humbul lying in the grass.

"Humbul!" Sephine reaches for him but before she can get to him the trackers grab her from behind and cover her mouth. Though Humbul is still sleeping, they bind and gag both of them. They attempt to put them in the wagon but discover the doors are locked. Instead, they leave them inside the stable and close the doors.

* * *

In the workroom, Tahvi's modified foot is coming together nicely but it's not quite tight enough.

"I am going to punch another set of holes in the three straps and that should make it fit much better."

Tahvi nods.

"Sheree, we're nearly done here. Why don't you check to see if your mother needs any help?" Evangelina suggests.

Sheree does as she's asked and walks quickly to the cooking room, where the house appears to be empty. She pauses for a moment and listens to see if she can tell which part of the house they're in but she can't hear them.

Finally she calls to them. "Mother? Humbul? Where are you?"

She sees the open door and remembers that Vertimus and Jabneh had just arrived and they're likely in the stable. She walks outside and Kallima is standing just beyond the door.

"Who are you?" Sheree asks.

"You must be Humbul's sister. You look like your brother, but only a little."

Sheree feels confused and disoriented. She shakes her head and puts her arms out to keep her balance.

"Come closer to me. I have some questions for you."

Sheree can hear the woman, but she sounds muffled and fuzzy.

"Where is the workroom? Where are Tahvi and Evangelina?"

Sheree speaks without realizing it, "Making … a … foot."

Kallima gives Sheree a strange look. *What's the matter with these children?* she thinks.

Sheree can feel something is not right. She tries to run but she can't feel her feet and she trips over them, landing hard in the grass.

"Pick her up," Kallima orders Balfor. "Take her to the barn. Secure her with the others and then return. We're going to have to find the workroom ourselves. We must be quick about it."

* * *

Tahvi sits patiently on the chair while his mother secures the final buckle that holds his foot on.

"How does that feel now?" she asks.

He moves his new leg and the false foot moves along with it. It doesn't move with the same mobility as his real leg, but it has the functionality that he needs. Tahvi will still have a limp but she suspects he will be able to move much faster than before. He may even be able to run.

"It feels comfortable."

"Is it secure?"

Tahvi puts his foot on the ground and presses on it. "Yes, I believe so. Shall I stand on it?"

"Yes, try that."

Evangelina puts a slip-shoe over it and stands back so Tahvi has room to walk when he stands up from the chair. Tahvi hops off the chair and begins to walk around near the furthest end of the room. His mother follows him in case the foot is not secure and he loses his balance. They do not hear Kallima or the trackers moving quietly down the stairs toward the workroom.

"Oh no!" Tahvi exclaims.

"What's the matter?" Evangelina asks.

"We forgot the rice bag. Sheree said it is mostly for comfort, but it will also keep the wood from—"

"I can't believe I forgot," Evangelina interrupts him. "It's to keep the wood from absorbing moisture."

Tahvi nods.

She motions for him to walk toward her. As he does he sees Kallima in the doorway. The look in his eyes reveals fear and confusion and Evangelina quickly turns around, moving herself directly in front of him. Kallima walks further into the room and the trackers follow closely behind her. Tahvi moves closer to his mother and grabs ahold of her dress. The table is between them and he sees the crystal spear next to the lamp. He quickly averts his eyes so no one sees what he's looking at.

"Mother, who are these people?" Tahvi asks.

"Why are you in our home?" Evangelina asks.

Kallima doesn't bother to answer her. "Take them both ... now," she says.

The three of them approach the table that divides the room. Evangelina looks at the table and sees the spear she had neglected to put back in her pocket. Kallima's eyes follow hers and she notices it as well. They both begin to move for it at the same time. As Evangelina reaches for the spear, Balfor and Pandarus are already moving toward her, each moving on opposite sides of the table.

Just as Kallima is about to grab the end of the spear before Evangelina does, the spear flies through the air and Tahvi catches it, moving in front of his mother. As he holds it, Evangelina grabs him around the waist.

"You will not hurt my mother," Tahvi says calmly, as if pandemonium has not broken out in the room. He says it in his own childlike voice but something about it frightens Kallima and she takes several steps back.

Suddenly the spear begins to glow and Kallima feels a change in the atmosphere around her. Heedless, the two trackers advance on Evangelina and Tahvi when Kallima stops moving. Evangelina pulls her son backwards while he's still pointing the spear at Kallima.

Then the air around the three intruders begins to solidify and becomes a translucent stone.

Kallima and Pandarus are frozen where they stand but Balfor, who is leaning forward, with only one foot on the ground, topples over in his stone prison. He falls down with a heavy crash on the end of the table and the weight of it lifts the other side of the table in the air, making everything fly off the table at once, including the oil lamp. The glass cracks when it hits the shelves and the flame races across the room. It instantly engulfs anything it touches and begins to spread so fast that even the wooden shelves begin to catch fire.

Evangelina stares at the intruders, wondering at their imprisonment. Then she feels Tahvi tugging on her dress and notices the room is filling with smoke.

"Tahvi!" she yells. Forgetting his newfound mobility, she picks him up and runs out of the room.

"Wait, I have to get my jar!" he yells.

"There's no time!" She carries him out of the house through the blaze. They make it safely to the front yard when Evangelina considers going back inside to save whatever she can.

Then she remembers the small barrel of oil that she keeps in the workroom.

Just then, there is an explosion and they watch in horror as the middle of their home collapses over the workroom and fire lights up the clear morning sky.

"Mother, where is everyone?" Tahvi asks.

Evangelina looks at him and then at the house. "No!" she cries.

Evangelina falls to her knees and holds Tahvi close to her. "They can't be inside, Tahvi. Pray that they aren't inside." Her eyes fill with tears and she can feel Tahvi shaking as he begins to cry with her.

He pulls away from her suddenly. "Mother, look!" he says.

Evangelina turns in the direction Tahvi is pointing and sees Sheree, Humbul and Sephine running from the barn, Kaco running ahead of them. Tahvi limps toward them.

Evangelina sits on the ground, crying, feeling gratitude that her prayers were answered and despair about their home.

When Sephine reaches Evangelina she helps her stand so she can move her farther away from the house. They hold each other.

"Where were you?" Evangelina asks Sephine.

"In the barn. Two men and a woman tied us up and left us there."

"When?"

"Not very long ago. We would still be there if Kaco hadn't

chewed through the ropes. Where did they go?"

Evangelina signals toward the house.

"The woman too?" Sephine asks.

Evangelina nods. "They couldn't have survived the fire." After she says this, she looks at Tahvi.

Sheree, Humbul and Tahvi are standing just behind Evangelina and Sephine. Tahvi is rubbing Kaco behind the ears, praising him for helping his family.

"They're not dead," Tahvi says.

"They're not?" Evangelina asks.

"They're … waiting."

Evangelina walks to Tahvi and kneels in front of him. "Tahvi, they're in stone. They can't breathe in—"

"It's not stone. It's a shielded blend of air and water. That's why we could see through it. It's as if they're sleeping. In several hours' time, the blend will dissipate and release them."

"How can you know this?"

"Because I've done it before, with stinging flies."

"Tahvi, I've not seen you do that." Sheree says.

"It's not something I've shown you."

Evangelina holds her son tightly, not knowing exactly what to say. She only knows that she feels an enormous sense of relief.

"I'm sorry if I scared you, Mother. I didn't know how else to help us."

"It's all well, Tahvi. I'm glad that they'll be … but wait, what about the fire?"

Tahvi shakes his head. "It can't harm the blend, so it can't harm them."

Just then the roof over Tahvi's room collapses. Tahvi stares at it as a wave of grief sweeps through him and he begins to cry. Evangelina holds him and does her best to console him, but she is weeping as well. There is nothing they can do but watch their home burn.

"The jar of grains. They were in my room," Tahvi whimpers.

"Wait!" Humbul shouts. He runs to the barn, grabs a leather pouch with a drawstring at the top, and brings it back to Tahvi.

"All you have to do is call to them, yes? If they didn't burn when they landed, how can they burn now?"

Tahvi is wiping his nose when he stops suddenly. He realizes

Humbul is right. Tahvi gives Humbul a brief but strong hug, then opens the pouch and points the open end at the house. He concentrates. Nothing happens at first. Then, what looks like thousands of pieces of glimmering ash rise out of the fire. They swarm together and then the swarm moves in his direction. In a most orderly fashion they form a long line that allows them to easily enter the pouch. When the last grain is inside, Tahvi pulls the drawstring closed and clutches the precious bag of grains close to him.

The fire has engulfed Evangelina's workroom and the rooms directly above it, including Tahvi's room, though it has not spread to the rest of the house yet. Everyone stands close to one another, watching the massive flames. There is nothing they can do to stop the fire—even if they had enough water, there are not enough of them present to help put out the flames.

"It's burning away," Sheree says, unable take her eyes from the fire.

Humbul is the only one who notices the horses. From behind them, he sees them approaching with great speed.

Vertimus and Jabneh are riding as fast as the horses will allow them to. They had seen the fire from a distance and had known that it must be coming from Evangelina's home. When they reach Evangelina and the rest of the group, they quickly dismount their horses.

"What happened?" Vertimus asks. He begins to take a count of everyone before waiting for an answer. Once he realizes everyone is safe he rushes to Evangelina, whose eyes are fixed on the fire. He turns her to him.

"Eva, what happened!" he asks again. This time his voice is louder, his tone firmer.

Evangelina looks at him, her eyes glossy, and says, "They tried to … to take Tahvi or the spear, I don't know. Tahvi stopped them. But … I don't know."

Vertimus lets her go and kneels in front of Tahvi. He grabs him the same way he grabbed Evangelina just moments before.

"Tahvi, do you remember what you told me about the fire?" Vertimus asks.

"I didn't intend to start it. I was trying to stop them from harming us," Tahvi says, still watching the fire. His voice is cracking, tears falling from his eyes.

Vertimus stares at him, confused. He realizes Tahvi is in shock and that he doesn't understand his question.

Vertimus turns the boy's head so that Tahvi is facing him. He takes the pouch from Tahvi's hands and sets it on the ground. Then Vertimus looks Tahvi in the eyes and puts his hands on the side of Tahvi's head and says, "Tahvi, I want you to listen to my voice. Fix your attention on what I'm saying. Can you hear me?"

Tahvi nods.

"Do you remember what you told me about the fire? The one you created on the morning of your celebration?"

"Yes," Tahvi whimpers.

"Good. One of your gifts allows you to partner with things. Those things include the elements. Do you remember?"

"Yes," Tahvi responds. When he speaks it sounds like a reflex, as though he hasn't really thought about the question. Then his head twitches and his eyes widen. He grabs hold of his uncle. The realization, or recollection rather, sends a shudder through his body and he almost topples over.

"You think I can stop it?" Tahvi asks.

"I'm not sure. But you must try, yes?"

Tahvi doesn't answer him. He lets go of his uncle and takes a few steps closer to the house. He looks at the fire, *into* the fire. He watches the flames, taking a moment to appreciate them. They move with such force, even though there's no wind to carry them. He notices the different colors: yellow, orange, brown and even specks of black in some places. The fire behaves differently depending on where he looks. The flames at the bottom don't seem to move as much, but the flames at the top … parts of them seem angry. Others are dancing fiercely, like they've been waiting for years to celebrate something. Tahvi closes his eyes and breathes deeply. In Tahvi's mind, the fire becomes smaller. It takes on the shape of a boy his size, but the form is not as defined. Its arms and legs are long limbs of flames. They begin to walk side by side, then Tahvi holds one of the hand-like limbs. It feels warm but it doesn't burn him. The fire seems happy to have company. It skips and holds its other hand-limb up to Tahvi. It's trying to tell him something but Tahvi can't understand. He listens closely until he hears a strange sound, like the sound he makes when he tries to talk under water.

Though the fire doesn't speak in words, Tahvi begins to

understand it and communicate with it. As he does, the fire-boy gets larger and larger until it's nearly the size of a house. Tahvi is still holding its hand but it feels cooler now and its color is starting to change. Tahvi can see specks of blue and white in random places throughout its shape. They flutter, like small pieces of papery falling from the sky.

* * *

Evangelina had heard Vertimus speaking to her son. Now she kneels beside Tahvi and watches as he uses whatever magical gift he has. The others watch too, waiting to see if Tahvi will be able to stop the fire. Tahvi's breathing has increased and he's sweating.

Sheree notices that Evangelina is nervous and she walks over to console her.

"This is how he looks when he does it," Sheree says.

"When he uses his … influence?" Evangelina asks.

"Yes."

"Have you ever seen it hurt him? When he uses it does it hurt him?"

"No. Sometimes it makes him tired," Sheree says. She reaches out to Evangelina and hugs her. Evangelina returns her affection.

"Do you see it?" It's Jabneh who asks the question.

Everyone looks at the fire except Tahvi, whose eyes are closed. They collectively see what Jabneh sees. The fire stops moving, as if it's been petrified. It lasts several seconds—just long enough for them to know it happened but abrupt enough for them to already start to doubt it.

When it begins to move again, it starts to shrink.

Evangelina rises slowly and begins walking closer to the house. She grabs hold of her dress with both hands but she can barely feel the material on her fingers. She thinks maybe she's dreaming. She watches the fire as it gets smaller, but it's the way it gets smaller that stuns her: it looks like the fire is being sucked into the ground. It wisps, turns and undulates with the same ferociousness that it had when it was ravaging the house, but now it does so on a lesser scale. As it dwindles it moves like a tornado, its force whipping up ash and debris as it rotates. The only things unburned and unmoving, in what used to be the workroom beneath the house, are the large, almost clear structures encasing the three uninvited guests.

Evangelina feels pressure around her arm. When she looks to her left Vertimus is standing beside her, trying to stop her movement. She hadn't realized how much closer she was to the house.

"Please don't go any further. The smoke can do as much damage as the fire," Vertimus says.

She turns to meet his glance and when she looks back at the house, the fire is gone. Much of the wood is still smoking, but even that is quickly dissipating. She looks at her son, whose eyes are still closed. He's sweating, but his breathing has returned to normal. Sheree and Humbul are standing close to him, looking like they've positioned themselves to catch him.

*How many times have they seen him do this?* she thinks.

Tahvi opens his eyes, using them to confirm what his mind already knows: that the fire is gone.

Vertimus walks over, kneels by his side and says, "You stopped it, Tahvi."

"I did," Tahvi says, just before falling into his uncle's arms.

* * *

Everyone is relieved to learn that Tahvi is not having another spell—it's clear that he's just exhausted. Though there's a lot of smoke, everyone has a view into the workroom, where they can partially see the three people trapped inside what look like clear stones. Still in disbelief, Evangelina gives a brief explanation of the events that led to the fire.

"The people there—you did that to them?" Vertimus asks his nephew.

"Yes," Tahvi answers.

"You should be proud of yourself for protecting your family."

"But I'm not proud," he says sadly. "I'm at fault."

Tahvi looks at the charred remains of their home and the parts that aren't burned. *It looks like a giant has taken a bite out of it*, he thinks. He's trembling. The trembling increases until he almost falls to his knees. Vertimus catches him before he does.

"Tahvi, you can't blame yourself for something you had no part in beginning," Vertimus says. "I'm not sure why these people are here, but I'm sure their intentions aren't benevolent. Do you believe that?"

"Yes," Tahvi answers.

"Then you must not accept blame for what had to happen. You, your mother and everyone are safe. That's what matters most. And if it were not for you, dear boy, the fire would have claimed your entire home. Do you agree?"

"Yes," Tahvi says. He turns toward his mother and she holds him.

"Vertimus, the woman is from Baldric. She's the one who sold the stone to me."

"Kallima?"

"Yes."

"Who were the men?"

"I have no idea. I hadn't seen them before today."

Vertimus looks at the men, trying to gauge their origins by how they're dressed and what they're carrying but Tahvi's "blend" isn't transparent enough for him to gather the details he is hoping to get.

"They must have tracked you here. If they were following you, I believe you would've noticed. Either way, they didn't come on foot, so their horses have to be close by. Let's see if we can find them."

It's Vertimus who sees the horses first, tied behind the barn. All of the adults except Evangelina are with him and they stop when they notice the gargantuan black horse.

"Look at that horse!" Humbul shouts and begins to run towards it.

"No, Humbul!" Vertimus stops Humbul when he's about five meters from the horses, "We know nothing about this horse and its master isn't here. Are you to approach a horse if its master is absent?"

"No, but … " Humbul stops without finishing his sentence. He knows Vertimus is right. He remembers that horses can be dangerous, especially if someone has trained them to be so. A horse of this size is likely even more dangerous.

"I can see by the look in your eyes that you remember now," Vertimus says.

"I've just … I've never seen a horse of this size."

"I know."

Vertimus asks everyone except Jabneh to wait while he approaches the horses. At Vertimus' request, Jabneh has brought some sliced apples. He walks near Vertimus and hands them to him as Vertimus asks for them.

The large black horse is the farthest from them, so Vertimus and Jabneh approach the other two first. They're both very friendly, eating the apple slices docilely as Vertimus sifts through their saddlebags. He finds three items in one of the saddlebags that he removes and gives to Jabneh. After Jabneh looks at the items he looks back at Vertimus, who can see the concern in Jabneh's eyes. Then Vertimus hands him a piece of leather from the saddlebag.

"Please wrap them in this," Vertimus says. Jabneh does as he's asked.

Vertimus approaches the large, dark horse slowly. He's close enough to see that the horse is male. When he's about two meters away, the horse starts to neigh and shuffle. It pulls on the reins, which are tied to a stake anchored in the ground, to move further away from him. Vertimus tries to coax the animal with the apple slices in his hand, but the horse continues to neigh and shakes his head back and forth.

Vertimus takes two smaller steps closer, moving even slower then he did before. The horse stops neighing. It stands its ground and beats its front hoof on the ground twice, with its ears pinned back. It makes a gruff braying sound and stares at Vertimus. The other horses move as far from the black horse as their reins will allow.

Vertimus stops, knowing he will not be able to approach the horse.

"Whoa, whoa," Vertimus says in a gentle voice as he begins to back away. He tosses the apple slices in the grass close enough for the large horse to eat them. The horse doesn't seem to notice. He keeps his eye on Vertimus. By the time Vertimus returns to where everyone is standing, the horse has not changed his position.

"Are you well?" Evangelina asks Vertimus.

"Yes. But if I'd tried to get any closer I wouldn't have been," he responds.

"That horse is as mean as it is big," Humbul says.

"Meanness is not its intention, it's well-trained. I haven't seen a horse like this one in years. These horses are trained to fiercely protect their masters. It would have attacked me if I have tried to get any closer."

"What did you find in the other saddlebags?" Evangelina asks.

Vertimus looks at Jabneh, who looks at Evangelina. He looks scared.

"What's the matter? What did you find?" Evangelina asks again, but this time she speaks slower and softer, as though she's confused by the question she's asking.

"I didn't find much food, but I found weapons. Evangelina, do you know what they wanted?" Vertimus asks.

"I'm not sure if they said what they wanted. I can't remember," Evangelina answers.

"They wanted us," Tahvi says.

"You know that? It's not a guess?" Vertimus asks.

"I heard the woman tell the men to take both of us," Tahvi says.

"I'm sure these men are trackers. Kallima probably hired them. They didn't bring much food, which tells me they didn't plan to travel very long. They've taken the time and trouble to track you from Baldric to Violetta to here," Vertimus reasons.

Evangelina seems confused. "Violetta? But we were there for some time. They would have had to be—"

Vertimus interrupts her, "Waiting. They were waiting for you. And when you left, they followed you here. You and Tahvi aren't safe here anymore."

# GOODBYES

Vertimus and Evangelina lead a discussion to decide what to do next. They begin by gathering as much information as they can about Kallima and the two men. Vertimus has a lot of questions and Evangelina, Tahvi, Sheree, Humbul and Sephine do their best to answer him. He asks for everyone's version of what happened, listening patiently and paying special attention to any details he believes might be important.

Though Sheree and Humbul can't remember exactly what happened, they share enough information for Evangelina and Vertimus to conclude that Kallima has the ability to influence others, so much so that they might answer any question she asks, even if they don't want to. After everyone has finished sharing their accounts, Vertimus asks Evangelina if she'll take a walk with him, away from the others.

Away from the still-smoking house, he tells her what he thinks their plan should be and he asks for her input. He also shares that whatever they decide, they need to resolve it now before they share it with the group. The news will be difficult for everyone to hear, especially the children, so it will be better received if the group knows Evangelina and Vertimus are in agreement. Evangelina listens to his plan and agrees.

As Vertimus and Evangelina walk back to the group, Evangelina sees Tahvi looking at her. His eyes seem full of awareness and she wonders if he knows what they've decided. Sheree and Humbul are standing next to him, one twin on each side. Evangelina sees Tahvi reach out for Sheree's hand and Sheree takes it in hers. Tahvi takes his handless arm, loops it around Humbul's and pulls each of them a bit closer to him. As he does, his mouth begins to tremble and tears fall from his eyes.

"Tahvi, what's the matter?" Sheree asks.

Tahvi answers her by squeezing her hand a bit harder and bringing it close to his chest.

Sheree sees that Tahvi is looking at his mother so her gaze drifts to Evangelina as well.

"We've decided what to do," Vertimus says. "Evangelina and I are going to leave for Encarta today. Tahvi will come with us, and everyone else will remain here."

Now it's Sheree who pulls Tahvi. When Tahvi moves closer to Sheree, Humbul follows by moving closer to Tahvi.

"Why is Tahvi not staying with us?" Sheree asks.

"I was about to ask the same question," Sephine says. Sheree's eyes are threatening tears and she's trembling. Sephine puts her arm around her, trying to comfort her.

"We know this woman and these men want Evangelina and Tahvi. We also know they didn't hurt any of you when they had the opportunity to." Vertimus looks at Sheree, Humbul and Sephine when he says this.

"It's a good sign that they didn't hurt anyone, but it's not a good sign that they planned to take Tahvi and me against our will. What we know for sure is that Tahvi and I are marked, but the rest of you don't have to be," Evangelina says.

"But what happens when they're freed from those … things they're in? Won't we all be in danger?" Sephine asks.

"I don't believe so," Vertimus says. "But we did consider that. Tahvi said this blend will last several hours. By that time, the three of us will be gone. We will stop by the sentry tower before we leave, give them a description of Kallima and her men and say that we caught them trying to steal Evangelina's horses. We won't mention the fire because we don't want them coming to the house … not yet."

"You don't want anyone to see them as they are now, do you?"

"That's right, Humbul," Evangelina answers.

"Sephine, we're asking that Jabneh stay with you in your home. We're hoping that tomorrow you'll advise the sentries about the fire. Tell them you don't know how it happened but that no one was harmed, as far as you know. We expect Kallima and her men to be gone by then," Evangelina says.

"What if they don't leave? If they want you and Tahvi, don't you believe they might stay in the village and try to find out where you are?" Sephine asks.

It's Vertimus who answers her. "We considered that as well. That's why we'll tell the sentries they tried to steal Evangelina's horses. It will destroy their integrity and keep the sentries from sharing information with them. And because of our accusation of thievery, they'll be forced to leave the village or confined if they resist. They'll likely assume we've all left together, but in case they don't, we're going to stop by the carrier post. I plan to message two of my most trusted friends who will acts as guards for all of you until we return. Based on where they are now, it should take them less than two days to arrive. In the meantime, stay inside your home and don't come back here, even to tend to the animals, without sentries as an escort."

Sephine takes some time to think about this. She considers all the options and then realizes this is the best plan to keep her family safe. "I will do as you ask," Sephine says.

"But I thought you said Tahvi wasn't well enough to go!" Sheree cries. "And if you're sending guards here then why can't they protect Tahvi just as they protect us! I don't understand!" Her hands are clenched, the cords in her neck standing out.

Her sadness overcomes her anger. She begins to weep, reaches for Tahvi and wraps her arms around him. He does the same to her and Humbul joins them, holding Tahvi from behind. Sheree looks at Evangelina and Vertimus, eyes pleading, but she can see they've already made up their mind and there's nothing she can do to change it.

It's not long before Tahvi and Humbul begin to weep as Sheree does. Rather than trying to help the children understand their decision Vertimus and Evangelina stay silent, knowing there are no words or explanations that will comfort them. They allow the children to feel what they need to and eventually they kneel next to them and join the children in their hug. Sephine and Jabneh do the same and they stay huddled together for some time, in a close circle, not wanting to let go of one another.

* * *

Before saying their goodbyes, they discuss the final details and finish packing the last few items in the wagons.

Vertimus and Evangelina ask Jabneh to stay with Sephine until they return. They explain that because Kallima and her men followed them from Violetta, they might return there. They ask him to message his apprentice Nahele and tell him he's visiting a village other than Padhraig and he expects to be gone for weeks. If anyone asks Nahele about Jabneh's whereabouts, they will think he's somewhere other than Padhraig.

Sephine's husband Gaelan is expected to return in less than three days. Vertimus' friends will have arrived by that time and if Jabneh needs to return home for any reason, one of them can return home with him while the other stays with Sephine and her family.

Vertimus will leave a message for Exos at the carrier post advising him to go straight to Encarta when he returns. He will also direct him about how to find Sephine's home, in case there's anything he needs before he makes the trip and to check on the others.

Evangelina gathers all the remaining coin she has on the land, which she's kept in a hidden compartment in the barn. She gives some of it to Sephine and packs the rest into the wagon with the coin that's already there.

Once the adults have finished packing the wagon, Evangelina nearly panics when she doesn't see Tahvi or the children.

Sephine notices Evangelina's reaction and gently touches her shoulder. "They're over there," she says, pointing in the direction of one of the trees near the barn.

Evangelina sees Tahvi sitting in the grass with Humbul and Sheree. Kaco is with them. She can see Tahvi's lips moving but can't hear what he's saying. The twins say nothing. Sheree is still crying. Humbul has his legs pulled close to his chest, with his arms wrapped around them. He's lightly rocking himself back and forth.

Evangelina hears someone say something from behind her, but she doesn't understand it. "What?" she asks, taken aback.

"The wagon is ready. Is there anything else we must do?" Sephine asks.

Evangelina looks at her friend and hugs her forcefully. "I'm scared," she says.

"I'm scared with you," Sephine replies.

\* \* \*

It's difficult for all of them to say goodbye but it's hardest on the children, especially Sheree, who can't stop crying. She feels scared— not only for Tahvi and Evangelina but also for herself. She can't imagine life without them, even for a short time. She and Tahvi hold each other for what seems like an eternity until Sephine and Evangelina have to gently separate them.

They agree they will write as often as possible, both by messenger, and if urgent by carrier bird, but no one knows when they will see each other again.

Jabneh, Sephine and the children use Evangelina's second wagon to go home, taking three of Evangelina's horses with them. Sephine's home is less than a half hour's ride, but Evangelina has asked that Sephine keep the wagon on her land until she returns. Sheree and Humbul are both crying again. As they ride away in the wagon they watch Tahvi for as long as they can, until they are too far away to see him. Sheree will cry now and then, for the rest of the day, until eventually she cries herself to sleep that night.

After the others take leave, Vertimus helps Tahvi get into the back of the wagon. Kaco is safe beside him. Vertimus looks back at the house and sees Evangelina standing close to the space in the ground that used to be their workroom.

Evangelina is looking at the people in their clear prisons and thinking of Baleel.

Vertimus walks over and stands next to her. "Evangelina, Tahvi is in the wagon. We're ready."

Evangelina continues to stare at the still people. "Tahvi says they're not in pain."

"Then I believe they're not."

"Do you believe they're still dangerous?"

"Yes," he says, without hesitation. "All the more reason to leave quickly."

Evangelina considers something she never thought she would. She looks at Vertimus and when he sees her eyes, he knows what she's thinking.

"They're only a threat to us if we stay here or if they know where we're going, so it's best we be on our way."

Evangelina begins walking towards the wagon as Vertimus stays behind. He thinks about his brother and how proud they had felt when they finished building the house. They'd celebrated by drinking wine and falling asleep under the large tree closest to the barn that hadn't been built yet. He starts to cry silently as he curls his hands into fists. For just a moment he wishes he'd had the opportunity to face these men, and even the woman—but he pushes the thought away before it enrages him. As he walks away, instead of thinking about these trespassers, he tries to think of what it will feel like to rebuild Evangelina's home once they've found all of Tahvi's stones.

Evangelina makes sure the back of the wagon is locked before she climbs into the front. The doors are open behind her and she can see Tahvi sitting with Kaco. Her son looks very tired. As they ride away, she looks back at her home. She can no longer see the three figures but she knows they're still there. The spear is tucked away safely in her coat pocket and the dagger that Vertimus gave her is in a sheath attached to a belt around her waist.

Vertimus rides alongside the wagon on his horse. They start toward the center of town and Tahvi looks back and sees the partially scorched structure. He sees the stable and the courtyard, where he recently celebrated his birth. He cries silently, understanding he is leaving the only home he's ever known, and wondering if he'll ever see it again.

\* \* \*

At about the same time that Vertimus is leaving messages at the carrier post, there is a crunching sound coming from behind the barn. It's Maddox, who is finally eating the pieces of apple that Vertimus had thrown to him.

It's not the only sound in the area. Birds are chirping, flying from one tree to another or to different branches within the same trees, making shuffling sounds as their wings clip the leaves when they rush by them. It's just before noon, with the sun star blazing brightly in the sky. It casts short shadows of everything on the land, including the charred pieces of wood and ruins in the center of Evangelina's home.

The quiet is interrupted by a splintering, followed by a clattering sound as a small piece of damaged wood that had been dangling for the last several hours finally breaks off and falls onto what used to be the workroom floor. It tumbles and turns over several times before colliding with the structure that encloses Kallima.

Shortly after the wood settles, a high-pitched squeaking noise comes into being. It's barely audible, sounding like a kettle of water that's just beginning to boil, but the volume is much, much lower. As the sound continues, moisture begins to form on the outside the structures that Tahvi created around Kallima and the two men. Within minutes, the small piece of wood resting against Kallima's is drenched in water.

Less than an hour later, Maddox begins to neigh and pull at his reins after hearing a sound that agitates him. Though it's muffled, and he can't register it as a command, he knows what it is. It's the sound of his master.

Broken

# APPENDIX (Pronunciation Tool)

1. Aaban [uh-ban]
2. Aahil [ah-hil]
3. Ascuns Loc [ahs-koons lohk]
4. Baldric [bawl-drik]
5. Balfor [bal-fohr]
6. Eldgeon [el-jun]
7. Evangelina [ee-van-jel-ee-nuh]
8. Fahvyl [fah-vihl]
9. Gabbirrel [gab-ih-rel]
10. Gadarine [gad-uh-reen]
11. Gaelan [gey-luh n]
12. Gentian [jen-tee-un]
13. Hadden [had-en]
14. Humbul [huhm-buhl]
15. Jabneh [jab-neh]
16. Kaco [keyk-oh]
17. Maezon [meyz-aw]
18. Maubud [maw-buhd]
19. Maryth [mair-ith]
20. Nahele [nah-heel]
21. Ocran [aw-kran]
22. Onym [oh-nim]
23. Orbis [awr-biss]
24. Pandatus [pan-dair-us]
25. Padhraig [pahd-rag]
26. Sabina [suh-bee-nuh]
27. Sheree [shur-ree]
28. Stefan [steh-fahn]
29. Tabarak [tab-uh-rak]
30. Tahvi [taw-vee]
31. Tadgh [tawg]
32. Telracs [tel-raks]
33. Thaumaturge [thaw-muh-turj]
34. Vertimus [vur-tim-us]
35. Violetta [vee-oh-let-uh]
36. Zaavan [zah-vahn]

# ABOUT *BROKEN*

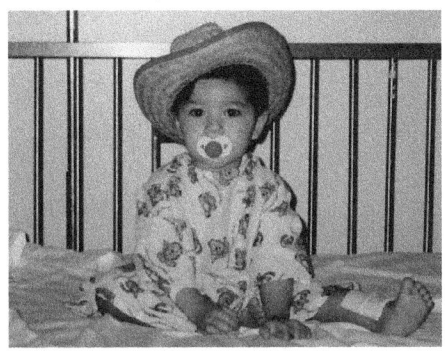

*My nephew Andy (the real Tahvi) was born with spina bifida lipomyelomeningocele, a condition that can cause a number of severe health complications. When my sister first told me about her newborn son's diagnosis, I wasn't sure she or Andy would be able to handle it. The years of surgery, limited mobility, danger of complications ... I was too scared to be hopeful for them. I had no idea that as Andy grew older, being part of their journey would change my life for the better.*

*Several years after he was born, I was talking with my sister as she and Andy were preparing for yet another surgery. Exhausted, she said to me, "I feel like my job is to turn this boy into a man, but I don't have all the pieces." This statement was so profound that I've never forgotten it. It was the birth of the idea for* Broken.

*I had always hoped to write and publish stories, yet both tasks seemed so unachievable. It was my sister's unfailing and uncompromising love for her son that compelled me to write a story about their relationship, about how love and family can overcome any obstacle. Over the course of his journey to live and thrive despite his difficulties, Andy has filled our lives with compassion, humor, adventure and hope—he showed us what life can be like when you refuse to let anything hold you back.*

*Eva and Andy—thank you for proving that through love, courage and perseverance, all dreams are possible.*

*C.H. Garrison*

Broken

www.ingramcontent.com/pod-product-compliance
Lightning Source LLC
Chambersburg PA
CBHW061131200626
46817CB00016B/684